Carolyn,

I am because we are
and we are because I am.

— African Proverb

A Flower
It Has Its Own Song

ℰ℘ ℭℬ

by
Dana Rondel

Bloomington, IN   Milton Keynes, UK
authorHOUSE™

AuthorHouse™
1663 Liberty Drive, Suite 200
Bloomington, IN 47403
www.authorhouse.com
Phone: 1-800-839-8640

AuthorHouse™ UK Ltd.
500 Avebury Boulevard
Central Milton Keynes, MK9 2BE
www.authorhouse.co.uk
Phone: 08001974150

This book is a work of fiction. People, places, events, and situations are the product of the author's imagination. Any resemblance to actual persons, living or dead, or historical events, is purely coincidental.

First published by AuthorHouse 6/20/2006

ISBN: 1-4259-3436-6 (sc)
ISBN: 1-4259-3437-4 (dj)

Printed in the United States of America
Bloomington, Indiana

This book is printed on acid-free paper.

Cover design by Brian Gaidry
Author Photo by Del Anthony

*This book is dedicated
to music—and to all
of God's children, each
of you a flower with
its own song.*

God is life…
Life is all and, too,
we see it as simply a word.
Yet words born of love, written, spoken or sung,
illuminate and redeem the human soul.
They become the rays of sunshine
that transform an ordinary day.

Love, blessings and thanks to each of you:

God, the root of every flower, the spirit of all life and the purest, most vital of love—the beating heart of humanity.

Mom, thanks for nurturing the seed that became my life, and for giving me a gift greater than all, love. If not for love I wouldn't be…

Dad, thanks for opening my eyes to hope and my heart to compassion. You teach not by words solely, but simply by being.

Charles H. Giscombe, thanks for just being, and for the music you are—a song so genuine and true. The melody of you breathes life into my existence and blends so perfectly with each beat of my heart. I am more because of you and with you.

Patricia Barlow, thanks for your wisdom and spiritual mothering. Your unceasing faith in me and undeniable acceptance of all that I am has elevated me to higher heights within myself. Woman, the divine architect, she is you.

Ludney D. Pierre, thanks for believing in me and my dreams. Your life for me was a mirror of truth reflecting most plainly an image of who I am, who I was and who I needed to become.

Greg Pazdersky, thanks for encouraging me to keep my story alive. From you I learned that my words created a story that is more than just mine; it became yours too.

Chandra Sparks-Taylor, thanks for your vision, your ability to know beyond knowing, and for the magic of your pen once in your hand—a hand guided by the divine.

Brian Gaidry, thanks for your pure, artistic brilliance. A rare jewel you are as an artist, but most importantly, as a man.

Del Anthony Thomas, thanks for your supreme and perceptive eye. You have the ability to capture a memory, making it become still and tangible. Memories are instrumental in writing our stories, which help us to grasp more definitely the purpose of our being.

Godchildren, nieces and nephews, you are hope in its truest form. You, too, are innocence that is never lost.

Family and friends, together you are a fountain of love overflowing, and a rainbow of authentic colors representing beauty and truth.

"…it is necessary to teach by living and speaking those truths which we believe and know beyond understanding. Because in this way alone we can survive, by taking part in a process of life that is creative, and continuing, that is growth."

—Audre Lorde

Sister Outsider

Music

Music, its song is the rhythm that flows within me. It, too, is the soft sounds of the piano, the humming of a human voice, a bird's melodious chirp, the blossoming of a flower and the sun's silent rise. It is the beating of the human and Nature's heart. It is the beginning.

My story began with the first beat of my own heart, or perhaps it was the sound of my first vocal cry, a high note—fading, softer, lower. I love the rising and setting of a piano's chords, high then low, but if life for me began with a beat, then the music of my heart had begun to blend with the beat of drums from the start. The blood within me flowed through my veins as a musical note flows out from the strings of a violin. I opened my eyes and listened to the tempo of the song that was now the breath and rhythmical movement of my body. The song was within me, and I was within the song. We had become one. Life is a vibration that had given birth to creation.

I am creation—a note, a lyric, a song—improvising within the music of life. Improvisation is the key to a harmonious blend of life's music with mine.

I was born an instrument being played within life's song. A jazz song. In jazz, instruments, which are what we are, sound together melodiously. But sometimes an instrument has to stand by itself to make its own music heard, but it can never stand alone for long because it is always a part of something much greater than it.

Our heart, too, is an instrument. It is nothing more than that lone instrument making its own music, wanting to be heard, then longing to be a part of that thing greater than it. For the human heart, that greater thing is the song of love. We all are in one way or another, a part of the same song, life. Within the song we improvise and try to keep with the rhythm and the harmony, sometimes leading, sometimes following and sometimes just creating together with the rest of life, like a jazz song. But we don't always succeed with our part—our instruments are not always in tune. When we fail in our part, we can blame it on the rest, put to sleep our instrument and choose to stay silent, not to be heard and not participate, or we can begin again, creating and continuing to create and possibly inventing something different and new. That's the song of love. The song of life. There is freedom in every song. The song doesn't have to change, just the way we choose to play it.

Chapter 1

"The seed already planted. It just have to be cultivated," my neighbor Mrs. Wise used to say. It didn't matter what the conversation was about. She would say it to grownups and to children. Around the time that I met her, in 1971, she was an older woman in her seventies—at least that's what I was told—with a lot of energy. She was an attractive woman with long, thick, pearly gray hair; an almond complexion; dark eyes the color of midnight; a prominent nose that sat perfectly on her oval face and soft, full lips that slightly curled when she smiled. She was indeed a pretty woman. Wise too. Age was her blessing.

When I saw her, which was mostly during the warmer seasons, she was crawling around in her flower garden digging, tucking, plucking, trimming, cutting, feeding, watering, humming or just plain ole talking to her plants. I guess they were like children to her because she didn't have any of her own. She handled them with a mother's touch, like a mother with a newborn child. She was always so gentle with them. Those flowers grew to be quite healthy, and there were so many of them—different shapes, sizes, textures and tones. So much color in one place made such a pretty rainbow. It was like magic. Only God knows how to create rainbows. But Mrs. Wise must've had some of God's magic because in her garden, there was always a rainbow.

When I was younger, I used to wonder why Mrs. Wise took such care with her flowers. I had never known anyone to love plants as much as she did. In fact, she was the only one that I knew in Hartsfield, Connecticut, with a garden. There were others who tried to make a garden and grow flowers, even a few different types of vegetables, but after the first few months or so, when nothing transpired, that would be the end of it. Folks would just throw up their hands, suck their teeth and walk away. Some would even go as far as spitting and trampling on the patch of earth where they had planted their seeds. They blamed the lack of growth on conditions such as the fact that we were living with mostly the poor. Most of the three-story tenements on East Street where I lived usually housed six families and were deteriorating inside and out. Either the vinyl siding was falling off their fronts or the paint was old, chipped and practically washed away enough that the original cement-gray and brick stones were exposed. Inside, it wasn't difficult to find cracks or holes in the hallway walls, collapsed or missing wooden steps and water bugs. The roaches came in all sizes—an army of their own—determined to take over the buildings, mostly the apartments. There were only a few three-family houses and one single family on our street. They made our street look less like the projects that surrounded us on the east and west sides. The houses made the area around us look better, but life may have been a little more pleasant if there were more trees, grass and flowers decorating the outside of our homes. There was mostly dirt, dandelions, which were always very pretty to me, and pavement.

Many people, especially those living outside of the urban city of Hartsfield, associated neighborhoods such as ours with ignorance and filth. They believed that nothing good or healthy could come out of that environment. This attitude had a tendency to negatively affect a great portion of city folks, but Mrs. Wise knew better than to adopt such a negative opinion of her own common people. She would tell those who had nothing good to say about our neighborhood that, "God take care of business here just like anywhere else. The sun shine and the rain fall in these parts too. God don't discriminate. What do God care about urban or suburban?"

Of course, folks would stand and scratch their heads, slightly baffled, before turning and walking away. They never would put up an argument against hers. Mrs. Wise, never stopping the process of tending to her plants, would just smile. She was always smiling.

I had never tried to make a garden myself, but at the inquisitive age of seven I was more than curious, and I wanted to know what it would take to plant one. In the summer of '71, early one Saturday morning, it must've been late June because school had ended only a week prior,

I walked next door to Mrs. Wise's house. It was a small, white house with sky-blue shutters and a bright-red door. She was in her front yard tending to her garden. She had on a worn-out straw hat with a sage-green ribbon tied around it just above the large brim. Pinned to the ribbon was a small yellow-and-blue silk butterfly with white speckles. Over her slim, frail shoulders she wore a knitted shawl of many colors: earthy browns, greens and beiges. There were also a few hints of red and blue. It looked as though the shawl was fairly old because the colors had paled, and it was covered with lint balls along the edges where it had begun to unravel. In the garden the bright colorful flowers became an embroidered floral design knitted onto an old cloth, making Mrs. Wise's shawl look new again. Beneath her shawl she wore a wrinkled denim jumpsuit with a yellow T-shirt, and her small, almond-colored feet, marked with the lines of time that also appeared in her face and hands, were bare. Mrs. Wise was on her knees at the edge of the garden picking up a handful of moist reddish-brown earth, rolling it between her palm and fingers. After gently massaging it a short while, she molded it into a small pile then began to flatten and even it out. She slowly pushed her index and middle fingers down into the soft earth and spread the particles of dirt. When the hole was large enough, she dropped a seed into it, poured a few drops of water then covered the hole. She did this several times while I watched. After a while, when there was only a small portion of seed left, Mrs. Wise inched back onto an empty patch of earth large enough for two and leaned up against a large oak tree. Its trunk was a grayish-brown, and it was fairly wide and tall and was standing on the front right side of her diminutive one-family house. The plants and flowers made a half moon around it.

Although East Street was busy and full of sound—the voices of young and old resonating in the air, children's laughter, bare feet and hard-sole shoes on pavement, an occasional chirp from birds in nearby trees and the murmur of car engines and police sirens that echoed from the adjacent Main Street—there was a peaceful silence that embraced Mrs. Wise and me. There were no words, just the meticulous movement of her small, wrinkled brown hands as she counted the remaining seed. Once she was done and seemed to be rested, she moved back toward the edge of her garden. She began to plant more seed. For several moments I stood above her looking over her shoulder then finally reluctantly I knelt beside her. I wanted to touch the earth and feel her warmth in the palms of my hands, but I was afraid that I might poison her just as the others did. I wondered if my touch would kill the seed that had been planted within her. I wondered if I would infect her with the same disease that caused the other gardens and plants in my neighborhood to die. I didn't want to kill the garden, its flowers or its new seed so I didn't open my hands. I didn't receive the precious earth until Mrs. Wise told me I could.

I was afraid to pick up the reddish-brown substance myself, so I waited for Mrs. Wise to pour what she had in her hands into mine. I didn't realize how soft, moist and warm the earth was until I touched it. I felt guilty holding it, so I didn't caress it between my palm and fingers like she did. I just held it. I studied it. There was a tiny earthworm burrowing its way to the surface of the small, dark particles. I touched it with the index finger of my free hand. It wriggled back down into the hole it had made. I hoped it would not suffocate or cause the seed that would be planted not to grow. Mrs. Wise looked down into my hand and said, "Worms is important for the earth and the plants. Ancient Egyptians—they our ancestors, you know—considered the worm to be a sacred thing. They necessary for the earth to stay healthy." I opened my hand flat and spread out the particles in search of the worm. When I found it, I picked it up then placed it in the earth between two small plants that had just begun to grow. Soon it disappeared.

Mrs. Wise sat up straight and looked out over her garden. "Life is a blessing. It sure is," she said as she pulled off her straw hat and wiped the sweat from her forehead and brow with the back of her hand. "Everything we need to know about life is right here in front of us. She always speakin' to us." She put her hat back on, studied my eyes for a moment then continued to speak. "She always speakin' to us. The earth, that is. Her word is a livin' word. Yes, it is. You got to listen very closely to hear it though. You got to observe her very carefully to understand it. You got to put your bare hands into her to know her love. You got to plant them like a seed. Her love is strong too. Yeah, it's strong. Ain't no other love like hers. Put your hands down into her." Mrs. Wise leaned forward and began to slowly and carefully dig into the earth. I, too, placed my hands first onto the surface then pressed my fingers into her. "See? Now we like a root within her. You know what a root is, right, child?" I nodded to let her know that I understood. "We connected to her now. We like a small child in our mother's womb." She continued to dig deeper and deeper into the earth while she spoke. "She the one who teach us about God, you know? Yup, she the one. What you know about God, child? What you been taught?"

I shrugged because I didn't know much about God, except that He made people laugh and cry and sometimes curse. I used to hear my grandmother thanking God, mostly on her knees with her hands clasped in front of her. Other times I would see her throw up her hands in supplication, pleading to God and blaming Him for all of her troubles. I was confused about God. I didn't know if He was a good or bad person or a person at all. I had never seen God for myself, so I didn't know what to think. Sometimes my own mother had been on her knees praying to God and asking for her prayers to be answered. I had heard her ask often, "Why me?" I used to think God was mad at her. All of these thoughts went through my head. I wanted to answer Mrs. Wise with words and tell her my thoughts but nothing would come out, so I remained silent.

Mrs. Wise shook her head and said, "You speak, child?"

I lifted my head, turned and looked at her. "Yes."

"I thought somethin' might've gotten your tongue 'cause you so quiet." Her shoulders shook as she chuckled.

"I can talk," I answered bashfully.

"Good. But I don't mind if you just wanna keep quiet and listen. Good listenin' is what help you to learn." The entire time she spoke, Mrs. Wise kept her hands buried in the earth. "Yeah, what was I sayin' before? Oh, yeah. This here is our Earth Mother, and she the one connect us to God. Some folks like to say Nature connect us to God. Somethin' about a communion or somethin' like that. I'm talkin' about the same thing— Nature, Earth Mother—it's all pretty much the same. You probably too young to understand what I'm talkin' about. One day you gon' know though. One day."

"How does the earth love us?" I asked.

"Oh, baby, in so many ways. She love us in so many ways. She gave us this life we have. We was born out of this earth. The grass, the flowers, the trees and all livin' creatures and things of God was born out of this earth. She the maker of life. I ain't takin' no credit away from God 'cause, you see, she can't do it without His help, but she the maker. She gave us our body and our blood. Her body is ours. That's why you got to be gentle with it. Her blood is ours; that's why you got to plant only good seed in it. And the water we put into the earth got to be blessed. We got to pray over it like we pray over the rain, the oceans, the rivers and the lakes. All of these is holy water, you see? This here in this jar—" Mrs. Wise unearthed her hands and picked up a large, clear glass jar by the handle and pointed at it—"this holy water. How I know? If it look like crystal, if it smell like fresh mountain air and it taste like spring then I know it's God's holy water. I ain't gonna put nothin' in my own body that ain't clean, you see? And if I can't put this water into my own body then I can't put it into my mother's body. That's how you have to think of things. You can't think about it no other way." Mrs. Wise pursed her lips and shook her head. "Mmm-mmm. People around here, they go puttin' any ole thing into they body. If they gon' pollute they own body without a care, then they can go and do the same to the earth. It ain't right, you know?" She shook her head again. "It ain't right. The earth is in us just like we in this earth. We share the same body and the same blood. I know it don't seem to make no sense to you, but it's true. We all connected."

I was still on my knees with my hands planted in the earth, trying to make sense of everything Mrs. Wise had said. Some of it I understood but most of it I didn't. The only thing that my young mind could discern was that I had to learn to love our earth mother in the same way Mrs. Wise did. Learning to love her would be the only way I could grow my own flower garden without killing it. I buried my hands deeper and deeper until the reddish-brown particles covered them entirely. I massaged the moist particles with my fingers and wondered if she would learn to love me too. She must have the ability to love things, I thought. If she didn't love then how could the grass and the flowers and trees grow to be so pretty?

"When you embrace her, she embrace you," Mrs. Wise said, pressing her fingers down into the earth. "Can't you feel her embrace? It's a good feelin', ain't it? You ain't never feel nothin' like it, I'm sure. There's a sayin' that I've heard people use before: Do unto others as you would want others to do unto you. Well the same can be said about our mother. You do unto her what you want her to do unto you. You plant good seed in her, and what grows in her and out of her is made good and healthy. Look at all these beautiful flowers. So many pretty colors. God's children. They beautiful, ain't they? Give us so much joy."

I smiled, nodded and replied, "Yes."

"She give us life. This garden here is life. She give us joy. All these bright and beautiful colors. When I ain't feelin' so good—and I do have those kinda days—I come out here and sit on the grass near my garden or on that patch of earth beneath the oak tree, and I just watch these here flowers. God be right here with me talkin' to me and showin' me things that can't nobody else see. It take a special kinda listenin' ear to hear God's word. That's 'cause it's a livin' word. God's word breathes. Oh yes, it does. It breathes. If somebody tell you different, don't believe it. No, sir. Don't believe it. If it ain't breathin' then it ain't God's word. Not only that, but it takes a special kinda seein' eye to see God's word. You see that flower over there?" Mrs. Wise pointed to a bright yellow flower.

"That one?" I asked, reaching toward a flower in the center of the garden surrounded by several others. It was the only bright yellow one there.

She gave a nod and smiled. "They call that a marigold. It reminds me of the sun. The written word say what is above is below and what is below is above. If that's the case, then this is my sun because it brightens up my day. I don't never have to look up at the sky to know how sunny it is because the light above is reflected in this flower. I watched the earth give birth to this flower. To see it was a glorious thing—a miracle if I ever seen one. After she was born, I watched her grow. Every day I would come out here to see her progress. I would talk to her and tell her how precious she was. She was my favorite. It was something about her. Don't know what it was. Maybe it was because she was different than all the rest. I don't really know. I can't begin to explain it. But let me tell you a little about what I do know. You see, when she was first bein' born, it was a little bit of a struggle makin' her way into the light of the world. I could see that for myself. At first, I didn't think she was gon' make it. The process seemed to take longer than it should have, so I would talk to her, and I know she was listenin' 'cause the spirit of God in all of us, you know? That's right. The same spirit that's in you and me is in this here flower. We all connected. God planted a seed in all of us. Some of us just don't know it yet. We don't all know about the power we have within. I didn't know much about it myself until I started makin' this garden in the spring of '68. It's been a long time since that day, but makin' this garden was the best thing that ever happened to my life. Before this garden I thought my husband—he dead now—was the best thing. I ain't takin' nothin' away from my marriage 'cause my husband was a good man, a loyal man, a hardworkin' man, and he loved me. Boy, did he love me. I loved him just as strong. We was married for over fifty years. He was my life. Oh yes, he was. Didn't think I was gon' make it after he died, but that all changed the day I started on this garden. I forget what happened to make me think about growin' these flowers. It must've been my spirit. Can't think of nothin' else. I know I ain't makin' no sense to you right now, but one day you gon' know what I'm talkin' about. God plants a seed in all of us.

"That experience—death—it woke up some things in me. It was strange. One day I was starin' it in the face then the next I felt like I had been reborn, like I had been given a new life. I think that's what made me love this flower so much. One day it looked like it was starin' death in the face 'cause it didn't look like it was gon' make it, but then one day it just started growin'. The same way I talked to this flower is the same way God talked to me. Sound crazy, don't it?"

I had remained silent and began releasing my hands from within the earth. I sat in the emerald-green grass and rubbed my hands into it, hoping to clean them. The reddish-brown stains underneath each of my nails caught my attention. I hoped that I could find a way to clean them before dinner.

Listening to Mrs. Wise talk about death made me keep thinking about it. I didn't know much about death. No one had ever talked about it with me. What I did know was that it was a bad thing that made people sad. I had never been to anyone's funeral, and I hoped I would never have to go to one. I didn't want to see death or sad faces or tears.

Mrs. Wise continued to speak without paying me much attention. On occasion she would look over and shake her head, give a nod, a smile or an intense stare as though she were trying to figure out what was going on in my young mind.

"Oh yeah, I kinda remember things now. What made me get this garden started? There was a voice. It spoke to me. I could hear it as clear as a sunny August day. It said, 'Love.' Thought I was hearin' things at first. Then it spoke again, 'Love.' I looked around the room and didn't see nobody else there. Wasn't nobody else there but me, the silence and the dark. I sat there for a minute with my eyes open. I was sittin' in the chair next to my bedroom window. The shade was down and the curtains were drawn. Didn't care nothin' 'bout seein' the day. Then I yelled out my husband's name, 'Mr. Solomon Wise? Is that you?' I didn't get no answer. Didn't believe in no ghosts or nothin', but I did hear the voice. I closed my eyes again and rested my head on the back of the chair. 'Love.' There was the voice again. This time I kept my eyes closed though. The voice spoke again, 'Love.' Finally I asked, 'God, is that you?' It had to be God. Couldn't be nobody but God, 'cause God is love, you see? And love is of God. That's what God was tryin' to tell me. Didn't need no long, drawn-out explanation either. Just one word was all God needed to say. I thought when my husband died he had taken all the love I had in me with 'im.

"It was like the hand of God snatched me out the dark that day. I wasn't seein' nothin' but the light. Really what it's called is a revelation. It was durin' my revelation that I had a vision about a garden. Ain't never had no children of my own to love. If I did, they could've made the hurt I felt less for me, 'cause then I wouldn't have been feelin' so lonely. But God showed me another way. I didn't fully understand at first until I started makin' this garden. These flowers and these plants gave me the answers I needed. Made things clear. Yeah, on that day, I heard the spirit—nothin' but God—speakin' to me. I hurried out my chair, pulled up the shades and opened the curtains to let the sunlight in. I ain't never closed them since. Ain't never thought 'bout death again neither."

Mr. Dickens yelled out, "Mrs. Wise, what you puttin' in that girl's head?" as he ran past to catch the city bus. He lived one building down from me and two from Mrs. Wise. He was known for keeping an eye on things in the neighborhood. If you wanted to know anybody's business, he was the man to tell it.

"That man there say he got the story on life, but he ain't got the right story until he have a conversation with God. That's what I do every day when I'm here tendin' to my garden. And you ain't got to do no real talkin'. It don't have nothin' to do with sharin' words back and forth. A conversation with God is nothin' more than a expression of love, and love is the language of the spirit." Mrs. Wise moved back toward the oak tree and rested against it. "I'm sorry I got a little sidetracked, child. I was supposed to be talkin' 'bout this here yellow flower, this here marigold. I did give her a name, you know? Her name is Mari. Whatcha think?"

"I like it. It sounds nice," I said, smiling.

"By the way, baby, what's your name?" Mrs. Wise asked with an inquisitive expression.

"My name is Rose," I answered.

"You got a last name? I might know some of your people. I do know some of everybody in this here city. You got features like the Averys from Pearl Street. Don't know if you familiar with 'em. They ain't too far from here. Maybe ten minutes away if you walkin'. Grew up with 'em, but haven't seen 'em in what seem like ages. They got a red tint to they light skin just like yours. That's the Indian in 'em. They eyes is small, dark and shaped like almonds, sitting right on top of they high cheekbones. Kinda like my kin. You got they eyes. And you got hair like 'em too. Most of 'em got long, curly, mahogany hair, 'cept the older ones. Theirs turn pearly-white. Put olive oil in it to keep it healthy and shiny." Mrs. Wise reached over and began to stroke my head and two long braids, one on each side. "I see American Indian, African and some white in there. I can see it all in you." Mrs. Wise moved her hand down to my shoulders then straightened my pink, floral, cotton blouse. "Your bones is slender like the older Averys. The young ones put too much junk in they body. Bigger than they supposed to be. Seem like the older generation take better care of themselves. It's a shame." Mrs. Wise shook her head. "I'm sorry, baby, what's your last name?"

"Rose Day Lee is my full name."

She thought for a moment then replied, "Nope. Don't think I know any Lees. Maybe if I think about it awhile, something will come to me, but I can't think of any that I know at the moment. How old are you?"

"Seven."

"You've only been in the neighborhood for a couple of weeks. Where'd you come from?"

"Maple Street. On the south side."

"You know what city livin' is all about," she said.

"I guess," I said, shrugging.

"Only difference is you on the north side now. People on this side is a little different, but we all people, and really when you think about it, we all the same. It's our experiences that make us different. It's some good and some bad that come with life. Dependin' on how you look at things, you either gon' turn out lovin' life or hatin' it. And dependin' on how you feel 'bout life will say a lot 'bout how you gon' feel 'bout yourself and how you gon' feel 'bout people in general. Anyway, well, it's good to meet you."

"Thank you," I said before being interrupted.

"Devilment. That's all that is. Nothin' but devilment." The voice was strange and distant. It belonged to an old man who I'd never seen before. He never looked our way. He kept walking with his nose in the air and eyes directly before him.

Several people walked by and looked over at us. A few gave indignant stares and whispered under their breath. Only one young man waved and said hello. Regardless of the expression and gestures given by the passersby, Mrs. Wise remained pleasant and presumably at peace. "Don't let people bother me," she said. "Usually I just give 'em what they need. Most times that's nothin' but a smile or a prayer. Sometime it's both." She waved her hand in the air. "So, who'd you come to East Street with? You got sisters or brothers?"

"I don't have any sisters or brothers. I moved here with my mother," I said.

"Father livin'?" she asked.

"Yes," I said.

"Come here too?"

"No."

"Won't ask too much about 'im, unless you feel like talkin' 'bout 'im some more," Mrs. Wise said, looking into my eyes.

I looked away. "Don't really want to talk about it right now." I hadn't known my father's whereabouts. After we moved I hadn't seen or heard from him, but each night I thought about him and hoped that wherever he was he was okay.

"That's okay, child. Some things is for ourself and God only," she said, looking away. "Beside gardenin', I find pleasure in readin' magazines. I mostly like the ones 'bout nature. I'm always interested in learnin' 'bout trees, the oceans, flowers, birds and bees. I like to know 'bout all we connected to. You like to read?"

"Yes," I said.

"What you like to read?"

"Different stuff. My father used to read to me all the time."

"What did he read?" Mrs. Wise asked, smiling.

"Everything," I said, shrugging. "He had a lot of books. They were all over our apartment. Sometimes he read them to me, and sometimes he made me read them to him. My father taught me how to read when I was three years old. That's what my mother told me. I learned about the Indians and about war and about the Africans that were brought here. The Indians and Africans were treated bad, but the white people learned a lot from them."

"We all learned from 'em," Mrs. Wise interjected.

I nodded. "We learned how to farm, build houses, and sing and dance and pray. My mother said my father was trying to teach me all about the world. Some stuff was good and some was bad. The bad stuff used to make him cry. Then I cried."

"Your father must be a good man, and a smart one too," Mrs. Wise said.

"He is." I smiled at Mrs. Wise. "He taught me how to write too. I have a journal."

"You do?" Mrs. Wise asked, brushing away a fly that had flown by her ear. "What have you written in your journal?"

"I have poems in it."

"Yours?"

"Some of them. One is my father's. But some I copied out of his books."

"Do you have a favorite poem?"

"Not really," I said, shrugging. "I like all of them. I have a poem about a flower. That's the one my father wrote."

"Can you tell it to me?"

"I don't remember all the words, but it's a nice poem."

"I'm glad you like it. I like poems too."

I had promised Mrs. Wise that I would share my father's poem, "To Paint A Portrait". And I did. It was written on the inside cover of my journal. The only part of the poem that continually remained in my memory was, "No blush betrays the likeness to a spirit that's my Rose." Perhaps it's because my father always put more emphasis around this line, especially when he said my name.

"Do you have a journal?" I asked.

"No," Mrs. Wise said, shaking her head, "but my garden is like a poem to me, 'cept it's livin'."

I inched over a little closer to Mrs. Wise. She reached for my hand and gently squeezed it as she stared at her flower, Mari. I looked at the bright yellow flower, too, and embraced the silence.

Mrs. Wise let go of my hand, reached toward Mari and softly stroked her petals. "Yeah, about this here flower. When it seemed like Mari wasn't gon' make it," Mrs. Wise continued her initial thoughts regarding her flower, "I started to pay more attention to her. I spoke to her every day. Some days I would just hum. I could tell she liked that. Well, as I said before, eventually she started to grow. It was a process though. Yes, it was. Even when she seemed to be full grown, she just wouldn't blossom like I knew she was supposed to. I looked at the picture of the other marigolds in *Garden Magazine*, and something just didn't seem right. In the magazine I saw morning's glory, the sun spreadin' open her wings to embrace the day. But in front of me was a summer bird whose wings were frozen in the cold and damp of a winter's night. All she had to do was see the light. It was within her, you see? That light would be those wings that would guide her into the mild summer breeze of freedom."

Mrs. Wise's tone became slightly higher as she uttered the words. At that moment, a beautiful red-and-black butterfly with tiny white speckles landed on a white tulip. Shortly after, a light breeze passed, and the butterfly spread its wings and ascended into the air. Mrs. Wise studied the butterfly in silence.

"Freedom come after the struggle," she said finally. "You got to go through the darkness before you can come into the light. Funny thing is the thought reminds me of childbirth. No matter how grown we get, we still like a newborn child 'cause we constantly bein' born. Within our struggles, old ways of bein' die, and after the struggle a new self is born. But for this flower I thought life itself was over. I guess I was wrong. Wouldn't be the first time. I didn't give up on Mari though. I'd still come out here every day and speak to her and share my song. When I'd be hummin', that's when I knew she felt my presence. God would put a melody in my heart, and I'd just hum it." Mrs. Wise chuckled.

"Struggle disguise itself. And it don't discriminate. It can creep up on you at any time. It's like a storm. One minute the sun shinin', the next dark clouds fillin' the sky and rain is comin' down hard. Everybody get caught in a storm every now and then. Sometime that storm is dark clouds, ragin' winds and heavy rains, and sometime it's the darkness of pain, a ragin' cry and the heavy burdens within us. When my husband died, the storm was within me. Didn't think I was gon' make it through, but my spirit kept me holdin' on. This here flower, it's been through some storms. The rain came down hard some days. Thought my whole garden would be destroyed 'cause that's how bad some of them was. But these here plants and these here flowers kept holdin' on. This here Mari, she kept holdin' on. The spirit is powerful, ain't it? Yeah, it is powerful. And God behind it all. You see this here oak tree? It got a story too. This tree is what gave my plants and my flowers shelter from the storm. Made it a little easier for them to bear it. That's how God is. God make it a little easier for us to bear the storms of life. God is like this oak tree, but God is the Tree of Life. You see this here flower? Mari? We the same. You a flower too. I know this ain't makin' no sense to you, but one day you gon' understand. The seed already planted. It just have to be cultivated. The sun gon' be goin' down soon enough. Let's plant a few more of these seeds and let God work some more miracles for us."

Chapter 2

The season changed. The hands of time stood still at autumn but the footprints of the living kept forward on their paths. The night grew longer and presented the living with the opportunity to observe the revelations that lie within her. One revelation being that life is change and change is constant. Mother Earth continued to create and sustain life in one form or another. And though the city streets were less flooded with human voices, Nature still sang her song. God was still busy at work too. He was still making rainbows. Mrs. Wise's flower garden with its various hues was slowly being put to rest, but the trees and their foliage would for a short while take its place and, too, indulge the senses. The spirit remained alive in all, and all in one form or another remained alive within the spirit.

As the old had begun to wane and the new had begun to emerge, I was steadily being carried away by the rhythm of my own life's song. I had made a new friend, although she was much older than me. Mrs. Wise didn't seem to mind that I was so young, so I didn't either. I learned how to make a garden and grow healthy flowers. I had recently turned eight, and I started the school year at a new school in Hartsfield. My teacher, Mr. Nathaniel, seemed to like me and decided based on reports from my former school that I should be placed in the honors group within our class. The honors group consisted of only two other students who had the ability to read on a twelfth-grade level, albeit we were only in the third grade. The three of us learned how to read at a very early age. Because I was in this group I, along with the others in my group, was always given more homework than the rest of the class. I thought it should be the other way around. If the rest of the class wasn't reading as well as I was, then they should've been given more homework so that they could learn more. I didn't voice this opinion to Mr. Nathaniel because he probably would've thought I was trying to tell him how to do his job. Regardless, I enjoyed reading and really didn't mind the extra work.

Each morning, Mr. Nathaniel would start by calling attendance. This process helped me to remember the names of the other students. Otherwise, I probably wouldn't have learned all of them because not everyone was as friendly and as excited to meet people as I was. Although I was shy and didn't introduce myself to others by walking up to them, shaking their hands and providing my name, I did manage to smile and say hello. If the person I spoke to smiled and spoke back then I would offer my full name. I would say, "Hi, my name is Rose Day Lee." Mrs. Wise told me I should always introduce myself by giving my full name just in case the person I was giving it to happened to be a friend of my family or a distant relative. But no one else offered his full name. After a while I started just providing my first name.

Once the attendance was complete, Mr. Nathaniel would ask the class to pull out their homework. First he would have May, Robby and me take turns and read out loud our assignment then answer the questions Mr. Nathaniel had prepared for us. May who was the most articulate of the group always answered every question correctly. Robby who was extremely shy seemed to struggle with his answers whenever Mr. Nathaniel called his name, but he never had a problem conveying his thoughts during our discussions. He was the most vocal within our tiny group. I always had an answer when Mr. Nathaniel called on me, but unless it was already in writing, I sometimes had difficulty articulating my thoughts in front of the rest of the class. On most occasions, when I didn't already have an answer prepared—at times Mr. Nathaniel would make up his own questions rather than use the ones in the back of the book—I would convince myself that any one would do whether it was right or wrong because it showed I at least made an effort. On a couple of occasions when I was wrong, Mr. Nathaniel shook his head and said, "Rose, you know the right answer. Just take your time and think it through. You don't always have to say the first thing that comes to mind. Plus, it's okay to say 'I don't know' if you don't know." I didn't think that it was okay. I was in the honors group, and more was expected of me, so I felt I should always have an answer.

Once Mr. Nathaniel was done with the honors group he would move on to work with the rest of the class. May, Robby and I would sit patiently and listen to the dialogue between our teacher and the other students. Mr. Nathaniel never seemed to have the same level of confidence and patience with the other students as he had with us. Once in class he made a girl named Shawna cry because she didn't have time to do her homework. She told him she had to baby-sit her younger brother while her mother worked. Mr. Nathaniel exclaimed, "That is no excuse. When I give you work to bring home, I expect you to bring it back the next day. Completed." Shawna tried to explain that her younger brother was sick and needed her attention, but it didn't matter because Mr. Nathaniel refused to hear any excuse regardless of how legitimate it was. I found myself growing angry with him during the incident. I liked Mr. Nathaniel and thought he was a nice man, but he had a tendency to treat people unfairly at times.

On another occasion he told a boy named Thomas he didn't understand why he was here. He said, "I don't know how you made it this far. It doesn't appear to me that you have any sense in that head of yours. Someone must've felt sorry for you. Well, I don't."

Thomas responded by scowling.

Mr. Nathaniel caught him and made him stand in the corner and face the wall the remainder of class.

I told Mrs. Wise about how Mr. Nathaniel treated Thomas. She frowned and said, "A harsh word is like a mighty sword. It has the power to wound a man for life."

On many occasions, May, Robby and I were teased and treated unfairly by other members of our class. I was sure it had to do with the harsh treatment they received from Mr. Nathaniel, among other things. Some of the kids would call us names, shoot spit balls, make nasty faces or try to bully us in the hallways during our restroom breaks or during lunch. May would either verbally threaten the offender or she would report him or her to Mr. Nathaniel. Robby took the abuse without uttering a word. Usually May would have to come to his rescue. My response would usually depend on whether I had had a long talk with Mrs. Wise the day prior. Sometimes I would respond with a kind gesture, and other times I would retaliate with words.

There was one boy in my class who seemed to like me the least. I heard Justin Romero mumble under his breath and say, "She ain't better than me." I wasn't sure what he meant by the remark, so I just ignored him. Every day in class I would catch Justin glancing over at me and mumbling. Other kids who sat near him would look at me and giggle. I eventually became annoyed by him so I took it upon myself not to look over at him, if I could help it. It worked for about a week then I grew curious and wondered what Justin's problem was. Mrs. Wise had told me that regardless of how a person treated me, to always remain cordial, so one day when I caught Justin staring at me, I smiled at him. I thought maybe he would smile back but instead he stuck up his middle finger. The gesture made me angry, but remembering what Mrs. Wise had told me, I smiled again then turned my head.

A few weeks went by, and nothing between Justin and me had changed. He would stare at me and make crude remarks and gestures. I would smile or simply ignore him, but one day that all changed. During a short restroom break, Justin walked past me in the hallway and rubbed up against my arm. Instead of ignoring him, I asked him to say excuse me. Because my tolerance had begun to decline, which he could hear in my tone, the incident led us to argue.

"I don't have to say excuse me to you," he proclaimed.

"Yes, you do. You hit me," I responded, aggravated.

"So what? I don't like you," Justin shouted.

"I don't like you either," I exclaimed, pointing my finger at him.

"You think you're smart. But you ain't," he retorted.

"You— "

Before I could get the rest of the words out, Mr. Nathaniel was standing in front of me. "Hey. What are you two arguing about?" he asked, looking at me. We remained silent. "I asked you a question. Rose, answer me."

"He started it," I replied as tears began to form in my eyes.

"I didn't ask you that. I asked what you are arguing about." Mr. Nathaniel held a twelve-inch ruler loosely between his fingers.

"He rubbed up against me." A tear ran down my cheek.

"I did not," Justin proclaimed.

"Yes, you did," I answered.

"I don't know what happened out here, but one of you started it." Mr. Nathaniel was patting the ruler on his open palm. "Both of you go back inside and sit in your seats. Tomorrow you will not get a morning restroom break." He turned and walked away. I followed him, but before I entered into the classroom I made sure to wipe away my tears. Justin was behind me mumbling. I couldn't hear what he was saying, so I proceeded to my desk without a word.

I went home that day and spoke to Mrs. Wise about what had happened in school. I told her I had tried very hard to control myself, but that Justin continued to instigate the fight with me. She told me I had done well and that she could see why I had gotten so upset.

"It's hard to ignore people when they start to crowd your space, but there's a simple solution to that. As long as you ain't stuck between four walls then that mean you got room to back up, move to the side or walk away," she said.

"But he rubbed up against me," I stated.

"Did he hurt you?" she asked.

"No," I replied irritably with my arms crossed in front of me and pouting.

"Then you just pretend that you didn't even feel it. If he didn't hurt you, it don't matter. You could consider something like what this young boy did a love tap." Mrs. Wise chuckled.

"Mm-mm." I shook my head in disagreement.

Mrs. Wise reached for my hand and held on to it tight. "Baby, all I'm tryin' to say is it ain't worth the aggravation. There's a lot you still too young to understand, but you ain't too young to know this: the pain ain't worth it."

I put my head down in disappointment. "I know."

"Don't worry over it, child, but next time you might not be havin' this conversation with me. It's your mother you gon' have to answer to. I don't know how she would handle this thing." Mrs. Wise squeezed my hand and said, "The world is like a field of weeds, and still gardens prosper, flowers bloom and a rose blossoms." Then she released my hand.

"What are weeds?" I asked.

"You see there?" Mrs Wise said, pointing at the sidewalk. "See the life comin' out of those cracks? Those are weeds. I once read a sayin' in my *Garden Magazine*. It said, 'a weed is a plant whose virtues have not yet been discovered.' Those was the words of a poet named Emerson. That answer your question?"

"Yes," I said.

"You run along now," she said. I smiled at her and pleasantly sauntered away.

That night before bed I wondered if my experience in school was one of the many storms of life Mrs. Wise had once talked about. I hadn't done anything to deserve the treatment I'd received from Justin, but Mrs. Wise said that sometimes people do strange things, especially when things are not right in their lives. She told me Justin might be dealing with some things at home and that I should continue to smile at him because it was probably the only one he received throughout the day. She also told me it was important that I try to put myself in the other person's shoes. If I did then I could understand the person better, and it would teach me compassion. But I wondered how I could step into another person's shoes and understand him better if I didn't know what the person was going through. I didn't think it would be right to walk up to the person and ask. Mrs. Wise said it didn't matter whether I knew what the person was dealing with. The only thing that mattered was that the person was a human being like me, the person had feelings like me and God loves everybody the same. She said when I stepped into another person's shoes, figuratively speaking, all it meant was that I was treating that person exactly the way I would want that person to treat me. God's seed, the spirit, has been planted in everyone. How far along it is within its growth cycle, nonetheless, is different for each of us. I should remember that God is love and that we are all of God whether we know it or not and that we all go through different things in life, but that all of our experiences are only to help us grow. God is just cultivating the seed within us.

While pulling the covers over me in bed, Mother knocked on the door then opened it before I could answer. "How things goin'?" she asked.

I shrugged. "Okay."

"I haven't had a chance to ask you about school 'cause work has been keepin' me busy. What do you think about your new school?" she inquired.

"I don't think I like it," I responded.

She sat at the foot of my bed. "Why not?" She still had on her green hospital uniform and white leather clogs. Mother was a nurse's aide at Hartsfield Hospital. She had long hours, which made it seem like she worked more than anything else she did. Her hair was short, curly and brushed back from her round, cinnamon-brown face. Her almond-shaped eyes looked as though she were squinting under my bright light. Her nose was round, and her lips were full and painted a shimmery red. Her hands, which she had resting in her lap, were short and stubby. She was a petite woman with a slightly healthy figure.

After giving her a quick once-over I answered, "Because the other kids don't like me. They're mean to me."

"What makes you say that? Why would they be mean to you?" she asked. She was wrapping one of my braids around her finger. I wore my hair mostly parted down the middle with one, long, thin, mahogany braid on each side. "Your hair's gettin' longer."

"They don't talk nice to me. The only one who talks to me like she likes me is May. She's in the honors group too. I had more friends at Foxgrove." I felt tears beginning to form in my eyes.

"I'm sorry you haven't been able to make new friends easily. I'm sure the other kids will come around," she said still playing in my hair.

"I don't know and I don't care." I rolled over onto my back then stared up at the ceiling.

"I don't like that attitude." Mother's tone grew higher. "It's not necessary." I refused to respond. I thought Mother should've put herself in my shoes. I needed her to understand how much it hurt me that the kids in school were so mean to me. I continued to study the images fading in and out on my ceiling while twirling the loose strand of hair just above my forehead around my finger.

"Are you ignoring me?" Mother looked at me indignantly. I remained silent. "I asked you a question."

"No," I finally answered.

"Sometimes I don't know what gets into you. Some days you're as pleasant as a ladybug, and other days you can be as irritating as a mosquito bite." Mother stood from my bed. "If you keep on with that attitude, you can be sure you won't make any friends. Now get up and get your clothes ready for school. Dinner will be ready in a minute." She walked out of my room, and though I could tell she wanted to slam the door, instead she pulled it closed without barely a sound, except for the minor squeaking caused by the loose metal hinges.

As soon as Mother turned to walk away, I rolled my eyes, sucked my teeth and muttered, "I don't like school anymore." I remained under my cover until I heard footsteps outside of my bedroom door. I quickly sat up and waited for Mother to enter. She didn't. I threw off the cover, stood, walked over to my dresser and begrudgingly began to sift through my shirts, which lay folded one on top of the other, and began to prepare not only my clothes but my mind for the next school day.

Chapter 3

I awakened earlier than normal the next morning. It was a Wednesday, the middle of the week and getting closer to the weekend. I looked forward to the weekends because it was the only time I didn't think about Justin Romero. I was contemplating whether I should pretend to be sick. Having a cold or flu or some other sickness was the only way to completely avoid Justin. I rubbed my eyes for as long as I could stand it, then I sat up just enough to view my face in the mirror. They were a pinkish red. I didn't think I really looked sick, just a bit tired. I wasn't sure what else to do to make my thoughts on being sick become my reality, so I lay there letting my hopes slowly escape into the distant sound of the early-morning vibrations. But within every moment, my mind would strike another chord, and as each one produced its own melody, it would inspire another idea.

I should find a way to transfer to Foxgrove. I'll still be in Hartsfield, I thought. The idea moved me. I slid out of bed and caught myself in the mirror again. This time there was brightness in my eyes.

My bedroom door opened slightly. "Are you up?" Mother asked, peeking into my room. I could hear music playing in the background. Mother always had jazz blaring from the stereo in our living room. It didn't matter how early or late it was, music was her love, and it seemed she couldn't live without it.

"I'm up," I answered groggily, making my bed.

"Wash up and get dressed so you can eat," Mother said before closing my door. I could hear her snapping her fingers while walking away.

"I'm going to wash up," I said drowsily. The thought of transferring to Foxgrove had me preoccupied. I was hoping I could somehow find a way to convince Mother it would be the best thing for me. As I made my way to the bathroom, I could hear her in the kitchen singing. Billie Holiday's "Good Morning, Heartache" was playing. I had heard it plenty of times, and although I had grown to love Billie, the song always made me sad. Mother started playing it more often right before we moved from Maple Street, late spring of '71. Some nights she would sit in the living room by herself with the lights off, quiet and listening. Other days she'd be in the kitchen at the sink washing dishes and staring into space with the song playing in the background. But most often she'd be in her bedroom with the door shut and the music low. If I knocked on the door to ask if everything was okay she'd just say, "uh-huh." Sometimes I'd stand there and listen just to make sure. Over the music I could hear her voice, but I could never make out what she was saying or who she was talking to.

While in the bathroom, I could still hear Mother singing. After a few moments, another one of Billie's songs played, and Mother's voice grew quiet. As I sat on the edge of the tub and began to undress, I heard Mother's footsteps approaching. When she reached the bathroom, she opened the door and poked her head in. "I'm gonna be leaving now. I put your breakfast on the table. Make sure you eat and lock the door when you leave." I nodded then dropped my gown onto the floor and took the wet rag from the sink. "Can I talk to you first?"

Mother sighed. "I don't have a lot of time. The city bus gonna be here soon."

Looking away from Mother, I began rubbing myself down with the wet, soapy rag. "I want to go back to Foxgrove."

"Rose," she said then paused for a moment, "we ain't in the right school district. Foxgrove is on the south side. We're on the north side. And there ain't no school buses that can bring you there from here."

"What about Mr. Bradley?" He was the father of a Foxgrove classmate.

"Mr. Bradley was nice enough to pick you up from downtown and drive you to school for two weeks after we moved. Two weeks is long enough. I would never ask him to go out of his way to do it for a whole year or more." Mother was growing irritable.

"I can take the city bus there," I said despondently.

"You're too young to take the city bus all the way to Foxgrove and back by yourself. It's too dangerous. Plus, the school won't take you back anyway. I told you before we ain't in the right district."

"I stay at home by myself," I said.

"You're in the apartment by yourself, but Mrs. Cooper next door, is always lookin' and listenin' out for you."

"I don't like Watson."

"Well, you gonna have to get used to it 'cause there ain't much I can do right now." Mother's voice was raised and mean.

"I don't know why we had to move anyway," I muttered.

Raising her voice louder, Mother said, "I'm not gonna get into this with you again. Don't blame me for the way things are. You wanna be mad at somebody, then be mad at your father. I gotta go." She slammed the door shut.

"It's your fault," I cried out. I threw the rag into the sink and slumped down onto the edge of the tub. I sat with my arms crossed, pouting. I heard the front door slam shut and Mother running down the hallway steps. The music was still on in the living room but playing low. After a while, the piano melody began to soothe me. I stood from the tub and wiped away my tears. After brushing my teeth, I picked up my gown and put it back on. I walked into the living room, turned up the music then made my way into the kitchen, dancing rhythmically to the musical tones, to eat my breakfast with only the company of Billie's voice crooning "God Bless the Child."

I had locked the front door to our apartment and was on my way down the stairs when Mrs. Cooper, our next-door neighbor, peeked out her door and said, "Make sure ya come straight home from school. I'll be here waitin', ya hear?" Without looking back, I nodded and kept on my path. When I walked out into the fall air I could feel the chill of the wind through my jacket, which was bright red with two small white butterflies knitted on the front just below the collar. Walking down the cement path onto the street, I remembered that Father had given it to me only a year before. It was supposed to be a surprise but I had found it in a brown paper bag behind the sofa in our living room on Maple Street. I was playing hide-and-seek with a friend. Father was slightly disappointed when I walked into the kitchen with the jacket in my hand, but he'd bought it for no special occasion so he quickly got over it.

"Try it on. Let's make sure it fits," he'd said, holding the jacket behind me as I slipped my arms into the sleeves. They were a little long, so he folded them back so that they weren't hanging over my hands.

"I like my jacket. It's pretty," I said.

Father had a pleasant smile on his face and nodded in agreement. "I'm glad you like it. I haven't shown it to your mother yet. Let's surprise her when she comes home," he said.

"Okay," I said, grabbing my friend Vanesha's hand and skipping out of the kitchen.

Father was rarely home during the day. He was usually out looking for a job or spending time by himself at the local park just down the street. Every now and then I would see him resting on a bench or reading the newspaper. Even in the cold or in the rain you could find him there. The time of day or season didn't seem to matter. Whenever I asked him what he was doing or why he spent so much time there, he would just say, "No reason in particular. Just need time to think."

Some nights I would lie awake and wait for him to come home. I would usually fall asleep waiting. In the mornings he was always gone before I awoke, but if I looked out my bedroom window and far enough down the street I could see him resting or sitting on the same forest-green bench. Sometimes on my way to school I'd first run down the street and give him a hug. He would smile and say, "Thank you. I needed that." Father always had a funny smell on his breath and in his clothes, but I'd still hug him for as long as he would let me.

My parents had always tossed words back and forth. Most of them weren't so nice. It didn't seem as though they knew how to have a normal conversation with pleasant words or smiles. When we were all home together, I spent more time in my room with the door shut than I did anywhere else in our apartment. When I was home alone with one or the other, that was the only time I could roam freely into the other rooms.

Mother worked two jobs while living on Maple Street, so she wasn't around often. She left the one at the department store soon after we moved. When Father was still with us he would come home early some days after I got out of school and relieve the babysitter. He would sit with me and help with my homework, read books and poems to me, teach me a new game or let me invite a friend over. If it was warm and windy enough outdoors he would take me to fly my kite. He wasn't around much on the weekends, so Mother would take me shopping with her or we'd go to the park and play on the swings, go swimming in the local pool or lay in the grass under the sun talking and laughing. In the winter, Mother and I would stay in listening to music, letting the rhythm of each song carry our spirits away. The day Father waited at home to surprise Mother with my new jacket was the last time I saw him. Shortly after that, Mother and I were packing our things into brown cardboard boxes and watching as they were being loaded onto a big white truck by strangers. Mother said moving away was the best thing for us. If it was, I wondered why she didn't bring her heart along.

On my way to Watson, I couldn't help but think about the last time I had seen Father. My red jacket reminded me so much of him. I also thought about the times before then when I would meet with him at the local park. I deeply missed him. And more than ever I missed Foxgrove. It was during my walks to my old school that I'd stop and visit him at the park. Mother never knew I saw Father. She always thought I was going to meet Vanesha so that we could walk to school together. On my way to the park, I would see Vanesha and tell her to keep walking, but slow, so I could catch up. When I did finally meet up with her, I was usually out of breath and we'd only have a block left to go before stepping onto the school's grounds. Vanesha would just look at me and smile. She'd stopped asking me where I went or what I was doing because my answer was always the same: nothing.

As I drew closer to Watson, I began to feel butterflies in my belly. Several times I thought about turning around and heading back home. But either Mrs. Cooper or Mr. Dickens, who lived in the building next to mine, would have spotted me. Mrs. Cooper would've heard me in the hallway coming up the stairs or unlocking my door. She would've probably stuck her head out to see who it was. I'm sure she would have called Mother at work to let her know I was home quite early for a school day.

Mr. Dickens would have announced my absence from school to the whole neighborhood and would've probably thought I was up to no good. He wouldn't have said a word to me. He would've just followed me with his eyes until I disappeared into my building. As soon as Mother stepped off the city bus, someone would've been in her ear telling a story that had only half the truth. Taking all of this into consideration, I knew it was a bad idea to miss school, so I continued up the long paved walkway. Before I knew it, the school bell rang. The other kids were stampeding into the building with me behind them, and soon I was sitting in class looking into Justin Romero's face and dreading his crude remarks and mean gestures. The only thing that seemed to help me through the day was my dreams. Every opportunity I got to drift off into another time and place, I did.

My last dream wasn't as pleasant as all the others. It scared me, because in it I had found my father dead. It was a winter morning, dark and raining. I was on my way to Foxgrove, my old school, and saw my father on the bench, face down, in the park by our building. I walked over to where he was and called his name. I thought he was sleeping. He didn't wake up to answer me. I shook his body and called his name over and over, but he still didn't answer. I started to cry, then I heard a voice. I woke from my dream. Mr. Nathaniel was at the door talking to another teacher. It was his voice I had heard. When I lifted my head from my desk a tear dropped onto my sleeve. I quickly wiped away the dampness flooding my cheeks.

Chapter 4

Foxgrove Elementary was a large school with more than one thousand students. The population was fairly diverse. I had the whole rainbow in my second-grade class. Everyone got along, and we were all reading on the same level and working out of the same mathematics books. My second-grade teacher's name was Mrs. Carey. She was a petite woman in her mid-thirties with dark brown hair and eyes. She had two young children of her own and was married to a firefighter. She'd give us quizzes every Friday on one of the assignments we worked on during the week, and whoever received the highest grade would get a gift that was donated by the Hartsfield Fire Department. One time I won a stuffed dog called Spot. He was mostly white with big black spots all over his body.

Mrs. Carey was patient, kindhearted and loved to teach. She treated all of her students equally and never had to punish any of us, even when we acted out in class, which is something we did every now and then. She'd walk up to the offender and whisper softly in his or her ear. The offender would usually smile. Then she'd walk away and resume class. Once I had interrupted the class while she was in the middle of working out a math problem. She was writing out the numbers on the blackboard when I began to talk to a classmate. She turned around and caught me, looked at me for a moment with disappointment, then she walked over to my desk and whispered, "Little girls are gifts from God. He makes them pretty and polite. It isn't polite to talk when I'm teaching." She softly patted my head then walked back to the blackboard and began to write. She didn't have to talk to me again for a while after that.

At Foxgrove I learned about the different colors of the rainbow. My parents were the first to teach me. They bought me a box of crayons and made me draw lines on a piece of paper. They would say each color then make me repeat it, then I would have to give an example of something that represented that color. My favorite color was red because I was named after a red rose. In school my lessons on color were taught in other ways. First were the crayons, coloring books or drawing paper then there were my friends and Diversity Day. None of my friends looked the same. We were all unique in our own way, but no one made a fuss about it. Mrs. Carey told us that it was important that we learn to celebrate our differences. Once a month she would dedicate a day to cultural diversity. Each child was asked to bring to class something from home that represented *our* culture. American culture. Mrs. Carey would start Diversity Day by reading a piece taken from literature or displaying a work of art. Once she told a story about Jesus. She said he was a remarkable teacher who possessed great wisdom, compassion and love for humanity, as well as a great devotion and love for God. She said he was an example that all should live by. As she talked more about his life, she wrote on the blackboard:

If we say we love God, but hate others, we are liars. For we cannot love God, whom we have not seen, if we do not love others, whom we have seen. The command that Christ has given us is this: whoever loves God must love others also. —1 John 4:20, 21

When she finished writing the text on the board she said, "These were words inspired by Jesus." She continued her dialogue regarding his life and work and explained further the words that she had written.

On another occasion she brought in a picture of Mahatma Gandhi. Below his portrait the words *My Life Is My Message* were inscribed. Mrs. Carey said that Gandhi was another great teacher and leader and that his life and many of his writings inspired such prominent leaders as Martin Luther King, Jr. As she talked about Martin Luther King, Jr., who had died only three years earlier, in 1968, she made reference to his well-known speech entitled, "I Have A Dream." Mrs. Carey said she would recite the speech during our next Diversity Day. After learning so much about it, my classmates and I were very excited to hear it. The next month finally rolled around, and Mrs. Carey was well prepared to share Dr. King's famous words. Before she began the first word, tears started to well in her eyes. "I'm sorry but I get so emotional every time I read it," she said, dabbing at her eyes with a piece of tissue. "On August 28, 1963," she began, "Martin delivered these very words, which affected the hearts and minds of every human being around the world." During the speech she'd momentarily pause between words and sometimes her voice would grow higher. She read:

> The marvelous new militancy which has engulfed the Negro community must not lead us to distrust all white people, for many of our white brothers, as evidenced by their presence here today, have come to realize that their destiny is tied up with our destiny and their freedom is inextricably bound to our freedom...
>
> I have a dream that one day this nation will rise up and live out the true meaning of its creed: "We hold these truths to be self-evident: that all men are created equal." I have a dream that one day on the red hills of Georgia, the sons of former slaves and the sons of former slave owners will be able to sit down together at a table of brotherhood.... I have a dream that my four children will one day live in a nation where they will not be judged by the color of their skin but by the content of their character. I have a dream today.

Mrs. Carey continued reading. After the very last word of the speech, she turned away from the class, walked to her desk and sat down. She remained silent for several moments before she spoke. "Well, class. That was Martin's speech. It was a powerful one too. I know you're still too young to fully comprehend every word, but you're not too young to understand its meaning. If you don't remember anything that I said today, just remember this; We all are God's children, and we all were created to be equal." She put her elbows on her desk, clasped her fingers then rested her chin on her hands. "Okay, who's next?" Miles Bradley, a white boy with curly red hair and bright blue eyes, raised his hand. "Come on up to the front," Mrs. Carey said, waving him toward her.

"I brought music," he said.

"What kind of music?" Mrs. Carey asked.

"Jazz," he replied.

"Oh! I love jazz. Let's pull out the record player so we can hear it." Mrs. Carey walked to the storage closet at the other end of the room. She opened it then rolled out a small wooden table with a record player sitting on top. She plugged the cord into an outlet. "Hand it over," she said, holding out her hand.

Miles handed the vinyl disc to Mrs. Carey. "Nice. Louis Armstrong." Miles smiled. "Which song do you want us to listen to?" she asked. Miles shrugged. "I'll pick one," Mrs. Carey said. She studied the record's jacket for a few seconds then slid it under the base of the record player. "Okay. Here we go. The song is called 'What A Wonderful World.'"

I was sitting in the front row of the class observing Mrs. Carey while she listened to the song. I could see that she wanted to cry again. Her eyes were glistening, but this time she held back her tears. I found myself near tears. I couldn't help but remember the day when my parents danced to that song in our living room. Father was swinging and dipping Mother. She had laughed and laughed.

I thought, *if the world is so wonderful, why are my parents always arguing? Why is my father sleeping on a bench in the park?*

While I became engrossed in my thoughts, Mrs. Carey started toward the record player and asked "Well, did you like the song?"

The class answered in unison, "Yes."

While removing the black vinyl from the record player, Mrs. Carey asked Miles "What's so important about jazz?"

Miles took a minute before answering. "My father told me to bring this record."

Mrs. Carey paused for a moment. "Okay, but why is jazz important? Why is music important?"

Miles reflected for a moment longer then said, "My father said jazz is, uh, uh a language that—"

Mrs. Carey handed him the record and completed his sentence, "A language that the world understands. It is universal. Very good. You may be seated." Mrs. Carey sauntered over to her desk and sat on the edge facing the class. "Music, like other art forms, is a deep expression of the human spirit. It gives voice to human emotion. Sometimes it's hard to put emotion into a simple vocal expression. The song that we just heard had words, very meaningful ones, but the music itself not only gave voice to emotion, it spoke to us about the human experience.

Music with or without words is the closest we come to knowing the truth about ourselves, dependent and independent of culture, race and identity, and the truth about our American experience. Jazz is the American experience. The American experience is jazz." I didn't quite understand Mrs. Carey but I did know that music could make people laugh, cry, dance and remember things good and not so good.

"Who's next?" Mrs. Carey asked. I raised my hand. "Rose, what do you have for us today?"

I picked up my bag and brought it to the front of the class. "I have a quilt." I pulled it out the bag and let it roll down to my feet. It was sewn together by my great-grandmother. She gave it to my mother shortly before she died. My mother said my great-grandmother made the quilt when my mother was a young girl. She had helped cut out the patterns.

"Wow. That is pretty," Mrs. Carey said. The colorful quilt was made out of pieces of cloth. Some were a solid hue and others were designed with various patterns. All of the cloth had been cut into square patches and sewn together. Embroidered within the center of the quilt was a group of people, a house, a sun, a few trees and flowers.

"My great-grandmother made it," I said, trying to straighten it out.

"Here. Let me help. I'll grab the other ends." Mrs. Carey walked over and held the other two ends. "What does this quilt represent?"

"It represents family and love," I said.

"What else?" she asked.

"Hope," I said with excitement.

"Life, hope, community and freedom," Mrs. Carey said. "Women, particularly black women—slaves and free—were able to create the lives they dreamed of within their quilts. To dream was to experience a form of freedom. Quilts also told a story about the reality of their lives. That reality was good and bad." Mrs. Carey grabbed the two ends I held. "Let's leave this sitting out for a while. We'll let the other students observe it a little more after we're done." I nodded, grabbed my bag and headed back to my seat. "Next," Mrs. Carey said.

The remainder of the school day was spent viewing and discussing various cultural artifacts and art that included literature and music. In one way or another, each artifact or art form represented an aspect of our American culture. Poems and writings by Frederick Douglass, Langston

Hughes, Ralph Waldo Emerson, Gwendolyn Brooks, Phillis Wheatley, Sojourner Truth and others were read.

A Native American named Dakota in my class brought in a rug with a sandpainting. It was multicolored with several significant symbols, including what Mrs. Carey referred to as the swastika. Mrs. Carey said that the design went back thousands of years in human culture. It is one of the oldest symbols made by humans and dates back to the time of cave paintings. It was said to have originated in India.

As Mrs. Carey related the history of the swastika, a Jew named Walter yelled out, "That's a bad sign."

Dakota frowned.

Mrs. Carey saw Dakota's expression and said, "It's alright. We need to explain to Walter what this symbol originally signified for Native Americans." Dakota nodded. Mrs. Carey proceeded to explain the symbolic meaning of the design. She said that although most of the world, particularly those from the Western Hemisphere, frown upon the symbol because of its association with Adolf Hitler and his National Socialist Party, it is a symbol that was designed within many artistic creations. For Native Americans it represented abundance and prosperity. Mrs. Carey asked Walter to come up to the front of the class and join her and Dakota. He did. While there, Mrs. Carey had Dakota explain the significance of the other symbols designed within the sandpainting and how they each related to one another.

We learned that our American culture was infused with, not only modern works of art and literature created by some well-known and not-so-well-known people, but it was also influenced by ancient beliefs, traditions and rituals that were practiced by natives and those who migrated from distant lands, including Africa and Europe. Mrs. Carey began to discuss Egyptians and their many contributions to the world. She said that mathematics, science and many of our religious and spiritual practices were heavily influenced by or originated within ancient Egyptian culture. The bell rang before she could elaborate further.

When I talked to Father about what I learned in school that day, first he smiled then he frowned. "Whites stole everything from us," he said. "What they couldn't steal they tarnished. It pains me that their blood is running through my veins and through yours." Father slammed his fist down on the kitchen table. "It pains me." He walked away from me and stared out the window. "Sometimes I don't know who to blame more—whites for their evil or the rest of us—blacks, coloreds, negroes, or whatever we want to call ourselves—for our weakness and stupidity. Don't know if we'll ever figure out where the blame lies." I sat at the table in silence and just listened. Father continued to speak, but mostly as though I wasn't there.

Chapter 5

I was visualizing a miniature stone model of an Egyptian pyramid and hearing Mrs. Carey's last words before the bell—"One of the seven wonders of the world hidden truths of life…"—when I heard a man's voice in my ear. My teacher at Watson, Mr. Nathaniel, a dark, tall and stocky black man with salt-and-pepper hair and thin wire-rimmed glasses, was standing in front of my desk asking, "Rose, do you know the answer?" I looked up, surprised to see him. I still had pyramids on my mind. "Well, do you have an answer for me?" he asked impatiently.

"No," I answered nervously.

He turned and walked back to the board. "Well, at least you're honest. But that doesn't mean that you're off the hook. On page thirty of your math book you'll find the answer." I could hear the other students turning pages. My book was still closed. I quickly grabbed it from underneath my reading book and turned to page thirty. There were ten math problems on the page. Below each were three answers, but only one was correct. "Just in case you don't know, we're working on problem number five," Mr. Nathaniel said. "So Rose, what is your answer?"

Already embarrassed, I studied the problem for several seconds then finally answered, "Twenty-five."

Mr. Nathaniel turned toward the board and wrote the answer underneath a math problem he had already written out. "Perhaps. Does anyone else have an answer besides this one?" Several students fidgeted in their seats. No one answered. "No one? I'm not surprised. Is twenty-five the right answer?" Still no one said a word. "Okay, I'll have to call on someone. Thomas, what about you? Is twenty-five the right answer?"

Thomas squirmed in his seat. "Huh? Yeah. I think so," he said.

Mr. Nathaniel walked over to Thomas's desk and picked up his math book. "Doesn't look like you did your homework."

Thomas fumbled with his pencil and reached for a torn piece of paper that was on his desk in front of him, quickly replying, "Teacher, I wrote my answers on this paper."

"Let me see that," Mr. Nathaniel said, grabbing for the torn, stained, white sheet. He studied it. "Looks pretty good. Not bad. Now tell the class your answer for number five." He handed back the paper and began to walk away.

"Twenty-five," Thomas said confidently.

"Thomas, you've been surprising me over the last couple of days. Good job. That is the right answer," Mr. Nathaniel said, circling it on the board. "Rose," he said, turning to face me. "Now that everyone is on the same page and we have confirmed that the number you gave us is right, why don't you tell us what you were daydreaming about. I'm sure the rest of the class would be interested in knowing."

Mr. Nathaniel's request caught me by surprise, especially because I thought I was off the hook considering I had given the right answer. I didn't know what to say, so I looked around the class then studied Mr. Nathaniel's face for a moment, hoping I could think of something quick. I couldn't, so I decided to be honest. "We should have Diversity Day once a month."

Mr. Nathaniel chuckled. "Diversity Day," he repeated. "And what would we do on Diversity Day, Rose?"

"Celebrate our differences by sharing them with one another," I said.

"Celebrate our differences? And what are our differences?" Mr. Nathaniel asked inquisitively.

"We're not all the same."

"Okay. And?" Mr. Nathaniel replied. He appeared slightly confounded.

"If we accept our differences, we can get along better," I said.

"Who taught you that?" Mr. Nathaniel asked.

"Mrs. Carey."

"Mrs. Carey? Help me to remember who she is," he said.

"My second-grade teacher."

"Oh yeah. That's right. I spoke to her on the phone. She was a very friendly woman. She had a lot of nice things to say about you. So, Mrs. Carey says if we accept our differences, we can get along better?" He paused and scratched his head. "Well maybe we can learn to get along better in the classroom if we have Diversity Day, but what about the rest of the world? Do you think they have Diversity Day?"

I shrugged. "I don't know," I said.

"My job is not to teach you about diversity or acceptance. Each one of you is a person of color, regardless of how light or dark you are. There isn't one white child or Asian child or Indian child in this school. Most of you are black with the exception of a few Latin children in this classroom and others. So, my job is not to teach you about diversity. My job is to teach you about survival. The rest of the world hasn't learned to celebrate our differences. The rest of the world has only learned to fear our differences. So, until we, as people of color, have been accepted and loved by the rest of the world, we will have to master the skills of survival," Mr. Nathaniel explained irritably.

"Justin doesn't like me," I said. I looked over at Justin and frowned. He frowned back.

"The world will never fail to teach us that we all are not equals. Some of us have been afforded better opportunities than others. At Watson, we are lucky to get the grade of textbooks we have. They're used and have been handed down to us by one of our sister schools, but they're all we have, so we'll have to make the best of them. At Foxgrove you were afforded the luxury of acquiring new and upgraded textbooks each year. Your teachers were sent to summer workshops to strengthen their skills and to stay abreast of new discoveries in teaching. At Watson, we're lucky the school is still open and that we have jobs. So the only answer I have for you and Justin is that we do the best we can at Watson. Furthermore, if Justin is concerned that you're smarter than he is, perhaps he should pay more attention in class and focus on completing his homework assignments each night."

Mr. Nathaniel seemed slightly perturbed as he articulated his thoughts. He looked away from Justin then over at me with a stern expression as though he were waiting for me to answer.

Feeling myself growing angry with Mr. Nathaniel, I stared back at him. I mumbled, "I want to go back to Foxgrove."

"Excuse me, Rose? Did you say something?" Mr. Nathaniel asked.

"I heard her," Justin yelled out.

"I didn't ask you, Mr. Romero," Mr. Nathaniel stated angrily.

"Nothing," I said.

"Sure you said something. Repeat it for the rest of the class," he said.

"Nothing," I muttered.

"If I have to ask you one more time, that corner is where you will be sitting for the rest of the day," he said, pointing a long, dark finger at a space near the exit.

"I said I want to go back to Foxgrove." I held my head down while answering.

"Rose, to be honest with you, I wish we all could go to Foxgrove, but we can't, so get used to Watson. Get used to the real world." Mr. Nathaniel walked over to the door and opened it. "It's time for lunch. Starting with the farthest row, stand and make a line in front of me. If I hear one word, you will be spending lunchtime at your desks."

Not much changed during the remainder of the school year, except that Mr. Nathaniel grew sterner each day. Many of us got used to the corner of the room. It seemed that everything, regardless of how minor it was, irritated him. On a few occasions, he went as far as using a ruler to punish us by hitting us in our opened palms. I experienced that form of punishment once and made sure never to experience it again.

Justin and I had gotten into a wrestling match in the cafeteria. First, we were sent to the principal's office and almost suspended then we had to face Mr. Nathaniel for further punishment. I cried for almost half the day. Justin turned red and gave our teacher a nasty scowl. If he wanted to cry, he didn't. It probably would have been best if he did because he ended up receiving more hits with the ruler than I did. He missed school for three days after that. Mr. Nathaniel tried to get in touch with his parents, but his family didn't have a phone. Because I had cried for so long, Mr. Nathaniel decided not to call Mother. He probably had begun to feel sorry for me. At the end of the day, once the rest of the class was dismissed, he walked over to the corner where I was, turned me toward him, looked me in the eyes then wiped away my tears. He didn't say a word to me, except that I, too, was excused.

After that day, I was ambivalent about whether I liked Mr. Nathaniel. I would usually talk over these types of matters with Mrs. Wise, but I was too embarrassed to tell her why I had gotten into trouble in the first place. If I'd told her I had gotten into a fight with Justin, I knew she'd be disappointed in me. I wanted Mrs. Wise to be proud of me, so I only told her the good things. Sometimes I would tell her the bad things, but only if they didn't involve me. Plus, I knew that she'd tell me to put myself in the other person's shoes. For a very long time, it was difficult for me to put myself into Mr. Nathaniel's shoes and to empathize with him when he said or did something that made me angry. Sometimes I thought he was a monster from another planet. But one day that all changed, when he cried in front of the whole class. I had only seen one tear. It had escaped before he could catch it.

Mr. Nathaniel had come into class late that morning. When he walked through the door, he didn't bother to acknowledge our presence as he usually did. Normally, the first thing out of his mouth was, "Pull out your homework. Honors group, you know the routine." But this day he didn't say one word for a whole hour. Surprisingly, the class remained quiet. Before Mr. Nathaniel walked through the door, it sounded as though we were having a party. The only thing we could hear during that hour after he walked in was the raindrops on the windows and whispers. On occasion we could hear Mrs. Crawford teaching the fourth-grade class next door. Sometimes she would get excited during teaching. Suddenly, I had heard Mr. Nathaniel clear his throat.

His voice sounded raspy when he spoke his first words to us that morning. "It was today that I lost my family." He put his head down for a short while then lifted it again. I heard the rain hitting the glass, but I didn't hear any other voice in the room. All was quiet. Mr. Nathaniel stood from his seat and walked over to one of the windows. He stared out, watching the rain fall. Someone giggled in the back of the room. Another voice said, "Be quiet." Then Mr. Nathaniel began to speak again. "It's May fifth. It was exactly three years ago, on this day, in 1969, that I lost my wife and child.

"I found out one week before my release date. I was serving in the military. I had served for twenty long years. Didn't like it, but I had to make a living somehow. I had a chance to buy my family a house and other things that we could never afford before. My wife spent most of her time fixing it up and making it a home. My son was only four years old. It took my wife almost three years before she could finally conceive. Giovanni was a good child. My wife spoiled him. She would send me pictures of him every year so I could see how much he had grown while I was away."

He continued to stare out the window. "She'd sent me pictures of the house too. She had always had an eye for interior decorating. That's what she wanted to do. She thought that everyone's home should be their sanctuary. She was right. But three years ago on this day, I received a call that would change my life forever. My wife and child were struck by a car. They had just left Hartsfield Hospital. Only about an hour before, my wife had called and left a message for me saying she had good news. She would tell me when I reached home. The military was nice enough to release me early. They said they still needed me, but they understood I had duties at home and had to go. After the funeral, I thought about re-enlisting, but my spirit wouldn't let me. Instead I decided to become a teacher. I wanted to make a difference in another child's life. I wanted to save our children from the streets. I know it's what my wife would've wanted." Mr. Nathaniel was quiet for several moments. He then turned to face the class. "Pull out your homework. Honors group, you know the routine," he said. It was then I witnessed the tear. And though he had quickly wiped it away, it was that tear that had made me realize his humanness.

Chapter 6

The third grade was finally behind me. During the last month of school, I became eager for summer's return. I was in need of a break from homework, Justin Romero and Mr. Nathaniel. Although I had begun to develop more of an understanding for my teacher, mostly because of my talks with Mrs. Wise, I still hadn't gotten used to his harsh tone and occasional physical threats with a ruler. I supposed it was the only way he could maintain order and control in class and perhaps within his life. After all, much of his experiences were garnered within the military, and before that he was being raised by a father who had spent most of his life in the navy. Within these institutions they had been taught that order and control were integral to one's survival. And patriotism meant engaging in wars to defend one's country and oneself against the enemy.

For Mr. Nathaniel his war was no longer on the battlefield, it was an internal one. It was a war for which he had to engage his own internal demons—his own prejudices against his black skin and his fear of love. In Mr. Nathaniel's eyes, to be black was to be less than. He was a black man, but it seemed that his life experiences had taught him that his life had little worth. And the self-image within the looking glass was a constant reminder. That image didn't speak love. Love was a human quality. To be less than was to be less than human. In the military, it was an important lesson to learn for survival. After he lost his family, it was a lesson that was further ingrained.

I was too young to understand it at the time, but I learned a lesson on patriotism the day I witnessed the tear falling from Mr. Nathaniel's eye.

It took a lot of courage to become human again. Life can do that. Life has a way of stealing every ounce of self-love, worth and dignity one can have. And then something as simple as a kind word, a gentle touch, a child's smile or even a human tear can restore it all. When Mr. Nathaniel was looking out of the window, something must've caught his eye. Whatever it was touched his heart. I don't think it was the rain, although Nature has a way of reminding us how precious life is, but I do think that it might've been each of us children. Instead of looking at his own reflection through the glass, he was seeing ours. And just as his son, Giovanni, was a gift of life from God, so was every child. I know he could see Giovanni in each of us. But instead of loving us, he spent most of his time trying to save us—not from a speeding car, but from the cruel world. Perhaps this was his way of expressing to us what was in his heart. If it was, there came with his kind of love some gain but more loss.

We had been out of school for less than a month when I learned about Justin Romero's death. Mother told me about it after reading Justin's mother had killed him. The article said he was found dead in his bed with a large bump on the back of his head. Mother remembered I had complained on numerous occasions about Justin Romero being a pest and how much I disliked him. After that day, him being a pest didn't matter to me anymore. I only wished I could take back every unkind word and gesture toward him. More than anything, I wished I could go back to the day when we wrestled in the cafeteria. If I could've relived that day, I would've walked away instead of pushing him after he pulled my hair. I broke down after Mother finished reading the article. I also cried for a few days after that. Mother was working most of the time, but when she was home, she was more than kind and understanding toward me. We hadn't done much talking, but she held me when I needed her to. I didn't go to Justin's funeral. I couldn't bear it to see him dead.

I'm sure Mr. Nathaniel read the article. If he did, I know he felt extremely bad. He was very tough on Justin. When Justin was in school Mr. Nathaniel was always scolding him. Justin spent more time in the corner than anyone else in our class. He definitely received the most discipline with the ruler. And each time he would stay away from school for days at a time. Mr. Nathaniel would send him to the principal's office when he was back. He threatened personally to visit his home on a few occasions. Those were the only times that I saw tears in Justin's eyes.

Nothing else could seem to make him cry. It appeared those were the only times that Mr. Nathaniel felt sorry for him. But it never stopped him from being tough on Justin.

After Justin's death, I confessed to Mrs. Wise everything that had happened during the school year between Justin and me, as well as between Justin and Mr. Nathaniel. Mrs. Wise shook her head. She looked as though she wanted to cry, but she didn't. She said, "Love. That's what the boy needed. It might've saved him. He was just lookin' for love. Cryin' out for it. That's what the actin' out was 'bout. That's all it was 'bout. A sad story. A sad, sad story indeed." I knew that Mrs. Wise wanted to remind me how important it was to step into another person's shoes. She didn't though. I'm sure she knew I felt bad enough. The only other thing she said was, "You gotta let the bad memories go. First you gotta forgive yourself for doin' what you did then you gotta forgive him for makin' you do what you did." I didn't visit with Mrs. Wise for very long that day. I needed some time to myself.

I saw May, who was in honors group with me in third grade, later that day. She lived across the street from me. When she saw me sitting on the steps in front of my building, she called out my name. She was in her front yard playing double dutch with two other girls. It looked as though they were having a lot of fun. I jumped up and ran across the street to join them.

May asked, "You know how to play double dutch?"

"Just a little," I said.

"You want us to teach you some more?" she asked.

"Okay."

"This is Tanya and Patrice," she said. I hadn't met them prior to that day.

"Hi," Tanya said.

"Hi," I replied.

"Hi," Patrice said.

"Hi," I said.

May walked over and took the ends of both ropes from Tanya. "Tanya's gonna show you how to jump in. She knows how to jump better than me." Tanya stood to the left of Patrice and carefully watched the movement of the two ropes as they moved up and down. Patrice and May simultaneously moved their hands in a circular motion. After a moment

Tanya leaped between the ropes and lifted her feet one at a time. She turned around and jumped up then slapped the ground and was back up again. She looked like she was having a lot of fun then suddenly the rope stopped and was tangled between her feet. "Shoot," she said.

"You wanna try now?" May asked me.

"You go first," I answered.

"Okay. You know how to turn the ropes?" May asked.

"I remember a little," I said.

"Here. Take the ropes and start turning. I'll show you how." May stood behind me and held tightly on to my hands. She was portly and slightly taller than me. She moved my hands in a circular motion while Patrice did the same on the other end. "Watch Patrice," she instructed. As I looked at Patrice and allowed my hands to move within May's, I could feel the ropes becoming lighter, and soon I was beginning to master the technique of turning rope for double dutch. When May felt comfortable enough with my turning, she released my hands. "See. It's easy," she said. I nodded. Soon May was in the middle of the two ropes jumping up and down, one foot lifting at a time. She didn't try any of the same tricks Tanya did, but she remained between the ropes for a while before she jumped out and gave Tanya another turn. Soon we all had had a turn turning and jumping. It took a few tries before I could make it into the middle of the ropes without them hitting me and becoming tangled between my legs. After a couple of successful tries, nothing could stop me, except the next girl who jumped in behind me, which was an indication my time within the ropes was up.

We played double dutch for at least an hour before we grew tired of it. Once we were done, we decided to sit on May's steps and talk about school and boys and other interesting games like hopscotch, jacks and kickball. "Oh, wait a minute," Patrice said. She reached into her pocket and pulled out several plastic jacks and a small red rubber ball.

"Let's play," she said.

"Okay," the rest of us answered. While playing jacks on the wooden steps, May announced she would be attending another school for the upcoming year. I wasn't happy to hear the news. I expressed my disappointment by throwing down my jacks.

"What's wrong with you?" May asked.

"I don't want you to go," I said, frowning.

"Why not?" she asked.

"Because I don't have any other friends at Watson. Nobody else likes me," I said.

"But I don't like it at Watson. I didn't like Mr. Nathaniel, and my parents said he wasn't a good teacher. They think everybody there is just like him. He had a bad attitude," May said.

"Sometimes he was okay," I said.

"No he wasn't." May shook her head. "I didn't like him."

"Mrs. Crawford might be nicer," I said. She was one of the fourth-grade teachers at Watson. Her class was next door to Mr. Nathaniels.

"Don't matter. My parents already signed me up at my new school. The bus gonna pick me up right there," she said, pointing down to the corner of East and Main streets. "Plus, I can get a better education at a white public school. My parents said the state don't care about blacks. That's why we don't have no money for new books. We'll probably be reading the same books next year in Mrs. Crawford's class."

"We'll be taking the bus together, right, May?" Patrice asked.

"Yup. And we're going school shopping together too," May said.

"I'll be your friend," Tanya said, looking at me.

"Okay," I said, looking over at Tanya. "What grade are you gonna be in?"

"Fifth," Tanya replied. "I only have one more year at Watson."

"We can walk to school together," I said.

"Okay," Tanya said.

"See, now you have a new friend. Y'all can go school shopping together too," May said.

"My mother don't like to take me school shopping. She brings my clothes home from her job," Tanya said. Patrice put her hand over her mouth and giggled.

"That's not funny," May said sternly.

"Whatever." Tanya rolled her eyes at Patrice, who looked away.

"Where does your mother work?" I asked.

"The Salvation Army. They have some nice stuff there. My mother got this from there," Tanya said, tugging on the strap of her jean dress. There was a single pocket on the top front center of it. A large pink heart was knitted onto the pocket. The stitching around the heart had become unraveled. The top edge of the heart was falling away from the dress.

"Your mother can't afford to go school shopping. That's why she get your clothes from her job," Patrice said.

"Your mother's fat and sits around the house all day," Tanya replied.

"Your mother ain't no better than mine," Patrice retorted.

"Both of y'all need to be quiet. Y'all always arguing. Make me sick," May shouted. "Come on, Rose. Let's go upstairs." She jumped up from the steps.

"I can't. My mother won't know where I am," I said.

May marched to her front door. "I'm going upstairs. I'll see y'all tomorrow." She opened the door, walked into the hallway then slammed the door shut.

"Whatever," Tanya shouted.

"She always gettin' a attitude. We was just playin'," Patrice said.

"Y'all wanna finish playin' jacks?" I asked.

"Yeah," Patrice and Tanya answered at the same time.

The three of us remained on May's porch playing jacks until I saw Mother walking up the street from the bus stop. I saw that she needed help. She had grocery bags in her hand. "I have to go. My mother is coming," I said, placing my jacks down and jumping up from the porch then running down the steps. "I'll see y'all tomorrow." Patrice and Tanya waved good-bye. Mother was struggling with the two bags. I quickly ran up to her and grabbed for one of them. "Be careful," she responded.

"I'll help," I said.

"Okay, but these bags are heavy. Here, grab my pocketbook instead." Mother tilted her shoulder toward me. "I can manage the bags myself," she said.

I took the strap of mother's worn black leather pocketbook and slid it off her shoulder. I managed to remove it from her arm without making her drop either bag. I placed the strap onto my shoulder and let the pocketbook fall to my side. I clutched the strap and sauntered up the street beside her. The sun was still shining bright although it was getting late. It was close to dinnertime, and the street was quiet. Mrs. Wise was no longer in her front yard tending to the garden when we passed. Patrice and Tanya had disappeared down the street, and my neighbor, Mrs. Cooper's silhouette within the second-floor window of my building had gone away.

While walking with Mother, I started to think about school again. My heart began to beat faster and I felt my face becoming warm. I didn't like that May wasn't coming back to Watson. It wasn't fair, I thought, that she was leaving and I had to go back. I slowed down my pace and let Mother walk ahead of me. Her pocketbook slipped off my shoulder and hit the ground, making a loud noise. Mother turned around and looked down at her pocketbook then looked at me. "If you weren't slouching and dragging your feet, maybe it would stay on your shoulder," she said.

"May isn't coming back to Watson," I said angrily. I knelt down, picked up Mother's pocketbook and let the strap fall hard onto my shoulder.

"What does that have to do with you, Rose?"

"Why do I have to go back?" I said, pouting.

"Because you do," Mother answered while turning back toward our building.

"Why?"

"Rose. Please," she said, struggling with the bags.

"I don't wanna go back," I said still dragging my feet.

"It's not up to you," Mother said, walking up the steps. She pushed open the door with her body. "Hurry up. These bags are heavy."

"When school starts I won't go," I said, stomping up the stairs.

"Don't test me, Rose." Mother let the door go before I was through. She turned back and looked at me when I kicked it wide open with my foot.

"You wouldn't go if it were you," I shouted.

"If I had no choice, I would have to go. You don't have a choice, and that's why you have to go back to Watson." Mother moved her feet quickly and loudly up our hallway steps.

"You're not a good mother," I shouted.

Mother threw her head back and stared into my eyes. "You're gonna mean those words if you say one more thing to me. You're gonna mean those words." Mother continued to stare at me. I could see the anger in her face, but I didn't look away.

Chapter 7

I was turning the key in the lock of our apartment door when Mrs. Cooper stuck her head out her door. "How's ya doin', Mrs. Lee?" she said.

Mother placed one bag down next to the wall then turned around. "Oh, I'm fine, Mrs. Cooper. Just tired. How about you?"

Mrs. Cooper opened the door a little wider then stuck out the upper part of her body along with her head. She was a large-framed woman who wore a dark brown wig and thick glasses. The wig was always on slightly crooked, so I could always see her thick gray hair. Every time I had a chance to talk to her face-to-face I would stare at her wig. I always wished I could straighten it out for her.

"The day was fine, Mrs. Lee. No complaints. God give me another day to thank Him for," she said with a southern drawl.

"I'm glad to hear it," Mother said. "And please call me Maxine. We're friends, I hope, and you're in charge of watchin' little Rose while I'm away, so please call me Maxine."

Mrs. Cooper smiled. "Yes, indeed. I'd like to say we friends. I think you's a nice woman. Different from the rest 'round here. Minds nobody business but your own. That's the way to be 'cept when you tryin' to help people," she said.

Mother nodded. "Well, you have a good evenin'. Thanks for keepin' an eye on Rose for me. I'm gonna make us some dinner before it gets too late," Mother said.

"Good evenin'," Mrs. Cooper replied then slid back into her apartment and shut the door.

I was already standing with our door wide open. Mother leaned forward and picked up the brown paper bag then walked through the door.

"Why is she so nosy?" I asked, shutting the door then locking it.

"What do you mean?" Mother asked, walking into the kitchen.

"She's always stickin' her head out the door when I leave and when I come home. And she's always watchin' me out the window when I'm outside talkin' to Mrs. Wise or playin'," I said, following Mother.

"She's supposed to do that. She's in charge of watchin' you while I'm away. You can either sit in her apartment and keep her company or you can come and go as you like as long as she can see you or you can hear her," Mother said, dropping the bags onto the kitchen table. I placed her pocketbook down onto one of the kitchen chairs then began to sift through one of the brown paper bags.

"When am I gonna be able to go to the park?" I asked.

"What park?" Mother inquired.

"The park in the back, up the hill," I said, pointing toward the corner of our kitchen.

"You're still too young to travel up there by yourself." Mother began emptying the contents of one of the bags.

"Other kids go," I said.

"Yeah, and they're older," Mother said. "Do me a favor and turn on the radio."

"I see kids my age," I said, turning to walk into the living room.

"Rose, I'm too tired to argue with you," she said, putting a container of orange juice into the refrigerator.

"You can take me," I said before reaching the living room. "You used to take me to the park."

"Rose, I don't have time," she replied loud enough for me to hear.

I walked over to the radio and hit the power button. "You used to," I mumbled. The dial was already set to the jazz station, WJAZ 107.1. A song had just begun to play. A man's voice, deep and raspy, came on the air. "And this next tune is one of my favorites. It's called 'Yesterdays.' Yeah. Miles Davis is on the trumpet giving us an earful of sweet notes. Candy. Yeah. Yeah." The voice faded, and the music grew louder. I turned to walk back into the kitchen. I slowly sauntered past the sofa, grazing it with my fingers. I had been silenced by the man's voice and the almost melancholy song. When I reached the kitchen, Mother was at the sink washing ears of corn. I sat down in one of the chairs and stared at her.

"What is wrong with you?" Mother asked, looking over her shoulder at me.

"I miss my father," I said.

Mother turned away and was silent for a moment. "Rose, I don't know what to say," she said.

"I want to see him," I said.

"You can't," she said.

"Why?" I asked.

"Because he's sick, and I don't know where he is," she answered.

"What's wrong with him?" I asked.

"I don't want to get into it right now," she said. She began peeling another ear of corn. She tugged at the husk and tore it off, throwing it into the sink.

"But I want to know," I said, becoming irritated.

"One day you will know," she said.

"I want to know now," I said.

Mother threw the corn she held into the sink. She turned toward me. "Didn't I say I don't want to talk about it?" she yelled.

"I want to see my father," I yelled back.

"Rose, get out of my face right now." Mother pointed at the entryway of the kitchen, which lead back into the living room.

"You left him alone. That's why he's sick," I screamed, quickly rising from the table then running out of the kitchen.

"You have too much mouth, little girl," Mother yelled after me.

I ran into my room and slammed the door. I plopped face down onto my bed and started to cry. "I hate her," I mumbled. "I want my father."

I had cried myself to sleep. When I opened my eyes again, the day had become only a portrait of colorful memories. Now that it had gotten darker outside, the night had begun to capture moments of my being within the dim reflection of light. My silhouette had shown itself on my ceiling and walls. Outside of my bedroom window, I could see the moon was half full, and the stars were clear and bright. I rolled off my bed, stood and walked over to the chair beside the window. I sat and rested my chin in the palm of my hands while leaning with my elbows on the windowsill. I didn't bother to turn on the light because the moon and stars provided enough for me to see. The shadows on my wall were busy. I imagined they were angels that had come to keep me company. I could still hear the radio in the living room. The music was playing softly, and I could hear the sounds of a piano. While listening, I drifted deeper into my imagination, thinking about all sorts of things, but mostly I wondered if the angels were watching me and heard the words I had silently expressed. I needed God to let my father know I missed him and we needed him. Since we had moved, Mother was always depressed, and she never made time for me. I missed going to the park, playing on the swings or talking in the grass. I also missed going shopping with her on the weekends. She used to be so much fun. And when Mother wasn't around to do those things with me, Father would spend time with me, even after he stopped coming home at night.

I hadn't known that Father was sick. That night I hoped he was okay and God was taking care of him wherever he was. The times I had visited him in the park before we moved, I could see he wasn't his usual self. Most of the time Father's eyes were red, his clothes were wrinkled and dirty, and his breath smelled funny. Once he tried to stand from the bench but fell back down.

I asked him, "Father, you okay?"

He looked at me, grinned and said, "I'm dandy."

I hugged him, kissed him on the cheek then ran away. Each time I'd seen him, I thought he looked so bad because he was tired. I knew that wherever he was spending his time he wasn't getting a good night's rest, and I knew he wasn't working. Mother always argued with him about finding and keeping a job. She used to say if he spent less time dreaming and more time working then maybe he could keep a decent job. Because he didn't have one, I guessed he couldn't afford to buy any clothes. A few times I thought about taking some of his stuff from the drawer in Mother's old room on Maple Street and bringing them to him, but I knew she would catch me. I decided to sneak his toothbrush and comb instead, hoping they would help him to keep himself up a little more. I don't think he ever used them because his hair remained disheveled, and his breath still smelled the same—like grapes that had gone bad.

Once, when Father and I had been outdoors flying my kite, he said before I was born he had been trying to save enough money to travel around the world. He wanted to learn more about other cultures and to live like the tribal Indians who were very spiritual and in touch with the higher spirits. They always talked to the spirits about peace, love, Nature and community. He said the tribal Indians were a kind people and worshipped the earth. He once carved miniature people called gnomes out of wood as a gift to the Indians. He showed them to me and told me these tiny wooden people were preservers of the earth. Father wasn't an Indian himself, but he used to spend a lot of time outdoors sitting in the grass with his legs crossed and his hands cupped around each of his knees. Sometimes I would hear him making sounds. I could never understand what he was saying.

While at the park one day I had gone off to play. When I came back to join Father, he was sitting in the grass making the same noise I always heard him make. I had snuck up behind him and listened for a while. Then I tapped him on the shoulder and asked, "What are you doing?"

He opened his eyes and looked over his shoulder at me. "I'm chanting," he said.

"What for?" I asked.

"I'm communicating with the spirits," he said.

"What spirits?" I asked.

"The spirits that are up above and all around us," he said.

"I don't see them," I said, looking up and around me.

"They're invisible," he said.

"If I talk to them, will they hear me?" I asked.

"Sure. You can talk to them by praying," he said. "Tonight before bed we'll say a prayer."

"Can I talk to them now?" I asked.

"Sure. Sit here beside me and put your hands together like this," he said. He placed the palms of his pale hands together. I sat down and emulated him. "Close your eyes." I closed my eyes. "Now, praying is like when you blow out your birthday candles and make a wish. No one else has to hear that wish. It's between you and the spirits."

I kept my eyes closed and made a wish, then I opened them and said, "I'm finished."

Father hugged me then kissed me on my forehead. "That's a good girl."

That was the last time I made a wish, but on this night, as I sat looking into the sky, I thought about the spirits Father talked about and wondered if they also dwelled among the moon and stars. If so, I wondered if they could deliver my prayer to God. I closed my eyes, placed the palms of my hands together in front of me and made a wish. If Father was traveling the world, I hoped he had found the Indians and they were taking care of him.

Chapter 8

Mother lightly knocked on my bedroom door then opened it. She walked in, looked around, saw me at the window then turned on the light. I quickly put my hands over my eyes until they adjusted to the bright light. Mother walked over to where I was, stood in front of me and stared out of the window. "Why are you sittin' in the dark?" she asked. I shrugged. "Did you hear me callin' you?" Still gazing into the night sky I shook my head. "What are you thinkin' about?" I shrugged again. "I guess you're still mad at me," she said. I still didn't respond or gesture. "Well, I was just comin' to let you know dinner is done. I know you're hungry. It'll be waitin' for you when you're ready," she said then turned to leave.

She walked out of my bedroom but left the door open. I wished she had shut it. I was still not prepared to step out into her world. It was becoming more and more unpleasant there—a place of silence and sadness. It was as though she had somehow lost her voice and her joy. I had witnessed her as a woman who always spoke what was in her heart and on her mind. It didn't matter who the person was, Mother always knew how to express herself so that the other person knew just what she meant. She could make a kind word easily soothe your pain, and she could make a harsh word deepen your hurt.

In the last days of our living on Maple Street, I knew her as a woman who mostly made the pain hurt more. It seemed like the more she made others hurt, she would hurt just as much or maybe even more. I knew this because, after she argued with Father or screamed at me for the smallest things, she would break down and cry. Sometimes I would try

57

to say something nice to her so she could feel better but she'd just tell me to go to my room. I don't think Mother liked for anyone to see her cry, but after she was done, she would come to my room and say something kind to me. She never directly said she was sorry, but I knew that was her way of letting me know.

After thinking about Mother for some time I decided to sit at my window awhile longer. A warm summer breeze softly stroked my face. The gentleness I had felt softened my heart. It reminded me of the softness of both Father's and Mother's love. I remembered my father's lips pressed gently and briefly against my forehead and Mother's touch when she ran her fingers through my hair or wiped away my tears. I could feel myself struggling to smile. My lips parted slightly, until I was reminded by the sudden stillness how little I'd received that affection since we'd moved shortly over a year ago. I sat there longer, refusing to step out into Mother's world, but it was slowly inviting itself into mine.

Eventually I found myself sitting at the kitchen table with a warm plate of food in front of me. Mother had kept it in the oven until I was ready. I had no appetite, so I only picked at the contents on my plate. I did have a hunger for answers so I asked, "Do you still love me?"

Mother looked up from the garment she was sewing. "Of course I do. That was a foolish question," she said.

"I don't think so," I said, still picking at my food.

"You don't think I love you?" she asked, placing the garment on her lap. "Or you don't think it was a foolish question?"

"I don't think it was a foolish question," I said.

"Why wouldn't I love you?" she asked, searching my eyes.

"I don't know," I said, shrugging.

"There's a reason why you asked," she said.

"You never smile," I said.

"I'm too tired to smile," she said, picking up the garment from her lap. She looked away from me and continued sewing.

"You're always tired," I said.

"It ain't easy workin' my long hours. I gotta come home and make sure you're taken care of too," she said.

"Why you have to work so much?" I asked.

"So I can keep food on the table, clothes on our backs and a roof over our heads," she said.

"You can't do that working less hours?" I asked.

"Besides food, clothes and shelter, I gotta pay bills. We need light to see, gas to keep us warm in the cold and to cook with and a phone just in case of an emergency. Livin' ain't free, you know?" she said, shaking her head. "And to be honest with you, I can barely afford livin'." Mother sighed. "There was a time when the natural things of life was free for everybody, but folks made claims and now everything costs. Even water."

"I know," I said.

"Sometimes I'm not sure you do," she said. "Seem to give me a hard time about things."

"I don't like it here. You ain't the same," I said.

"We ain't the same. Time and circumstances have changed us. And sometimes that change is hard to get used to," she said.

"I haven't changed," I said.

"Sure you have," she said.

"How?" I asked.

"Your mind is growin'. It's because you're learnin' more things about life. The more you learn about life, the more you become aware of things. The more you become aware of things, the harder it becomes to live life in this world. I can tell already that livin' is becomin' harder for you. And you still young. The only thing that makes livin' easier is by keepin' your heart shielded. The only way to do that is to toughen your heart. You see? Your father and I spoiled you. All the lovin' we gave you made your heart tender. Now don't get me wrong, I still love you the same and more, but we set expectations that the world ain't gonna be able to live up to. You gonna expect the same kinda lovin' you got from home from the world. Expectations like that only gonna make you experience a whole lot of hurt. Deep, deep hurt," she said, shaking her head.

"Is that what happened to you?" I asked.

"Things was a little different for me as a child. Your grandma never set false expectations for her kids. She didn't spoil us with hugs and kisses and a whole lot of kind words and things like that. It wasn't because she didn't love us. She knew how cruel the world could be, and she knew the rest of the world wouldn't treat us the same. I guess she figured she'd make life a little easier for us by lovin' us the tough way. I didn't always like it, and a lot of the time I resented her for the way she made us feel.

We felt unloved. At home it always mattered to me, but when I walked out into the world and somebody did me wrong, it didn't matter because my heart was already prepared." Mother sighed again.

"There's good people in the world. Mrs. Wise said so," I said.

"Oh yeah, there's good people in the world. Good black people and white people and more, but it ain't always easy to come across those kinda people. And some people you come across, you can't really tell if they good or not because they make it hard to get to know 'em." Mother chuckled. "That's what your father said about me. He said when he first met me, he didn't think I had a heart. When he found out I had one, it took him a long time before he could thaw it out. Your father had a lot of patience. Most people in this world don't have the kinda patience he had. There was a lot of good things about your father. The only thing was he had a sickness. If it wasn't for his sickness, things might've been a little different."

Mother sighed. "We still wouldn't have had much money though." She chuckled. "Your father was always dreamin'. He always wanted something different than what he had. Nothin' could keep him happy for long. Because he was never happy with what he had, he became dissatisfied with life. Eventually he started doin' things that wasn't right. He ended up hurtin' himself and hurtin' me. Wasn't long before I started to harden my heart again. The only thing was it was too late. The hurt was already there, and it was already deep."

Mother was looking down at the garment and fidgeting with the needle. She was quiet for a moment, then she said, "Life ain't fair. For the first time, I thought I had somethin' good and that your grandma was all wrong about life. My relationship with your father made me resent her more than I had as a child. Well, I quickly learned. Your grandma knew somethin' I didn't, so now all I'm tryin' to do is make things easier for you. I don't want you to feel the kinda hurt that I'm feelin'."

"But I'm already hurt," I said.

"That's 'cause things are different. You ain't used to how things are yet. When you get used to the way things are, the hurt will start to go away," Mother said.

"When are you gonna get used to the way things are?" I asked.

"In time. In time," she said. The persistent look of consternation in Mother's eyes had seemed to question her own answers and views on life and love. Confusion was still twirling around in my own head. I had already known love. I wanted to know it again.

Mother and I sat at the table in silence for a long time. She was busy sewing, and I was busy playing with my food and making various patterns on my plate with the sauce from my spinach. "Your father once quoted a verse from the Bible to me," she finally said. "It was a long time ago though, before we married. It was from the Gospel of John: 'Anyone who does not know love is still in death.' After reading it to me, he said, 'we live to love, we don't live to die. Ain't no life in death. You got to live so you can experience love. You got to love so you can experience life.' It seems he forgot this when times was hard. I must admit I had forgotten what he said myself."

Mother sighed, put her head down and placed the garment on her lap. "Sometimes I feel I've become so familiar with death that I've forgotten about the simple joys. Like watchin' the sunrise." Mother smiled softly to herself then resumed her sewing.

After dinner, Mother asked me to wash the dishes. It was the first time she requested my help in the kitchen. She said, "Now that you're older, it's time that you learn more responsibility. It's just the two of us now, so I'm gonna need your help."

I didn't mind. I was ready to help more around the apartment, and the time spent by Mother's side was something I cherished. We rarely had the opportunity to be in each other's presence for long periods. While washing dishes, I began to think that things could be the way they used to be. This was the kind of change I could get used to.

Mrs. Wise once said life was like a circle. I took it to mean that things go around and come back around. Mother and I used to have good times, then we had bad times. Maybe we could have good times again. The only thing I didn't like about life being a circle was that if we had bad times once, then we would probably have bad times again. It wasn't a thought I wanted to hold in my head for long, so I quickly let it go. The only thoughts I wanted to keep in my head, like a picture on film that I would revisit every now and then, was that Father was coming back, and love would make life good again. Mother said she had to do the things she did to toughen my heart because life and love hurt sometimes. And when it hurt, it hurt deep down at the core of the soul. While I was washing dishes and probing, not for any answer but for truth, she said the hurt can make a person lose it.

When I asked her what *it* was she said, "your spirit."

"How do you lose your spirit?" I asked.

She didn't answer right away. She kept scrubbing the top of the stove. At first I thought she hadn't heard me. Finally she said, "You lose your spirit when you stop trustin' God."

I probed a little further. "Why do people stop trusting God?"

"I suppose it's because the tests of life are hard," she said.

I went to bed that night thinking about God and spirits. *Is God a spirit?* I wondered. Mrs. Wise had talked about the spirit within us. She also said God was inside of us. *If God is inside of us why are there so many bad people in the world? Bad people make the world bad,* I thought. Don't people want to live in a good world? I guessed that everyone wanted to live in a good world. Mrs. Wise once said people have good experiences and bad ones in life. Sometimes the bad can make people mean. I guessed that the bad experiences are the tests Mother was talking about. The tests of life. I guessed they made people forget about God, the spirit inside of us. Mrs. Wise had said God is where our strength comes from. If God is inside of us, then I figured our strength must come from inside us too.

Chapter 9

I lay awake in bed for hours that night. It was hard to sleep with all my thoughts about God, but once they began to dissipate, I began to hear voices outside my bedroom window. One of the voices sounded like Mr. Dickens's. The other sounded like a young girl's. They were talking low, so I couldn't hear what was being said. Afraid that I might get caught if I peeked out, I decided not to leave my bed. After a while the voices grew quiet. I heard the door shut beneath my window and light footsteps in the hallway. There was another set of footsteps on the pavement outside of my building. They grew fainter, then there was silence. When I turned to look at the clock on the end table at the foot of my bed, it was half past midnight. I began to wonder why Mr. Dickens was out so late and who he had been talking to. I gathered it must have been Tanya, the only other young girl in my building, who lived with her mother and younger sister on the first floor.

When I awoke the next morning, I remembered the two voices. It wasn't the first time I had heard people talking outside of my bedroom window during the night, but I had never paid much attention before. The man's voice was high like a woman's. The only man I knew who sounded like a woman was Mr. Dickens. I still wasn't sure whether the other voice was Tanya's. If it was her outside with Mr. Dickens, she was too young to be out so late, I thought. She was nine years old, only a year older than me.

Mother knocked on my door before entering my room. "Rise and shine," she said. I pulled the thin floral sheet over my head before she opened the door, pretending I was still asleep.

Mother pulled the sheet down from my face. "Come on, sleepyhead. It's time to get up. I'm leavin' for work, and breakfast is on the table." I opened my eyes and stared at Mother. She looked different this morning. She had on makeup, including ruby-red lipstick.

"You look pretty," I said groggily.

"Thank you," she replied with a smile. "I'm surprised you're still asleep. Why are you so tired?"

I rolled over on my side, yawned and stretched. "I couldn't sleep," I said.

Mother sat at the foot of my bed. "I hope I didn't worry you last night. You're still young and don't need to think too many big thoughts in that little mind of yours. I know things are tough for us right now, but we'll find a way to work 'em out."

"I'm not worried," I said.

"What kept you up then?" she asked.

"I was wondering about God," I said.

"Yeah, I was thinkin' about God myself. Some of what we talked about made me question my faith," she said.

"Faith?" I asked.

"It's kinda like what I said about trust. When you stop trustin' God, all that means is you lost faith in Him," she explained.

"Oh," I said, yawning. "Do you think you can trust God again?"

"I'm workin' on it," she said, gently patting my foot. "Now let me go before you make me late."

"Why do you have makeup on?" I asked.

"I got tired of lookin' at that same ole ugly face in the mirror every mornin'. That's all," she said.

"Your face isn't ugly," I said.

Mother smiled. "It's just a figure of speech," she replied. "Listen, I have to go. I just wanted to tell you that if you need me, you know how to get in touch with me. Your lunch is in the fridge, and Mrs. Cooper will be keepin' an eye on you, so don't give her a hard time." Mother stood from my bed. "Ya hear?"

"I won't," I said, yawning again.

"Boy, you must've stayed up pretty late," Mother said, walking out my bedroom door.

I stayed in bed for a short while longer. I heard the front door to our apartment shut then Mother's footsteps hurriedly walking on the pavement outside of our building. I got out of bed and sat at my window. The jazz station was on, and the music was playing low. I had forgotten what day it was, but it was 7:15 a.m., according to the voice on the radio. It was a little after Mother usually left for the bus. Mrs. Wise was already in the garden watering her flowers, and Mrs. Cooper was with her. Patrice, who May had introduced me to and who lived down the block, was coming up the street with a jump rope in her hand, and Mr. Dickens was sitting on the stoop in front of his building, listening to gospel music on a small black radio with silver knobs. He looked like he was waiting for someone. Patrice walked into May's front yard and sat on the steps. She made me think about May. I remembered the fun we used to have together in Mr. Nathaniel's class. I knew I would miss her at Watson when it was time to go back.

Patrice looked over then saw me in my window. "You comin' out?" she yelled from across the street.

"I have to wash up and eat first," I answered. Mrs. Wise and Mrs. Cooper looked up at me and waved. "Hi," I responded.

I jumped up from my chair and scurried around my room looking for clothes and my sneakers. I rushed out of my room and into the bathroom. After washing up I ran into the kitchen and grabbed the cold, hard toast off my plate, took a bite and gulped down my orange juice. I took a few bites of my hard-boiled egg and threw what I didn't eat into the garbage. I rinsed off my plate and left it in the sink. I would wash it with the rest of the dishes after dinner. I turned off the radio, grabbed my keys off the coffee table and ran out the door. Patrice was jumping rope when I got outside.

"May said she'll be out in a little while," Patrice said.

"Is Tanya coming out?" I asked.

"I don't know," Patrice said, shrugging then handing me one end of the rope.

"She never comes out early 'cept for school."

"Oh," I said. "Why?"

"She always talkin' 'bout she tired," Patrice said.

"She probably stays up too late," I said.

"I don't know," Patrice said.

"Hey, y'all!" May yelled. She was standing on the second-floor porch of her parents' three-family house.

"You comin' down?" Patrice asked.

"Hold your horses. My mother gotta finish braiding my hair," May said.

"Hi, May," I yelled up to her.

"Hi, Rose. I'll be down in a little while." May rushed from the porch.

"Look at this," I said, picking up a bright yellow dandelion.

"It's just a dandelion," Patrice said, walking toward me.

"I betcha I can tell if you like butter," I said

"How?" Patrice asked.

"Lift your chin," I said. Patrice did what I asked. I held the dandelion a couple inches away from Patrice's chin. "There's a yellow spot underneath your chin. That means you like butter."

"Let me see if you like butter," Patrice said, taking the dandelion. She held it underneath my chin. "You like butter too," she said, giggling.

"When May comes down, let's see if she likes butter too," I said.

"Okay," Patrice said. We walked toward May's porch then sat down. "Let's play another game."

"Which one?" I asked.

"Simon Says," Patrice said. "I'll be Simon."

"Okay," I said, standing. I walked toward the street, turned around and faced Patrice.

"Simon says put your hands on your head." Patrice demonstrated. I copied her.

"Simon says stand on one leg." Patrice did this and started swaying trying to catch her balance. I stood on one leg.

"Put your finger on your nose." Patrice placed her index finger on the tip of her nose. I moved one hand from my head then lost my balance while reaching for my nose. Patrice and I laughed.

"I didn't say Simon says," Patrice said, still laughing. "I got you."

"It's my turn now," I said.

"Hey, y'all." May rushed out the door. "I'm ready to play double dutch."

"We were playin' Simon Says," Patrice said.

"I don't wanna play that. I wanna play double dutch," May said.

"First, I want to see if you like butter," I said.

"What?" May wrinkled her nose.

"Let me see if you like butter," I said, walking toward her. I picked up the dandelion Patrice had thrown on the grass and placed it underneath May's chin. "You have a yellow spot. That means you like butter," I said.

Patrice ran over to look. "Let me see," she said.

"Let me see if you like butter," May said, taking the dandelion.

"She likes butter. I already did it," Patrice said.

"I wanna see," May said, placing the dandelion underneath my chin. "I see the yellow spot. You like butter. You like butter," she said, running away with the dandelion and laughing.

"Let's play tag. You're it," Patrice yelled after hitting May and running away.

"I don't wanna play tag," May said, standing with her hand on her hip.

"You don't wanna play because you're it," Patrice said.

"I don't wanna play because I feel like jumping," May responded, sucking her teeth and rolling her eyes.

"Rose, what do you wanna play?" Patrice asked.

"I don't care," I said, shrugging.

"Come on then. Let's play double dutch before May has a baby," Patrice said, picking up the ropes from the ground.

"I ain't gonna have no baby," May retorted.

"Whatever," Patrice said, handing me the ends of the ropes. She walked over to May then handed her the other ends. "I'm going first."

"I don't care," May said, frowning. We started turning the ropes and waited for Patrice to jump between them. When she made it in, they became tangled within her legs.

"You did that on purpose," Patrice said, looking at May.

"I did not," May yelled.

"I'm going again," Patrice responded.

We played double dutch for at least an hour before we heard Tanya's voice across the street. "Hey, y'all!" she shouted.

"Hey, Tanya," we all said.

"Can y'all come across the street? My baby sister's asleep, and I have to listen for her when she wakes up." Tanya shared her bedroom, which was in the front of our building, with her younger sister. She had the two windows raised.

"Where's your mother?" May asked.

"She had to go to the store," Tanya answered.

"We can come across the street," I said, taking the other ends of the rope from May and folding them up. Patrice, May and I ran across the street.

"I wanna play double dutch," Tanya said.

"I'm tired of jumping," May said.

"So what we gonna play?" Tanya asked.

"I don't know," Patrice and I said at the same time. We looked at each other then laughed.

"I don't know either but I'm tired of jumping," May said.

"Let's step," Tanya said. "You know how to step, Rose?"

"No," I said.

"Come on, y'all, let's teach her," Tanya said.

"Stand next to May," Patrice said, grabbing my shoulders and moving me closer to May. We stood next to each other. Patrice stood on the other side of May, and Tanya faced us.

"Move your foot like this," Tanya said, doing a light, rhythmic stomp.

I watched Tanya's foot then moved mine in synchronization with hers. Patrice and May watched then began stomping with us.

"Now clap your hands like this," Tanya said. I watched her then started to clap. We were all moving our feet and hands harmoniously. "Now just listen to us, then the next time we step you can say the words too," Tanya said.

"I'll start," May said.

"Let the queen go first," Patrice said, rolling her eyes. Tanya and I laughed.

"May, before you go, guess what?" Tanya said.

"What?" May asked.

"Today is my birthday," she said.

"For real?" Patrice said.

"Yup," Tanya said.

"Happy birthday," I said, smiling.

"How old are you?" May asked. "I know, I know, don't tell me. Um, ten. Right?"

"Yup," Tanya said. She stopped stomping and clapping. "Look at my first birthday present." She pulled a small, gold heart charm attached to a thin chain from underneath her shirt. "My mother went to get me a cake."

"That's pretty," May said.

"Who gave that to you?" Patrice asked.

"My friend," Tanya said.

"Your boyfriend?" I asked.

"Nope. Just a friend," Tanya said, blushing.

"What's your friend's name?" Patrice asked.

"I can't tell you," Tanya said.

"Why?" May asked, rolling her eyes.

"Because I just can't," Tanya said, sucking her teeth.

"Aren't you too young to have a boyfriend?" I asked.

"I don't have no boyfriend," Tanya said.

"Whatever. I don't know who gonna give you a charm like that unless it's your mother or a boyfriend," Patrice said with her hand on her hip.

"Since it's such a big secret then forget it," May said. "Let's just step."

"You don't have to get a attitude," Tanya said. May turned her back on Tanya and then turned back toward us.

We began to stomp and clap again. Tanya said, "May, I thought you wanted to go first."

"Humpty Dumpty dump," May sang out loud.

"A little louder now," Patrice and Tanya sang.

"Humpty Dumpty dump." May sang louder.

"Straighten up your back," Patrice and Tanya responded.

"What did Humpty do?" May sang.

"Humpty Dumpty sat on the wall. Humpty Dumpty had a great fall," Patrice and Tanya said in synch.

"My name is May."

"Humpty Dumpty dump."

"I'm nine years old."

"Humpty Dumpty dump."

"I'm a Scorpio."

"Humpty Dumpty dump. Humpty Dumpty sat on the wall. Humpty Dumpty had a great fall."

"My name is Tanya."

"Humpty Dumpty dump."

"I'm ten years old."

"Humpty Dumpty dump," I joined in.

"I'm a Leo."

"Humpty Dumpty dump. Humpty Dumpty sat on the wall. Humpty Dumpty had a great fall."

"My name is Patrice."

"Humpty Dumpty dump."

"I'm nine years old."

"Humpty Dumpty dump."

"I'm a Gemini."

"Humpty Dumpty dump. Humpty Dumpty sat on the wall. Humpty Dumpty had a great fall."

"You know this one now, right?" Tanya asked.

"Yeah," I said.

"Okay, let's do, um, Hotel Motel," Tanya said.

"That's a nasty one," May said.

Tanya laughed. "No, it's not. It's just words."

"Let's go in the same order," Patrice said.

"Hey, May. Where did you go? Where did you go last night?" Tanya and Patrice sang.

"I went to a party hardy freaky deaky," May sang.

"She went to a party hardy freaky deaky," Tanya and Patrice repeated.

"I went to a party-hardy-freaky-deaky."

"She went to a party-hardy-freaky-deaky."

"Hey, May. Where did you sleep? Where did you sleep last night?"

"I slept in a hotel, motel, Holiday Inn."

"She slept in a hotel, motel, Holiday Inn."

"I slept in a hotel-motel-Holiday Inn."

"She slept in a hotel-motel-Holiday Inn."

"Hey, Tanya—" Patrice and May began before a man's voice interrupted.

"Y'all know better than that mess," Mr. Dickens shouted from the stoop next door. He was waving his finger. "Lookatcha. Movin' 'em bodies like grown ladies and talkin' that nonsense. Whatcha know about a party and a hotel?" He blew cigarette smoke from his mouth. "Gonna have these boys comin' around thinkin' ya easy. Next thing ya know somebody gonna wind up pregnant. This how it starts. Yesiree. I betcha ya mamas don't know y'all out here talkin' that nonsense. It's a sin whatcha doing. It ain't right. No, it ain't right." He shook his head. "It ain't right."

Tanya had a surprised expression. She turned toward us and said, "Come on, y'all. Let's play double dutch."

"I'm going home," May said. "I don't like him."

"I'm coming over," Patrice said.

"I'll stay with you," I said to Tanya.

"Okay. Let's sit on the steps and play jacks," Tanya said, walking toward the steps in front of our building.

"I'll see y'all tomorrow," I said to Patrice and May.

"Bye," May said and waved.

"I'll be at my aunt's tomorrow, so I won't be able to play with y'all," Patrice said. "She's having a cookout."

"I'm coming," May said.

"I have to ask my mother if you can come," Patrice said.

"Okay," May said then began to walk away. Patrice followed.

I started toward my front steps. Mr. Dickens was still sitting on the stoop in front of his building blowing smoke rings and watching us. I wondered if he would really tell our mothers. I also wondered what he was doing outside of my building so late the night before, and if it was Tanya that he was with. I thought about Mrs. Cooper, too, and hoped she didn't hear us stepping. She had already left Mrs. Wise's garden and she hadn't stuck her head out, so she probably hadn't. Tanya was already sitting on our front steps. She looked over at Mr. Dickens. I looked again too. He was staring back at her like an angry parent who had just caught her doing something wrong. Tanya looked at me. "You ready?" she asked.

Chapter 10

Tanya and I played jacks without saying much of anything. Every now and then she'd look over to see if Mr. Dickens was still sitting on his steps. It seemed like she was afraid to make a sound while still in his sight. As soon as he disappeared from his steps, it was like God breathed air into her and she'd suddenly come back to life. She jumped up from the steps and said, "Let's go around back real quick. I wanna show you something."

I stood from the steps. "I can't stay long," I said.

"I can't either. My sister gonna wake up soon," she said.

"Whatcha wanna show me?" I asked.

"Wait 'til we get there," she said, running around our building toward the back.

Tanya ran over to the wire fence in our backyard. On the other side was a vacant community center that had been boarded up, and the park was around the back and up the hill. "See all 'em boys up there?" she said.

I walked up to the fence and looked through. "Yeah," I said.

"Sometimes I go up there and watch 'em play ball," she said.

"Your mother let's you?" I asked.

"She don't know. Nobody know. I sneak up there," she said, still looking up the hill. We could hear the faint sound of male voices, and with every minute that passed, a body would appear at the edge of the court near the basketball hoop.

"You gonna get into trouble if your mother find out," I said.

"She ain't gonna find out," Tanya said, holding on to the fence. "There's swings and a monkey bar up there. Sometimes I play on the swings or climb the monkey bar. Sometimes I'm the only girl there. I don't mind though."

"You don't get scared up there by yourself with all 'em boys?" I asked.

"Nope," she said. "Come on. Let's go before we get caught back here." Tanya ran away from the fence and back toward the front of our building. I ran behind her. We sat down on the steps.

"Wanna play another game?" she asked.

"Let's play Simon Says." I jumped up from the steps. "I'll be Simon first," I said excitedly.

"Umm-umm," Tanya said, shaking her head. "I don't wanna play that."

"Why?" I asked.

"'Cause I always do what Simon says," she said, shaking her head.

"It's only a game," I said.

"Mmm-mmm. Simon real," she said.

"No he isn't." I sucked my teeth. "It's just a game."

"Yes, sir. Simon is real. Simon live right there," she said, pointing at the building next door. "He the one who screamed at us."

"Mr. Dickens?" I asked.

"Yup. His name is Simon Thurgood Dickens," she said confidently. "Everybody else call 'im Mr. Dickens, but he always tellin' me to call him Simon. But only when we alone together."

"Y'all be alone together?" I asked.

"Can you keep a secret?" she asked.

"Yes," I said.

She waved me toward her. "You promise you won't say nothin' to nobody?" she whispered.

"I promise," I said, looking her in her eyes.

She looked away and lowered her head. "Simon the one who gave me this heart charm." Tanya pressed her hand against her chest. The small, gold charm was buried underneath her shirt. "He promised it to me. He always say, 'if you do nice things for me, I'll do nice things for you.'"

"What does he ask you to do?"

"I'm not suppose to tell nobody," she said.

"I won't tell anybody. I promise."

"Sometimes when he ain't working, he ask me to come over," she said. "He got a nice place. He got a TV and one of those big radios that play records and tapes. Sometimes we sit together on the sofa and watch TV. He pull me real close to him and hold me. Sometime he put a record on, and we dance together. We dance real close. I don't like the way it feel when he dancing close to me though."

"How does it feel?"

"He hold me tight. I be in front of him, and his thing be pokin' me right here," she said, pointing to a spot below her navel.

"Do you tell 'im to stop?"

"Nope. He said if I'm good and do what he say, he'll do nice things for me, so I just keep my mouth shut," she said.

"What kinda nice things?"

"He let me watch anything I wanna on TV. I see all the pretty ladies on TV. And sometimes they be kissin' a man. The white ladies be kissin' a white man and the black ladies be kissin' a white man too. I don't see no black woman together with a black man. One time I did, but they was fightin' each other. The black people I see on the TV always mad," she said.

"My mother doesn't let me watch TV. She said it's too negative and it brainwashes people," I said. "My father used to let me watch cartoons, but only if they didn't have violence in them."

"I like TV. I wanna be just like those white women. They got all the pretty clothes and jewelry and things. They got nice, long hair and pretty eyes. They beautiful. I wanna be beautiful just like 'em," Tanya said, smiling and stroking her hair.

"I like green eyes 'cause green is pretty," I said.

"I seen a white lady with green eyes. She had long hair way down her back, and she was real skinny. I think she was a model. That's what I'm gonna be when I get bigger. Simon said I'm already pretty. He be rubbing my face and kissin' me on the lips," she said.

"You let him kiss you on the lips?" I asked, twisting my own. "That's nasty."

"Uh-huh. He said he gonna bring me around the world if I let 'im kiss me. He work for the bus company. He said he gonna pick me up one day, and we gonna travel all over on his bus." She stretched her arms in front of her.

"You should tell your mother on him," I said, frowning.

"I can't tell. He said if I do I'm gonna get in more trouble than him. He said my mother gonna send me away forever, and I ain't never gonna see my sister again. Plus, it ain't all that bad. I'm gettin' a little used to it now. You should see all the pretty things he gave me. I have 'em in a shoebox under my bed. He gave me some pencils with my name on 'em and a big heart lollipop and some red heart earrings. I can't wear the earrings though, my mother might see 'em, so I just keep 'em in my shoebox. I go and look at 'em every day." Tanya smiled. "Next he gonna buy me some pretty dresses for school," she said, still smiling.

"I don't like Mr. Dickens. He's not a nice man," I said.

"He ain't that bad," she said. "He like a father to me. I ain't never had a father."

"I have a father," I said.

"Where he at?" she asked.

"He's travelin' the world and livin' with the Indians," I lied.

"The Indians kill people. That's what they show on TV," she said.

"My father said the Indians are good people. They only kill the people who try to take their land," I said.

"I seen the African people on TV. Simon said white people try to take they land too. They have diamonds and stuff. He said the white people bring diseases over there to kill the African people quicker. They land rich but the people is poor. Seeing how poor they was on TV made me cry. Simon wiped away my tears. He said I don't have to worry about being poor 'cause he gonna get me whatever I want." Tanya was looking between her legs at her feet and twisting her shoestrings around her fingers.

"My second-grade teacher, Mrs. Carey, said white people brought the Africans over here and made them slaves. But she said the African slaves are the ones who taught us about family and community and hope and love," I said. "My father said the same thing. He used to read to me and tell me all about them."

"My mother said what the white people did to the slaves was bad. She said we still suffering from it. She said things ain't really changed that much, and we still slaves." Tanya stood from the steps and began walking toward the street.

"I ain't no slave," I said.

"Me either," she said. "Here come Mud Pie."

"Mud Pie?" I asked.

"Her real name is Violet, but people call her Mud Pie because she so dirty. Her family real poor. They live in that building down on the corner with the boarded-up windows," she said.

"People live in that building?" I asked.

"Uh-huh. It stink real bad in the hallway too." Tanya walked back to the steps and sat beside me. "Mud Pie ain't nice. She like to fight everybody, but she don't bother me no more because I gave her a bloody nose the last time we had a fight," she said.

"Hey, Tanya," Mud Pie yelled, walking toward us.

"Hi, Mud Pie," Tanya replied.

"Whatcha doin'?" Mud Pie asked.

"Nothin'," Tanya said.

"Oh. Who's that?" she asked, pointing at me.

"My friend Rose."

"Rose? What kinda name is that?" Mud Pie rolled her eyes at me.

"It's a name," Tanya said, sucking her teeth.

"Hi," I said, looking at Mud Pie. She had on a dingy white floral dress with large brown stains on it. Her shoes were completely worn and too big and her hair was matted.

She looked at me then looked away. "Tanya, you wanna play double dutch?"

"I have to get my ropes." Tanya stood then walked into our building.

"You just moved around here?" Mud Pie asked.

"Last summer."

"I never saw you before."

"I didn't come out a lot."

"You live here?" she asked, pointing at my building.

"Yes."

"You act like you got a attitude problem," she said, putting her hand on her hip.

"I don't have an attitude," I said. The way Mud Pie looked at me caused butterflies in my stomach.

"You don't have to say it like that," she said, rolling her eyes. She looked me over. "Your mother black?" she asked.

"Yes."

"Why you so light then?"

"I don't know."

"Your mother light skinned?"

"No."

"Your father light skinned?"

"Yes."

"He white?"

"Half white."

"That's why you got that good hair?" My hair was braided on both sides, but the ends had unraveled and curled.

"My mother said there's no such thing as good hair."

"Yes, it is. White people have good hair."

"No, they don't," I said. "They just have a different texture."

"Don't tell me. I know. My mother said they got good hair." Mud Pie rolled her eyes again then looked away.

"I got my ropes," Tanya said, coming out the building.

"She know how to play?" Mud Pie asked, pointing at me.

"Yeah," Tanya said.

"White people don't know how to play double dutch," Mud Pie said.

"She ain't white," Tanya said.

"Her daddy is."

"No, he ain't," Tanya said. Then she turned and looked at me. "Your daddy white?"

"He's half white," I said.

"He black then. If you got black in you then you black," Tanya said. "My mother told me that before."

"She ain't got black people's hair," Mud Pie said.

"Just 'cause she ain't got hair like you don't mean nothin'," Tanya said. "Why don't you just leave her alone? She ain't botherin' you."

"I ain't botherin' her," Mud Pie said. "I'm goin' first."

"I don't care," Tanya said then looked over at me. "She botherin' you?"

"No," I said.

"If she do, let me know," she whispered. I nodded.

"I know you ain't talkin' 'bout me," Mud Pie said.

"Ain't nobody thinkin' 'bout you, Mud Pie. You always startin' trouble. You need to leave people alone," Tanya said, handing me the ends of the ropes.

"I can't help it 'cause her daddy a zebra," Mud Pie said, removing her shoes then jumping into the rope. Her scaly brown feet were covered with open sores and scabs.

"My father ain't no zebra," I said, turning the ropes faster.

"Yes, he is," Mud Pie said then jumped out of the rope. "If that rope would've hit me you would've been in trouble." She pointed a finger at me.

"I wasn't tryin' to hit you," I said, rolling my eyes.

"She wasn't tryin' to hit you," Tanya echoed.

"Yes, she was." Mud Pie walked up to me and looked me in the eyes. "Your daddy a zebra."

"No, he ain't." I said, glaring at her.

"You better leave her alone," Tanya said.

"I'm leavin'," Mud Pie said, turning away. She slipped her shoes back on, kicked the ropes that were on the ground and walked away.

"She always startin' trouble," Tanya said. "Come on. Let's just play by ourselves."

We walked back to the steps and sat. We watched Mud Pie as she sauntered down the street kicking a crushed soda can in front of her. I was quiet and still feeling nervous inside. Mud Pie was a little shorter than I was but she was portly and looked strong and mean. When Mud Pie was out of our sight Tanya leaned back onto the cement steps and folded her hands in front of her.

"I'm bored," she said.

I remained quiet, drawing invisible circles on the step below me. Tanya sat up straight. "I hear my sister." She jumped up. "I have to go. Bye," she said, pushing the door open then disappearing into our building.

Without looking up and still drawing invisible circles on the step I said, "Bye."

Chapter 11

I was sitting on the steps still nervous and angry at Mud Pie. Mostly, I was upset because she called Father a zebra. I hadn't heard the expression before but I guessed it was a name given to people who were mixed with black and white. I didn't think it mattered if a person was mixed, except during slavery. Mrs. Carey had shown our class a picture of mulatto children born during slavery. In many ways they resembled Father as a child in pictures Mother kept in her top drawer on Maple Street. Most of them were light complected with fine, wavy hair. Mrs. Carey said that although mulattos were the byproducts of white slave owners and black slave women, they were still treated as slaves. Sometimes, they were treated better and given more privileges than the darker slaves, but they were never treated equal to the white ones. She said children learned early that the color of their skin could be a blessing or a curse.

I had never really thought about my own skin tone or hair type until Mud Pie had made me aware of them that day. Mrs. Wise mentioned that I resembled the Averys, people she had known since living in Hartsfield, but I still hadn't thought much about my own features. When Mud Pie looked at me, I guess she saw the resemblance of white faces she had learned to hate. But since I wasn't one of them I had begun to wonder if white people would see the resemblance of black faces when they looked at me and hate me too. I had learned to love all the hues of the rainbow. Some you couldn't see until you mixed different colors together. I used to like doing this because I could take a plain white sheet of paper and fill it with a whole lot of beautiful tones. One time I had done this, and

Father hung up the picture on the wall of my bedroom on Maple Street. He said it reminded him of America.

Mud Pie made me think of one of the black slave children in a photo I had once seen in one of Father's books. She had downcast eyes, knotted hair and worn and dirty clothes. Father read to me that poverty was a condition of oppression, which was a condition of slavery. If poverty and oppression were conditions of slavery then why were black people in America still so poor? Slavery was over. Mother always talked about our lack of money, but if we were poor, I didn't know it. I didn't think that living in a community with poor people meant that we were poor too. Once I heard Mrs. Wise complain about the garbage pollution on our sidewalks and streets. She said, "The city like to pretend the poor don't exist. Our taxes pay for the garbage collectors, too, but seem like I'm always pickin' up my own garbage off the streets."

I had also heard that Mrs. Cooper had fallen down a flight of stairs in our hallway because the wood had rotted out and given way under her weight. She ended up with a broken leg that eventually healed, but she was never able to get rid of her limp or her cane. It took the owner of the building three weeks to fix the steps. The second and third-floor tenants had either to climb over them if they could or use the back steps to enter and exit the building. At night it wasn't usually safe to use the back stairs because there was no lighting.

While sitting on my front stoop thinking about how current conditions reminded me of slavery, Mrs. Wise walked out onto her porch. She looked up into the branches of the large oak tree, watching two birds. I decided to go over and keep her company. Walking up to her steps I asked, "Why are you watching those birds?"

Mrs. Wise smiled. "Music, baby. I hear music. The flowers appear on the earth; the time of the singin' of birds is come. The Song of Solomon."

"They're just chirping," I said.

"No, baby, that's music," she said. "Ain't nothin' like the music of Nature and God's creatures." She began descending her steps. "You come to help me with my garden?"

"I wanna ask you a question," I said.

"What's that, baby?" she said, walking to the edge of the step then sitting. She patted the area next to her. "Come and join me." I sat beside her. "What's your question?"

"Are we poor?" I asked.

Mrs. Wise looked at me contemplatively. "Well, if you think about it from a perspective of money, we ain't rich, but we ain't completely poor neither. We survivin'."

"We're surviving? What does that mean?" I asked.

"Even though it's hard to, we still affordin' the basic necessities. You got food to eat when you're hungry, right?" she said.

"Yes."

"You got clothes to keep your body covered, right?"

"Yes."

"You got a place to rest your head, right?"

"Yes."

"You get up every day 'cause you still breathin', right?"

"Yes."

"That's pretty much what I mean when I say we survivin'. Some of us do a better job at it than others, but in one way or another, we all strugglin' to survive," she said.

"What about Mud Pie? Why does she live in that boarded-up building? And why is she so dirty and why does she have sores all over her feet?" I asked.

"Life is harder for some of us than it is for others," Mrs. Wise said.

"Why are there poor people in the world?" I asked, feeling angry. Father had once explained it to me, but I still didn't understand.

"What you seein' is a glimpse into the ugly face of capitalism. American capitalism make a few folks rich, some folks comfortable and many folks poor. Most of the ones who is comfortable is workin' mostly to make the few that's rich stay rich. But they slaves to the system just like the poor. They just managed to get one leg higher up the ladder than we could. They biggest job is keepin' the rich safe from bein' too close to us. That's really what they gettin' paid for."

"Is it white people's fault that black people are poor?" I asked.

"Some people like to blame it on just the white folks. They like to say it's the white folks that keep us black folks down. I listen to Mud Pie's mother, Sister Lily, complainin' all the time 'bout how they so poor 'cause of white folks. It's true. In America the white folks have the biggest piece of the pie and some of 'em do anything to keep it, even kill, but the black folks who want a piece of the pie can have it too. It might only be a small piece but it's a piece. The other thing is it ain't white folks who own that buildin' they live in, you know? A black family got that buildin'. They've had it for a long time now. Instead of reinvestin' they money and usin' some of it to make it livable, they go spendin' it on fancy cars and stuff so they can feel important. But every time they come around and see the condition of that buildin', I know it make it harder for 'em to sleep at night. Oh, yes it does. Because it ain't human to keep it like that, especially with people livin' in it." Mrs. Wise nodded. "Most of the houses and buildings on this street is black owned. So it looks to me like black folks managed to get a piece of the pie, but it look like they just lettin' it go to waste."

"Why don't the people move out?"

"'Cause we used to bein' the victims. And we too busy lookin' at other folks like the white folks and seein' what they doin' instead of lookin' at ourselves and seein' what we doin' to ourselves. We used to bein' the victims, but we don't always have to be. The reality is can't nobody help us until we start helpin' ourselves, you know? Our own minds keep us poor. The way we think about things keep us poor. Ignorance keep us poor. Ignorance is one of the worst kinda oppressions there is," Mrs. Wise said. "And the hate we have in our hearts is what keep us slaves."

"Father read to me about slavery and oppression. What exactly does oppression mean, again? I don't remember," I said.

"Oppression is anything that keep us from empowerin' ourselves," she said.

"Empowerment? I heard that word before too."

"God is empowerment," Mrs. Wise said. "God teach us how to love ourselves. We just need to find God inside ourselves first. God teach us how to love our own mind that's filled with the wisdom of life. God is life. That's why we got to love life. And God teach us how to love our own heart. Our hearts is what make us human. God teach us how to love our bodies and cherish 'em. It's our bodies, the senses of our bodies, that remind us we human. What we think, feel and know is 'cause of the senses we was born with. The senses of the body. And the spirit." Mrs. Wise looked out in front of her. Mr. Dickens, our neighbor in the building next to mine, was walking by. He waved. Mrs. Wise smiled back. "The spirit. Yes, yes. Spiritual empowerment is the strongest weapon we have to defeat our enemy."

"Is the devil our enemy?"

"The enemy is ourself," she said. "The worst kinda enemy there is. We got to learn to love self again. Every part of us. Slavery taught us different, but it ain't got to be that way no more if we don't want it to be."

"I wish everybody could be rich. Maybe people would be happier and would love themselves more," I said.

"Money ain't the answer to everything, baby. It's nice to have but it don't teach us to love, and it ain't what make folks happy. Learnin' to appreciate the simple things in life is what make folks happy. When you learn to appreciate the simple things then you'll always be rich. The only time I feel poor is when I forget this, you see? This the kinda wisdom I was talkin' about earlier. If you pay close enough attention to life, it teaches you this simple truth. I've spent enough time around rich folks. One thing they taught me is money ain't what keeps a person happy. People look at me funny when I say to 'em that the best things in life are free. I know you done heard this plenty of times though you still young." I nodded. "Next time somebody say it to you, listen closely 'cause it's true. We forget this though. We got things like television tellin' us the best things in life is the stuff most of us black folks can't afford. Television real good at playin' tricks with the mind. Keep us in the mindset of believin' we poor. Yeah, it got folks doin' all kinda things just to live a lie. That lie is a powerful one too. It make folks kill themselves workin' hard for it, give up they lives for it, lose they values for it, steal for it, only to find out that the lie wasn't worth the price that was paid for it. And believe me when I tell you, the few at the top sufferin' just as much as those on the bottom. Maybe in a different way, but they is sufferin'. You see? It don't matter if you lose a material thing like money 'cause it can be replaced, and it can't make you poor. What makes you poor is when you lose everything you got inside of yourself. American capitalism has made many a man lose his complete self 'cause what they believe give 'em power ain't doin' nothin' but makin' 'em empty inside. When you lose your complete self, when you empty inside, you ain't human no more."

"What are the simple things?"

"It's too many to name, but a smile is a simple thing. I love to see my folks smilin'. Makes my heart happy to see my folks smilin'. Birds singin' makes me happy too. Sometimes I think they singin' to me just 'cause I'm alive. This tree," Mrs. Wise said, pointing at the large oak tree. "Is a simple thing. Ain't nothin' like the shade from this tree when the days are burnin' hot. Don't need to spend a whole lot of money tryin' to keep myself cool 'cause my tree does the job for me. Look at my garden. Pretty, ain't it? No matter how bad the world is, my garden reminds me there's still beauty in it. And Mari keeps me believin'. Keeps my faith strong. There's other things too. I'll give you a little secret of mine. Don't mind if you share it though." Mrs. Wise leaned a little closer. "When I'm feelin' a little weak inside, like things ain't right with me, I have a cup or two of my favorite drink. It ain't nothin' but a little apple cider vinegar and honey in my water. Usually have a cup a day. Have two when I ain't feelin' right. Just need a tablespoon of each in your water. Do the trick. Keep the body clean so you don't need all kinda doctors and stuff playin' with you. Takin' your money when they ain't done what really needed to be done to cure your illness."

"What else?"

"Well you don't have to pay nobody to love. The earth don't mind if you love it. The butterflies and the birds don't mind if you love 'em. Folks don't mind either. The ones that act like they mind is the main ones that need love the most. When you come across folks like that, give 'em all the love you got inside even when it's hard to." Mrs. Wise stood. "I'm gonna play around in my garden before it starts to get dark. I could use a helpin' hand, if you don't mind."

"I don't mind," I said, standing and following Mrs. Wise down the steps.

She removed her sandals and placed them in the grass underneath the oak tree. "If you gonna help, you gotta remove your shoes this time. Let the earth get to know you some more."

I pulled off my sneakers and placed them in the grass next to Mrs. Wise's sandals. We knelt at the edge of the garden and began planting new seeds.

Before I left Mrs. Wise that day, Mrs. Cooper joined us, and we planted a row of new seeds. Mrs. Cooper planted daylilies. She said they were her favorite. Mrs. Wise said it would take time before they would grow and become fully mature. I planted a single seed within the row without any help or direction. It would be the one that I alone would cultivate and grow into a flower. Mrs. Wise asked me to name the flower that I had just planted, although it hadn't started to grow yet, and to call her by her name whenever I talked to her. I had decided to name her Love. Mrs. Wise said everyone needed love. God is love. And love is the greatest of all things. I had wished that I could plant a flower in everyone's garden and call it Love. Mrs. Wise said that I could. She said there's a garden in everyone's heart and that I could plant a seed in it called Love. She said it wouldn't be easy because there were a lot of polluted hearts in the world that would need some cleaning up first. She also said it would be wise for me to practice with my own garden first. I wasn't sure if she was talking about the one where I had just planted my flower seed or the garden in my heart.

Chapter 12

I saw Mother sauntering up the street just as Mrs. Wise, Mrs. Cooper and I stood to wipe the soil from our clothes. Mother had a radiant glow on her face. Seeing her happy made me smile. I thought that she was feeling so good because of our talk after dinner the night before. Maybe she was learning to trust God again. After talking to Mrs. Wise, I knew that having faith in God meant trusting life again and love. I had also seen Mr. Girard, who lived on the next street over, standing on the corner smiling and watching Mother.

When she reached us, Mother said, "Good evening, ladies. Hi, Miss Rose."

"Hi," I said, waving.

Mrs. Wise and Mrs. Cooper turned to face Mother. "Good evenin'. How you doin'?" they asked in sync.

"Oh, I'm fine," Mother said, looking down at Mrs. Wise's garden. "It's beautiful out here."

"Yes, indeed. It is beautiful," Mrs. Wise said. Mrs. Cooper nodded. "Just gettin' home from work?" Mrs. Wise asked.

"Unfortunately," Mother said. "I wish I could enjoy my summers more."

"You gotta take some time for yourself. Work gonna always be there," Mrs. Wise said.

"Yes, it will." Mrs. Cooper nodded again.

"You right about that. It ain't goin' nowhere," Mother said, chuckling.

"Rose been helpin' me with my garden. She doin' a good job too," Mrs. Wise said, slipping on her sandals.

"I was hopin' she wasn't bein' a bother," Mother said. I was walking over to my sneakers to put them on. I looked up at Mother and wrinkled my nose.

"She ain't a bother at all. Miss Rose and me learnin' a lot of things together. It's a lot you can learn from a child," Mrs. Wise said.

"Ain't that the truth," Mrs. Cooper said. She was pouring water over the seeds she had just finished planting.

"Oh, I know. The questions alone make you think long and hard about things," Mother said.

"Yeah, they always got a lot of questions," Mrs. Wise said, chuckling. "Well, I'm gonna take myself in the house now. I think I'm 'bout ready to eat some dinner. Mrs. Cooper, you gonna join me?"

"Think I will," Mrs. Cooper said.

"Enjoy, ladies," Mother said. Mrs. Wise and Mrs. Cooper waved good-bye. "Are you ready for dinner too?"

"Yes. I forgot to eat my lunch," I said.

"Rose, you know better than that. You can't go the whole day without eatin' something. That'll make you sick. You already nothin' but skin and bones," Mother said. "Come on. Let's go."

I grabbed Mother's hand and began walking beside her. "I planted a flower seed today," I said.

"You did?"

"Yup. Her name is Love."

"Love?"

"Yup. Mrs. Wise said I should name my flower and talk to her every day," I said.

"Why'd you name her Love?" Mother asked, smiling down at me.

"'Cause everyone needs love. So I named her Love."

"I guess that's a good enough reason."

"Do you need love?"

"I guess I do. Sometimes."

"Not all the time?"

"I don't know. I don't always think about it."

"I do."

"Well you shouldn't. I may not tell you that I love you often but I do," Mother said. We walked up the steps and into the dimly lit hallway of our building. "All these questions about love makin' me think I treat you bad."

"You don't treat me bad," I said, taking two steps at a time. "Father said he loved you. He told me when we were at the park once flying my kite."

"He did? Well things have changed," Mother said, climbing the stairs behind me.

"Maybe he can love you again," I said when I reached the top of the stairs.

"There's a lot of things that would have to happen before that time," Mother said.

"Like what?"

"Your father would have to become a different man. I don't think that he's capable of doin' that right now."

"I like him the way he is."

"I like a lot of things about him, but there's a lot of things I don't like about him," Mother said, unlocking the door.

"Like what?"

"Not now, Rose," Mother said, waving me into our apartment.

"Then when?" I asked, shutting the door and locking it.

"One day when you're old enough to understand…" Mother said.

"I am old enough," I said, slumping on the sofa.

"I had a good day. Let's not change that," Mother said, walking over to the radio and turning it on. Ella Fitzgerald was singing "Now It Can Be Told." Mother dropped her pocketbook onto the love seat and started singing.

Mother fell onto the love seat. "I met someone. A real nice man." I gave her a strange look. "Why you lookin' at me like that?"

"If it ain't my father I don't care," I said, leaning back on the sofa.

"The attitude ain't necessary, little girl," Mother said, looking at me sternly. "And no, it ain't your father."

I crossed my arms in front of me. "Then I don't care," I said. Mother bit down on her lower lip and stared at me. "I hope it ain't that man, Mr. Girard, who was staring at you."

"Clarence?"

"Is that Mr. Girard's name?"

"That's his first name. His full name is Clarence Girard," Mother said.

"I saw how he was looking at you when you was walking up the street," I said.

"How was he lookin' at me?" Mother asked, smiling.

"Like he like you."

"Really?" Mother asked, grinning wider.

"I don't like him."

"You don't even know him."

"I see him sometimes on the corner watching everybody who walks by, mostly women."

"Yeah, he is a big flirt."

"He's a big ugly flirt."

"Watch your mouth now," Mother said, waving a finger at me. "I told you about that mouth of yours. That wasn't nice. You don't know the man, so don't say nothin' mean about 'im. He hasn't done one thing to you."

"I wish my father was here," I said, pouting. "If he was here, you wouldn't be talking to that man."

"Your father ain't here, and he ain't comin' back," Mother said, rising from the love seat. An instrumental jazz tune was playing on the radio. I could hear the piano in the background. Mother walked over and turned up the volume. "Maybe this will calm your attitude some." She grabbed her pocketbook and headed into the kitchen.

I remained on the sofa brooding. The music was playing loud in my ear. Soon I allowed my mind to escape into the soft sounds of the piano. When I opened my eyes again, the radio was playing low. While deep in my mind I hadn't noticed that the volume had changed. I was thinking about Mother and Mr. Girard. The thought didn't anger me as much as when she first mentioned him, but I was still worried he might take Father's place in our lives. Mother must've been lonely without Father and needed someone to replace the love she'd lost after Father was gone. Maybe it was time for her to unpack her heart and put it back into its rightful place. I had thought she'd left it behind during our move, but it seems it was sitting in a box with cobwebs just like some other things she never got around to unpacking. My mind was plagued with what might become of Mother and Mr. Girard.

Thinking about boxes, I had remembered the conversation I had had with Tanya and the shoebox under her bed. It was strange to me that Mr. Dickens would try to find love with a ten-year-old girl. I wondered why he hadn't tried it with a woman his own age. He had to be at least in his fifties. He looked old enough to be.

Does the heart make people do strange things? Mrs. Wise said there's pollution in some of our hearts and it needs to be cleaned out. I had hoped that Mother would clean whatever pollution was in her heart before she replaced it and that Mr. Dickens would clear out what was in his so he could leave little girls alone and find love with a woman. The only people I had met so far with clean hearts were Mrs. Wise and Mrs. Cooper.

Mother was in the kitchen preparing dinner. I thought about joining her, but I went into my room instead. I decided to pull out some old books that Father had left behind. They were ones he used to read to me when we were still together on Maple Street. I loved reading, too, at one time. I enjoyed the idea of learning everything I could about everything. Father taught me the importance of knowledge, but he also said I had to be careful about the things I read. He said some information could make me lose touch with reality and could shape my mind in the wrong way. Not all books had happy endings like some I had read. Not all stories told the truth, but then Father said truth is relative. He said that much of historical data contained facts, but one fact in history was that depending on who wrote it, people, places and events might change. Two people could be at the same place writing about the same person, and if the white man wrote the history book then most likely a white man would be the hero or the victim. If a black man wrote it, then most likely a black man would be the hero or the victim. The truth teller is few and far between.

"Artists are the truth tellers," Father said shortly before we moved from Maple Street. "They see beyond seeing. They know beyond knowing." He said one of the most important history books in the world is the Bible. Father used to get mad every time he picked one up though. He said it was suppose to promote love not hate, peace not war. Depending on the reader, it could do either. He had a hard time with religion.

Father said to a friend once and had written in one of his journals, "Spirituality and religion are not one in the same. Religion is an institution focused on promoting biased opinions that separate mankind. Spirituality is a state of being. It focuses on elevating the self to a higher self for the betterment of mankind and all living things. The experiences of life are our wisest teachers in this pursuit. Some religious institutions focus on spirituality while others focus on power and profitability. Jesus taught spirituality not religion."

Father's friend, Paul, who worked at the local hardware store near Maple Street, said he was a student of Jesus's teachings, a Christian. Father turned cherry red. He looked his friend in the eyes then called him a hypocrite. Paul never came back around our place again after that day. Shortly after Paul walked out of our apartment, my father picked up one of his books called *The Prophet*, opened it and read, "Your daily life is your temple and your religion." Perhaps that was partly what Father was really trying to say to Paul.

While in my room, pulling out old books from Maple Street from under my bed, I was most interested in reading one called *Those Who Ride The Night Winds* I had days before secretly unpacked from one of Mother's forgotten boxes. It was a book of poems by Nikki Giovanni. My favorite was "Love: Is a Human Condition." Father used to read it to me. I liked it because it had the word *love* in the title. I had only understood parts of the poem. After pulling the book out, I continued to read it so I could pick up its meaning. Each time I read it the words would mean something different to me. Father had been the one to always explain things I couldn't understand in books we read together. I had decided to copy the poem on a lined piece of paper. It was the same as learning the alphabet or learning how to write cursive. The more you practiced writing the letters or the words, the better you got at it. I thought maybe I could understand the words better if I wrote them enough times. The words on my sheet of paper were:

An amoeba is lucky it's so small…else its narcissism would lead to war…since self-love seems so frequently to lead to self-righteousness…

I suppose a case could be made…that there are more amoebas than people…that they comprise the physical majority…and therefore the moral right…But luckily amoebas rarely make television appeals to higher Gods…and baser instincts…so one must ask if the ability to reproduce oneself efficiently has anything to do with love…

The night loves the stars as they play about the Darkness…the day loves the light caressing the sun…We love…those who do…because we live in a world requiring light and Darkness …partnership and solitude…sameness and difference…the familiar and the unknown…We love because it's the only true adventure…

I'm glad I'm not an amoeba…there must be more to all our lives than ourselves…and our ability to do more of the same…

While writing the last word of the poem, I started to remember another one Father had once made me read out loud to him. It was named "Song of Self." I had asked him what it meant. He said, "It doesn't matter what it means to me. What does it mean to you?" It took me some time before I could decipher it. When I thought I had, I was still unsure as to whether it was the author's intended meaning. Perhaps Father would say the same about Nikki Giovanni's poem. What mattered is what I thought it meant. What did it mean to me? What did it mean to anyone who had read it or would read it? Did it mean the same thing to everyone, including its creator? What did it mean to me? I asked myself this question several times. I had to look up the word *amoeba* in the dictionary. It read, "a naked rhizopod or other amoeboid protozoan." The definition had totally confused me.

I looked up *rhizopod*. Its definition confused me even more. Finally, I looked up *protozoan*. The only word I had understood was *parasite*. It is a tiny organism that depends on another organism for its existence. I had heard someone call a lazy man a parasite. After getting stuck on the definition of amoeba, I didn't bother trying to decipher the meaning of the rest of the poem, but I still favored its title "Love: Is a Human Condition."

I pulled out my journal and slipped between its pages the sheet of paper with Nikki's poem. I kept the journal my father had given me under the bed with my books. In it, I would sometimes write out an entire poem, line for line, or I would write out just the words I couldn't understand or that I understood the most. Sometimes, using the words from another poem I would create my own. Once I wrote one that was only a single line. I had written:

God speaks to me through my own words.

I couldn't think of a title for my one-line poem so I didn't give it one. I had written a number of other things in my journal. I had my favorite songs written down. One of my favorites was called "Don't Let Me Be Misunderstood" by Nina Simone.

I stood from my bed, picked up my journal and held it in one hand. I remembered the music to the song in my head. I started to sing the words out loud. When I got to the words, "Oh Lord, please don't let me be misunderstood," I sang even louder. I pretended I had a microphone in my free hand. My stuffed dog, Spot, sitting on my bed was my audience. After singing my own rendition of the song three times, I finally laid back on my bed. I was surprised Mother hadn't heard me, but she was probably too busy with her own thoughts, which seemed to preoccupy her most of the time, or maybe she had been thinking about Mr. Girard again. Thinking about him made me write the word *ugly* in big black letters in my journal. Then I used each letter to create another word. I wrote *Unbelievabley God Loves You* down the page.

I had the words *African drums* written. Mrs. Carey, my second-grade teacher, said that African drums influenced all of the music we listen to: gospel, jazz, blues, R&B, rock and country. Although the piano was my favorite instrument, I always listened for the drums in every song I heard.

I also had the word *precocious* written in my journal. This was another word I had to look up. The definition read, "exhibiting mature qualities at an usually early age." One time Father told my first-grade teacher I was a precocious child. I always remembered the word, so one day I had decided to write it down. While sprawled out facedown on my bed with Nikki's book of poems still open and my journal on a half-full page, I wrote the word *darkness*. Then I wrote the word *secret*. Then I wrote:

A secret is dark(ness). Truth always comes into light.

Mrs. Wise had told me that secrets don't stay secrets for long and that the truth always comes into the light. She said, "As far as I know, the sun always gonna rise. Everything in the dark eventually come into the light." I flipped to an empty page. I couldn't write down Tanya's secret because I thought Mother might find my journal, so I decided to write something else. I wrote down *American capitalism*. Mrs. Wise had said the words to me but I didn't really understand them. I looked up each one. Then I wrote:

American—selfish   Capitalism—greed

I had seen the word *Indians* within the definition of American. Based on what I knew about the Indians, I thought it was very selfish that their land had been taken from them. If capitalism caused white people to steal the Indians' land for their benefit only, that was greed. Mrs. Carey had said that the Indians were treated similar to the Africans. With all that I had learned about capitalism, it seemed to make people do anything, even kill, for money. Maybe that's why we have so many wars, I thought.

I had begun to grow tired of reading, writing and thinking. I was ready to eat dinner. My stomach had begun to make all sorts of noises, but I knew dinner wasn't ready yet because mother hadn't knocked on my door. I put down my pen and flipped through my journal again. I stopped on a page where I had written *grass is itself a child*.

Children are grass. I am grass. I am green. The grass is green but it's not always greener on the other side. But I want to know what is on the other side. Will I like it on the other side? Will I like it better on this side? Does it matter what side I am on if the grass is green on both sides? Is the grass really greener on the other side or is it greener on the side that I am on? Do I really need to know? Why do I need to know? If I know, then I can choose what side I want to be on. Maybe? I like the sun. I like the rain. But I like the sun better than the rain. We need the rain too. So I do not choose not to have it at all. The rain helps to make the grass greener.

After reading what I had written, I decided to close my journal. It was green. On the front of it I had a sticker of a rainbow, a butterfly and a heart. In the center of my journal in big black letters I had written the word *music*. Underneath that I had written:

Words are my life. Life is my song. My song is music.

Chapter 13

September 21, 1972, was a day of new beginnings. It was my day of birth. Life opened its door and let me through again. Summer had retired, but only for a spell, and autumn was taking her place. But summer would not let us forget her easily. Traces of her magic were still present, and Love had never seemed to blossom fully until my day of birth. I turned nine years old. Mother came home from work with a special present. It was a milk-chocolate frosted cake with my name written in white letters in the center of nine red roses. It was a pretty cake, one I would never forget, especially because Mother had almost forgotten my birthday the year before. I didn't get a cake or a present on my eighth birthday, but I had gotten a special card a couple of days later. On the cover of the card was a picture of a woman holding a small girl in her arms. Below the picture were the words *I love you*. Inside, Mother had written:

I can never forget you. You are the reason why I live.

Love,
Mom

Mother had apologized several times for forgetting. Although she was already depressed, forgetting my eighth birthday seemed to depress her even more. She said after moving she had no more money saved and couldn't afford to buy me a cake or a present. It didn't matter to me because the card made up for everything. Plus, on my birthday, shortly before I left for school, I had gotten a call. I picked up the phone but there was no answer. I said "hello" several times but there was still nothing but silence. I thought about hanging up but instead I decided to ask, "Father, is that you?" No sooner than I asked, there was a dial tone. Something inside of me told me it was Father just calling to let me know he had remembered, on my ninth birthday too. The phone rang just as I was walking out the door for school. I picked it up and said "hello." There was no voice, but I heard noises in the background. I could tell Father was outside on the street somewhere. I heard car horns beeping, a siren was screaming in the distance, and there were muffled voices. I thought I heard a small child crying. This time I hadn't asked any questions, but I did say, "I love you." Then there was a dial tone. I didn't tell Mother about the phone calls. I thought if I did, she might think about changing our phone number. That was the last thing I wanted her to do. On my way to school, I told Tanya about my phone call and asked her to keep it a secret.

⁖⁃

The fourth grade was a lot different than the third. Mrs. Crawford was much nicer than Mr. Nathaniel. She was a petite, dark brown woman who wore lots of makeup and had red hair. Some of the kids in my class said she looked like a clown. I thought she would've been much prettier without so much makeup. I wasn't sure if the red hair was natural but it didn't look like it. Every time she read to the class, she would sit at the edge of her desk with her legs crossed, a book in one hand and the other stroking her hair. Sometimes it seemed like she paid more attention to her hair then she did the students, but she did care. She was patient with us and never used harsh words to discipline us when we acted out in class. Sometimes, I think the kids took advantage of her because she was so nice.

One time a boy named Joshua made her cry. While she was writing on the board, he threw a spitball in her hair. The whole class laughed, including me. When someone yelled out what had happened, she sat at her desk and started to cry. The class was silent. It seemed everyone felt really bad. Instead of sending Joshua to the principal's office, Mrs. Crawford made him stay after school and write one hundred times *I will not misbehave in class. I will not disrespect my teacher.* The experience taught Joshua a lesson. He never threw a spitball at Mrs. Crawford again.

Half the school year was gone before I realized Mr. Nathaniel had not come back to teach the third grade again. I asked Mrs. Crawford where he was. She said Justin Romero's death had sent him over the edge. He ended up in an institution for the insane. She said a few of his friends from the school had gone to visit him, but he wasn't accepting any visitors. Hearing about Mr. Nathaniel and his current condition depressed me. It made me remember the day he stood at the window and cried. The day I found out he was human. I wondered if he had shed anymore tears. If he did, maybe it had helped him some. Maybe he needed to cry all of the hurt out of himself. I had heard someone say crying tears can heal the soul.

Mother started coming home later than usual, or maybe it seemed that way because the days were growing shorter. Patrice, who I had met at May's and lived down the street, said she had seen Mother more than a few times with Mr. Girard. Mother had been sitting on his front porch talking and laughing. I didn't like the idea, and it had especially bothered me because Father had contacted me. In my heart, I believed one day I would hear his voice over the phone again, and soon after he would be back home with us. All that was needed was for the two of us to have a conversation. I would tell him how much I loved him and how much we missed and needed him. I would tell him how depressed Mother had been since we moved. I felt in my heart that, although Mother wouldn't admit to it, she wanted him back home too. One day, Father and I would surprise her by showing up together at her job, Hartsfield Hospital, with flowers, I thought. One day soon. But the only person who was surprised was me.

One evening in October, after dinner, I heard knocking on the door. Mother was in the kitchen washing dishes, and I was in my bedroom doing homework. I heard the soft tapping but I thought it was coming from next door. Mother hadn't heard it because she had the music on and the water running in the kitchen sink. The hallway was on the other side of my bedroom wall, so I could easily hear sounds coming from it. I put my ear to the wall. I could hear the light taps more clearly. After putting my ear to the wall, it sounded more as though they were on my own front door. I walked into the living room and looked out of the peephole. I saw a dark brown man with a bald head and bright yellow teeth. I jumped back from the door. The man looked like Mr. Girard.

I looked through the peephole again. The knocking grew louder. Finally I asked, "Who is it?"

The deep voice said, "It's Clarence."

I balled my fist and stomped my foot on the floor. Trying not to make it obvious to Mother we had a visitor, I said as low as I could, "No one is home. You have the wrong address."

Mr. Girard cleared his throat. "You home, ain'tcha?"

I backed away from the door because I thought I heard Mother coming. When I didn't see her shadow in the kitchen, I walked back up to the door and said, "You have the wrong address."

Mr. Girard cleared his throat again. "I don't think I do. Is Maxine in?"

I kept silent. I hoped he would just go away. The knocking continued. I walked over to the radio and turned up the volume then walked back into my room and shut the door. I pretended the noise coming from the door was nothing but the beating of a drum within my ear.

Shortly after plopping back down onto my bed, I heard Mother's voice. Then I heard a man's voice. I jumped back up and cracked open my door. I could hear Mr. Girard explaining to Mother that someone had answered the door but never opened it.

Mother sounded as though she was confused. "Are you sure?" she asked.

Mr. Girard cleared his throat again. Maybe he had a cold. It seemed he had to do that each time he opened his mouth to talk. "I'm sure. Maybe it was your daughter who answered," he said.

Mother walked over to the radio and turned it down. "Rose is doin' homework. She would've told me someone was at the door," she said.

"I don't know. Maybe it was the music or just my imagination," Mr. Girard said as though he was a little irritated.

"Well, I'm sorry for the confusion. Let me find out if Rose knows anything," Mother said. I could hear Mother's footsteps approaching my room. I hurried and eased my door closed then dived onto my bed. I picked up my pencil and began writing numbers on my worksheet. Mother knocked on my door then opened it.

"Rose, did you hear someone at the front door?" she asked. I gave her a blank look.

"No," I answered. She opened my door wider then stood for a moment, thinking.

"Are you sure you didn't hear anyone at the door?" she asked.

"I said no," I replied.

"Clarence was knockin' on the door. He said someone answered but didn't open it. That someone wasn't you?" Mother asked.

"I'm trying to do my homework," I answered impatiently. "I already answered you."

"You didn't tell Clarence no one was home and that he had the wrong address?" Mother asked.

"Nope."

"If I find out you're lyin' to me, that's gonna be your behind," Mother said, upset. "There's a lot of things I tolerate from you but I won't tolerate lyin'. You hear?"

"Yes," I said without looking at her.

"Look at me when I'm talkin' to you." Mother said, raising her voice.

"He's lying," I said, raising my voice.

Mother walked into my room and shut the door behind her. "I don't know what your problem is, but you better fix it before I do." She controlled her voice, trying not to yell.

"I don't have a problem," I said, moving away from her.

"I don't wanna embarrass either one of us tonight, so I'm gonna leave you to yourself," Mother said, grabbing the doorknob and pulling the door open. "Hurry up and get your homework done. The next time I walk in here, your lights better be off and your eyes closed. First thing in the morning, I'll check your homework." She walked out of my room and pulled the door shut as hard as she could without slamming it.

"I don't want him here," I yelled, pressing my head into the palms of my hands as tears began to well. It hurt me that Mother was letting another man take my father's place.

Mother started to see Mr. Girard more regularly. Initially, he would only visit her in the evenings after dinner then he began walking her home from the bus stop, eating dinner with us and spending the night. I stopped speaking to Mother for almost two months. The only time

I exchanged words with her was when we went over my homework. At first, Mother didn't seem to mind my silence, but after almost two months of it, she became bothered. She threatened to spank me if I continued to ignore her. When the threats didn't work, she decided to just talk to me until I was ready to respond.

One night she walked into my room and sat on the bed near me. "Clarence is a good man," she said. "He wants to help us. I've been strugglin' alone for a long time now. Every day that I wake up it seems like the price bein' charged to just live has gone up again. Water ain't even free. I don't know how we're expected to get by sometimes. It don't matter how many hours I work, the pay still ain't enough. I never considered myself poor, but lately I've had to reconsider. You think times are hard for you because another man has taken your father's place in my life, but baby, you don't know hard times until it becomes a struggle for you to put food into your own child's mouth. It's the worst feelin' ever, and quite frankly, if I can help it, I won't let that day come. If that means starvin' myself then so be it. Clarence said he ain't gonna let that happen though. He's a decent man, and he means well. You may not be able to love him like your own father, but he deserves to be loved just like any person. Try to be different. Don't punish me for needin' more." Mother stood to leave.

"I'm sorry," I said without looking at her. Then I raised my eyes and looked into hers.

Mother's eyes began to water. "I'm sorry too," she said. "I wish it didn't have to be this way. Believe me, I do."

"It's not your fault," I said.

"Partially it is. Maybe if my anger didn't always get the best of me, I could've been there for your father when he needed me most, the times when he had really been sick. Maybe we could've helped each other. I don't know. Maybe I should've just done more with myself."

"You're okay the way you are."

"No, I ain't. I should've made more of myself," Mother said, looking toward the window.

"You are more," I said. "You're my mother."

"Everybody can't wear the title, and sometimes the title don't fit me. But I do try hard to be what you need me to be. It don't seem like it, but I do." Mother walked out my room and shut the door.

I remained on my bed, sitting with my shoulders against the wall. I leaned my head back, rested it on the wall and closed my eyes. I wished I could do more to help. I would've tried to find a job, I thought, but at nine I was still too young. Maybe accepting that Mr. Girard was a part of our lives was the best way I could help. I decided I would be nicer, but I would never let him take my father's place.

After accepting Mr. Girard into our lives, the first week with him was extremely hard. At the dinner table, Mr. Girard sat across from Mother, and I sat at the head. Because he wasn't directly in front of me, I didn't have to look at him if I didn't want to. Sometimes I would look at him from out the corner of my eye and make a mean face. I don't think he ever knew but Mother did. A few times she had to give me a gentle kick under the table. I thought about responding by yelling a bad word, but I knew that the price would've been too high. It wasn't worth giving Mr. Girard the satisfaction. The last thing I wanted him to think was that Mother was choosing him over me. When Mr. Girard tried to have a conversation with me, I either ignored him or responded with one-word answers to let him know I wasn't interested. Mother told him after our third night at dinner together, "Just give her time. She'll come around." Mr. Girard just smiled and showed his yellow teeth. He smoked cigarettes, but Mother would never let him smoke in our apartment. His breath always smelled like cigarettes though. After our first week at dinner together, I decided to be nice to him. One evening when he started a conversation about school and asked how I was doing, I said, "I'm doing good. I like Mrs. Crawford. She's very nice, but I don't think she gives us enough work."

"I ain't never hear a child complain about that before," he said, looking at Mother and chuckling. Mother looked over at me and smiled.

"My father said that an idle mind is a useless mind. Idle minds promote laziness," I said, staring Mr. Girard directly in his eyes.

"That's not always true," Mr. Girard said. "Everybody got to rest their minds sometime. That don't mean they lazy."

I didn't like that Mr. Girard was challenging my father's words. "The only time a person's mind can afford to rest is when they're sleeping," I said, slightly piqued.

"Yeah, sleep is necessary. That's true. We got to sleep," he said. He looked over at Mother. "That's a bright girl there."

"Yeah, she's a smart one," Mother said, giving me an admonishing eye. I rolled my eyes and looked away.

"You must get good grades in school," Mr. Girard said.

"Most of the time I get A's," I said, "but if I get bored with the work then I get B's. I used to—"

"She should be gettin' A's all the time, even if the work is borin'," Mother said, interrupting me.

"I used to be in the honors group, but Mrs. Crawford said she doesn't like separating the class into groups. It can cause resentment. It can," I said, nodding. "It did in my third-grade teacher Mr. Nathaniel's class. Some of the kids didn't like me. They used to tease me and the other two that were in my group. I didn't like that." I put the last forkful of green peas into my mouth. "What do you do?"

"Don't talk with food in your mouth," Mother said.

Mr. Girard cleared his throat. "I work for a warehouse," he said.

"What kind?" I asked after swallowing my food.

"Furniture. I drive the movin' truck. I deliver the furniture to the people's homes," Mr. Girard said, pushing his plate toward Mother. She stood from the table and picked up his plate then hers and mine. She walked to the sink and placed them in.

"Do you have to move real heavy stuff up a lot of stairs?" I asked.

"I used to do it all the time, but I let the younger boys do that now. I just give the orders. It's like I got folks workin' for me now," he said, leaning back in his chair and sticking his hands in the waist of his pants. He had a gold pinky ring on his left hand. "I'm the big black boss."

"You so silly," Mother said, giggling. She sat back down at the table.

"Any dessert?" Mr. Girard asked, looking at Mother.

"Not tonight. Didn't have the time," Mother said.

I hope he doesn't think he's the boss of this house, I thought. "You don't have any kids?" I asked.

Mr. Girard cleared his throat again. "Had a son. He passed away when he was just a newborn baby. His mother was real sick when she was carryin' 'im. Had cancer. My son lived for only three days after he was born. My girlfriend died the next day," he said, averting his eyes.

"What kinda cancer did she have?" I asked.

"Rose, that's enough questions. Don'tcha got homework to do?" Mother asked.

"That's okay. Inquirin' minds want to know, so I'm gonna answer," Mr. Girard said. "She had lung cancer. Smoked too much."

"You smoke," I said.

"Yeah, that's right, I do. I been smokin' most of my life. Started when I was about thirteen years old."

"How old are you now?" I asked.

"You ask a lot of questions, don'tcha?" Mr. Girard said.

"Rose, homework time," Mother said.

"Let me finish answerin' her questions. We just tryin' to get to know each other, that's all. I'm forty-two years old."

"You ain't scared of getting lung cancer?" I asked, wrinkling up my face.

"No, I ain't scared. I ain't scared of dyin'. I figure if I do, I ain't got much to lose anyhow," he said.

"Well you got us now," Mother said.

"Yeah, that's true. Maybe 'cause things is changin' for me I can let the habit go now."

"You gonna stop smoking?" I asked.

"I'm gonna try. That's enough about me. What type of things you like to do?" he asked, removing his hand from his pants and resting them in his lap.

"I like to read and write poetry," I said excitedly. "And I like to listen to music."

"Sounds like you got a lot of talents. You gonna go far in life. Make something of yourself," Mr. Girard said, smiling.

Mother stood from the table and walked back to the sink. She started the water for the dishes. "Rose, it's time for homework. It's gettin' late."

"You want me to do the dishes?" I asked.

"No. I want you to get started on your homework," she said.

"Well you better listen to your mother this time. Got to get that homework done for school. We got to make sure you stay on the A list." Mr. Girard chuckled.

I stood from the table. *My homework is not your responsibility*, I thought. "Well, it was nice talking to you," I said. "Mom, you coming to help me with my homework?"

"I'll be there in a short while. We'll do some tonight then I'll check the rest in the mornin'," she said, and blew a kiss into the air.

"Okay," I said, looking over at Mr. Girard one last time. *He ain't nothing like my father,* I thought. I walked out the kitchen toward my room. The music was playing low on the radio in the living room. Mother had the Roy Ayers album on. The next song that would play was called "Love Will Bring Us Back Together." I kept my door open so that I could hear it. I laid back on my bed and faced the ceiling as I sang along.

Instead of opening my books to do homework, I thought about Mr. Girard. He made my heart beat faster and my face turn red and warm each time I was in the same room with him. I could always hear the pounding in my chest and feel the heat penetrating my skin. It even seemed that my eyes quickly grew tired from just one look at him. He had to know that I didn't want him near us. Nothing in my behavior displayed otherwise. Even when he told us about his newborn son and girlfriend dying, I couldn't bring myself to feel completely sorry for him. He looked like a liar to me. Mostly, because he always wrinkled his brow when he was telling us about things that had happened in his life. They were always sad. I think he made up stories just so Mother could feel sympathy for him and keep him around. But something inside of me wouldn't allow me to trust him, especially with Mother.

Chapter 14

The school year was racing time. It seemed to move faster than the hours within a day, especially if you were one to count the seconds. School hadn't stood still for even a moment. Just as quickly it had been coming, so was it going. All the frenzy around Mrs. Crawford's perceived nervous breakdown while the year encroached upon its end made it hurry along even more. Nothing slowed down, not even during the week Mrs. Crawford was absent from our class. When she came back her hair was dyed bleach blonde. She even changed the colors of her makeup. At the beginning of the year, she mostly wore green eye shadow, pink blush and red lipstick. Eventually, she changed everything to bright pink. With her blond hair she wore powder blue eye shadow, bronze blush and gold lipstick. Her attire was always black.

She once told us that she was an artist. She brought in a few of her oil paintings. When she came back from her week off, she brought in another oil painting. It was different from the rest, which were more scenic. This one was of a caged bird. The cage was painted bronze, and the bird within it was bright yellow with aqua streaks in its wings. The cage had a small silver lock on it, and there was a small brass key on the bottom. The painting was called "Freedom Is The Key."

Outside of school, I spent most of my time indoors working on homework, writing in my journal and reading. One weekend I found a box labeled *dad's stuff* tucked away in our kitchen pantry along with several others. Most of the boxes contained literature. Some of the books belonged to Mother, but most of them belonged to Father. While searching through Father's box, I found his favorite book, *The Prophet* written by Kahlil Gibran. He quoted from it almost every time he had a conversation with one of his close friends. During most arguments with Mother, Father would also use quotes from the book. Once he yelled at the top of his lungs, "Reason, ruling alone, is a force confining; and passion, unattended, is a flame that burns to its own destruction" after Mother burned their wedding picture. Then, he fell to his knees and began to cry like a baby. Mother, still in her nightgown, stormed out of our apartment and slammed the door behind her. It was the middle of winter. Almost two hours passed before she came home. Father was sitting in the same spot on the kitchen floor. Their anger made my heart pound. I remained in my room hidden underneath my bed with my crayons, drawing stick people without eyes, ears or a mouth.

I read *The Prophet* three times within one week after I found it. I wrote words from the book and looked up the ones I didn't understand. I also copied various lines into my journal. One of my favorites was in the section entitled "Freedom." It said, "And what is it but fragments of your own self you would discard that you may become free?" It reminded me of something Mrs. Wise had once said to me: "Everything that we hate and fear makes us a slave to it. If we hate our own skin, we become a slave to it. If we fear others who are different from us, we become slaves to them. Hate and fear by themselves make us a slave."

I wondered if people also feared love. Mother said love hurts sometimes. The deeper you love, the deeper it hurts. Kahlil Gibran said, "When love beckons to you, follow him, though his ways are hard and steep. Even as he is for your growth, so is he for your pruning. Even as he ascends to your height and caresses your tenderest branches that quiver in the sun, so shall he descend to your roots and shake them in their clinging to the earth. All these things shall love do unto you that you may know the secrets of your heart, and in that knowledge become a fragment of Life's heart."

Did this mean it was okay for Mr. Girard to hit Mother?

On the night of April 13, 1973, Mr. Girard had come by really late. Mother and I were already asleep. Earlier that evening we had gone to his place to look for him. He wasn't home. Mother was worried, but she said he was a grown man and could take care of himself. He pounded at our apartment door late that night, awakening both Mother and me. She answered the door. Mr. Girard stumbled into our apartment, smelling like alcohol and cigarettes. Mother backed away from him and screamed at him to leave. He wouldn't. Mother kept screaming and tried to push him out of our apartment. Next thing I knew, Mother was on the floor holding the side of her face. Tears were rolling down her cheeks. She screamed, "Get out. Get out."

Mr. Girard knelt next to Mother and said he was sorry. Mother kept screaming at him. Finally he left. I stood there in shock the entire time. I could feel anger boiling in my blood. I was growing to hate Mr. Girard even more. When he was gone, I slammed the door and locked it. I stood over Mother and asked her if she was okay. She averted her eyes. "Go to bed," she said.

Mr. Girard stayed away for a week. While he was gone he sent various gifts by children in the neighborhood. When I arrived home from school, I would find notes or candy and other small things, usually in an envelope, in front of the door. A few times I moved his gifts, without the notes, over to Mrs. Cooper's side of the hallway. If he had sent candy, I would throw it away. Mother barely spoke a word during the time he was gone. I hoped she would never let him come back.

But she did. He was more apologetic than ever when she first let him in. I had a hard time accepting his apology. I hadn't picked up a book nor did I write in my journal for almost three months after the incident. I was confused and didn't know what to think or believe. At the dinner table, I continually ignored Mr. Girard's attempts to talk to me. My anger wouldn't subside. I couldn't talk to anyone about my feelings. The only way I could channel my anger was by staying silent.

School finally came to an end. After only a week of being away, I already missed Mrs. Crawford. After her perceived nervous breakdown, she was a different person. She started talking about God and said He could deliver us from anything, so I tried to convince myself to believe her. I thought, *I have faith Father is coming back and Mr. Girard will leave. I still have faith in love.*

When summer arrived, I began to visit Mrs. Wise's garden again. My flower, Love, had just begun to sprout. One early morning after Mother left for work, I sat down at the edge of the garden and began to talk to Love. I said, "I have faith in Love." I sat there for a long time and talked to her. I learned from Mrs. Wise that the growth of a flower from a seed was sometimes a slow process. Patience was always necessary. It was also important for the rain to be gentle, the sun to smile often and the wind to be kind. All of this was needed for Love to grow.

Mr. Girard was still trying to find ways to make up to Mother. He eventually began to bring bigger and more expensive presents to our apartment. First he brought us a new stereo for the living room. The speakers were larger and much louder. Three weeks later, he brought a record player for my bedroom. He told me I needed to have my own so that I could listen to music anytime I wanted in private. My conclusion was he wanted me to stay in my room more often. Two months later, he brought a floor-model TV. Mother told him we were hardly interested in TV and didn't need one that big. He said if we didn't watch it, he would. He always had sports on during the weekends. After the TV, there were other smaller things, like a toaster oven and a blender. Mother liked both of them. Before the toaster oven she made toast by placing the slices of bread on the wire rack in the oven. We had eaten burnt toast for breakfast several times.

When we received the blender, we made milkshakes with fresh fruit. My favorite was strawberry-banana. Before the blender we made milkshakes by hand with mostly vanilla ice cream and milk. On the weekends Mother always made milkshakes for Mr. Girard. He liked to have one while he watched sports.

Even though Mother and Mr. Girard were on speaking terms again, their relationship was never the same. I remember their first argument— at least it was the first that I knew about. Over the winter, on Christmas of '72, Mr. Girard had gone out early. Christmas was in the middle of the week, and Mother and Mr. Girard worked the day prior and the one following. The day before Mother had come home completely exhausted. She fixed dinner then went directly to bed. Mr. Girard came over late that night. He missed dinner, and Mother was asleep by the time he arrived. He was gone before either of us was up the next morning. Mother was upset that Mr. Girard was already gone when we awoke on Christmas Day. She fixed breakfast for the two of us then I opened the few presents I had under the tree. Mother gave me a used paperback of *My House* by Nikki Giovanni. She said that what mattered was not the way the book looked on the outside but the substance inside. "Never judge a book by its cover. Same goes for people," she said. There was a bookmark stuck between the pages. When I opened the book, Mother

said, "That winter poem is for you." "Winter Poem" was the actual title.
I read it out loud:

> once a snowflake fell
> on my brow and i loved
> it so much and i kissed
> it and it was happy and called its cousins
> and brothers and a web
> of snow engulfed me then
> i reached to love them all
> and i squeezed them and they became
> a spring rain and i stood perfectly
> still and was a flower

When I was done reading the poem, Mother said, "I just love that poem. It makes me think about you when we used to go to the park in the winter. Your father taught you how to make snow angels. If there was snow on the ground, that was the first thing you did when we got there. And sometimes you used to stick out your small hands to catch the snowflakes. When they melted in your hands, it used to make you sad 'cause you liked lookin' at all the different shapes and designs. I used to just look at you and smile. A flower. That's exactly what you were. My little rose." Mother sighed. "Memories is all I got of my happy days."

My last two presents were albums. A single called "To Be Young, Gifted and Black" by Nina Simone and another called "Someday We'll All Be Free" by Donny Hathaway. "Let's play them," I said.

Mother smiled. "That's a good idea. I could use a little music this mornin'." I stood and walked over to the stereo. I turned it on then put one of the black discs on the player. I placed the needle on the record then turned up the volume. As soon as the words to Nina Simone's song started, Mother and I began to sing.

Mother grabbed my hand then twirled me around and caught me in her arms. She pulled me close, and we slow danced and laughed together through the song. It was the first time we had danced together in more than three years. As soon as the music stopped, Mr. Girard knocked on the door, opened it and walked in. Mother had forgotten to lock it when she first awoke.

Mother let me go then sat by the tree. I walked over to the stereo and lifted the needle from the record. I had planned to play Donny Hathaway, but Mother didn't seem to be in the mood to sing or dance anymore. I pushed in the button for the radio. It was already on the jazz station, which was playing an instrumental version of "Oh Christmas Tree."

Mr. Girard looked tired. His eyes were red, small and puffy. He had a brown bag in his hands. He cleared his throat. "Merry Christmas," he said with little excitement. Mother began cleaning up the torn wrapping paper I had removed from my gifts. She didn't bother to look at Mr. Girard or speak.

"I said Merry Christmas. Maxine, you ain't speakin'?" Mr. Girard asked.

"Don't have nothin' to say," Mother said.

"Why is that?" he asked.

"What do you want me to say?"

"At least Merry Christmas, good mornin', how ya doin', something," he said.

"Yeah, Merry Christmas, good mornin', how ya doin'?" she said, still looking away.

"Come on, Maxine. What's this about now?" he asked.

"You know what it's about. Gettin' hard to manage your schedule lately, huh?" Mother said, stuffing the paper in a bag.

"Been workin' overtime, tryin' to save up for Christmas."

"Hope you was able to buy the things you wanted with all the overtime you been doin'."

"Yup, got the stuff right here in this bag," Mr. Girard said, holding up the brown bag. He reached inside and pulled out a box wrapped in shiny red paper with a green bow. "Rose, this for you." He handed me the gift. He reached into the bag again and pulled out a smaller box wrapped in the same shiny red paper with green ribbon tied around it. He handed the box to Mother. She didn't accept it, so he placed it on the floor near her. I walked over to the Christmas tree and reached for the gift wrapped in silver paper. It had *Merry Christmas* written across the top in red letters. I picked it up then handed it to Mr. Girard.

"Thank you," he said.

I walked over to the love seat and sat with my present. "Can I open it now?" I asked.

"Go on," Mr. Girard said. "Maxine, you gonna open your gift too?"

Mother picked up her gift. "Rose, open yours first," she said.

"Okay," I said, tearing the paper from the box. Inside was a white baby doll with blond hair and blue eyes. The doll was holding a bottle in her hand. "She's pretty," I said.

"I can't believe you walked in here with that," Mother said angrily. She stood then started toward me.

"Whatcha talkin' about?" Mr. Girard asked, looking at the doll, perplexed.

"Give me that doll." Mother snatched it from my hands. She threw it into the bag with the torn wrapping paper I had removed from my other gifts. "Black kids in this world have a hard enough time as it is identifying with they own brown skin. Last thing they need is to try to identify with something they ain't and never gonna be. Rose gonna learn to love her own brown skin, regardless of how hard that is for some of us, before she learn to love some white doll. Keep it around long enough, next thing I know she'll be tryin' to look like it."

"You ain't got to go throwin' the baby in the trash. I'll give it to somebody else who might appreciate it." Mr. Girard put his hand out for the doll.

"You know any white kids around this neighborhood?" Mother asked. Mr. Girard dropped his gift back under the tree and walked out of the room.

"Rose, I'm sorry, but this world already makes it hard for us to love ourselves. And ain't nobody in this house gonna make it harder." Mother walked out the room and into the kitchen. Mr. Girard was sitting at the kitchen table smoking a cigarette. Mother made him leave the apartment.

Soon after Mr. Girard left, I put on "Someday We'll All be Free." I sat on the love seat and listened to the music and started singing the words to myself.

After Mr. Girard and Mother's argument on Christmas, he stayed away more often. When he did visit, he would usually come by late in the evenings after dinner and leave early in the morning. Once I heard him say, "The less I'm around, the better for both of us. Misery do okay by itself. Don't need my company."

Mother yelled something obscene. I don't know what made Mother more miserable: Mr. Girard staying away or coming around. When he stayed away, she fussed at everything in her sight, and when he came around, she fussed at him. Sometimes she would fuss at me, but I would usually turn the music up loud then go into my room and shut the door. Once mother was fussing at the wall while she was in the kitchen. I wondered if that was normal. Did people always talk to walls when they were mad? I supposed they did when no one else was around to listen. Maybe it was healthy to do that. It was probably better to let the hurt and frustration out some way rather than keep it in. I had heard Mrs. Wise say something like that before.

During the spring of '73, I only saw Mr. Girard on the weekends. He was usually stopping by just to say hi. But his visits would last the entire three days. Most times, I would find him on the sofa engrossed in a game. Mother usually let him stay because the TV he was watching was the floor model he had bought us. Mother would usually say, "Somebody got to use it 'cause I ain't." It seemed when he started coming around less they got along better. They didn't argue as much. But their resentment toward each other was still pervasive. It flooded their hearts. You only had to observe the body of each, its language, to know that something wasn't right between them. Even their smiles were artificial. I wondered why Mother still allowed Mr. Girard in, not only into our home but into our lives. I also wondered what kept him coming back. It had to be more than just the floor-model TV. Even though Mother tried to keep me ignorant of some things, I knew about the other times he had hit her.

Usually it happened late at night, after I was asleep. Mother's screams would always wake me. Sometimes I'd lie awake for hours listening to them yelling, and at the same time repeatedly play "Sinnerman" by Nina Simone. Other times, I would sneak out of my room and sit on the love seat in the living room, hoping Mr. Girard would walk out the door and never come back. But even when he did leave, he would eventually return.

Mother packed up and moved us when she was fed up with Father and his troubles. When would she pack up and leave this time?

Chapter 15

Secrets are hidden within silence. God whispered the secret of time to Nature, and life was created with no beginning or end. In silence, I watched Nature and learned that the beginning was the end. The end was the beginning. The past, present and future are only words. Words created in dreams. Dreams have a language of their own. They speak to us in metaphor. I was told that life itself is only a metaphor for God. God is life. The only way to understand life is to learn its secrets. Secrets are hidden within silence. In silence, I learned how to make time stand still. Within the winters of my life, I experienced summer. Within the summers of my life, I experienced winter. All else, spring and fall, are just one of the same season, reminders that in time there is change. Time has no truly quantifiable beginning or end. Only change. But change is born of living and dreaming. Dreams are born of the mind and felt in the heart. Secrets are hidden within silence. Silence is truth unspoken. It, too, has a language of its own. All is made known in time.

My secrets silenced me. Silence had begun to taunt me and forced me to learn to see, think and feel things differently. In silence, truth is unspoken, but in other ways is revealed. Could someone else know about Tanya's shoebox under the bed, the desires of grown men for little girls, Mr. Girard's empty liquor bottle under the sofa and Mother's screams in the night? Could someone else know the secrets I kept hidden within my silence? I had learned the secrets of Nature just by watching.

Mrs. Wise said, "It takes a special kinda listenin' and seein' to know the secrets of Nature." Most people in the world didn't know the secrets, but Mrs. Wise knew, and she had taught me. If we knew, there must've been others who did too. Mrs. Cooper, who lived across the hall from me, was always watching me. She always studied me with a strange eye. Did she know my secrets? I always looked Mrs. Cooper straight in the eyes whenever we talked, but I couldn't any longer. The secrets wouldn't let me. During the school year, when I left for school, I hurried down the stairs when I heard Mrs. Cooper opening her door. After school, I tiptoed up the stairs, hoping she wouldn't hear me. Sometimes, when I turned the key in the lock, she would open her door and peek out.

"How was your day?" she'd ask.

I never turned around to look at her. "Fine," I'd say then quickly walk into my apartment, shut and lock the door.

Now that it was summer of '73, and I was older and more mature than I was in June of '71 when Mrs. Cooper and I first met, I tried to come and go without her knowing, but she always knew. When walking down my hallway steps, it seemed like she felt my presence, even behind her closed door. I had always felt hers.

On most days in the summer, I would sit at my window, read and write in my journal. Other days I would listen to music almost the entire day. The secrets and silence were always there, but the company of words, poetry and music made the guilt of burying hidden truths inside less. Some words are like darkness; they made the light within my own soul dim.

Although the summer constantly exposed her abundant beauty to the world, I mostly kept to myself. Some days I spent with Mrs. Wise in the garden. While she tended to her flowers, I would sit and watch Love. She was taking her time to grow this summer. Mrs. Wise told me it was because I wasn't talking to her. She told me if I couldn't find the words, it was okay to hum instead. Music was good for Love. I couldn't hum as beautifully as Mrs. Wise, but I tried to. I would listen to her then hum along with her, trying to create the same harmonious melody. "That's it, baby," she would say most of the time when I hummed on tune.

Once, while we were sitting under the oak tree humming, my mind drifted off. I grew silent again. "It's summer but winter still in your heart," Mrs. Wise said, looking over at me. "Dream, baby. Dream it away. Dream until the silence that's holdin' you still is broken and your heart and spirit is free to sing again. Live the music. It's inside of you. It's always inside of you. As long as you got music inside of you, you got life, and life don't stand still so you got to move with it. When the melody of life changes, move with it. You got to move with it. The song doesn't have to change, but sometimes the melody does. Dream, baby. Create your own melody. Time and the rest of this world may stand still, but you gots to create your own melody and move with it. When the world standin' still in sorrow, create your own melody and call it joy. When the world standin' still in fear, create your own melody and call it courage. When the world standin' still in hate, create your own melody and call it love. When the world standin' still in death create your own melody and give it life. Play your melody loud. Let it be heard, and move with it." Tears had begun to form in my eyes. Mrs. Wise pulled me closer and held my head to her bosom. She began to hum again.

On the days I visited the garden, Mrs. Wise always had a word or a speech for me. It seemed she knew my secrets even though I hadn't shared them with her. Every now and then, she would say something that would bring peace to my heart and mind. The guilt of knowing dark secrets would never allow me peace. While with her, I always experienced the pleasures life had to offer rather than the chaos that seemed inherent in life. It was as though I had stepped into a foreign world that was completely different from the one I shared with others. Mrs. Cooper's stare reminded me of the guilt I held inside because of the secrets I had hidden within my silence. Sometimes silence is nothing but a lie. Mother and Mr. Girard made me doubt and question love. Tanya, who lived below me and shared a clandestine love with Mr. Dickens, reminded me that young girls are sometimes just as guilty as grown men. Her deep, almost insatiable desire, mostly for love, oftentimes dictated her bite into forbidden fruit. But grown men know better. They know better than to kindle a young girl's passions. Life allowed them enough experiences to know that the taste of sweet fruit can be poisonous.

Sometimes desire made people want the wrong things. Most don't know what they need until they have it. Life was sometimes tricky that way. We had to experience it to know what we did and didn't need. Listening, seeing and knowing was a part of experiencing life. That was a lesson I had learned but didn't always adhere to. Sometimes I had to possess within my own hands forbidden fruit, so I could feel its sensation. Seems like the feeling itself let me know things listening and seeing couldn't. Life is never without a lesson. And every lesson affected my feelings about life.

I avoided my friends over the summer as much as I could, but the world is too small. We were always bumping into one another someway and somewhere. I couldn't hide in my apartment because regardless of how I was feeling, summer days just wouldn't let me do that. The soft whisper of the wind was always inviting me out. A summer wind's soft whisper is always so calm. The bright smile of her sunshine was always tugging at my spirit and teasing me. So was Mrs. Wise's humming. When I closed my eyes and rested my head on her bosom, I could feel the vibrations of summer. Within the subtle breathing and beats of her heart, I could hear birds singing and a river flowing only in the way they do when the season has changed. Hers was the embrace I had in every moment thereafter longed for. My heart always longed for summer.

One July morning, as I was sitting on the cement steps in front of my building, Mr. Dickens, who lived in the building next to mine passed by. It was the first time I had seen him since the warm season began. When he looked my way, I lowered my head, averted my eyes and pretended I was tying my sneaker. He didn't bother to speak like he usually did. Maybe he knew Tanya shared their secret with me, I thought. I hoped he did. Several times when I ran into him over the winter, I thought about telling him that I knew about his covert meetings with Tanya, but each time I remembered she might get sent away. I had nothing to rely on except Mrs. Wise's words: "The truth always comes into the light." I was ready for the truth to unveil itself. I tried to think of ways I could bring it out, but my mind kept telling me it would have to expose itself.

School was becoming a faded image, and summer was fully unveiled. Tanya now had to resume the responsibility of babysitting her younger sister, Zinnia. I could hear Tanya's sister calling Tanya's name through the wide-open window. Because Zinnia's voice was young and soft, she made Tanya's name sound so innocent, so pure. I guess any child could do that. But Tanya's had a maturity to it. Nothing in her tone changed, but what was behind it had. Even the look within her eyes, although a child's eyes, didn't have the glow of innocence, of pureness. Maybe Mr. Dickens had noticed the woman inside masking herself as a child. It was probably the combination of woman and child that enticed him. When he said Tanya's name, he wasn't calling out to just any old child. He was calling out to a woman who gave to him love in the unconditional way of a child. That's what illusion led him to believe.

I guessed Tanya would be outside any time. Instead of going to Mrs. Wise's garden, I decided to wait for Tanya. After waiting for a while, I went to knock on her door. Tanya's sister opened it. "Hello," she said. She was barefoot with an oversized T-shirt on and two pigtails sticking out the sides of her head.

"Hello. Is Tanya here?" I asked.

"Yes," Zinnia said. She remained in the door staring at me.

"Is Tanya here?" I repeated.

"Yes," Zinnia said. She stood there smiling then ran away from the door after hearing Tanya's voice.

"Who's that?" Tanya shouted from another room.

"I don't know," Zinnia said.

"You just gonna open the door for strangers? I'm tellin','" Tanya shouted. "Who's at the door?"

"Rose," I answered, peeking into the overcrowded apartment. The furniture in the living room was old and worn. Most of it was a pale blue with a brownish tint. It looked to me like faded denim jeans that had been worn plenty but hardly washed. A pair of women's stockings stuck out from between the two cushions of the sofa, and a violet church hat with white feathers glued to the front rested on the armrest.

"Hey, what you doing at my door?" Tanya asked still shouting from the other room.

"Are you comin' out?" I shouted back.

"I'm tryin' to fix Zinnia some food," Tanya said, walking into the living room. She was stirring a pasty cream-colored mixture in a yellow bowl. "I'm fixing Cream of Wheat. We ran out of milk so I'm tryin' to make it soft with butter."

"I like Cream of Wheat," I said. "My mother fixes it for me sometimes."

"You want some?" Tanya asked.

"No. I ate already. Can you come out after?" I asked.

"Yeah, I'll be out in a little while. Wait for me outside," Tanya said, walking back out of the room.

"You want me to shut the door?" I asked.

"Yeah. Zinnia gonna get in trouble for opening it without lettin' me know first," Tanya shouted.

"Okay," I said, closing the door. I walked back out of the building and sat back on the cement steps. There were other kids running up and down the street playing. Two younger boys were kicking a bright orange ball back and forth in the middle of the street. Another boy named Tommy was chasing after a dingy mutt. Patrice was spending the summer with her aunt. May had gone to summer camp and wouldn't be home until mid-August. I hardly knew the other kids on my street and in the neighborhood. The only other person who came around every so often was Mud Pie. I tried my hardest to avoid her. She was never nice to me when we saw each other.

Almost an hour passed before Tanya made it outside. "Hey." She ran out the door of our building and surprised me.

"What took you so long?" I asked, standing.

"I had to put Zinnia in the bed. She needed a nap 'cause she was gettin' on my nerves. She wouldn't even eat the food I made her." Tanya was standing akimbo, rolling her eyes.

"She didn't eat anything?" I asked, concerned.

"I let her eat some jelly bread. That's all she'll eat sometimes," Tanya said, still rolling her eyes.

"Wanna play double dutch?" I asked.

"Ain't nobody else around to play."

"Ask one of those girls down the street."

"I don't play with them. Me, Patrice and May had a fight with them one time. That's why they don't come up here," Tanya said, walking down the steps.

"What do you wanna play then?" I followed her.

"Simon Says," Tanya said, laughing. She was joking about playing the game. She hated to play it because it reminded her of Mr. Dickens.

"Whatever," I said, waving my hand and rolling my eyes. I knew she was joking.

"You still remember the secret I told you about me and Simon?" Tanya asked.

"Yes."

"I'm gonna be eleven in a couple weeks. Simon says he's gonna get me something real nice and expensive." Tanya strutted toward the street.

"What is he gonna get you?"

"He said it's a surprise." Tanya stopped where the sidewalk met the street.

"I don't know why you're messing with that grown man."

"Because he buy me nice things."

"So? What he's doing isn't right."

"Ain't nobody business," Tanya said, stepping into the street. The orange ball came rolling toward her. She kicked it as hard as she could onto the other side of the street. One of the boys yelled at her and stuck up his middle finger. "Up yours," Tanya screamed.

"What if somebody finds out about y'all?" I asked, plucking a dandelion from the small patch of grass between the sidewalk and curb.

"Nobody gonna find out unless you tell," Tanya said, plucking a dandelion. "Let's make a wish." We closed our eyes, made a wish then opened our eyes and blew on each of our dandelion's soft white feathery hairs. We threw down our stems.

"I'm not gonna tell," I said, "but one day somebody's gonna know."

"No, sir. I already made a wish. Nobody ever gonna find out," Tanya said, stepping up and down from the curb. "What did you wish?"

"I wished for a vanilla ice cream cone with rainbow sprinkles," I said.

Tanya laughed. "You lyin'." She hit me and ran away.

I chased after her. "I'm not lyin'." When I caught up to her, I hit her and yelled, "Tag. You're it." I ran away as fast as I could.

"I'm gonna get you," Tanya said, laughing and chasing me into our backyard. When I reached the wire fence, I stopped. Tanya ran up to me and slapped my shoulder. "I got you."

"I let you," I said, leaning on the fence.

"No you didn't. I would've caught you even if you didn't stop."

"No you wouldn't have. I'm too fast," I said, climbing onto the fence.

"Where you going?"

"Nowhere. I'm gonna sit on top."

"Wanna go to the park?"

"I can't," I said, balancing myself on the top of the fence.

"Why not?" Tanya asked. "Only for a few minutes. I gotta be back before Zinnia get up."

"I'm not supposed to," I said, climbing down from the fence.

"No." Tanya grabbed my legs. "Just for a few minutes."

"Okay. Just for a few minutes." I climbed back up the fence.

Tanya followed. I jumped over onto the other side then she joined me. She grabbed my hand. "Come on before somebody see us."

"Mrs. Cooper's gonna be lookin' for me soon if she doesn't see me somewhere around that front yard," I said, running alongside Tanya.

Tanya pulled me up the hill behind her. "You hear that?" she asked.

"What?"

"All those boys?"

"Yeah."

"It's some cute ones up there."

"They're too old for us."

"Not for me. I'm gonna be eleven soon," she said, stopping at the top of the hill.

"When you gonna be ten?"

"September."

"You gonna be eleven next year. Then you gonna be old enough to come up here by yourself," she said, walking toward the swings. A group of teenage boys were running up and down the basketball court. A few younger ones were sitting on the sidelines.

"My mother said when I'm in junior high school I can start coming to the park by myself." I said, sitting in a swing. Tanya walked up behind me and gave me a push. She sauntered over to a swing near mine and sat.

"You only got two more years. That's not long," she said, pushing herself.

"My mother's always saying time flies. Two years is gonna fly by, and I can't wait," I said in full swing.

"Whatcha gonna do when you get to junior high school?" Tanya asked now in full swing.

"I don't know."

"Look at that cute boy over there running with the blue shorts." Tanya pointed to a cream-complected boy with curly hair and deep brown eyes. "That's gonna be my boyfriend."

124

"He's too old for you," I said, coming to a stop.

"He way younger than Simon," Tanya said, jumping off her swing. "Come on, let's climb the monkey bars."

I ran behind her. "Do you know how old that boy is?" I asked.

"He in high school," she said, climbing onto the monkey bar. "I think he a sophomore."

I started to count on my fingers. "He's four years older than you." I climbed up the other side of the bars.

"That's not old," she said. "Let's see who can make it to the other side first. If you make it to my side first, I owe you five two-cent candies. If I make it to your side first, you owe me seven two-cent candies."

"Why will I owe you more?" I asked.

"'Cause I'm older."

"You're only one year older. I'll owe you six two-cent candies if you win," I said.

"Okay. You ready?" Tanya asked, positioning herself to start the race.

"I'm ready."

"Go." As soon as Tanya started, she fell off the monkey bar. I jumped down behind her. "I scratched my leg," she said, pouting.

"It's only a little scratch."

"So. It hurts," she said, licking her finger then rubbing the spot below her knee.

"We've gotta go."

"You wanna race again?" she asked, standing and grabbing onto one of the metal bars.

"No. I already won."

"No, you didn't," Tanya said, rolling her eyes and sucking her teeth.

"Yes, I did. You fell off, so I automatically win," I said, standing akimbo.

"Whatever," Tanya said, walking away.

"Your future boyfriend saw you fall," I said, laughing.

"No, he didn't." Tanya slapped me on the back and ran down the hill.

I ran behind her. "Don't let me catch you," I shouted.

When we reached the bottom of the hill, Tanya stopped suddenly. I ran up to her and slapped her on the shoulder. "Stop," she shouted.

"You hit me first."

"Look," she said, staring toward our backyard.

I looked in the direction she was staring. Mr. Dickens was standing at the fence watching us. Tanya began to walk slowly toward him. I walked behind her. "You think he's gonna say something to you?" I asked.

Tanya shrugged. "He probably gonna be mad. He don't like me bein' around no other boys. He said it make 'im jealous."

"He doesn't have a right telling you what to do." I narrowed my eyes and balled my hands into fists as I gave Mr. Dickens a mean look. I was hoping he would leave before we reached the fence.

Tanya looked over at me. "Don't look at him like that. He gonna know I said something to you," she said worriedly.

"Hello, girls," Mr. Dickens said when we finally reached the fence.

"Hi," Tanya said, waving. I turned my head.

"Whatcha been doin'?" he asked.

"Playing on the swings and monkey bars," Tanya said.

"Hope you wasn't doin' more than that," he said.

"Nope. That's all," Tanya said, kicking a small rock out of her way.

"Your friend don't speak?" he asked.

Tanya elbowed me in my side. "Say something," she mumbled. I remained quiet. "She don't feel like speaking."

"Got something against me?" he asked.

"Say something," Tanya mumbled under her breath again. I remained silent.

"That's alright. We haven't had a chance to get to know each other. I'm a real nice person. Won't do you no harm. Ask your friend. She'll tell you I treat her real nice," he said with a grin.

"Yup. He treat me nice," Tanya said, climbing onto the fence. I remained still on the other side and stared at Mr. Dickens. "Come on. Mrs. Cooper gonna be lookin' for you." Tanya jumped down from the fence next to Mr. Dickens.

I climbed up the fence then jumped over. I made sure to land as far away as I could from Mr. Dickens. He looked over and smiled at me. I turned away and walked toward the front. Tanya followed me, and Mr. Dickens stood and watched us. "Tanya, we'll talk about whatcha was doin' at the park later." Tanya didn't respond or look back. She kept walking behind me.

When we reached the front of our building, we sat down on the cement steps. Mrs. Cooper was in her window. "Rose, I was just callin' ya. Everything okay?"

Without looking up I said, "Yes."

The days I wasn't at the garden with Mrs. Wise—sometimes Mrs. Cooper joined us, or by myself—I spent with Tanya. Some days she was stuck indoors with her younger sister. Tanya wasn't allowed to bring Zinnia outdoors while her mother, Ms. Ross, worked. Ms. Ross told Tanya she was too irresponsible. Once when Tanya had Zinnia outdoors she forgot about her, and when she remembered, Zinnia was a quarter of a mile up our street. East Street was at least a half a mile long. Tanya was put on punishment for a week. She wasn't even allowed to look out the window. Her mother kept the blinds down and curtains drawn. She threatened if Tanya even peeked out of the window while she was at work, her punishment would last even longer. Ms. Ross told Tanya she had spies. Tanya believed her.

Sometimes Tanya had a hard time getting Zinnia to nap, and she would have to find ways to tire her out. Once she got her to nap, Zinnia would usually be asleep for at least a few hours. Tanya used this freedom to her advantage. She dragged me to as many places as I would let her, mostly the park.

It was usually at night when Tanya met with Mr. Dickens. Sometimes it was out in front of our building when no one else was around, and sometimes it was at his apartment after Tanya's mother was deep into her sleep. Because Tanya's room was at the front of our building, Mr. Dickens would tap on the window or throw pebbles he found on the street. Ms. Ross's room was in the back of the apartment so she never heard the light taps on the window. Tanya said her mother woke up once because she thought she heard Zinnia crying. Tanya was in her window talking and laughing with Mr. Dickens. When her mother asked who she was talking to, she told her she was watching drunken Jack Black, who lived up the block, stumbling down the street and talking to himself. Tanya was always telling me stories, especially about her and Mr. Dickens. Every time she mentioned his name, I got upset. Even though I was spending more time with her, she still saw him whenever they had the chance. It made me hate Mr. Dickens even more, and sometimes I hated Tanya.

When Patrice came back from her aunt's and May was back from camp, they didn't spend much time with Tanya and me. Patrice had had a hard time her first year in a predominantly white school. She said the kids made fun of her and called her names because she dressed in African attire and wore her hair in locks. She said the kids called her Sista Kunta. Patrice's mother had sent her to live with her aunt for the summer because she was said to be a strong black woman who believed in black self-empowerment. She helped Patrice to raise her self-esteem and to bring her grades back up. Patrice's aunt told her she should be careful about the people she chose as her friends. It seemed as though Patrice was having a hard time deciding whether we were still her friends. She told Tanya she was fast and easy. Patrice's mother had told Patrice that the first day she met Tanya and me. Because I was friends with Tanya, Patrice's mother said I would end up just like her if I spent too much time with her. Patrice and May had grown apart during the school year. May was only nine, but she had gotten her first perm. Since attending her new school, she was always wearing her hair long and straight. She said no one at her school wore braids. On occasion May would sneak and wear her mother's foundation. It lightened her skin. She thought lighter skin made her fit in more with the white kids. Patrice said May was always embarrassed when she came around with her African attire and locks. When the other kids called Patrice names, May would laugh along with them.

The summer was almost over when I had my first physical encounter with Mud Pie. I had done everything Mrs. Wise and Mrs. Cooper asked me to, and I tried to put myself in Mud Pie's shoes when she acted ugly toward me and said mean things about Father. I knew she was only being nasty because she felt ugly inside. I acted as kind as I could toward her, hoping she'd realize all I wanted was for us to be friends. When she spit on my sneaker, I tried to ignore it and walk away, but when I turned my back, she'd hit me in the head with a small tote filled with coins. I grabbed her in a headlock and wrestled her to the ground. When I wouldn't let her up, she started screaming for me to let her go. I was too angry, so I held her head in the dirt and told her she had to apologize for calling Father names. Before I knew it, Mrs. Cooper was holding me by the back of my pants and pulling me off Mud Pie. When Mrs. Cooper finally gotten me off, Mud Pie reached forward and scratched me down the side of my face. I tried to go after her but Mrs. Cooper wouldn't let me go. She held me up against her with her cane shoved into my ribs. When Mud Pie ran off down the street and I finally calmed down, Mrs. Cooper grabbed me by my hand and led me to the steps in front of our building. "That ain't no way for a young girl to be actin'," she said, waving her finger at me.

I folded my arms in front of my chest and gave her a mean look. "She started it." I was pouting and still breathing hard.

"Don't matter who started it. You shouldn't be out here fightin' like this. Lookatcha face. It's all scratched up now. That mark gonna remind you of this day for a while. That long scratch down the side of your face is the price you had to pay for your anger. Could've been worse. You lucky your skin still young. Don't have to worry 'bout that mark bein' there forever."

"I didn't start it. She hit me in the head with a purse full of change," I said, looking Mrs. Cooper in the eyes. "She shouldn't have hit me."

"Now, now. I understand how you feelin'. It ain't easy to walk away from somethin' like that. Especially 'cause she hurt you, but there's other ways of handlin' these kinda things," Mrs. Cooper said, gently rubbing my head.

"How?" I asked, doubtful and frustrated.

"An eye for an eye and a tooth for a tooth ain't the answer. Courage and anger don't got nothin' in common. And showin' somebody that you can fight ain't courage neither. Courage is lookin' the person in the eye, just like you lookin' at me now, and sayin' nothin'. Nothin' at all. Just the look itself is enough to let a person know you ain't scared. The eyes do the speakin' by theyselves." I looked away from Mrs. Cooper and began kicking a pebble back and forth between my feet. "Sometimes folks make it hard for you to walk away. Just like this young girl just left did. But walkin' away takes a lot of courage, and it makes a strong statement too. Yes it does. Whatever she got goin' on inside herself to make her wanna fight, well, baby, that's her battle. It ain't yours, and it don't have to be. So don't make it yours. Just walk away, baby. Just walk away."

I looked up at Mrs. Cooper again. "But she hurt me."

"It hurt pretty bad, huh?" She was rubbing the area on my head where Mud Pie hit me with the tote of coins. I still felt the pain.

"Yes," I said.

"It hurt her just as bad. Probably even more. She got to live with the pain just as much as you do. 'Cause her judgment right now may be a little cloudy she might not recognize it right away, but the pain there, and she gonna feel it sooner or later. She gonna feel it. And that's a fact. Sometimes life makes us numb to things, but numb is a feelin' too." Mrs. Cooper placed her cane down on the steps and sat by my side. "There are lots of things in life worth fightin' for. Some of us fight for justice, some for respect and others for love, community, family. These is things worth fightin' for, but the only way to win the fight is with the heart and mind. I know it's some folks who don't have the right heart and mind. But only the heart can win over the heart and the mind over the mind. That's the truth. Sure is." Mrs. Cooper sighed. "There are times when you have to fight. Ain't got no other choice. That's when these—" Mrs. Cooper held up her fists—"is necessary. But wish hard, baby. Wish that you never faced with these kinda times. Wish real hard. You gonna know too. You gonna know. And these times ain't gonna be nothin' like what you experienced today. Nothin' like it."

I sat on the steps with Mrs. Cooper and listened to her explain her feelings about the importance of fighting our battles in life with our heart and mind and winning those same battles with a pure heart and mind. She showed me a scar down the left side of her face near her earlobe. I had never seen it until that day. She said she had almost lost half her ear in a fight she had as a teenager. She said the experience changed her attitude and her life, but I didn't fully realize how much the battles and wars between human lives affected her until she told me about the loss of her younger brother and husband. Both men died in war. Mrs. Cooper's younger brother was in school studying to become a science teacher when he was called off to fight in the Vietnam War. He was the first in the family to go to college. He never made it back to complete his degree and live his dream.

Her husband served in the U.S. Army for more than thirty years. He lived and died for freedom. Mrs. Cooper said it was only after his death that his freedom was realized. "Man is always a slave in war," she said. Before she left me that day, she lifted her two fists again. "These are weapons," she said. "They more dangerous than a gun. 'Cause they hold the gun. They pull the trigger. But the gun ain't innocent neither. It know exactly what it's made for. And it don't have no problem lettin' you know."

Chapter 16

Mrs. Wise was away visiting childhood friends the day I fought Mud Pie. I hoped she wouldn't find out, but I knew one way or another, she would. Especially with the long scratch being as visible as it was down the side of my face. Tanya was indoors taking care of Zinnia. She didn't find out about the fight until later that night. Mr. Dickens had watched the whole thing from his window. After the fight was broken up and Mrs. Cooper was leading me back to the steps in front of our building, I heard him yell from his window, "God don't like ugly." I gave him the meanest look I could. Mrs. Cooper ignored him entirely.

Shortly after Mrs. Cooper left me, I decided to go inside. I still couldn't feel any pain in my face, but I could literally feel the mark that was left. After I felt it, I grew angrier. It made me want revenge, but it had also made me regret I fought Mud Pie in the first place. My initial instinct was to give back what she had given. I wanted her to feel the same pain she had inflicted upon me. It seemed there was nothing else I could mentally process before my hands were around Mud Pie's neck. It wasn't until Mrs. Cooper made me see things differently that I realized I was wrong. It wasn't her words that had convinced me, it was the scar below her earlobe. It was an ugly one. It had spoken to me.

I had to face the looking glass again. It was nothing more than a mirror of truth that always shows it plain. The truth couldn't hide from itself. Mrs. Cooper's words were important, but they didn't become vital until I witnessed each mark—first hers, then mine. When I stood in front of my reflection, I could see her words and hear them much more clearly. What she knew and what I would eventually come to understand was that the long welt down my face was more than just a mark. Staring at the dried blood, I couldn't help but remember Mrs. Cooper's words again: "Could've been worse." It could have been. The mark on my young skin would eventually go away. I would, in a sense, be given another chance, and though Mrs. Cooper would live with a visible mark on her face for the rest of her life, she, too, was given a second chance. For many others, there wasn't another opportunity. Her own heart witnessed the indelible mark that was left upon the face of human lives. It showed itself as death.

The most visible mark, witnessed by the lives of so many, was left on the faces of America's states. States that have been united to form one body. United it seems for many a cause, but mostly for the wrong ones. Now there is only one, long, endless mark on her body. The body of our United States of America. It is the mark on the face of America that Mrs. Cooper and many others would see every day of their lives. The looking glass, the mirror of truth, too, is nothing more than the reality of our world. The mark did not always look the same though. It depended on whose eyes we were looking through.

When the first war was fought, the skin on the face of our united body was still young, but that mark, the wound on America's face, was reopened, and it grew larger and uglier. When I was younger, I had seen the pictures of the ugly wound of our wars. I came to learn at an early age that man himself is a deadly weapon. The fuel for his hate, greed and anger is supplied within his own heart. I also came to learn that wars are nothing more than a magnified reflection of the battles that rage in man's heart. Father taught me all of this.

I had listened to Father talk about war constantly. He despised it. The day he called his friend Paul, whom said he was a Christian, a hypocrite was the same day that Paul contended that all wars are God's battle against evil. Father said that was one of the biggest lies he had ever heard. "God's name is used to justify war, but men know in their hearts that no war is just. They only have to be face-to-face, looking one another in the eyes to know that the other is human, too, but most men are afraid to look within their own eyes. It's these same men who find peace unobtainable and war necessary. Peace will come after the war." Father laughed. "So they fight what they deem necessary wars and are still fighting them on and off the battlefields. They suffer. Always in the face of death, which comes with many disguises, but most of all they suffer because the two great commandments are written in the heart. And men can't run or hide from them." Sitting on the floor at his feet, I had asked, "Will the wars ever stop?" He had stared at me as though he were looking for the right answer—one that I would understand. "Wars will come to an end when the battles within man have ceased."

I had also read about war in Father's books, but it was mostly the pictures in them that helped me to understand what I read. Nothing scared me more than Father's words: "The whole world is at war." But war, I learned, was mostly within our own hearts. It appeared that it eventually found its way out, affecting the world. There were visible marks of these internal wars. They were everywhere. Poverty was the biggest mark on the face of my community. And it seemed to be growing and becoming uglier.

While still in front of the looking glass, reflecting on war, I began to wash away the blood on my face. Once it was gone, I noticed the mark was long and thin. My skin around the mark was discolored, but it wasn't as bad as it had first appeared when the blood was still visible. I wanted to completely hide it. I began to rub ointment on it, then thought about something else Father had once said: "America isn't able to completely hide any of her marks, and the only ointment she has is ignorance. It is better that people don't know the truth. Life, liberty and the pursuit of happiness are only afforded to the few." Another time, while he sat with a book opened on his lap, writing in his journal, he said, "Ignorance. That's all it takes for the few to keep us slaves."

That book in his lap painted the truth within its pages. There was a picture of an Indian and African in army suits pointing guns at each other. A white man on a horse was holding a globe of the world, looking down on them and smiling. Another picture was of a white man dangling a whiskey bottle from a stick with a long string tied to its end in front of an Indian and African. In that same picture, there was another white man walking away with both the Indian's and African's possessions. On another page, there was another picture. A preacher was holding an open Bible. It looked as though he was reading from it. The congregation, which was mostly black, had chains around their heads with locks dangling from them. Under the picture it read, *Slaves, obey your human masters with fear and trembling; and do it with a sincere heart...* The verse was taken from Ephesians, chapter six. I couldn't tell if the preacher was a white or black man. The page was slightly worn so the man's face was hard to make out. When Father and I were observing this picture, he said the infamous lie is that God is a white man and Jesus has blond hair and blue eyes. I first recalled his words when I noticed the blond-haired blue-eyed Jesus hanging up in Ms. Ross's, Tanya's mother, home. It was the first time I had visited her apartment. I also learned from my father that most black Americans believed God was white and that the white man is the only one equal to God. He said this is one reason why blacks fear and love white skin and why they hate and curse their own. What most of us were taught to praise resembled in no way the black face.

I read in one of Father's books on slavery that whiskey was used to keep the Indians and Africans ignorant and irrational. In this book they were referred to as drunken savages. Because of whiskey, they lost everything they owned, including their land. Some lost their lives. Whiskey as well as violence was a sure way to keep the Indians and Africans oppressed. It was doing the same for many in my own community. I had witnessed it for myself. On almost every corner in my neighborhood, there was a liquor store. Most of them were owned by black people. I wondered if the owners knew they were keeping their own people oppressed and in some cases killing them. It was true that liquor made people irrational. This irrationality had been in my own home, making me fear drunks. While still in front of the looking glass, my fears began to show themselves clearer.

When Mr. Girard had too much to drink, he became irrational and violent. He always seemed to talk more too. He would say things to Mother I had never heard him say while he was sober. Once he told Mother if he had the heart he would kill her. She told him he didn't need the heart 'cause all the liquor he drank was enough. I didn't want to take him seriously, but after reading about all the things whiskey did to the Indians and Africans and what it made them do, I had to. In Father's book, I had also seen a picture of two black men in army suits pointing guns at each other. Other blacks were fighting each other in the background. There was one black man lying on the ground dead. Another had his foot on top of the dead man's chest and was holding his gun in the air wearing a wide grin. He was shaking hands with a white soldier. Looking at the picture made me cry. Black people in my community were always killing one another, especially with guns. The media always said it was due to gang violence. But Mother said it was because we wanted to kill what we were taught throughout history to hate most: ourselves.

The evening after I fought Mud Pie, I was lying on my bed flipping through one of Father's books on slavery when Mother knocked on my door. When she entered my room, I quickly angled my face so she wouldn't notice the mark on it. "How was your day?" Mother asked, sitting herself on my bed.

"Okay," I said without raising my head from the book.

"Anything interestin' happen today?" Mother asked.

"No."

"I heard some kids were fightin' out front."

"You did?" I said, folding my page in the book.

"Any idea who they were?"

"Yes," I responded without raising my head. I began flipping through the pages again.

"Two young girls, I heard." Mother gently cupped my chin in her hand and turned it toward her.

"Yes."

"Did you know 'em?" Mother inspected my face.

"Yes."

"Who were they?" She inspected the long mark.

"Mud Pie and me," I said. Tears formed in my eyes.

"Why were the two of you fightin'?"

"She hit me," I said. Tears ran down my face.

"And you hit her back, right?" Mother looked into my eyes and began wiping my tears.

"Yes," I said, confounded.

"Until a few moments ago, I would've said you did the right thing. You defended yourself like you were supposed to. I would've said don'tcha ever let nobody put their hands on you and you don't strike back. That's what I was always taught. Protect yourself the best way you know how. If that mean you got to pick up something and beat a person down, you do what you gotta do. That's what I was taught, and that's what I did. I always hit back. Sometimes I would win my fights, and sometimes I would lose, but it didn't matter 'cause I fought back, and with everything

I had in me. Your grandmother was always fightin' too. She's the one who taught me to defend myself no matter what. 'Cause that was courage. Until a few moments ago, I believed that. As grown as I am, I've still been fightin', and every time I've lifted my hand to strike another I wonder why this way ain't gettin' me nowhere. I just feel more hurt inside after. Sometimes the pain inside is worse than the bruises on the outside, but a few moments ago, I figured it out.

"Really, Mrs. Cooper figured it out for me. She helped me to understand something inside myself I had never understood before. One of those things is that even when I thought I had won, I had really lost. 'Cause there would be a part of me that I would be losin' with every fight." Mother turned the book I had in front of me toward her and looked down at the picture. A young black slave woman was kneeling at the edge of a lake and staring at her reflection in the water with hatred in her eyes. She held a large sharp knife above her head. The blade was pointing toward her reflection. On the same page underneath the picture, it read, "We hate and desire to kill that part of ourselves that we see in others. That part that makes us forget we are human. Sometimes we see it—the thing we hate and desire to kill—in our own reflections, and sometimes we see it clearly in the face of another." Mother turned the book back toward me. "It's funny," she said. "The first thing I did when Mrs.Cooper mentioned to me that you were in a fight was start yellin'. I wanted to know who put their hand on my baby. I didn't even bother to ask who started it or nothin' else. It didn't matter to me if you was the one that was right or wrong. I just wanted to know who did it and that you fought back. I wanted to make sure you fought back. If you didn't, I was." Mother's eyes began to water. "I'm sorry."

"It's okay. I'm okay," I said. I picked up the book and shut it.

"I know. I know," Mother said, lowering her head. "I loved my mother, but I hate that I'm so much like her. Clarence reminds me every day how much I'm like her. Every time I try to forget, he's there to show me again."

"Am I like you?" I asked.

"I hope not," Mother said. "I hope not."

Chapter 17

Mother was depressed again. She had gotten good at hiding it, at least from the world outside. It seemed that every time she looked at my face, the mark on it reminded her of something she had been trying to forget. Sometimes she would just shake her head and walk away. She never said anything, but her look said everything. A few times she cupped my chin and just stared at me. I didn't know what to say to her, so I said nothing. I just waited patiently for her to let me go again. When she did talk, it was usually to an invisible figure. I eventually came to believe that maybe the wall had ears. Somebody inside it had to be listening. Mother would point at it to let it know exactly how she was feeling. Once she told it to fuck off while standing at the kitchen sink. Eventually she started screaming at it. Then she broke down and started crying. "Malcolm, it's because of you that I'm like this. It's all because of you," she said. Hearing the words sent chills through my skin. Mostly, the cold I felt was from hearing my father's name.

Mr. Girard caught Mother talking to the wall on a few occasions. He would always say the same thing: "Something in me told me there was some loose screws up there." He would laugh afterward and walk out. Mother ignored him. She just kept on talking. The only thing that seemed to calm her was music. She didn't play it as much as she had because Mr. Girard made his home in our living room where the stereo was. After the first time he hit Mother, he wasn't allowed to sleep in the bed with her anymore. He wasn't even allowed in our apartment, but he kept coming back anyway. If Mother really wanted him gone, she never changed the locks to keep him out. He must have known there was still a part of her that needed him. That part of her wouldn't let go and kept letting him in—not just into our home but into her heart. Deep down she must have cared about him. She had to love him in her own way, but something in him always brought out the worst in her. That ugly part of her always showed itself in his presence. I know there was a reason—one that I couldn't understand—why he kept coming back and she kept letting him in.

At night, I would lie in my bed listening for the music. I could hear it on my stereo, but I couldn't hear the music inside anymore. The silence was too loud. I tried to listen for it within the humming of my voice, but I still couldn't hear it. I could feel my lips move but nothing came out. Mrs. Wise had told me I had to create my own melody and move with it. But how? I was forgetting the song. My song. The beat of the drums in the music on my stereo had to take the place of my own heartbeat. Otherwise, there wouldn't have been any life in me. There wouldn't have been a song. Something had to remind me that I was still living even though the rest of humanity was dying. As far as I could tell, the rest of the world was already dead. Music was the only thing alive. It was the only thing whose heart beat.

I needed another song. Maybe a new one, or the same one, but played differently. Maybe I would just change the words and give it new meaning. I decided I would keep the same song, but give it another name. "Rebel" That's what I would call it, and the title would be the first lyric, I thought. Would probably be the chorus too. It seemed like the problem for the rest of the world was that it was too passive, so a song had to be created for it too. Passivity is what helped death do its job so well. People so easily shouted through the windows of their souls "I hate you." What they really wanted to do was sing through their hearts "I love you." I would write the words for them.

The world was teaching its thinking inhabitants how to be submissive to it, so we had been and still are. I had seen with my own eyes how the world treated people. Made them feel guilty for their own real feelings. The world only praised those who learned how to lie well. Black people made out to be white to feel good about themselves. Some pretended not to have any feeling at all. White people likened themselves to blacks in order not to feel guilty for their white brother's sins. Some acted out with hate toward blacks as a way to justify stealing what blacks had once owned—mostly their own hearts, minds and bodies.

Mothers feigned strength, hoping to protect their children from the world. But some had forgotten they, too, were part of the world, and therefore, had to protect their children from their own rage, caused by their weakness. Fathers masked their inability to listen, hoping that shattered dreams would be pieced together again and broken hearts would be mended, but words with deeper meanings were too easily forgotten by them. Children learned to act well, falsifying knowledge of themselves and the world. Most had no choice. The world raised them. Experience was their only truth, good or bad, and their only teacher. Women claimed to be happy living with only the image in their mirrors, and pretended to love only to survive. And men, they allowed themselves to be misled by passion to satisfy their desires, and allowed themselves to feel, but only for those occasions that required them to love and to be human. But pretending made people forget their own real feelings—how to love, how to live, how to be human. *Rebel! Rebel!* These were the words to my song. Not words for battle or war. They were words that meant only to love, live and be human in a world that worshipped death.

Mother feigned a lot of things. She mostly pretended that every lie she ever told was the truth. It was the pretending, which is nothing more than a lie, that made it easier for her to live with herself. Otherwise, death would have claimed her early, but she was afraid of real death, although she would never admit to it—at least not to me. She was always making life harder for herself. For her, that was living. What she knew more than anything else in her life was struggle, but living was harder than it had to be. She told herself that it was the only way, more like she convinced herself. "The only way to live is to learn how to survive. The world is tough, so the heart has to be tough too. Even the mind and the body have to be tough. Slavery taught us that. Slavery taught us how to survive," she said.

The lesson was passed down from generation to generation, from father to son, mother to daughter. Every decision she made was to keep her tough. Every choice with which she chose to live was to keep her tough, and almost everything she did was to keep her that way. And it all made her tough—to love and to live with. It was hard for her to accept for herself that she was human. She wouldn't let love or life show her that. She pretended too often. What she thought she didn't need is what she mostly desired: love. She had never learned true love, how to love herself, and life, at least in the way she understood it, hadn't taught her how to prepare for it. If love ever knocked on her door, she would never open it to receive it. Just a glimpse through the peephole would be enough. It would be too difficult to handle more. Love required more. It needed much more than she was willing to give to anybody, but mostly to herself.

Chapter 18

In early September, 1973, a summer storm hit hard. A big X, made by sticking together duct tape, marked most of the neighborhood windows to keep them from shattering to pieces if the wind hit too hard. Newspapers, radios and televisions all across Connecticut warned home owners and tenement dwellers to tape up and secure all glass doors and windows that would be directly exposed to the storm. Even those with an open window to the world, mostly those living on rooftops and alleyways, secured their belongings, in some cases only themselves, by taping together cardboard boxes and wrapping them in plastic garbage bags.

On the day of the storm, it was late in the afternoon, the sun was shining bright one minute then in the next, the whole street was overcome with darkness. Seemed like God just flipped a switch and the lights went off. I was sitting on the front steps of my building just watching. Mother was still at work. The thunder roared loud and shook the earth. The vibration of each booming rumble was enough to resuscitate the dead. And the lightning lit up the dark sky. If anyone ever said there was no beauty in darkness, God showed me different that day. Everyone had gone inside but me. I kept still. I was watching God. After a short while, the rain began to pelt the earth. I watched as each drop hit the cement in front of me, bounced up and split into smaller drops that sprayed into the air then eventually fell and flowed into the cracks in the cement. The cool drops that landed on me rolled down my skin, soaking into my clothes. If I were a weed growing within the cement cracks of life, my blessing had come.

It wasn't long before Mrs. Cooper was tapping on my shoulder with her cane. "Come on out the rain, child," she said. "It's gonna take more than a storm to wash heartache away." Imagining myself, first as a weed, then as a fallen leaf, I felt myself slowly being lifted and carried away. "Come on in, child. The wind gettin' too heavy to bear," Mrs. Cooper said, holding down the front of her dress. Already soaked from the rain, I stood then walked past Mrs. Cooper into our building. "Baby, this not the kinda weather you want to play with," she said, pushing my wet hair back away from my face.

"But it felt good," I said, pulling my clinging shirt away from my body.

"This more than a passin' shower. This a storm. Ain't no tellin' how it gonna leave things, and it don't have no mercy for the weak," she said, climbing the stairs.

"I hope it doesn't hurt Love," I said, following her.

"Don't know whatcha mean, child? Love?"

"My flower."

"If Love strong, it'll be okay," she said, almost out of breath. "These stairs get steeper by the day."

Once I reached the second-floor steps, I heard the phone ringing in my apartment. I ran up the last few stairs and brushed past Mrs. Cooper. "The phone's ringing," I said, pulling my key out of my pocket.

"It's probably your mother. Wanna make sure you okay," Mrs. Cooper said. "Let me know what she say when you get in."

"Okay," I said, pushing open the door. The phone was on a small end table just behind it. By the time I reached it, it had stopped ringing. I yelled out the door to Mrs. Cooper, "I missed it."

"Don't worry. She'll be callin' back," Mrs. Coooper said still out of breath.

Suddenly the phone began to ring again. I picked it up on the first ring. "Hello." Mother was on the other end.

"Where you been?" she asked angrily.

"In the front."

"Doing what?" Mother yelled. I pulled the phone away from my ear.

"Watching the storm," I said nervously.

"Watching the storm?" she asked. "Are you outta your mind?"

"No," I said still holding the phone away from my ear.

"Girl, I don't know what gets in to you sometimes." Mother had stopped screaming so I placed the phone back to my ear, but I could still hear the anger in her voice. "You just better be glad I wasn't there. Where's Mrs. Cooper? She supposed to be watching you."

"In the hallway."

"Doin' what?"

"Waiting to see if it was you calling."

"Tell her it's me. Did she have to go lookin' for you?"

"I was in the front."

"Why is she in the hallway?"

"I don't know."

"Let me speak to her."

I put the receiver down on the table then stuck my head out the door. "Mrs. Cooper, the phone."

Mrs. Cooper walked into my apartment. She shut the door then picked up the receiver. "Hello there," she said in a gentle, calming voice. Mrs. Cooper paused for a second then began to speak again. "She was just bein' a child. Curious that's all. Nothin' but curious." She paused again. I followed her lips with my eyes as she spoke. Mrs. Cooper smiled. "She a brave one. Got a mind too. Don't have to worry too much about this one." Mrs. Cooper smiled again. "Maxine, you enjoy the rest of your day. I'll be talkin' to ya. Good-bye." Mrs. Cooper hung up the phone and turned toward me. "Had your mother real worried, but she gonna be okay."

"I know," I said, twisting the bottom of my shirt.

"Take off those wet clothes and lay 'em on a towel over the edge of the tub. Put somethin' dry and clean on," Mrs. Cooper said, opening the door to let herself out.

"Okay."

"I know you's curious but keep away from the windows until the storm let up. You got lots of things to keep you busy, I know. Your mother said you like to read," Mrs. Cooper said.

"Yes."

"Good. You gonna go far in life," she said, gently patting my head. She stepped into the hallway. "Readin' help to build the mind, you know? If you got imagination, you don't got to go nowhere lookin' for nothin'.

Just bring the world right here to you. Make it how you want it to be. I wish I had learned to read better. Hmm. Things surely would've been different for me if I had. You still young. Got a good chance at makin' things different for you. That's what your mother fightin' for in her heart. Don't seem like it, but she is."

I looked at Mrs. Cooper and smiled. She didn't say anything else before she left me, but the expression in her eyes made me want to hug her tight and long. Too embarrassed to let her know, I said nothing as she walked out my apartment and shut the door. I locked it then walked into the bathroom and began to undress.

I decided to write a poem for Mrs. Cooper in my journal. I was planning to tear out the page and give it to her, but I never did. Mrs. Cooper was a wise old woman but she didn't finish school beyond the sixth grade. My fear was that she wouldn't be able to understand my thoughts.

Mrs. Cooper's gift was that she knew the inside depths of people. I learned this about her over the years, mostly through her talks with me and sometimes with Mrs. Wise. She knew things that only life itself and love could teach. Just seeing her alone, you wouldn't know this. Like most in my neighborhood, she was a lowly woman, but she had a rare gift and something books couldn't give you: common sense. She knew matters of the heart more than anything else. She had traveled through the smooth and more often than not rough terrains of the heart within her lifetime.

Once she said to me, "Most folks, upon hittin' the rough terrain in the heart, turn around hopin' to find an easier road, or just give up altogether. Yeah, sometimes there's an easier path to travel, but travelin' the rough road, learnin' it, is what make the rest easy. Folks too afraid to explore the heart and learn what's in it. Most of the beauty in the heart not on the surface. You got to travel down deep in it. That's where it is. The beauty in the heart down deep. And life don't make it easy for us to travel down there." It only took one look into my eyes and she would know what was in my heart.

After the storm passed, I looked out my window to see what it had done. Realizing it had slightly changed the world outside, I was inspired to work on my poem for Mrs. Cooper again by adding a few more lines. I wrote:

If life is a woman and woman is life
she is the sun and the rain,
the grass and the trees,
the ocean and the sky.
She is light and darkness,
the song and the dance,
the word and the poem.
She is all things moving and still,
old and new, known and unknown.
From her I learn that I am. I am.
I am the words that create poems.

The storm had changed lives. For some, their world had been turned upside-down, while for others it had been turned right side up. It all depended on how you viewed things after the storm. Some said the ways of Nature are like a woman. She has the power to make or break hearts, homes and the world. The storm had done just that. Some hearts were broken. And some homes. The world, which for many was nothing more than the happenings around them, was also broken. But the storm also had a way of making hearts, homes and the world new again. With the threat of death and disaster, a new appreciation for life emerged. The old was washed away, including grudges, habits and attitudes, and now there was room for the new. A woman could be spoken of in the same breath as Nature or the storm, but there was something more devastating or beautiful about the way a woman affected hearts, homes and the world. The pain or pleasure of her love ran deep into the core of souls. The change she made had a much more lasting effect, or at least it seemed. She could make a child a man and a man a child, the weak strong and the strong weak, the dying desire life and the living desire death. The storm shattered windows and tore limbs from trees. It had surely changed lives. But a woman has the power to shatter hearts and shatter dreams. She has the power. With it she can destroy or build the world.

The next morning, I visited Mrs. Wise's garden. A limb from the big oak tree had been torn off by the storm and crushed several of her plants and flowers. Mari was one of them. Mrs. Wise didn't seem too worried about it though. I helped her remove the limb and bring it to the back of the house. When we returned to the front, I checked on Love. She had been under the smaller part of the tree limb but wasn't affected. Mrs. Wise said, "Love survived the storm. Made her stronger, that's all." Although I was relieved, I was also disappointed that Mari had been crushed.

"What about Mari?" I asked.

"The spirit of Mari is still alive. That's the core. Take more than a storm to kill that," Mrs. Wise said, cutting away the stems of the crushed flowers and plants. She looked over at me and watched as I picked up the cut stems and placed them in a small bucket of water at my side. She then reached up and removed the small yellow-and-blue silk butterfly with white speckles from her hat. She carefully placed it in my hair.

"Thank you, Mrs. Wise," I said, reaching up to feel the silk butterfly. I then squeezed her as tight as I could. When I let her go, she cut Mari's stem then placed several petals in the earth, one in my hand and the rest of the crushed yellow flower in the same spot on her hat where the butterfly used to be. "That petal there is for faith. Put it in a special place so it's always remindin' you to believe," she said. Mrs. Wise started in her garden again. "The endin' is only the beginning of new things."

I spent the whole day working on the garden with Mrs. Wise. While cutting, pruning, turning over soil and planting new seeds, I forgot about the mark on my face. It had almost disappeared, although it was the first thing I saw in the mirror every morning, but Mrs. Wise didn't fail to remind me of it.

The first time she had seen it, she just shook her head and said, "The seed already planted. It just have to be cultivated." I took that to mean that whatever needed to be said had been already. Everything Mrs. Wise ever spoke to me about had taken root within me, but knowing and doing hadn't yet been integrated into one common thread of mindfulness. This time, though, she cut directly through the silence. "I had a talk with Violet's mother." As soon as I heard Mud Pie's name—Mrs. Wise always called her by her real name—the mark on my face was visible to me again. It even became enlarged and uglier than it first appeared while still stained with blood. The day it all happened was one big colorful picture in my mind. I felt a stirring sensation in my stomach.

I kept on with what I was doing. "Mud Pie?" I said, swallowing the name with my saliva uneasily.

"Don't like the name so I ain't gonna use it myself," she said. "But yes, that's who I'm talkin' about exactly. Had a talk with her mother, Ms. Lily."

"What did you say?"

"Well, first thing is I wanted to do somethin' nice for Mrs. Lily. I brought her a small arrangement of my very best tulips. Put a smile on her face. Then she invited me into her place, and we started to chatterin'. First, we talked about the flowers and my garden. Then, after a while, when she got a little more comfortable with my visit, we started speakin' about our community."

"Does Ms. Lily have furniture?"

"Now why is you concerned with that?" Mrs. Wise asked, dropping her hands onto her lap.

"I don't know." I shrugged. "Tanya said Mud Pie's family doesn't have furniture."

"It's a lot of things they don't have, baby. But what it is they have is more than the rich can afford." Mrs. Wise shook her head.

"I didn't say it." I lowered my eyes. "I was just telling you what Tanya said."

"I know. I know," Mrs. Wise said. She kept silent for a few moments while she dug up more earth for new seed. "We is a community. We a group of folks who more the same than we are different. This what I really wanted Ms. Lily to know. It's important you know it too. Even our callin' is the same, to serve. That's right, baby. To serve the people of this earth the best way we know how. We have to work together to build the world around us. Make it better than we know it's been. Ain't been a good place for a while now. All kinda things has happened and not happened to this community and the people in it. Attitudes has changed. And I ain't talkin' about no small change neither. Folks just discouraged. Heartbroken. And it don't take much to lead 'em astray. Even when the wind blow a little hope back around to these parts, something else come and just take it away."

"Why are people discouraged?"

"Because there ain't nothin' that ain't been said or done to make the black people of this community think they ain't worth the trash they walk past every day."

"I ain't discouraged."

"Hope. You still got hope," Mrs. Wise said, pushing away particles of earth from a small budding shoot. "I understand all the trouble Ms. Lily havin'. It's real hard in this world, I know. And it's even harder when you got a family to raise. But she don't have to do it alone. Folks like me and Mrs. Cooper don't have no problem helpin' at all. Didn't wanna volunteer no other names 'cause you never know with some folks, but it's some good people in the community that really don't mind helpin'. Some of 'em keep to themselves 'cause they don't want nobody thinkin' they tryin' to pry, but they ready to help out when you let 'em know. I think Mrs. Lily might've been a little embarrassed with what I was sayin' to her. Sometimes we ashamed to ask for help when we need it, but I told her she needn't be ashamed. Times have been tough for us all."

Mrs. Wise removed the straw hat from her head and began to fan herself, then she placed it back on her head. "We talked a little more about this until I could see that she understood what I was meanin' about us bein' a community." Mrs. Wise scooped up some of the earth and began to sift through it. She picked out a small fragment of glass then put it in her apron pocket. "Community is real important, you know?" She placed the earth back onto the ground. "Well, it was gettin' late, so the last thing I told her was rememberin' and forgettin' equally important in our world. After I said that, she said she was real sorry for the trouble Violet caused you. She hopes you can forget it all."

"How do you forget?"

"Choose to. That's all it is," Mrs. Wise said. "Violet gone away, you know? She gone away."

Forgetting didn't always come as easy as when the words *choose to* were first spoken by Mrs. Wise, but when she said Mud Pie had gone away, I could feel the change inside of me. A window opened within me, and the sun was let in, making all the hard, cold spots soft and warm. Butterflies emerged from the darkness of their cocoons and spread their delicate golden wings to fly. Flowers pushed upward far beyond their roots and unfolded themselves like the awakening of a spring day. Birds made music, melodious music, within me. Forgetting didn't always come easy. I would come to learn this more and more with the passing of each season, but knowing I had the choice made summer last longer. Forgetting made it summer year round.

Chapter 19

I heard music. When he spoke to me, it was early on a Sunday morning, a few days before my tenth birthday. I was surprised he called as early as he did. There was no explanation given, mostly just silence and music. Church bells were ringing. I held the phone to my ear as close as it would go and listened. Sounded like God was singing to me. Father must've been standing all the way at the top of the church right under those bells, but when I thought about it more, he couldn't have been. I don't think they have pay phones up in a church tower. The ringing was loud though. When Father finally spoke, he said only a few words: *I love you.* They were the lyrics to a song. I kept the words and the music that made the song in my heart and head that whole day. Nothing could make me forget it. Not even Mother and Mr. Girard could make me forget the song. They awoke shortly after I hung up with Father. Mother walked out of her room with disgust on her face when she saw Mr. Girard sprawled out on the living room floor with an empty liquor bottle in his hand. She didn't say one word. When he opened his eyes and looked up at her standing over him, he just shut his eyes and went back to dreaming again. I knew he was dreaming because I heard him cooing like a baby. The sound he made was low and soft like a dove.

Mother walked into the kitchen and rattled the pots and pans. The noise was sure to give Mr. Girard a headache if he didn't already have one. If Mother wanted anyone to know how disturbed she was that morning, the cacophony of pots and pans was a clear indication. When she was done making noise, she cracked four large brown eggs, let them spill out of their shells into a small white bowl, and she beat them for a long time—a real long time. She was still beating them when Mrs. Cooper knocked on our door almost thirty minutes later. She had asked Mother the night before if she could bring me along with her to church service. Mrs. Cooper attended the Baptist church on Saint John Road, a few blocks away from East Street, next door to the fire house. Some people said it had to be close to the fire house because most people in the church were bringing the fire from hell with them. I had never been to a church service before, but Mother didn't mind me attending. I was almost ready to go, except I hadn't eaten. Mother hurried and fixed me two slices of buttered toast, then poured me a glass of orange juice. I was to meet Mrs. Cooper down in the front of our building once I was done eating. Before Mrs. Cooper left, she said to Mother, "God for everybody, you know?"

Mother wiped her hands on her apron and started messing in her hair. "God is in my heart," she said.

Mrs. Cooper smiled. "Seems like you havin' a hard time findin' Him nowadays. A little church might help you some."

Mother averted her eyes and pursed her lips. "Church ain't for me. Never helped me before. Don't see how it can help me now."

"The church is for showin' us the right way, but it can't move your feet for you," Mrs. Cooper said, looking Mother in her eyes.

Mother turned toward Mr. Girard who had fallen back asleep. "My feet have taken me where I needed to go and back just fine."

"Well, I'm sure glad you lettin' Rose attend church with me. She'll be good company," Mrs. Cooper said.

"Don't have no problems with Rose attendin' church with you. It will do her some good to get out from around here for a little while."

Mrs. Cooper offered a friendly smile. "God bless," she said. Mother nodded then shut the door.

When we walked into the old school building, the hallway was dimly lit. I could hear the choir singing in the distance, something about wanting to be a Christian. We walked down the long hallway until we reached the metal auburn doors that read *Auditorium* in white letters.

"Church right through those doors," Mrs. Cooper said, pointing with her cane.

"This doesn't look like a church," I said.

"Don't matter what it look like on the outside, baby. Only thing that matter is what's on the inside. When we walk through these doors, you gonna think you in a big white church on the top of a hill. Gonna put the same feeling in you. Praise God, praise God, praise God." Mrs. Cooper pointed to the silver door handle with her cane. I grabbed it and pulled open the door.

The female usher put out her arm. "Pastor Starks praying. Give 'im a second then I'll walk you to your seats."

Mrs. Cooper nodded then lowered her head and closed her eyes. I looked around the packed auditorium. There was a rainbow of black faces with their heads lowered and eyes closed. The pastor was a diminutive cream-complected man with salt-and-pepper hair. He had a low-pitched monotone that echoed throughout the auditorium. He stood behind a pulpit at the center of the raised stage. Before him was an open Bible whose thin, leafy pages he smoothed as he recited Psalm 123.

When he got to the end, he raised his voice in a loud cry. "Have mercy on us, O Lord. Have mercy on us, for we have endured much contempt. We have endured much ridicule from the proud, much contempt from the arrogant." He laid his hands on the pages of the Bible. "Amen. Amen. Amen. Can the congregation say 'amen?'"

The congregation cried out, "Amen!"

Mrs. Cooper grabbed my hand and squeezed it hard. "Yes, yes, Lord. Have mercy on us," she said. The female usher with white gloves and a kind smile handed us a folded program then led us to our seats.

As we sat, the choir stood. The rest of the congregation joined them. Mrs. Cooper remained in her seat. I remained in mine too.

Mrs. Cooper looked over at me and said, "Stand, child. You still young. My feet can't bear the pressure on them for too long." She handed me a hymnbook then I stood. The people in front of me blocked my view, so it was hard to see the pastor and the choir. Pastor Starks asked the congregation to turn to page 364. Then he said, "My brother in Christ will sing for us this glorious morning 'Amazing Grace.' Now we have all heard our brother sing for us before." The congregation responded with "amen" or "yes, yes." "God has blessed him with the spirit of song. Yes. What a gift he has. Let's welcome Brother Dickens to the front."

The congregation nodded and shouted "amen" and "yes, sir."

I stood on the tips of my toes and looked over the shoulder of a man standing in front of me. When I saw Mr. Dickens, who lived in the building next to mine, walking to the front of the stage where a single microphone was located, my heart nearly stopped. It was hard to believe my eyes. I was looking at the same man who was messing with Tanya, a girl way too young for him.

"Yes, God has blessed him," Pastor Starks noted once again. Then Mr. Dickens began to sing.

The congregation eventually joined in.

A woman two rows in front of me began to shout and cry, "O God. O Lord. Thank you. Thank you." When I looked to see who it was, I saw Ms. Ross, Tanya's mother, waving her hands. After every verse, she would begin to shout. Tanya and her sister, Zinnia, who lived on the first floor of my building with their mother, sat on each side of her. Next thing I knew Ms. Ross began a dance that made her whole body shake. Then she was out into the aisle running to the pulpit and back. I had never seen anything like it, so I thought something was wrong with her.

I looked over at Mrs. Cooper and asked, "What's wrong with Ms. Ross?"

Mrs. Cooper leaned over and whispered, "She filled with the Holy Spirit."

I began to watch Ms. Ross again. "The Holy Spirit make you do that?"

Mrs. Cooper's eyes got small. "Hush, child, and listen," she said.

When the song was over, Pastor Starks walked back up to the pulpit. "That was beautiful. Brother Dickens did a fine job. Now didn't he do a fine job, church?"

The congregation clapped and shouted. Those who had already taken their seats stood and began to clap and shout, joining in with the rest of the members. Ms. Ross was spread out on the floor in front of the pulpit. Mr. Dickens was standing over her with a fan, waving it back and forth.

"What's wrong with Ms. Ross? Why is she on the floor?" I asked Mrs. Cooper.

"She overcome with the spirit, baby."

I looked back up at Mr. Dickens and watched as he waved the fan over Ms. Ross's head. I sat back down in my seat. "The devil sing too?"

Mrs. Cooper grabbed my hand and squeezed it. "That wasn't nothin' but God. Nothin' but God. You mind your mouth now."

Pastor Starks preached a sermon on God's grace and mercy. He said there's a seat in heaven beside the throne of God for everyone. "It doesn't matter how much we as blacks suffer on earth because life in heaven will be different."

Why do blacks have to die first before things are different? White people don't wait to get to heaven to enjoy life, I thought.

"Blacks will again be kings and queens, and milk and honey will be abundant," he said. I wondered if Mr. Dickens would get into heaven. I had also wondered why blacks had to wait until we got to heaven before we could be kings and queens. We already had kings and queens on earth. Mrs. Carey, my second-grade teacher, had taught me that. And there's plenty of food on earth, so who cares about milk and honey in heaven? I already had both at home. Anyway, I would probably be tired of milk and honey by the time I got there, I thought. I wanted to ask Mrs. Cooper about some of the things Pastor Starks said, but she had already asked me to hush too many times. Pastor Starks also said that all of our past and present wrongs would be forgiven if we repented. "God forgives all," he said. I wondered if we did the same wrong thing every day then repented right after or the next day God would still let us into heaven. Does God let murderers and thieves in? Does God let white people in? How was Mr. Dickens going to get in?

When Pastor Starks finished his sermon, he began to shout and dance around the pulpit. Others within the congregation stood, shouted and danced with him. Mrs. Cooper started to cry, and her body began to shake. When her hands flew into the air, a honey-brown woman in the front of her and another in the back held hands and encircled her. I wondered if she was having a seizure.

"Is someone gonna call the ambulance?" I asked.

"No, baby, she filled, that's all," the woman in front answered. I looked back at Mrs. Cooper. She was sweating all over.

"What is she filled with?"

The woman sucked her teeth and rolled her eyes. "The holy ghost," she said.

"Ghost? Is that the same thing as the holy spirit? Is the spirit a ghost?" I asked.

"Yeah, little girl. You ask too many questions. This ain't the time now. Ain'tcha never been to church before?" The woman in front began to wipe the sweat from Mrs. Cooper's forehead with a napkin.

"No," I said.

She looked at the other woman in the back of Mrs. Cooper. "That's a sin," she said. The other woman who wore a lime-green hat, lime-green gloves and a Sunkist orange dress nodded.

"You oughta think about gettin' saved," the woman in black said.

"Saved from what?" I asked.

"From goin' to hell," she said.

"Why am I goin' to hell?" I asked as Pastor Starks made his way back to the pulpit.

"'Cause you ain't been baptized. You ain't a Christian. If you ain't a Christian then you ain't got no chance for heaven. God gonna look right past you when the time come for Jesus's return," she said.

Pastor Starks began to talk again, and the two women sat back in their seats. The woman in the lime-green hat looked over at me and shook her head as Mrs. Cooper rocked back and forth in her seat. Tears rolled down her face.

"Please open your bibles to Psalm, chapter twenty-three," Pastor Starks said. Mrs. Cooper reached for her bible. She flipped through the pages until she reached Psalms. She handed the Bible to me. "Turn to twenty-three," she whispered.

"If everyone has it say 'amen,'" Pastor Starks shouted to the congregation.

"Amen," the congregation shouted back.

Pastor Starks read:

"The Lord is my Shepard; I have everything I need.
He lets me rest in fields of green grass
And leads me to quiet pools of fresh water."

"Yes, yes. O Lord," the woman in black said.

"He gives me strength.
He guides me in the right paths, as he has promised.
Even if I go through the deepest darkness,
I will not be afraid, Lord, for you are with me.
Your Shepherd's rod and staff protect me."

A man who sat three rows in front of me jumped up and waved his hand in the air. "O Lord, give me strength. Give me strength. For I can't do nothin' without you." He sat back in his seat, bowed his head and clasped his hands.

Mrs. Cooper's leg began to shake. "Give me strength in my legs again, O Lord. And let your strength forever be inside of my heart and spirit," she said.

Pastor Starks continued reading:

"You prepare a banquet for me,
Where all my enemies can see me;
You welcome me as an honored guest
And fill my cup to the brim.
I know that your goodness and love
Will be with me all my life;
And your house will be my home
As long as I live."

The woman in black looked back at me. "It's a sin," she said and turned back to the front. Pastor Starks closed his bible. "It is time," he said. The congregation began to shout and clap. "It is time. It is time," he said again.

The congregation stood and shouted, "Yes, Lord."

Pastor Starks picked up three small baskets from the side of the stage then passed them on to three men who wore white gloves. He walked back over to the pulpit. "It is time to collect the tithes and offerings." The congregation remained standing. "Give only what you got, but make sure that you don't give less than ten percent. If you give less than ten percent, you ain't doin' nothin' but stealin' from God." Pastor Starks wiped the sweat from his brow. "And let's give an offering for the men and women without homes, for the children without food for their small bellies, for the crippled and the blind. God has ordered us to serve Him. The only way to serve God is by serving the people of this congregation. The only way to serve the people of this congregation is by making sure the pastor of this congregation is taken care of. Amen. This church that I have built for each of you is our home. The Word that I have fed you this morning is your food, and I have healed the crippled and the blind by renewing their spirits with the gift of song and praise."

One of the men in white gloves passed the basket to an old man with a checkered suit and shiny white shoes at the end of our row. The man dropped change into it and passed it on to a dark brown woman with honey-blond hair beside him. I wondered if he had put in his ten percent.

The woman with the basket rolled her eyes and sucked her teeth. "I can't give what I don't got," she said then passed the basket on to Mrs. Cooper who dropped in a pink envelope then passed the basket to me.

"I don't have any money," I said.

Mrs. Cooper went into her purse then pulled out two quarters. "Here ya go, baby," she said, passing me the quarters. I dropped the change into the basket then passed it to the woman beside me who wore a big candy apple-red hat and a matching suit with black silk gloves and patent leather shoes. She looked inside the basket. "I need change," she said to the man with the white gloves.

"What you need?" he asked.

"I need four twenties," she said with a devilish smirk. She was holding a ten-dollar bill.

"You won't find it in there," the man said.

"Can't give no money then," the woman said, placing the ten-dollar bill back into her wallet. Her expression read, she had no intention on tithing.

"Ain't nobody's cross to bear but your own," said the man with white gloves.

"I done already been to hell and back—several times. I'm 'bout used to it now."

"Suit yourself," the man said and reached for the basket. He then walked up to the front with the other two men.

Pastor Starks began a silent prayer over the baskets. Once he was done, he began to sing "The Bible Tells Me So." The rest of the congregation joined in.

Pastor Starks raised his hand toward the congregation. "God looking for a soul to join this church today. You ain't only doing it for yourself. You doing it for God. We don't know when Jesus is coming back for us, but He is coming back, so today is the day to prepare for His return.

When you walk out those doors today, walk out saved not a sinner. Come on now. God is waiting for you."

While the congregation sang, I remembered the song in my own heart. Father had already put it there earlier that morning. And nothing could make me forget it, not even the thought of going to hell.

Chapter 20

On my way from church, I picked dandelions. I made wishes while I blew on them and watched the soft white feathery hairs float in the air then blow away. My very first wish was that God would save me from burning in hell. My second was that God would keep me from sinning. Only sinners go to hell. I thought about that for a while as I walked quietly alongside Mrs. Cooper. I wondered if the whole world was going to hell. I didn't know very many people who didn't sin except for Mrs. Wise and Mrs. Cooper. But Mrs. Wise wasn't saved. Did that mean she was going to hell too? She always talked to God. He talked to her too.

Mother was sitting at the kitchen table when I returned from church. Mr. Girard was already gone. The eggs were still in the ceramic bowl in the middle of the table uncooked. Mother was picking the feathers from the chicken wings she had bought a few days earlier and staring out the window. The sun was out and the day was young, but the look in Mother's eyes was old—almost ancient—depending on how you counted the days and the years. I decided to save a dandelion for Mother so she could make a wish too. Maybe she would ask for a new life and God would give it to her. First, she had to get rid of Mr. Girard. As long as he was around, she would always remember the old, the past. It seemed to always find its way into the present and the future. Mother was staring out the window into another world filled with rays of light and hope— promise. Maybe this was heaven. If so, it was obtainable. Seemed like all she had to do was stick out her hand and she could touch a cloud, move it to the side and find the rainbow behind it, but the shattered glass bottle on the table reflected a sharper image of blinding light, almost enough to fill the room with a certain darkness, that I knew could not be in heaven. In Mother's eyes, there was no light, no color, no rainbow.

Mother didn't hear me enter the kitchen. When I stretched out my arm and placed the dandelion in front of her, I startled her. "You must've lost your mind," she said with a strange look in her eyes. She picked up the wing she had dropped into the silver cooking pan in front of her. "People get hurt that way, you know?"

"I didn't mean to scare you," I said, holding the dandelion in front of her.

"What's this?" she asked, oiling the skin of a wing.

"A dandelion. I brought it home so that you can make a wish."

"A wish?"

"Yes."

"What kind of a wish?" she asked, wiping her hands on her apron.

"Any kind," I said, handing her the dandelion.

"Let's see," she said, taking it from me. "What do I want?"

"Whatever you want, God will give it you," I said.

"Is that what you learned in church this morning?" she asked, getting up from the table.

"No. Mrs. Wise told me that," I said, following Mother to the window.

Mother stuck her hand out the window then closed her eyes and blew on the dandelion. The soft feathery white hairs floated into the air then slowly began to drift away. Mother opened her hand and watched the stem as it fell onto the cement below. "There. I'm done."

"What did you wish?"

"I can't tell. It's between me and God," she said. Mother walked back to the table and began to pick up the small fragments of clear glass that lay across it.

"What happened?"

"It slipped right out my hand. Don't know how it happened, but I got so frustrated, I just left it here. Don't have the patience nor the tolerance for much these days, you know?" Mother emptied the pieces of glass into a small brown paper bag then placed the bag on the floor at the side of the sink. "How was church?"

"Okay," I said, pulling a chair out from the table.

"Just okay?" Mother asked, picking up the pan of wings.

"I didn't like it that much," I said, sitting at the table. "What are you going to do with these eggs?"

"Thought about pourin' them down the sink, but they still good. I guess I can use 'em for batter." Mother placed the pan into the sink and began to run water into it.

"They're not spoiled?" I asked, turning up my lip.

"Beaten to death, maybe," she said, picking up the bowl of eggs, "but not spoiled." Mother began to beat the eggs again. She then placed the bowl on the sink and turned off the water. "So tell me about church," she said, wiping her hands on her apron.

"I didn't like it that much," I said, drawing an invisible circle on the table.

"Why not?" Mother asked.

"'Cause mostly everybody in church is going to hell. Some people have already been there," I said, drawing invisible flames below the bottom of my invisible circle.

"That's not nice to say," Mother said without turning to face me.

"It's true. One lady said it herself. She lied in church, and she said she already been to hell." I drew a stick woman with a large hat, a long pointy tail and a pitchfork in her hand. "Another lady told me that I was going to hell because I wasn't saved."

"Somebody said that to you?" Mother asked, turning toward me with a surprised expression.

"Yes. She made me angry, but I didn't say anything bad back to her." I drew another stick figure in the middle of my circle then drew an invisible X over it.

"Well, I'm glad you didn't say nothing bad back. Sometimes you have to learn to ignore people, especially those overly religious ones. They the worse kind." Mother walked back over to the table with the silver pan and sat down.

"What's the purpose of religion?" I asked.

"That's a good question. Don't really know how to answer it. Depending on who you ask, you'll get a different answer. But I think everybody needs something to believe in. Something that's bigger than our own lives."

"God?"

"Yeah, God is bigger than us."

"Can you only find God in church?"

"God too big to be only in the church. God too big. Much too big," Mother said, dropping a wing into the egg batter.

"Where is heaven?"

"Wherever there's a rainbow," Mother said. "Wherever there's a rainbow."

&⁊Ɒ

The next day in Mrs. Delgado's fifth-grade class, she quizzed us on Puerto Rico again. "What does Puerto Rico mean?" she asked. No one raised their hand although Mrs. Delgado had been asking the same question since the first day of school, which was more than a month ago. It was the middle of October. Everyone knew the answer but we all hoped that she would stop asking. When no one raised his or her hand, Mrs. Delgado picked on me. "Rose, what does Puerto Rico mean? Come and write it on the board for me. It's important that we all know because Puerto Ricans are a part of our American culture. The schools and colleges want to teach Spanish, but they know nothing about the history of the Spanish-speaking people. They know nothing about Puerto Rico. They know nothing about Puerto Ricans." Mrs. Delgado spoke with a thick accent, and each word fluidly rolled off her tongue. When I reached the front of the room, I picked up a piece of broken white chalk and wrote on the board *Rich Port*. Mrs. Delgado waved her hand at me, which was a sign for me to go back to my seat. "Why the name Puerto Rico, or in English Rich Port?"

I raised my hand once I was seated again. "Because in 1511, gold was discovered there."

Mrs. Delgado nodded. "Very good. Who discovered the island before it was named Puerto Rico?" Mrs. Delgado walked to the board and picked up the same broken piece of chalk. She wrote, *Christopher Columbus*. She turned toward the class, lifted her brow then turned back to the board and underlined the name. "Who agrees with this?" she asked. No one spoke. "I will take the silence to mean that no one agrees. Good. I don't agree either." She drew a line through the name. "How can Mr. Columbus discover an island that is already inhabited by its native people?" Mrs. Delgado walked toward a girl named Lorraine Montez who sat in the front row. "Lorraine, do you have an answer for me?"

164

Lorraine looked up at Mrs. Delgado and smiled. "No, teacher," she said.

Mrs. Delgado walked away and sat at her desk. She began to shuffle papers. "I don't think the man who wrote the history book has the answer either. Take out your reading books, and let's begin our next assignment."

The rest of my days in the fifth grade were no different than the first week. Mrs. Delgado always began her class with a history lesson on Puerto Rico. By the end of the school year, I could answer all of her questions although it was rare that I volunteered. There were four Spanish-speaking students in my class, but none of them knew any of their history until the fifth grade with Mrs. Delgado. She was very proud that during the school year they had learned more and retained facts about their ancestors' culture.

The sixth grade came and went just as quickly as the fifth grade. There was nothing significant about it except that it would be my last year at Watson. On graduation day, Mr. Price, my sixth-grade teacher, celebrated the fact that seventeen of his twenty-one students were passing on to junior high school. Everyone received, along with their diplomas, a blue ink pen with their first names engraved in gold. This was a small token of Mr. Price's appreciation for being one of his most cooperative classes during his ten years at Watson. In the middle of his speech, he almost broke down and cried when he talked about how difficult it was for black kids in predominantly black schools to learn. Mr. Price turned bright red and could barely finish his speech. He stroked his blond curls several times then finally said, "Thank God for this blessing."

The summer after the sixth grade seemed like the hottest one ever. That was in 1975. It rained only six times during the season. In between those times, the air was dry, and when the wind moved across the city, it took everything that was once attached to something with it. Paint peeled off the exterior of houses and melted into the scorching-hot cement. Old and worn shingles dropped one by one off rooftops. Leaves bristled loudly, detached from the limbs of trees and turned into dust before they touched the earth. Blades of grass, unprotected by the shade of tree trunks, turned into thin, tan strips of paper that crackled under the soles of human feet. This kind of summer was unusual for the northern hemisphere. It made men, women and children testy. In order to keep civil and the neighborhood at peace, people kept their shades down, windows closed and doors locked after sunrise.

It rained six times, but I only saw the rainbow twice. If the rainbow is a glimpse into the realms of heaven, this season was mostly a hot summer in hell. Mrs. Cooper said she dreamed about the underworld. She said all she could see was red in her dreams. "Nothing but hell," she said. "Last time I saw red in my dreams, a man used to attend my church was burned alive in his own bed. His only child set him on fire. Nobody ever learned the truth why she did it. The truth gone under with 'em both. The fire took the girl too." Six days after Mrs. Cooper dreamed about hell, the liquor store a block over on the corner of Main and Kent went up in flames. Two abandoned tenements inhabited by dope dealers and users burned down with it. Nothing was left of the buildings but ashes and a shiny metal medallion found under the debris. Engraved in the medallion were the words, *Vengeance is mine, I will repay, says the Lord.* —*Romans 12:19.*

The neighborhood speculated for days about who did it. The only truth was speculation. A woman who lived across Main Street said she saw it all. "The owner of that store did it," she said. "Insurance money is what he after." Someone else said he saw a woman walk by and throw a lit match into the window. Many reasons for the burning of the buildings were shared among the community, but after the medallion was found, it was said by the mass who gathered around the ashes to view it that it was nothing but God.

Every Sunday succeeding the finding of the medallion, local churches more easily found new members. Those who had already given their lives to God studied their bibles more frequently and prayed more fervently to be forgiven for their sins. Mrs. Cooper began to speak in tongues and was heard shouting in her apartment thanking God for the healing of her legs that hadn't come yet. Ms. Ross began to teach bible study class in her living room on Tuesdays at 7:00 p.m., but her only students were her daughters, Tanya and Zinnia. Tanya said after three months she had learned the entire book of Revelation. It was the only book Ms. Ross taught during the one-hour study. Mr. Dickens anointed his apartment with olive oil and rubbed what was left of the small bottle on his body, making sure not to miss any external organs. Tanya said when he slid his hand down into his pants, he asked God to forgive him for being a man.

If the hot days of summer were cursed by the tongues of men and women, they began to bow under the rays of the sun and worshipped the power of God. Jack Black who converted from the neighborhood drunk to a born-again Christian walked up and down East Street with his bible in hand. "God gonna raise the Christian up and out of this here hell. There is a place in heaven for us. There is a place in the green pastures of heaven for us. Sinners will perish. But the people of God will live. I once was lost. But now I'm found. Hallelujah."

Mrs. Wise, who had only heard about the medallion, shook her head every time Jack Black walked by her house.

"Sinners will perish," he would say, clutching his bible and averting his eyes. "Hell has come to claim us, but God will save us. There's a place in heaven for us all."

One day while I was visiting the garden, Mrs. Wise stepped down from her porch and stood on the cement walkway in front of her house. Jack Black who was coming down the street with his bible crossed over to the other side of the street. "Good evening, Mr. Black," Mrs. Wise said with a wide smile.

Jack Black paced, turning the pages of his bible. "There's room in heaven for all who are faithful," he said.

"How long you gon' wait for this heaven you speak of?" Mrs. Wise asked.

"God already done showed me the pearly gates. He already done showed me," he said, still pacing and fumbling through the pages of his bible.

"The kingdom of heaven is here on earth. It's in the heart of every man, woman and child," Mrs. Wise said.

"The devil is a liar. The devil is a liar," he yelled.

"I couldn't agree with you more. The devil is a liar." Mrs. Wise turned away and walked back up to her porch. "Baby, pass me the hose over there. The garden of heaven could use a little more water."

Mrs. Wise's garden still prospered although rain was minimal and the air was dry. Each morning before sunrise she prepared the garden for the day. Early in the evenings, she would come out to check on her garden again and water it after the sun had long dried the surface of the earth. Mari had been brought back to life, or at least another flower that looked just like her had risen out of the earth and had taken her place. Mrs. Wise gave her the same gentle care and attention she had given to Mari. Love was growing too.

Mrs. Wise didn't speak of the burning buildings or the medallion that was found under the ashes. Once I had asked her if it was God that burned the buildings down. "Evil destroys itself," she said.

"Mrs. Cooper and everybody else said it was God," I responded.

"Maybe it was," she said.

"Why is everyone so scared then?" I asked. "Isn't God good?"

"God is good," she said.

"So why is everyone so scared of God?"

"Truth is God," she said. "People scared of the truth."

"The truth?" I asked.

"The truth," she said without any further explanation.

That same evening May, my friend from the third grade and who lived across the street, was out sitting on her front porch. She was reading a book called *To Kill a Mockingbird*. I had never heard of it before, but the title sounded interesting. As soon as she saw me, she put the open book facedown by her side. She jumped up and ran down the steps toward me. "Hey," she said, embracing me.

"Why are you so happy?" I asked, pulling away.

"Because I haven't seen you," she said. "Why are you acting so stuffy?"

"I'm not acting stuffy," I said. "I'm just not used to you being so touchy-feely, that's all."

"People change," she said, pulling a tube of red lipstick out of her purse. "How do my lips look?"

"The same as they always look."

May gently glided the tube of lipstick around her mouth. Then while looking into a compact case with a mirror, she pulled out a small, beige powder sponge and patted her nose and forehead.

"Why do you wear so much makeup?"

"I don't," she said, placing the compact back into her purse.

"You look pretty without all that makeup," I said, picking up her book.

"Do not lose my page," she said. "I have to read that for school."

"School is over," I said, thumbing through the pages.

"I know, but it is required reading for the seventh grade. We have to write a paper on it, so I am reading it early," she said.

"That makeup makes you look white."

"No, it does not," May said angrily.

"Yes, it does," I responded. "Your skin isn't that light."

"Yes, it is."

"I bet you it isn't." I licked the tip of my finger, so I could remove some of her makeup. "Let me see."

May leaned away from me. "You better not touch me."

"I'm not gonna touch you," I said, wiping my finger on my shirt.

"Why are you starting trouble with me?" she asked.

"Why are you talking that way?"

"What way?" she asked, wrinkling her nose.

"Talk regular," I said. "You don't sound like May."

"What do I sound like then?"

"White."

"Aren't you half white?"

"No. My father is."

"You still have white blood in you."

"That doesn't mean I have to act white."

"You talk proper too."

"I've always talked this way. You haven't."

"Yes, I have."

"No, you haven't."

"Whatever." May waved her hand. "Besides the way I talk, how am I acting white?"

"You don't look the same. I guess it's that makeup." I wrinkled my face.

"You are just jealous." She crossed her arms in front of her and turned away. "I am learning things that you will never learn living in this neighborhood. Plus, you are at a black school where nobody cares."

"I am learning things that you will never learn."

"Like what?" she asked, placing her hand on her hip.

"Things," I said, frustrated.

"I am not listening to you anymore," she said, snatching her book away from me.

"What's that book about anyway?"

"People," she said.

"What kind of people?"

"Mean white people, good white people and dumb black people."

"What about them?"

"Some white people have a conscience and some of them don't. Black people don't think at all."

"What do you mean?"

"My grandmother said conscience is the voice of God. If black people had a conscience then they would be different. Look at all the black people around here. Hardly any of them are doing anything with their lives." May placed a marker in the book then closed it.

"That's not true. Anyway," I said, shaking my head, "what else did your grandmother say about the voice of God?"

"She said when you are looking for the truth, listen to the voice of God. But some people have more than one voice inside of their heads. Some have as many as twenty." I sucked my teeth. "It's the truth, but when the voice of God speaks, everything inside of you is at peace." May placed the book on the step next to her.

I picked it up and opened it. "What do the mean white people do?"

"They act real ugly and do real ugly things. They look real ugly too." May was pointing her index finger at me while she spoke.

"What do the good white people do?"

"They tell the truth no matter what," she said. "My favorite character is Scout Finch, but she acts too much like a boy."

"Why is she your favorite?"

"Because she is not afraid of anything. And she is a humanitarian." May jumped up from the steps and grabbed the book from me.

"Are you afraid of anything?" I asked as Jack Black came up the street with his bible, yelling out the Ten Commandments.

"I do not want to end up like him," she said, pointing. "I am a thinking person." She slumped down onto the step.

Chapter 21

Though the summer was hot, the neighborhood frenzy had cooled, but not enough to cast down the heat of tempers, particularly Mother and Mr. Girard's. Most of their arguments were torrid as ever. If you stood too close to either one of them during one, you were likely to get burned.

"Those burnin' buildings is a sign." That's what Mr. Girard told Mother after the medallion was found, only two weeks earlier. She just waved him away. He had a half-empty liquor bottle sticking out of his back pocket when he said it. "That liquor store didn't burn down for nothing. Had to be God. Ain't no black man gonna burn up no sweet candy. No, sir. Too sweet. Got to get rid of the sweet tooth first. Even that ain't gonna help. The smell too strong," he said, pulling the bottle out of his pocket. He unscrewed the top and took a whiff. "The smell too strong to resist. Got to burn every liquor store down if you wanna keep me away from this."

"You're a pitiful man," Mother said.

"And you a nutcase," Mr. Girard responded after taking a sip of his liquor.

"I guess we a match made in heaven," Mother said.

"A lost cause maybe," Mr. Girard said, handing the bottle to Mother. She waved it away. "Might help your senses a little."

"Ain't helpin' yours," Mother said, tossing the wet, soapy sponge into the sink. "If those burnin' buildings is a sign, they haven't stopped you from drinkin'."

"I'm already dead and gone to hell," Mr. Girard said, stuffing the bottle into his back pocket.

"Rose, don't you got something you can do, besides listenin' to us?" Mother asked, walking away.

"No," I said.

"Time you find something else then," she said, heading into the living room. Mr. Girard walked over to the window and pressed his forehead against the glass.

"It's too hot to go outside," I said, rising from the kitchen table.

"Hotter than hell in this place. Can't be no hotter outside," Mother said, walking over to the stereo. She blew the dust off the top.

"Nobody else is out there," I said.

"Well then go and read a book," she said, annoyed. She wiped the knobs of the stereo with her apron.

"Don't be mad at me."

"Rose, not today." She turned on the radio.

"Not any day," I said, falling back onto the sofa.

"Can't even remember when I last turned this thing on," Mother said, sifting through her records. "Looks like I'm missing some."

"You are. I have some in my room." I was watching Mr. Girard make his way into the bathroom. The door slammed.

"I want music not noise," Mother yelled at him.

"Fuck music," Mr. Girard yelled back.

"One more word like that, and your ass is on the street." Mother was facing the wall with her hand on her hip. "Today is not the day," she said, pointing a finger at the wall.

"What's on the radio?" I asked.

Mother turned the knob until she heard the sounds of jazz. "Let's see what they got for us," she said. I heard the musical notes of the clarinet. Mother began swaying her head. "Sounds like Benny," she said.

"Who's Benny?" I asked.

"Benny 'the Swing King' Goodman," Mr. Girard said, buttoning his pants and walking into the living room.

"I know this song," Mother said. "Sounds like 'I Ain't Got Nobody.'"

"And you wonderin' why?" Mr. Girard said, falling onto the love seat.

"That's the name of the song." Mother turned up the music.

"I like the clarinet, but my favorite instrument is the piano," I said.

"Naw, baby. The trumpet is boss," Mr. Girard said.

"I like everything as long as it sounds good," Mother said.

"Wait a minute," Mr. Girard said, struggling to his feet. "My man Louis got something for you." He walked over to the radio and pressed in the button for the record player. He then knelt and picked up a record. He placed the black disc on the turntable.

"The radio ain't good enough for you?" Mother asked, annoyed.

"Just wait a minute," Mr. Girard said, moving Mother to the side with his hip.

"Don't touch," Mother said angrily.

"Calm yourself, woman," Mr. Girard responded while putting the needle on the record. The music began to play. Mr. Girard backed away from the stereo and closed his eyes. He wrapped his arms around his shoulders and began to sway. Mother was staring at Mr. Girard with a perplexed look. Then, suddenly after a few words of the song, Mr. Girard began to hum.

"You should know the words by now," Mother said.

"I do all my life through I've been so black and blue," he sang.

"Always feelin' sorry for yourself," Mother said, still staring at him. He continued singing.

"Boo-hoo," Mother said, wiping invisible tears.

Mr. Girard began to hum again as he continued swaying. The record continued to play. He began to sing again.

When the song ended, Mother shoved Mr. Girard out the way with her behind then removed the needle from the record. Mr. Girard sat back on the love seat. "I got something for you," Mother said.

"Play me another Louis Armstrong song," Mr. Girard said, leaning his head back onto the love seat and closing his eyes.

"Got something else for you," Mother said. "My lady Ella Fitzgerald."

"Yeah. I like her too. That was my woman. You didn't know we had a thing goin' on once, did you?" Mr. Girard talked with his eyes closed.

"In your dreams," Mother said. She placed the needle on the record. "The song I'm gonna play for you is 'Pick Yourself Up.' And when I sing the words for you, I mean it literally. So you just make sure you listening carefully." The song began to play. Mother began to sing along.

Mother turned up the music. Mr. Girard was lying back on the love seat with his eyes still closed and his mouth hanging wide open. Mother walked over to the love seat, leaned over closer to Mr. Girard's ear and began singing the words louder.

Mr. Girard turned so he was facing away from Mother, but she leaned down closer. Mother reached over Mr. Girard's shoulder and pulled his ear. "I know you listenin' to these words," she said.

Mr. Girard began to snore. When the song ended, Mother walked back over to the stereo and removed the needle.

"Let the rest of the record play," I said. "I like Ella Fitzgerald."

"I'm gonna turn the radio back on. They usually have a pretty good selection on WJAZ. He ain't listenin' anyway." Mother pushed in the button for the radio.

"I was listening," I said, feeling slighted.

"Are you gonna keep changing these records every time they're at the end?" Mother asked.

"I will," I said.

"Let's just make things easy for everybody today. Let the radio play," Mother said, walking back into the kitchen.

" 'Let's make things easy,' " I mimicked.

"I heard you," Mother said. "I told you today is not the day."

I rose from the sofa and went into my bedroom. It was hot, dark and stuffy. The shades were drawn, and both windows were closed. Mother said it would be cooler in the dark, but it still felt hot and empty. I pulled on the string for each shade and watched them rise to the very top of each window. They rolled up so fast that one fell off and landed on the floor. I left it there. The sun was still shining bright. East Street was empty though. The two boys who always played kickball in the middle of the street were not out either. Seemed like nothing could keep them in, not even the biting cold of winter, but it was a torrid summer day. Stifling hot. Hot enough for my breath to be sucked right out of my body if I had let the air outside in. Looking through the glass of my bedroom window, for the first time, I wanted summer to disappear behind the blanket of powder-blue sky and melt back into spring.

Every winter I wished for the myriad blessings of summer, which gave birth to the wide-eyed song birds, rainbow-colored butterflies and dancing honeybees. I wanted summer in the world but mostly in my heart. God must've had a different plan for the living this time around, because it wasn't easy for us to experience the blessings of summer in '75. What was God trying to open our eyes to? If Mother Earth had had her way, I know things would've been different, I thought. There definitely would've been more rainbows, but we had hardly gotten rain. Mrs. Wise said God was just getting rid of the old and making room for the new. But Mrs. Cooper said she saw red in her dreams. Maybe it was the devil she was seeing, coming to keep the idle minds and hearts company.

I could feel the hot air suffocating me in my dream. I stood over my body and looked down at it. It was flat and lifeless. Then, I started to cry. Everything turned white and cool, and my body disappeared, but when I awoke from my dream, there were no tears, just the sweat on my face that rested against my window. And there was music.

Chapter 22

Jack Black, the neighborhood drunk turned born-again Christian, changed his name to Proverbs. It was said he did it when the first autumn leaf dropped. He waited for it. It was another sign. "The bible says those who depend on their wealth will fall like the leaves of autumn," he said, pacing under a maple tree on upper East Street in early November of '75. Proverbs despised the wealthy who made their living off the hard labor of others. He was always heard quoting from Proverbs 11:28 among others. Once, he walked twelve miles and stood in front of the house of Mr. Thomas Vanhurst, an old, rich white man, and quoted the entire book of Proverbs.

On an early winter morning in December, I ran into Proverbs. He was resting in a fetal position under the same maple tree he was seen under on more than one occasion quoting the book of Proverbs. As I was passing him, he said, "Proverbs chapter six, verses sixteen through nineteen: There are seven things that the Lord hates and cannot tolerate: A proud look." Proverbs quickly rose from the cold, wet ground. He walked in a circle around me with his head held high. I froze and followed him with my eyes. "A lying tongue. You smell like cow shit." He held his stomach and laughed. "Hands that kill innocent people." He threw his hands behind his back. "Not these hands, young lady," he said. "A mind that thinks up wicked plans." He placed his index finger on his temple and raised his brow. "Hmm," he said. "Feet that hurry off to do evil." Proverbs ran up to me and looked me in the eye. "What's in that bag, young lady? Where are you going?"

I held my book bag tighter and said, "School."

Proverbs circled me again and looked me over from head to toe. "A witness who tells one lie after another and someone who stirs up trouble among friends. Do you have any friends?" he asked.

I began to walk again. "Yes," I said.

"Where are you going so fast?" He jumped into my path.

"School," I said, stepping off the sidewalk into the street.

"Scared of me, are you?" he said, walking behind me.

"No."

"The road the righteous travel is like the sunrise, gettin' brighter and brighter until daylight has come." He continued to follow me. "This road leads nowhere."

"It's taking me to the bus stop," I said, becoming annoyed.

"Where's school? There's only one teacher," he said, pointing upward. "The Almighty."

"Where? Heaven?" I asked.

"Through the pearly gates, my dear," he said. "Why is a clever person wise? Because he knows what to do. Why is a stupid person foolish? Because he only thinks he knows."

"Are you wise?" I asked.

"I am Proverbs," he said.

"What does that mean?"

"The teachings of Proverbs are wise," he said, taking off his worn and stain-spotted hat then bowing his head. He stuck out his hat and said, "If you want to be happy, be kind to the poor." He began a two-step dance in front of me. "What is the richest city? What is the richest city?"

"I don't know," I said, shrugging.

"Generosity," he said, sticking out his hat again. "If you oppress poor people, you insult the God who made them, but kindness to the poor is an act of worship. What is the richest nation? What is the richest nation?" he asked then twirled and stopped directly facing me.

"I don't know," I said, stepping back onto the sidewalk.

"Donation," he said, placing his hat in front of my face. "It is better to be patient than powerful. It is better to win control over yourself than over whole cities."

I looked into Proverbs's hat and saw crumpled dollar bills stuck within the lining. I only have change," I said.

"Any amount will do," he said, pointing into his hat. "The rich have to use their money to save their lives, but no one threatens the poor."

I stopped, placed my book bag on the ground between my legs, pulled out my hand purse and opened it. Proverbs shoved his hat back into my face. "Truth, wisdom, learning and good sense, these are worth paying for, but too valuable for you to sell." My purse dropped from my hands and two quarters, a dime and a small round mirror fell onto the ground. When I reached for the purse, Proverbs leaned over and looked into the mirror, which landed face up. He jumped back as though he was startled.

"What's wrong with you?" I asked, frightened.

"Who was that?" he asked, crushing his hat against his frail chest.

"Who are you talking about?" I asked, picking up the change.

"That person in there," he said, pointing at the mirror.

I picked up the mirror and looked into it. I pointed at my reflection within the mirror. "This person?" I asked.

Proverbs leaned over and looked into the mirror. He jumped back again. "That other person," he said, squeezing his hat in his dark, bony hand.

"That was you," I said.

"Don't know who that is," he said.

I pointed at him. "You," I said, walking toward him with the mirror.

Proverbs backed away. "Keep that thing away from me," he said. "I don't know that person. He a stranger. Don't like the way he looked at me."

"What are you talking about?" I asked, placing the mirror into my purse.

"Don't like his eyes," he said.

"Those are your eyes."

"No," he said, shaking his head. "Don't like those eyes. Stranger eyes. Don't like the way that glass show 'em to me." He placed his crumpled hat back onto his head.

"Proverbs, those were your eyes," I said, picking up my bag.

"Don't like what I saw in those eyes," he said.

"What did you see?" I asked.

He scratched his head and looked from side to side as though he were making sure no one else was around to hear. "The truth," he whispered, backing away. "The living truth." Proverbs turned from me and began to walk away.

"Do you still want change?" I asked, holding out two quarters and a dime. Proverbs kept walking and he began to sing:

> Can I have a dime
> Yeah, in this cup of mine
> Right here, clinkety clink
> Gonna pay for my next drink

I thought about Proverbs the entire day while in school. I couldn't help but wonder what he saw in my mirror that frightened him. What was the truth? He had seen it with his own eyes, but what did he really see?

Mrs. Amos, my seventh-grade homeroom teacher, was a tall, lanky woman who wore a short afro and colorful dashikis. During homeroom she always talked about the rich continent of Africa and the sun-baked earth people who dwelled there. She said when our African ancestors were taken from their homeland, they left behind their true identities. "Descendants of the African earth people have come to know only a part of that identity. Pieces of it were buried within the ancient dust of time. We are now responsible for discovering a new identity within our inner spiritual world."

When she had completed her last sentence, I asked, "How do we do this?"

"Life will teach you," she said.

I raised my hand again and asked, "How?"

"Experience will bring you face-to-face with life. Life will bring you face-to-face with yourself," she said.

I thought about raising my hand again but the bell rang for first period. I wanted to ask, "What if you're afraid of yourself?"

There were six periods in junior high school—seven, if you included lunch. I enjoyed every class except math. English, reading, science, art and gym were much more interesting. All of my teachers were nice and always seemed excited about the subjects they taught. My two favorite subjects were English and art. The poems written by famous authors that were read in class by the English teacher, Mrs. McFerguson, were intriguing, but I especially liked the poems we had to write for homework. These we shared in class. Some poems were funny and some sad, but they were all good. There was a girl in my class who could barely read, so she memorized songs she made up then sang them a capella.

Mrs. McFerguson had to work longer hours with the students who were still learning how to apprehend words. I loved to read, but after a few months, reviewing the same material bored me. We were studying *The Basic Fundamentals of English Grammar* instead of reading novels. May, who was in the honors group with me in third grade, had already read two novels in her English class within the first two months of school. When she was done with *To Kill a Mockingbird* and *Invisible Man*, I borrowed them. She said the next required book was *The Bluest Eye*. When I told her we didn't read novels in my English class, she said, "Most black kids in the inner city can't read anyway."

In art class, we glued together Popsicle sticks, and the girls made jewelry boxes and pretended they were princesses who owned fancy ruby and emerald rings, and we made flowerpots out of clay for planting seeds that would bring life to spring. The boys made Popsicle-stick airplanes and dreamed about white sand and aqua-blue oceans. I made a flowerpot for Mrs. Wise and jewelry boxes for Mother and Mrs. Cooper. I drew a rainbow on the flowerpot and a butterfly on both jewelry boxes.

Mrs. Wise loved the flowerpot so much I decided to make one for myself and glue the silk butterfly she had given me on to the side of it. I showed it to her, she smiled and said, "Use this for planting your dreams. Water them with hope and watch 'em grow." The first things I put into my flowerpot was the one yellow petal of faith from Mari and seven red petals I had taken from my flower, Love.

There was a boy named Paton at Brown Middle School. He was in the eighth grade. I had first seen him in the lunch room. Then, I began to notice him more often in the afternoons on my way to sixth period. His class was right next door to mine. Paton was dark chocolate with short, curly black hair and eyes that were the shape of half moons. The first time I spoke to him was at the water fountain outside of the lunch room.

"Hello," I said.

He lifted his head and turned to look at me. "What's up?"

"Nothing."

Paton put his head back down and began to drink from the fountain again. "I'll be done in a minute," he said, lifting his head again. I remained in back of him and watched as the cold, clear water met his lips. When he was done, he picked up his book bag and walked away. I pretended I was thirsty and stuck my head into the fountain and began to drink the cool sweetness of his voice into my memory. The next day I saw Paton in the hallway after sixth period. I followed him until he turned the corner to leave the building. I watched him as he faded out of my sight but not out of my dreams. Every night before bed and in the mornings before school I dreamed Paton to life. He became my first true love.

In the mornings before school I rushed out of bed, in and out of the bathroom and through breakfast. I always arrived at the bus stop earlier than the other kids. Although it had gotten colder, since we were now into the winter season, the weather didn't bother me as much as it used to. I rarely looked forward to or enjoyed the cold days of winter. Once I had rushed out without my coat. If Mrs. Cooper wasn't in the window watching out for me, I probably would've made it to the bus stop without one. She stuck her head out the window and shouted, "Where you goin' without a coat, child?"

"Nowhere," I said, stopping at the curb in front of our building.

"Must be tryin' to catch a cold or flu or somethin'," she said, shivering.

"No," I said, turning around.

"Go on back up those stairs and put a coat on your body."

I ran back up the stairs to our building and pushed open the door, then threw my book bag down in the hallway and leaped up two stairs at a time until I got to my apartment. I had forgotten that my key was in my book bag. I stomped my foot then ran back down to get my key. By the time I made it back up to my apartment I was out of breath. I stuck my key into the lock and opened the door. I had forgotten to turn off the radio. It was playing "Day Dreaming" by Aretha Franklin.

Chapter 23

My first true love rose into the heaven of my dreams. He floated on top of a sugar-coated cloud and became honey drops of rain. Wherever he was, I could smell his sweetness. At twelve, I was still too young for a boyfriend, but I always thought about Paton. The scent of him dulled the sour feelings of resentment building within me. Father hadn't called for my last two birthdays. More than anything I had begun to miss the one thing I had grown to look forward to—the song Father put inside of me. It was a gift greater than any. Dreaming was the only thing keeping the song alive. I dreamed of golden church bells ringing at the top of mint green–crested mountains. They hung from a willow tree, and I dreamed of the melodious voice of a hummingbird rising within a distant field of confectionary white daylilies. When I awoke from each of my dreams, I could hear the musical notes faintly until again I closed my eyes and the music would grow louder.

Paton became the music in my dreams—candy-coated musical notes that lingered in the honeydew-scented air. Paton filled my dreams with the myriad scents of sweet fruit, cocoa, lavender, rose and vanilla. When in his presence, his smell drew me nearer to him where I remained until my craving for sweetness was satisfied. After school, he held my book bag and walked me to my bus. Every night and on the weekends we talked on the phone and discussed our first real date. It would be at the movies where we would share caramel-covered popcorn or at a diner for breakfast where we would order French toast with strawberry maple syrup or a park where we would sit in the shade under a tall tree and feed each other fresh mango and pineapple. At night, in my window the silver moon and northern star became his eyes, watching me while his voice created a different song with every word.

Tanya wanted to know. Everything. First thing she wanted to know was if I had kissed Paton. I blushed when she asked. I had never kissed a boy before. She said she had, besides Mr. Dickens, and it gave her goose bumps. She said Mr. Dickens never gave her the same sensations when he kissed her on the lips or in the mouth. The boy she kissed was named Wells. He was tall, bony with red hair, freckles and light brown eyes. She said his red hair reminded her of the small red seeds in a pomegranate. She had never eaten a pomegranate but she had seen one on television. I had only eaten one once when I was five. Father brought it home for dessert because he refused to eat any other sugar except for that of fresh fruit. Tanya said Wells's tongue was soft and tasted like pink bubble gum. She said every time she chewed a piece, it reminded her of the times they kissed. Wells lived on the other side of town, in walking distance of Brown Middle School. He lived only two streets over from Paton.

On a sunny autumn day after school Tanya and I missed the bus. We walked home with Paton and Wells that day. We had planned to catch the city bus home before dark. Paton lived in a single-family house between other single-family homes on Cinnamon Lane. His mother worked for the state, and his father was a doctor. He was an only child, and he was the only kid I knew who had a king-size bed. When we walked into his bedroom, he told Wells and Tanya they could have the foot of the bed and he and I would occupy the head. As soon as Tanya sat on the navy-blue down comforter, Wells stood in between her legs and began rubbing her breasts. Tanya gave a devilish smile and opened her legs wider. I turned my head and looked in the other direction while Paton moved in closer to me.

"Let's kiss," he said.

"Don't know how."

"Me neither."

"You never kissed a girl before?"

"On the lips."

"Who?" I asked with a tinge of jealousy.

"Nobody worth tellin'," he said, rubbing my arm. Tanya hadn't mentioned there were other ways to get goose bumps. "You nervous?"

"No," I said.

"Why you got goose bumps then?"

"I don't know. Maybe I'm cold."

"Let's do what they doin'," he said, looking into my eyes.

I peeked over Paton's shoulder at Wells and Tanya. Wells was lying on top of Tanya with his tongue in her mouth. Paton blew on my neck and smiled.

"I'm a little cold," I said, drawing my arm in closer to my body.

"I'll warm you up."

"Can we go upstairs? I'm a little thirsty," I said, sliding down from the bed.

"Thirsty?" Paton said. "I'll quench your thirst." Paton pulled me closer and pressed his lips to mine. His soft, wet tongue pried its way into my mouth. He pushed it farther in and moved it around in circles. My tongue froze, and I couldn't move it.

"You ain't gonna kiss me back?" he asked after removing his tongue.

"Yes," I said nervously. Paton pushed his tongue into my mouth again. I kissed him back but I didn't feel goose bumps.

"Let's lie down," Paton said, pushing me back onto the bed.

"I don't want to."

"Why not?"

"I'm not ready to do that."

"We don't have to take our clothes off."

"I know."

"They doin' it."

"It's gettin' late."

"My mother ain't coming home yet," Paton said, pressing his body into mine.

"We've gotta catch the city bus before it gets dark," I said, sliding away.

"You scared of me?"

"No."

"This our first date. We suppose to kiss and stuff on our first date."

"We're suppose to eat caramel-covered popcorn, French toast with strawberry maple syrup or fresh mangos and pineapples on our first date," I said, walking away from the bed.

"If you don't let me kiss you again, I'm breaking up with you."

"Y'all talk too much," Tanya said.

"She ain't lettin' me touch her," Paton said.

"Why not?" Tanya asked, looking over at me.

"It's gettin' late," I said.

"We still got a little time," Tanya said.

"We need some privacy," Wells said. "Can we go upstairs?"

"Y'all could stay down here. We going upstairs to my parents' room," Paton said, grabbing my hand.

I walked behind Paton toward his parents' room. He looked back at me and smiled. "You gonna kiss me now?" he asked.

"Maybe."

"If you don't, I'm gonna break up with you."

"I'm gonna kiss you."

"Can I lay on top of you?"

"I'm not ready for that."

Paton walked into his parents' room and turned on the small lamp on the end table near the bed. He took off his shoes and jumped up on the king-size bed. "Take off your shoes," he said.

"I'm not gettin' on top of the bed."

"How am I suppose to kiss you then?"

I shrugged and leaned against the bed post. "We shouldn't be doin' any nasty stuff," I said.

"Sex ain't nasty."

"Yes, it is."

"If you don't let me lay on top of you, I'm gonna tell everybody at school we had sex," Paton said then laughed out loud.

"That isn't funny. Anyway, I'll just tell everybody you're lyin'."

"Ain't nobody gonna believe a seventh grader."

"Yes, they will."

"How you figure?"

"'Cause I'm a girl."

"That don't mean nothing," he said, jumping down from the bed.

"Boys lie all the time."

"Girls lie too," he said, grabbing my arm.

"Let me go," I said, snatching my arm away.

"I'm breaking up with you," Paton said then stormed out the room.

"I don't care. I don't like you anymore anyway," I yelled at him.

"I don't like you neither," he yelled back.

"I'm leaving."

"Well get out my house," Paton said, walking back into the room. He grabbed his shoes then pushed me out of the room.

"Don't put your hands on me."

"Get out my house," he said, opening the front door.

"Give me my book bag and coat first."

"Wait outside," he said, walking downstairs, back into his room.

"I'm waiting right here," I said, crossing my arms and tapping my foot.

Paton stomped out his room, up the stairs, then threw my bag and coat down at my feet. He walked back into his Parents' room and slammed the door. I walked onto the front stoop and sat to wait for Tanya. Ten minutes later she walked out the door.

"What took you so long?" I asked.

"Wells wouldn't let me up," Tanya said with a grin.

"I'm not missing the bus with you anymore," I said, walking toward the street.

"What happened?" Tanya asked, following me.

"Paton wanted to do the nasty."

"With your clothes off?" Tanya asked.

"No," I said, tossing my book bag over my shoulder.

"Then why you didn't let him?"

"'Cause I didn't want to."

"Did he break up with you?"

"Yup."

"He gonna get another girlfriend if you don't let him."

"I don't care. I don't like him anymore," I said, crossing the street.

"Why you walking so fast?"

"'Cause the bus is coming."

"It ain't coming yet," Tanya said. "You don't care if Paton get another girlfriend?"

"Nope."

"I don't want Wells getting no other girlfriend, so I let him do what he want, but I don't let him take my clothes all the way off." Tanya was combing her hair back into place with her fingers. "Plus, I'm still a virgin. Simon said he'll know if I let somebody else touch me down there."

"I hate Mr. Dickens," I said, walking faster.

"He ain't do nothing to you."

"He's a devil."

"He ain't no devil," Tanya said. "He take care of me and always doin' nice things for me."

"He shouldn't be messing with young girls," I said, dropping my bag on the grass near the bus stop.

"I don't know why you dropping your bag. Here come the bus," Tanya said.

"Simon said he love me."

"Why can't he love somebody his own age?" I asked, picking up my book bag.

"'Cause nobody make him feel the way I do," Tanya said, picking a blade of grass. She began to blow on it.

"If he's so good to you, why are you messing with Wells?"

"'Cause Simon don't give me goose bumps when he kiss me," she said, rubbing her face with the blade of grass.

The bus stopped in front of us and opened its doors. The driver smiled and said hello. I smiled and followed Tanya onto the bus. We dropped our change into the glass case then proceeded toward the back. We sat at the rear and waited for the doors to close and for our journey back home to begin.

"I didn't get goose bumps when Paton kissed me," I said, looking out of the window.

Chapter 24

Mother noticed the change that evening after I left Paton's house. I first noticed it when the pain began, which was sometime around the beginning of the school year. My breasts had begun to grow. I stared at my naked body in the mirror every morning and every night before bed. I didn't dare touch myself because I thought I might make the pain worse. At first I thought something was wrong. I had heard of breast cancer before and wondered if I might've developed it somehow, but after thinking about the possibilities more, I realized I was still too young and hadn't quite developed enough breasts to attract that much attention to them. But I did catch Mother's eye at the kitchen table one night. Thank God Mr. Girard had decided not to join us that evening. Mother made a small scene. And she made sure that God was the next one to know.

"Oh my God," Mother said, staring at my developing breasts.

"What?" I asked, pulling a piece of broccoli I had intended to bite away from my mouth.

"You gettin' breasts," she said, walking over to me.

"Is that what these are?" I asked, moving my arms in front of my chest.

"You know what those are," Mother said. "We're gonna have to buy you a couple of bras."

"A bra?" I asked, looking down at my chest.

"Trainin' bras."

"What's a trainin' bra?"

"You're just startin' to grow. You don't have enough to fill a bra for mature breasts yet," Mother said, touching the small mounds on my chest.

"That hurts," I said, pulling away.

"It's gonna hurt for a while," Mother said.

"It hurts even when I don't touch them."

"That's normal. Those little things tryin' to sprout," Mother said, smiling.

"Don't tell Mr. Girard," I said, feeling my face turn red.

"Why would I do that?" Mother asked, sitting down at the table.

I shrugged. "You told God," I said.

"God knew before either one of us knew," Mother said, laughing.

"How did God know?"

"Oh girl, God knows it all. You'd be surprised. Ain't much you can keep from God," Mother said.

"Does God know everything that goes on in this apartment?"

Mother gave a questionable look. "What do you mean?" she asked.

"Can God see us using the bathroom?"

"I suppose He can," Mother said.

"Oh," I said, wondering if God watched me during the times I examined myself in the mirror.

"There are no secrets with God. None," Mother said as she stood again. She walked to the sink and began to run the water for the dishes.

"I'll do the dishes."

"Don't you got homework to do?"

"I finished it already."

"When?"

"On the bus."

"Must not have been a lot."

"It was a long—"

"A long what?" Mother interrupted.

"Bus ride."

"It's only a ten-minute bus ride from the stop to school and from school and back," Mother said, looking over at me.

"The driver went the long way today."

"Why was that?" Mother asked inquisitively.

"Um. There was a lot of traffic," I said, getting up from the table.

"Traffic, huh?" Mother said, still looking at me.

"I think there was an accident or something," I said, placing my plate in the sink.

"Accident, huh?"

"I think so, but I don't know for sure," I said. "I'm gonna get my clothes ready for school."

"If I find out different, your behind is mine. You hear me?" Mother rolled her eyes and looked away.

"Yes," I said. I stood in the same place for a moment and watched Mother's expression. She was pensive. I wondered if she already knew.

While in my room, I stood in front of my mirror. I pulled my shirt up above my breasts and examined them again. They looked like two small round lumps. Although they were sore, I decided to gently press them. I felt something hard inside. I wondered what it was, but then the thought that I was being watched began to plague me. Biting down on my lip, I looked up at the ceiling. Was God watching me? I pulled my shirt down and sat on my bed. I began to think about Paton. Did God see him stick his tongue into my mouth? I didn't know whether God saw him, but I made him stop. Then I thought about him kissing me again. I made him stop, not because God was watching but because while kissing me he pressed his hand hard into my breasts and began to rub them. The pain almost brought tears to my eyes. Although Paton hadn't known he was hurting me, I grew angry with him because of the pain and because I had a different dream for us, a candy-coated one filled with music. But the sweetness of my thoughts had grown sour, and I no longer desired the smell of Paton.

I pulled a pair of jeans out of my drawer and spread them on my bed. They were my favorite ones although they lacked character, except for the hole in the knee. When I first noticed Paton, I decided I would retire them. No boy would desire a girl who wore loose-fitting jeans with a hole in the knee, I once thought, but now things had changed again. I would do whatever I could to avoid Paton and to force him to avoid me. If I made myself ugly and plain, he wouldn't dare tell anyone he had sex with me—at least, I hoped. The thought turned my face red. I stood again in front of my mirror and noticed the two small lumps protruding underneath my shirt. I wanted to hide them. I pulled a thick wool sweater from the lower drawer and placed it on top of my pants. This would be my attire for the next day.

ᴈᴑᴄᴈ

Tanya heard it first. I wasn't a virgin anymore. Wells had told her so. Paton bragged about our having sex in his parents' bed. He said because it was my first time and because he was hurting me, he stopped. That's why it only took a few minutes and why I was angry and left. Tanya smiled and wanted to know more details about my first time. She was saving herself for her husband. That's what she said.

"Are you going to marry Mr. Dickens?" I asked without responding to the lie Paton told.

"Maybe." Tanya shrugged. She pulled me into the corner by the lockers. "Did it hurt bad?"

"No," I said, feeling the heat rise into my face.

"It didn't?" Tanya asked, surprised.

"No."

"I heard it hurts the first time and blood gets everywhere."

"I didn't bleed."

"You didn't?"

"No," I said with a stoic expression.

"Wow. I hope it don't hurt the first time I do it."

"Me too."

"You already did it."

"In Paton's dreams," I said angrily.

"For real?" Tanya said, placing her hand on her hip.

"Paton is a liar."

"Ooooo. You wait until I tell Wells," she said, walking away.

"You wait until I see Paton," I said, walking behind her.

"I don't know why Paton lied," she said.

"You wait until I see him," I said.

"He told Wells you had those big jeans on because after the first time you can't wear nothin' tight. It'll make it hurt more." Tanya ran through the door. "You wait until I tell Wells."

When Tanya reached the corner where Paton and Wells were standing, she pulled Wells away by the hand. I walked in the other direction to catch the school bus. When I looked back, Paton was

192

following me with his eyes. I stuck up my middle finger and kept on walking.

Mother came home with two training bras that night. She asked me to try them on while she was still in the room. I shook my head and told her I would try them on later.

"You don't have nothin' I haven't seen before," she said. "I'm the one who changed your diapers."

"I know," I said, embarrassed by the thought.

"Well I need to know if they fit," she said, sitting on the bed.

"Do I have to try them on now?"

"Why not now?"

"I'm doing my homework."

"It will only take a few minutes. Plus, I have to show you how to wear it."

"I know how to wear a bra."

"You haven't worn one before." Mother pulled out the bras from the bag. "Here you go. Go ahead and try on one of 'em. I'll turn my head until you're done." Mother handed me one and looked away.

"Do I have to?" I whined.

"Go ahead, girl," Mother said, losing her patience, still facing the other direction.

I pulled off my shirt and gazed into the mirror at my naked breasts. I became embarrassed at the thought of Mother seeing me in a bra. I pulled it around me and hooked the two sides. I pulled the straps up onto my shoulders and looked into the mirror.

"You have it on yet?" Mother asked.

"Yes," I said, looking away from the mirror.

Mother turned toward me. "Look at you. You look like a little lady," she said, staring at me.

"No, I don't."

"Yes, you do," Mother said, smiling. "I can't believe how fast time is flying by." Mother's eyes became glassy.

"Can I take it off now?" I slouched.

"Stand up straight. You're gonna mess up your posture slouching like that." Mother rose from my bed. "The idea is to wear the bra. You can take it off before you go to bed."

I reached for my shirt and slipped it over my head. "Do I have to wear it every day?" I asked.

"Do you want saggy breasts?" Mother asked.

"No."

"Well then it would be a good idea to wear it every day," she said. "And by the way, just because you're wearin' a bra don't make you grown."

"I know," I said, looking into Mother's eyes.

"I hope so," she said, walking out my room and shutting the door behind her. As I turned to look into the mirror again, Mother opened the door.

"Yes," I said.

"What happened to your little friend?" Mother asked.

"Who?" I asked, pretending not to know who she was talking about.

"Parson," she said.

"His name is Paton."

"He hasn't been calling."

"I don't like him anymore."

"Why not?"

"I just don't."

"I hope he hasn't done anything wrong to you."

"No."

"Well, you're still young. You have all the time in the world for boyfriends."

"I know," I said, averting my eyes.

"Dinner will be ready shortly."

"Okay," I said, sitting back on my bed. I opened my book and began my homework again.

Mother stood in the door and watched me. "I'll call you when dinner is done."

"Okay."

Mother stood silent for a moment then reluctantly closed the door.

Chapter 25

Paton avoided me during the rest of the school year. After Tanya told Wells the truth, she said he walked up to Paton and laughed in his face. Paton said I was a lying bitch then walked away. He didn't speak to Wells for a week. Tanya said he walked a different route to school and home in order to escape Wells's ridicule. After a week, Paton and Wells's relationship was back to normal. After the many attempts to break Tanya's virginity, Wells realized he had more in common with Paton than not. By the end of the school year, he lost all patience and broke off his relationship with Tanya. She didn't mind. Mr. Dickens was becoming more and more suspicious of her. He said if she kept coming home from school late he would hire a private eye to watch her. She believed him.

It had been months since I saw Mrs. Wise. The last time we didn't do much talking. I mostly watched as she knelt over her garden and hummed a sweet tune. I leaned my head against the oak tree, sat Indian style and began to hum along with her. She looked over and smiled kindly then went back to making miracles. Everything Mrs. Wise touched was like magic. My eyes were a witness to them. Even the ones made within the chilling days of winter. Mrs. Wise said life itself is a miracle simply because it is.

It was a cold winter day in '76 when I next saw Mrs. Wise. She was standing over her garden and watching life as she always did. "Most people can't see it," she said.

"See what?"

"Life," she said, looking down at her garden.

"I can't see anything but frozen plant stems."

"That's what most people would see," she said, pulling down her bright yellow knit hat over her ears.

"What do you see?"

"Beginnings."

"Beginnings of what?"

"Life."

"I don't understand," I said, looking perplexed at the bare plant stems.

"Only life can explain itself," she said. "But you got to be active in life, creatin' with it and makin' change."

I looked at Mrs. Wise as she studied her garden. She remained still and quiet as the wind blew through the loose, fine strands of her hair. As I thought more about what she had said and had not said, I began to think about Father and Paton. "How does love feel?" I asked.

Mrs. Wise stood quiet for a moment longer. "Like sunshine. Feels like sunshine," she said.

"Warm?"

"Warm," she repeated.

"Sometimes hot?"

"Sometimes hot, indeed," she said, nodding.

"Does love always feel like sunshine?"

"Yes. I think so," she said, kneeling to remove a frozen water droplet from one of the bare plant stems.

"I don't always feel the sunshine."

"But it's always there. Even when you can't see it or feel it directly," she said, looking down at the water droplet as it slowly melted in the palm of her hand.

"If you can't see it or feel it, how do you know it's there?"

Mrs. Wise looked over at me then back down at the small wet spot in the palm of her hand. "Change don't ever mean the end of things," she said. "The days look different, but they still got sunshine in them." Mrs. Wise and I stood awhile longer in front of her garden. While she studied the bare plant stems, I looked into the sky in search of the sunshine. It was there. It was always there—just hidden behind a cloud. On that day, right before I left Mrs. Wise, she reached for another frozen droplet. Like the first one, it melted in the palm of her hand. "Look into my hand, baby," Mrs. Wise said.

I looked down into her palm. "The frozen tear melted," I said.

"What do you see inside my hand? Right there." Mrs. Wise pointed to the wet spot in the middle of her palm.

"I see a melted teardrop."

"Look again. Look a little closer."

I lowered my head and studied the wet area. "I still don't see anything else," I said.

"Close your eyes then open them again," she said. "When you open them, look into my hand until you see it."

I looked more intently into Mrs. Wise's hand. "I see, umm. I don't see anything," I said, becoming frustrated.

"What would you like to see, baby?" Mrs. Wise asked.

"I don't know," I said, shrugging.

"Think about it for a moment. What would you like to see?" she asked again.

"Umm. A rainbow," I said, looking up into Mrs. Wise's eyes.

"Go on and look into my hand. Keep looking until you see it," she said.

I closed my eyes again then reopened them. I looked into the small wet area of Mrs. Wise's hand. "I think I see it now," I said.

"Well keep lookin' until you see it clearly," she said.

I kept looking into Mrs. Wise's hand until I could see my rainbow. "I see it now. I see my rainbow."

"Do you really see it, or is you just makin' it up?"

"I see it. It's pretty too. All the colors of the world."

"That's right. It's a pretty rainbow. All the colors of the world."

"Do you see it?"

"I see it," she said. "I see it too."

"It's really pretty," I said, smiling.

"A thing don't always show itself clear at first," Mrs. Wise said, "but if you really want to see it, whatever it is, you can. You just got to look a little harder. See things a little differently."

I gave Mrs. Wise a tight squeeze. "Thank you."

She held my head to her breast and softly whispered, "Dreams is real too."

Chapter 26

What keeps us living and struggling when all about us is weak and broken? For some, it is fear. The fear of dying, especially when one has seen beauty. And when one has known love. Even in a world where there is constant pain, suffering and loss, there is in this same world eternal beauty, hope and love. What keeps us living and struggling? For others, it is our dreams. We have seen beyond this world, beyond the here and now. Beyond today. As a child, in the midst of my tears, I could still see a rainbow, even if it were not really there. And within the murky clouds of turbulent skies I could still see the sunshine. Dreams. Dreams for which I lived.

Yet, though my mind paints portraits of other places and times, and my eyes witness what no other can, there are still those things that are beyond my knowing, beyond my understanding. There are still those things that dreams cannot keep hidden. Because this world, too, is real.

Mother said it was me only that she lived for. I was her perfect dream. She said she tried to imagine bigger than what anyone she knew had. But the days had shown her there was no bigger dream than to live for the one thing worth dying for, if it came to that. She didn't say any of this to me. I overheard her talking to Mrs. Cooper in the hallway one Sunday morning, in October of '77. Mrs. Cooper was telling Mother in the most polite way she could that it was time Mother started making herself a better example and give her life back to God. Mother said what I always heard her say, "God is in my heart."

"Can't be so," Mrs. Cooper said.

"You ain't never looked inside my heart so how you gonna know?" Mother said.

"Everything around you is a reflection of what's in your heart. I don't see nothin' resemblin' God around you, Maxine."

"You don't spend your days and nights with me, so you don't know," Mother said. "Anyway it ain't your duty to know what's goin' on around me."

"Guess you right, Maxine. Guess you right."

"I told you already. I live for one thing. One thing only, and that's my daughter. She my only dream. My biggest one. Having her always in my mind and heart, I am livin' the best way I know how," Mother said.

Mrs. Cooper remained silent for a moment. "God can help you dream bigger, Maxine. That's all I'm tryin' to say."

"Ain't no bigger dream than the one that's right inside this door, and God the one gave her to me."

"I suppose you right. I suppose you right," Mrs. Cooper said. There was silence again. I listened through my bedroom wall, waiting to hear if Mrs. Cooper had anything else to say. "Well," she said, "guess I should go now. God waitin' on me."

"Have a good day," Mother said.

"You too, Maxine," Mrs. Cooper said. "And tell the young one I said God bless."

"Yes, I'll do that."

Mother walked back into our apartment and shut the door. After that, all I could hear was Mrs. Cooper's footsteps going down the hallway steps. I ran to my window to see her. It was a while before she made it out the front door of our building. When she finally made it down the front steps, I could see she was limping much more than she had in the days before. Mrs. Cooper had buried her cane after the medallion was found within the ashes of the burned building. She said she didn't need it anymore. God had delivered her, but Tanya said Mr. Dickens had to unearth it after she complained about feeling weak again in her legs. That was only a few days later.

Mother knocked on my bedroom door. This time she didn't open it like she would normally do. She waited for me to answer. Now that I was older—a teenager in high school—she thought it necessary to give me a little more privacy. I was fourteen and in the ninth grade.

"Come in," I said, still sitting at my window.

"Thought you might still be asleep," Mother said, shutting the door behind her.

"No, I'm awake," I said, without turning away from the window.

"What are you lookin' at out there?" Mother asked, making her way over to me.

"Watching Mrs. Cooper."

"What's wrong with her?" Mother asked, adjusting the shade.

"She can barely walk. I feel real bad for her."

"Yeah," Mother said, staring down at her. "I feel real bad for her too. Sometimes age is a curse, and sometimes it's a blessing."

"If she hadn't fallen again, a few weeks ago, down those stupid steps in our hallway, she wouldn't be suffering so much."

"Those stairs had a big part in the pain she's been experiencing lately. That's for sure," Mother said, walking away from the window. She sat on my bed.

"Why did we stay here, in this building, so long?"

"Don't know. I ask myself that question too sometimes." Mother lowered her head. She stared at the space on the floor between her slippers.

"Ain't hardly anything here, except for Mrs. Wise and her flower garden. And Love."

"I forgot about that flower of yours. How's Love doin'?"

"She still grows every year. But she looks different. Sometimes she has a whole bunch of bright red petals and sometimes she has just enough for you to know she's a rose. It's strange." I looked out the window again. "I asked Mrs. Wise about it."

"What did she say?" Mother asked, leaning back on her elbows.

I rested my head against the glass and watched a small bird flutter by. "All that makes the world what it is is what makes things change, she said, but there's still strength in Love. That won't change. That's all she said."

Mother leaned forward again. "All that makes the world what it is is what makes people change too. Sometimes for the good. Sometimes for the bad." She shook her head. "All that I need to change me is real love. I'm waiting for it. I'm waiting for the change."

I looked into the sky far beyond my window. "Love's always making us change, isn't it?"

"I don't know. Sometimes I don't know," Mother said. She rose from my bed. "I didn't come in here to make you sad. I really didn't."

"I'm not sad," I said, still looking into the sky.

"But you ain't happy neither," she said. "I can see you ain't happy, and I know I'm to blame."

"I just wish..." My hands dropped into my lap. "I don't know."

"Say it. I know whatever you got to say, I need to hear it. Go on and say it." Mother sat back down.

"I just wish you would throw him out. For good. He isn't right for you. He isn't right for us," I said.

"I hear what you sayin'. I've been hearin' it for a long time, even when you haven't expressed it in words, but somethin' keeps me from doin' what I know is right. Don't know what it is. I guess I just haven't found the strength in me."

"But you said God's in your heart. Doesn't God give you the strength?"

Mother gave me a surprised look. She stared at me for a long while without any words. She stood again from my bed. "God? God is in my heart, but—"

"But what?"

"I don't know," Mother said, opening my bedroom door. "I don't know." She walked out and closed it behind her.

I stood from my window, walked over to my bed and threw myself down onto it. I could feel the tears begin to well in my eyes. I wiped my eyes then rolled onto my back. I looked up at the ceiling and mumbled, "Mrs. Wise said it's not enough that God is in our hearts. It's not enough. We have to be in the heart of God."

ชา๗

I was a freshman in high school. It was my first year at Webster High. I hated it. The students there were hard to talk to and most would only talk to others they already knew—kids from their own neighborhood. Tanya was the only one I knew well, but she was a grade ahead of me. She didn't ride the same school bus, since the students were split up according to our last names or take any of the same classes with me. It was frustrating trying to make a new friend. It was even more frustrating trying to become friends with someone who had the same interests. I still loved reading, and music had become much more of a passion.

Once in a while, I would run into Paton in the halls, but we rarely spoke. I never really forgave him for telling Wells and Tanya that we had had sex. I was a virgin then and was still a virgin in the ninth grade. I thought I should wait until college before I gave myself to someone in that way. I had heard people say that two people—a boy and a girl—don't fall in love until college. I thought I would wait until then when I was in love. Maybe I would wait until I graduated from college. By then, I would be ready for marriage and children. Mother said I should wait until I was married before I gave myself to someone in that way. I asked her about kissing, but it seemed she found it hard to talk to me about that too. She said it would lead to other things. Things I had no business thinking about or doing. Tanya said the same thing. She said kissing made her lose her virginity. She was only fourteen and in the ninth grade when she lost it. That was last year.

I didn't find out Tanya had lost her virginity until a little over six months after. I found out by accident. Tanya was telling me about all the boys she had had a crush on at Webster High. There was one boy she talked about named Morris. He was a senior on the basketball team. She said he was the cutest boy she had ever seen. I saw him for myself. He was cute. Probably the cutest I had ever seen too. One day after school Tanya said she had the opportunity to kiss Morris. Morris and Tanya made out behind the school building. She said they tongued for a long time. While kissing he put his hand down her pants and began to play with her private. She said it felt good but it made her nervous because she was still a virgin and wanted to remain one—at least until her relationship with Mr. Dickens was over. She had been thinking about ending it since it began, but he was always able to convince her to change her mind and heart.

When things got hot and heavy between Morris and Tanya, she decided she had to do something about her relationship with Mr. Dickens, so she did. She finally let Mr. Dickens take her virginity.

She said he was gentle, but it still hurt the first time. They had sex every day during the first week. After that, she told him she wanted to have sex only twice each week and that she preferred weekends. She wanted to save herself for Morris during the school week. Mr. Dickens told Tanya she needed to start taking birth control. She thought if she started on pills her mother would find out. The school nurse told her they usually made the body change. Mr. Dickens wasn't happy about wearing condoms. Sometimes he didn't, and Tanya always had to let him know when she was having her period. Morris wore one every time they had sex. It was his decision. When Tanya first told me that Mr. Dickens had sex with her, it made me hate him more. He knew I hated him. He could never look me in the eye in passing. One day I saw him on the street. He was walking toward me. "Good day," he said with a smile.

"Not anymore," I said, lowering my eyes.

"God don't like ugly," he said.

"I guess God doesn't like you then."

"Why you hate me so much?" he asked, stopping in front of me.

"I've got my reasons."

"What reasons are those? I'm a nice man. A God-fearing man. Don't mean no harm to nobody."

"Just to young girls," I said, turning to walk away.

"Wish I knew whatcha was talkin' about. Maybe you might want to explain it to me," he said, following me.

"God knows. That's all that matters," I said, stopping then turning to look Mr. Dickens in the eyes.

"Don't look at me like that. God knows I'm a good man," he said. "That's what God knows."

"I already talked to God about you," I said, still staring Mr. Dickens in the eyes. God knows the same things I know. And one day, everybody's gonna know."

Mr. Dickens turned to walk away. "You is a devil child. Always knew you had the devil in you. Always knew it. Read too many of 'em books. Make your mind think real ugly. Real ugly."

"I don't have to read books to think real ugly"—my lips began to quiver—"or to see real ugly."

Before entering into his building, Mr. Dickens turned toward me. He looked at me for a moment. "Jealousy is a evil thing," he finally said, then walked through the door. I wanted to chase after him and scream in his face, but no words would come to mind. My anger had left me speechless.

There was a knock on our apartment door the very next day. Mother hadn't come home from work yet, and I was in my bedroom reading for class. I thought it might be Mrs. Cooper but the knocking was too heavy.

"Who?" I said, while walking toward the front door.

"Me," a girl's voice said.

"Me? Who is me?" I asked before reaching the peephole.

"Tanya."

I opened the door. "Can I come in?" she said.

"Maybe," I said, smiling. "It depends on what you want."

"I need to talk," she said, frowning.

"What are you mad about?"

"Can I come in?"

"Come on."

Tanya came into the apartment. "Anybody here with you?" she asked.

"No." I shut the door.

"I'm mad at you," she said, walking toward the sofa. She dropped onto it and slumped over.

"What for?"

"You said something to Simon," she said, still frowning. Tears had begun to well in her eyes. "He said if my mother or anybody else find out about us." Tanya paused. "He said he gonna make sure my mother send me away."

"He can't do that," I said angrily.

"Yes, he can. He told me what he gonna do."

"What's he gonna do?" I asked, twisting my lips and raising my brow.

"I don't wanna talk about it. I can't say nothin' anyhow." Tears began to run down Tanya's cheeks.

"Tell him to leave you alone," I said, walking toward the love seat. I fell backward onto it.

"You need to just mind your business. That's all I came to tell you." Tanya quickly rose from the sofa.

"You don't have to be so mad," I said, rising from the love seat.

"We ain't friends no more. I don't want to be friends with you no more." Tanya walked to the door and opened it. "Next time, just keep your mouth shut." She walked out the door and slammed it.

I glared at the door. Tears began to surface. Again, I was left speechless.

I walked back into my bedroom. I picked up the books on my bed and slammed them on the floor then kicked one across the room. It flew open and ended up on a page with a photo. I walked over to it and looked down to see what the picture was. It was a man whose face, chest and private parts had been scratched out. I had erased each area on the man because he reminded me of Mr. Dickens. I did it after our last encounter the day before. At first, I only scratched out the face and area between his legs, but then I realized, the man no longer needed a chest either, he had no heart for it to hide.

Chapter 27

I completed the remainder of the ninth grade without talking to Tanya. I also hadn't made any new friends. After starting my period over the winter break, it seemed everything made me cry. Everything and anything more easily affected my mood. I preferred being alone reading a book or listening to music, which is what I did when I wasn't confined to doing homework. Mother noticed the change in my demeanor. She could barely bring herself to talk to me because every time she entered my room, I snapped at her. Eventually she developed the habit of slamming my bedroom door. The doorknob loosened and began to wiggle. I was pretty sure it would eventually become loose enough to fall off completely. It didn't bother me that it was loose until it began to slightly hang. When that happened, it was easier to see into my room through the hole that had become visible.

I finally gathered enough strength to ask Mr. Girard to tighten it back on. It was the hardest thing I had to do considering I had hardly spoken to him in almost three years. It was easy to avoid him, mostly because he hadn't changed his habit of only coming around on the weekends. Mother still tolerated his visits. Why she did was still beyond my knowing, beyond my understanding. The day he worked on tightening my doorknob, I thought to ask him. Maybe he could explain it. He must have known the reason. But it was too much for me to ask. It was too much for me to look into his face for more than the few seconds I did the day I asked him to fix my doorknob.

I remember the day my period started. It was on January 7, 1978. I wrote the date in my journal. I hadn't felt any cramps or any of the other symptoms I had heard most women experience. It just came. I wasn't prepared for it, but it came anyway. When I saw the blood in my panties, although it wasn't much, I started to cry. I wept like a baby. I wasn't ready to be a woman yet. Being a woman was too hard. Remaining a child was easier, I thought, at least for a little while longer. When I was ready for marriage and for children, I could accept being an adult. Only then would I be fit to be a woman. For the first few months of my period, I stuffed toilet tissue into my panties. I folded the sheets into a neat square, creasing the sides and turning them under so that it would fit and wouldn't move when I walked. My periods were light enough to use tissue, and I was too embarrassed to tell Mother about my menstruation. She made such a big deal about my chest when it began to grow. Seemed like the whole world knew I was growing breasts when she made the announcement to God. If God knew what was going on inside my panties, too, it was better that I didn't know He knew.

My secret lasted for six months. Mother found the sanitary napkins under my bed. She said she was looking for a book I had borrowed. I didn't believe her. Along with my napkins, she was holding one of Father's journals. I hadn't had a chance to read much of it yet. I had hidden it under my bed and had forgotten about it until I saw it in her hand. Most of what I had read was about war, slavery and crime in America. On the very first page Father wrote, "If white people could make it a crime to be black in America, they would." He wrote a bunch of other things, too, about blacks, whites and racism. Until I started to read his journal, I didn't know white people had as many fears as they did. It seemed their biggest fear was equality, or maybe it was something more. I hadn't had a chance to read enough to find out, but I did read that white people feared that the inferior would begin to read more, think more, ask more...The inferior would not forever remain voiceless or remain inferior. After reading some of Father's thoughts, I thought maybe he hated white people, but I'm not sure he did because many of his friends were white.

Mother had almost forgotten about the box of sanitary napkins. I had directed her attention to Father's journal when I asked for it back. "I don't want you reading this stuff," she said, waving the journal in my face.

"Why not?" I asked, holding out my hand.

"Because I said so." Mother placed the box of napkins into my hand. "Here you go."

"What's so wrong with knowing the truth?"

"Whose truth?"

"How many truths are there?"

"It depends on who you ask."

"So are you saying that everything written in Father's journal is a lie?" I put out my free hand.

"I'm not sayin' that any of it is a lie." Mother put the journal behind her back.

"So why can't I read it?"

"'Cause some of what's in here might not be your truth."

"I'm black," I said, still extending my hand.

"That don't make it your truth."

"Is the stuff written in there your truth?"

"Most of it's my truth. Yes, it is." Mother turned away from me.

"So why isn't it my truth?"

"'Cause times change." Mother placed Father's journal on the kitchen table. "Don't touch it," she said, waving her finger.

I sat at the kitchen table and rested my hand on top of Father's journal. "How much have times changed? Wars still exist. Racism still exists. Poor people still exist."

"I said don't touch it," Mother said, slapping my hand away.

"How much have times changed?"

"Enough for some of what is written in that journal not to be your truth," Mother said.

"Isn't knowledge the key to making things better and different, especially for me? Shouldn't I learn as much as I can about the world and its ways? I need to read more, think more and ask more. That's the only way I can make things different."

"Your own experiences will teach you. What you're livin' every day is teaching you. Don't get me wrong, your experiences include reading, thinking and asking, but some things… Some things you got to figure out on your own. Some things you just got to find out for yourself." Mother walked over to the table and picked up Father's journal. "Knowledge is your friend. And knowledge is your enemy. I want it to always be your friend."

"So far it's been my friend," I said. "I like knowing."

"You do, huh?"

"Yes."

"I like knowin' too. What's with the box of sanitary napkins? You been hidin' something from me? I already know whatcha been hidin'. I'm just wonderin' how long you been hidin' this new thing that's come about."

"Not that long," I said, embarrassed.

"Not that long? What's not that long?" Mother asked, cupping my chin and lifting my face toward hers.

"Um." I shrugged. "Maybe six months."

"Ain't no maybe six months," Mother said. "It's been six months."

Tears began to well in my eyes. "I don't want to talk about it."

"Why not?" Mother let go of my chin. She wiped my eyes.

"Because I don't," I said, backing away.

"It's nothin' to be embarrassed about," Mother said, walking toward me. "Does it hurt when you bleed?"

"No," I said, looking away.

"Do your breasts get tender?" Mother asked, looking into my face.

"No."

"Then what's the problem?"

"I'm not ready to be a woman yet."

"What's with the tears? Don't cry about it. You're becomin' a young lady, that's all." Mother wiped away my tears.

"I'm not ready to be a lady," I said, backing away again.

"There are some things in life that don't give us a choice. Be proud about it. You earned the right to be a lady. More of a right than most women I know."

"I'm not ready to be a lady. It's too hard," I said, looking into Mother's eyes.

"What do you mean?"

"Look at you," I said, still looking into Mother's eyes. "Ain't it hard being a woman?"

"It ain't always easy." Mother turned back toward the kitchen table and placed the journal on top of it. "But it don't have to be hard. It don't have to be hard for you."

"How do I make it easy then?" I sat back down at the table.

"You make it easy by knowin' what you want out of life and demanding it." Mother banged her fist down on Father's journal. "Demand it from life."

"Don't you know what you want?"

"I suppose I do."

"So why don't you demand what you want? Isn't that what you just said? You have to demand it from life."

Mother's eyes began to glisten. She pressed her fist down harder on Father's journal. "Never had the courage to demand it." Tears rolled down Mother's face. "Never had the courage. I've only taken what life has chosen to give me."

I stood from the table, wrapped my arms around Mother and pressed my head softly into her shoulder. "Is it too late?"

Mother continued to press her fist into Father's journal. She wiped the tears from her face. "I suppose it isn't."

"It's not too late," I said, squeezing her tighter.

Mother sat at the table and continued to wipe away her tears. I stood over her, rubbing my fingers through her hair. "I suppose it isn't," she said.

I remained in the kitchen with Mother for a long time. We hadn't spoken for what seemed like hours. Mother stared out the window, and I stood over her, running my fingers through her hair and studying the worn, black cover of my father's journal. The cover was blank, except for a few deep creases along the corners and edges. I was surprised Father hadn't stuck to it anything such as a white label with typed print indicating its title. It was unusual for him not to give his journals a name. The emptiness shown on the outside of Father's journal made me long to know what more was in its pages. Perhaps it would be something meaningful—enough that it would fulfill the void I felt inside.

Chapter 28

It was the summer of '78. Mrs. Lily, Mud Pie's mother, was in the garden with Mrs. Wise picking tulips. She started visiting Mrs. Wise's garden on the very day God gave the world a glimpse of spring again. Sometimes Mrs. Lily would be sitting under the leaves of the oak tree in Mrs. Wise's garden. Mrs. Lily would be listening to the singing of birds and observing the birth of new life. Sometimes Mrs. Wise would find Mrs. Lily kneeling at the edge of the garden with her nose gently pressed into a flower. Mrs. Lily had never touched any flowers in the garden, not until Mrs. Wise picked the first yellow tulip of the new season for her. She said Mrs. Lily laughed with all the joy she had in her. It was the first time Mrs. Wise had ever seen Mrs. Lily laugh that hard. Every day of the spring and summer, Mrs. Lily was present to help Mrs. Wise with her garden. She even brought some of her own flower seeds. Mrs. Lily said she always wanted to make her own garden, but she didn't know how to make the seeds grow.

Mrs. Lily planted violets. When they started to grow, she danced like a child under the leaves of the oak tree, and she laughed more than she had after receiving the first yellow tulip of the season. Mrs. Lily took great care with her violets, making sure they received all the love and nurturing one woman could give. She had learned how to grow her seeds by observing Mrs. Wise. Mrs. Lily told Mrs. Wise, "God giving me a second chance." Mrs. Wise smiled like she always had and just continued to hum.

"I been missin' Violet, you know?" Mrs. Lily said, pressing her nose gently into the petals of a bright-colored violet. Violet, most of us knew her as Mud Pie, had been sent to a home for girls farther south of Connecticut. Mrs. Wise nodded and continued to hum softly, sweetly.

I was sitting under the leaves of the oak tree picking away the small bright yellow petals of a dandelion. "He loves me. He loves me not." Father had been on my mind heavily over the last few days.

"She ain't come home to see me in a while, you know?" Mrs. Lily said. "Don't think she still mad at me. It's been some years now since I sent her away. Was the best thing for her. I know it was."

"I'm sure it was," Mrs. Wise said, planting new seeds.

"Don't think she would've made it around here. It wasn't right for her livin' the way she did, angry and fightin' all the time and all."

I plucked another dandelion from the grass. "He loves me. He loves me not. He loves me."

"No, it wasn't right," Mrs. Wise said.

"She in a better place now, you know? A place for young girls who tryin' to make somethin' of theyselves." Mrs. Lily picked up a small pebble from the earth. She rolled it between her fingers. "She ain't really like it at first. Every weekend she come home, tears was in her eyes. Made my heart real sad. Didn't know if I should've just let her stay and never go back, but inside I knew it was the right thing for her. I knew it was."

"Where is she?" I asked.

"She in a home," Mrs. Lily said. "A home for girls down in this small town called Riverton. Real nice place. Quiet there all the time. Ain't had a chance to go myself, but I seen pictures of it. Look real pretty and quiet. The picture alone put peace in me."

"Where's Riverton?" I asked.

"Right outside of New York." Mrs. Lily picked up another pebble. She tossed both pebbles between her hands. "Ain't that far from here. Maybe a hour drive or something like that. Mrs. Shirley—she the head of the place—she drive Violet there. Used to bring her home on the weekends and pick her up and take her back. Real nice white lady. Ain't never thought there was any nice white people before, until I met Mrs. Shirley."

"What do they do at the home?" I asked.

"They learn all kinda stuff," Mrs. Lily said. "Learn how to read big books with big words and make all kinda nice things. Violet made me a sweater. Knitted it all by herself. Real pretty. Lavender. Make me think of her every time I wear it."

"Why doesn't she like it there?" I asked.

"Don't know if that's still the case." Mrs. Lily placed the two pebbles in her apron pocket. She clasped her hands together and placed them in her lap. Mrs. Wise was moving to and fro along the edge of the garden still humming, softly, sweetly. "Think she might be feelin' different. When she first went there, she wasn't used to bein' around so many white people. I ain't never teach her anything good about white folks. Ain't really never had a reason to say or feel nothin' good about 'em. It kinda made me feel bad. All the bad stuff in her head and heart about white folks just made things harder for her."

"When you talk to her again, tell her I said hi." I picked another dandelion. I twisted it between my fingers, making it dance.

"Sure will." Mrs. Lily smiled. The white of her eyes began to glisten. She unclasped her hands and placed one on top of mine. "She real sorry for what she did. I know she didn't mean it. She got goodness in her, just didn't know how to make it come out, that's all. She different now though. I hear it when I talk to her. She different now."

Mrs. Wise looked over at me and smiled. "Love forgives all offenses," she said.

I smiled back at her. "I don't think about my fight with Mud Pie much anymore."

Mrs. Lily squeezed my hand. She looked up toward the sky. "God is good."

Mrs. Wise reached over and held on to Mrs. Lily's hand. She looked over at me and smiled again. Mrs. Wise closed her eyes and began to sing "In the Garden." It was a song by Mahalia Jackson that Mrs. Wise would sing sometimes.

Mrs. Lily held my hand tighter and closed her eyes. She began to sing along. I closed my eyes. And I listened to the song, to the women, to their song.

"Hallelujah." Mrs. Lily squeezed my hand tighter and raised it in the air. Mrs. Wise continued to sing. Mrs. Lily finally let go of my hand and

Mrs. Wise's and clasped her hands together in front of her, raising them up. "Thank you," she said. "Thank you."

The mark that had been on the side of my face was no longer visible, but it wasn't until that day at the garden, that I was able to fully forgive Violet. I hadn't realized until then that she was only living the hate and fear that had been instilled in her. A seed had been planted inside her long ago, but it had yet to bring forth a flower.

The next morning, the sun sprinkled its golden dust into our windows. Mother was sitting on the sofa listening to music. I watched her for a moment before making my presence known. She was singing "Take My Hand, Precious Lord." Her voice was almost a whisper.

Mother rose from the sofa and walked over to the window. She rested the palm of her hand on the glass. She began to sing again. She pressed her hand more firmly onto the glass and continued to sing in a whisper.

"Mother?" I walked over to her.

"Yes," she said, still facing the window.

"What's wrong?"

"Just felt like I needed church in my spirit today."

"You not going to work?"

"Not today," Mother said, placing the other hand onto the glass.

"What's wrong?" I pressed my hand next to hers.

"My spirit is weak."

I stood with my hand on the window. The glass was warm from the sun's rays. The music was still playing low. "What song were you singing?"

"'Take My Hand, Precious Lord.' It's one of Mahalia Jackson's songs."

"That was pretty," I said. I looked out into the sky. "God's pouring gold dust onto the world."

"Yeah, pourin' a lot of it today." Mother closed her eyes and began to listen to "His Eye Is On the Sparrow." She pressed her body against the warm glass and rested her face on her forearm.

I rested my head against Mother's shoulder. I closed my eyes and listened to her sing.

Mother and I stood in front of the window for a long while. We rested there with only the whisper of her voice and the rhythm of words together with song to penetrate the silence. It seemed as we rested there that God was drawing us nearer. Mother had not made her way to church in all these Sundays passed, but it appeared that church was making its way into her heart. Something inside of her was changing. It was difficult for me to express in words. I tried to write earlier in my journal, but all I could say was: Love has its way....

As I stood there with my eyes still closed, the words came to me again. I thought, *Love has its way. Love has its way. Love has its way.* Later that evening, I wrote:

Fear robs us of our greatest strength to be human. And yet love has its way.

Chapter 29

Mrs. Cooper died before sunrise on July 12, 1978. How the women of East Street knew was beyond any explanation, but they all knew she had died. It wasn't a normal Sunday morning—at least that's what Mrs. Wise said. Mrs. Cooper hadn't stopped by to wish her a good day like she usually did before her short, and on most occasions, jubilant journey to church. Mrs. Wise picked a daylily that morning, removed its petals and distributed them over her garden. Next she called Hewlett's funeral home. When Mrs. Cooper's body was removed from her apartment, all the women in the neighborhood stood outside the building and shook their heads.

"Yeah, you right, Sister Wise. It was before sunrise. You could see it in her face," Ms. Ross, Tanya's mother, said.

Mrs. Wise, without opening her eyes—she was praying—said, "In darkness before the light."

"Yes, Lord. In darkness before the light," Mrs. Lily said.

Mother stood silent. She reached out when the body was carried past her then her hand dropped lifeless to her side. She walked a little way behind the men who carried the body. She parted her lips to speak but instead said nothing.

Mrs. Wise grabbed her hand and squeezed it. "It's gonna be alright, Maxine. She in a good place."

Mother nodded then she looked at Mrs. Wise and said, "Can I...can I keep one of those petals for myself? I know the daylilies for Mrs. Cooper. Those belong to her. I wouldn't feel right pickin' one from your garden, so if it's alright, I'll just take one of those petals and put it in my bible." Mother looked sullenly into Mrs. Wise's eyes. "She gave it to me. The bible."

Mrs. Wise nodded and smiled. "Yes, it's alright." She walked over to the edge of her garden, leaned down and picked up four silky white petals. Mother was watching as the doors of the hearse were closed. Mrs. Wise walked back over to Mother and lifted her hand. She placed the soft white petal in her palm then gently closed it. Then she said, "This is for rememberin'." Mother lowered her head and closed her eyes. She held her hand up and pressed it against her heart. Mrs. Wise walked over to me and extended her hand. The other petals rested in her palm. "Hope," she said. "These three here is for hope."

"Thank you," I said, taking the petals from Mrs. Wise. Shortly after, I left the women, including Mother, who were still congregating in front of my building. I went up to my room, walked over to the window where my flowerpot with Mrs. Wise's silk butterfly rested on the sill. I placed the three silky white petals in it along with the one yellow petal for faith and the seven red petals from Love.

Later that day, I visited Mrs. Wise at the garden. She was sitting under the leaves of the oak tree cooling herself with a handmade bamboo fan. I walked over and sat beside her. "Hot today, baby," she said, looking over at me.

"Yes," I said, leaning back against the large trunk of the oak tree.

"Something on your mind?" Mrs. Wise asked.

"Sad, that's all," I said, folding my hands on my lap.

"Life always bringin' change," Mrs. Wise said. "Always bringin' change."

"I saw her yesterday. We talked for a little while. When we were talking, she said she was ready—to cross over to the other side of the river."

"She there," Mrs. Wise said. "Arrived just before sunrise."

"She was ready to die?"

"For new beginnings, baby. Just new beginnings," Mrs. Wise said.

"But she's not here with us anymore."

"She here still." Mrs. Wise moved over to the edge of the garden nearer to the daylilies. "Her seed been planted." She poured water over each of the lilies. A yellow butterfly landed on one of them then quickly flew away.

"I've never been to a funeral before."

"Been to plenty of 'em," Mrs Wise said. "Serve as reminders."

"Reminders of what?"

"Really, funerals just make you appreciate things," Mrs. Wise said.

"Like what?"

"The beauty that's in life but that we most times forget about," she said. "The simplest of things."

"So why do people cry?"

"We cry 'cause we've forgotten."

"I haven't forgotten," I said, unfolding my hands and moving over to the edge of the garden near Mrs. Wise.

"Some people and some things make it harder for us to forget. Sister Cooper made it hard." Mrs. Wise began to hum.

I looked down at the white lily petals that were resting on top of the earth beneath the other flowers. They had begun to change color and form. Change, I thought. But what they represented for each of us, for Mrs. Wise, for me and for the other women of our community would never change. For us they represented hope. Hope is what Mrs. Cooper brought to life through her words and in the way she lived.

The next morning, a strange white man stopped by looking for Mrs. Cooper's residence. He walked up to the oak tree, leaned against it and took his hat off his balding head. He wiped his brow and said, "It's real hot out here today." He loosened his tie.

Mrs. Wise turned to face him. "Yes, it is," she said. I had already seen him before he reached the oak tree. It was the first time I had seen a white person in our neighborhood. I observed the man without responding.

"I'm looking for Mrs. Cooper's residence," he said.

"Used to live on the second floor of that building there," Mrs. Wise said, pointing over at my building.

"Right there?" he asked, pointing in the same direction.

"That's right. Second floor. Window right in the front used to be hers," Mrs. Wise said.

"It's real sad that she passed," he said. "I heard she was a kind woman. Church-going woman."

"She was a kind woman," Mrs. Wise said. "Godly woman."

"Had a big spirit, I heard." He put his hat back on.

"She had the spirit of an angel," Mrs. Wise said, standing. "Would you like a glass of cold water?"

"That would be nice of you," the man said. "My name is Mr. Thatcher." He extended his hand.

"I'm Mrs. Wise." She grabbed Mr. Thatcher's hand and gently squeezed it. "This is Rose."

"Hello," I said, standing and extending my hand.

"It's nice to meet you both," he said, squeezing my hand.

"I'll be right back," Mrs. Wise said, heading up the steps.

"That's a beautiful flower garden," Mr. Thatcher said, walking away from the tree to observe the garden more closely. He bent forward and began to smell the roses. "I haven't seen a garden this beautiful in almost twenty years. My mother had a lovely garden. It didn't last too long after she passed, however. No one in the family had a green thumb like hers. It was depressing watching it die away like it did, but I guess it didn't matter after a while because we sold the house."

"Where did your mother live?" I asked.

"She lived out in the country," he said.

"How far is that from here?"

"Long ways away. With all the back roads, I'd say it would take about an hour to get there." He walked over and sat on a step.

Mrs. Wise walked out of her house with three glasses of cold water. "Miss Rose, come and help me with these," she said.

Mr. Thatcher sprung up from the step. "Let me assist you with that." He reached for a glass. I walked up a step and reached for another one.

"So, Mr. Thatcher, what's your duty in these parts today?" Mrs. Wise asked, pulling her sundress above her ankles then sitting on a step.

"I'm here to assess the value of Mrs. Cooper's belongings. She has a relative down South who is interested in having a few items shipped down." Mr. Thatcher took off his hat and scratched his head.

"Not aware of any relatives of Sister Cooper's down South," Mrs. Wise said. "I'm sure she would've mentioned 'em to me."

"Not sure they stayed in touch frequently, but of course Mrs. Stone is aware of Mrs. Cooper's recent death."

"Yes, happened right before sunrise yesterday mornin'." Mrs. Wise crossed her ankles. "I must say you quite efficient, Mr. Thatcher. Stoppin' by in so little time."

Mr. Thatcher averted his eyes and placed his hat back on his head. "Mrs. Stone was really upset about the death when I talked to her earlier this morning." He passed his empty glass to Mrs. Wise. "Thank you."

"Not a problem. Wouldn't mind gettin' you another glass if you need it," Mrs. Wise said.

"That won't be necessary," Mr. Thatcher said.

"Is Mrs. Stone plannin' to attend Sister Cooper's funeral on Wednesday? The women of the community is plannin' it for her. None of us was aware of any relatives. Had we known about Mrs. Stone, we would've called to let her know. I'm sure she would've wanted to be a part of the service." Mrs. Wise placed the two empty glasses on the porch beside her.

"Didn't hear Mrs. Stone mention being present for a funeral, but I did hear her say she would send a real nice bouquet of flowers." Mr. Thatcher loosened his tie a little more. "I really need to get going now. Mrs. Stone is awaiting my call. You said Mrs. Cooper lived in that second-floor apartment?" He pointed to the empty window again.

"Yes, indeed I did," Mrs. Wise said. "Please let Mrs. Stone know that plenty of fresh flowers will be available for the funeral. Most of 'em Sister Cooper planted herself." Mrs. Wise rose from the step. "The women of the community are making some lovely wreaths to decorate the church Mrs. Cooper attended. That's where the funeral will be held."

"I'll let Mrs. Stone know," Mr. Thatcher said.

"And Mr. Thatcher?" Mrs. Wise walked down the steps toward him.

"Yes, Mrs. Wise?"

"I have a letter here." Mrs. Wise pulled out the letter from her side pocket. "Something like a will. It was given to me by Sister Cooper."

Mr. Thatcher removed his hat and scratched his head. "What does it say, Mrs. Wise?"

Mrs. Wise removed the letter from a white envelope. "The letter says, in summary, that the women of the community will inherit all of Sister Cooper's belongings. Everything she owned should be shared between the women and distributed according to need."

Mr. Thatcher placed his hat back on his head. "In that letter is there any mention of a brooch that was owned by Mrs. Cooper?"

"As a matter of fact, there is." Mrs. Wise unfolded the bottom half of the letter. "Accordin' to this letter, Sister Cooper inherited from a Mrs. Olivia Randolph Thatcher a brooch made of rubies. An angel with wings. It says it should be given to Mrs. Lily 'cause it would remind Mrs. Lily of the angels that is watching over her daughter, Violet, while they apart."

Mr. Thatcher sat down on a step. "If you don't mind, I would like to see that letter."

"Sure. Says it in the sentence right above Sister Cooper's signature." Mrs. Wise handed the letter to Mr. Thatcher.

"That brooch belonged to my mother." Mr. Thatcher folded the letter. "She inherited it from her mother. It's worth a lot of money."

"Wasn't no money specified in the letter." Mrs. Wise reached for the letter. "Wasn't really sure how much it was worth but it is a pretty brooch. Sister Lily owns it now."

Mr. Thatcher handed back the letter as he rose from the step. "I would love to have it back. It would really mean a lot to the family, especially my sister."

"Don't have it to give back." Mrs. Wise put the letter back into the envelope. "Already belongs to Sister Lily. Made her real proud to have it too. That brooch really meant a lot to Sister Cooper. Not sure Sister Lily would want to part with it."

"I can write her a check for a hundred dollars. I'm sure she can do much more with the money." Mr. Thatcher removed his tie and swung it over his shoulder.

"Doubt that she would take it," Mrs. Wise said, putting the envelope back into her side pocket.

"Don't appear to me that you people around here have a lot. I'm sure she could use the money." Mr. Thatcher reached into his jacket pocket. "What about two hundred dollars?"

"Doubt that she would take it," Mrs. Wise said, sitting.

"Are all of you people this difficult?" Mr. Thatcher pulled out a pen and opened the small leather checkbook. "You black people are always making things hard for yourselves. What about three hundred dollars?"

"Doubt that she would take it," Mrs. Wise said. "Rose, hand me that water pot over there." She pointed at the silver pot resting in the grass at the edge of the garden.

I walked over to the edge of the garden, picked up the water pot and handed it to Mrs. Wise. Mr. Thatcher was writing out a check. When he was done, he ripped it out of the checkbook and handed it to Mrs. Wise. "This is my final offer," he said.

Mrs. Wise placed the silver water pot on the porch beside her. She leaned toward Mr. Thatcher, clasped her hands and rested them on her knees. "Sister Cooper gave this pot to me a long time ago. It was a gift." Mrs. Wise unclasped her hands and sat upright again. She picked up the silver canister. "She had my initials engraved on it right above these three flowers." She rubbed her finger over the small, thin engraved letters. This is one of a few gifts I own that is priceless. Come a little closer, Mr. Thatcher." Mr. Thatcher, still holding the check, walked up the stairs, closer to Mrs. Wise. "Let me show you something," she said. She turned over the silver water pot. "See here?"

Mr. Thatcher pulled his glasses out of his pocket and placed them on. "I see," he said.

"These initials belong to Sister Cooper's grandmother," she said.

"I see," Mr. Thatcher said, leaning in a little closer.

"And these initials, they belonged to Sister Cooper's great-grandmother," she said, pointing to another set of letters. "And these initials belonged to her great-great-grandmother." Mrs. Wise rubbed gently her finger over each area that was engraved with the small, thin letters. "And see these initials?"

Mr. Thatcher nodded. "I see," he said.

Mrs. Wise rubbed her finger over them. "These belonged to the woman who owned Sister Cooper's great-great-grandmother," she said. "Now let me show you something else." Mrs. Wise turned the water pot around to the back. "You see what it says here?" She pointed at the words engraved deep into the silver pot. "It says, 'In every heart there is a garden with a flower that longs to bloom.' These words were put here for all the women who put life into the garden of someone's heart." I moved in closer to Mrs. Wise to see for myself the words that were engraved on the silver pot. Mr. Thatcher stood and removed his glasses. "You see? That's what Mrs. Cooper did for Mrs. Olivia Randolph Thatcher. She put life into her heart. There was a flower in there longin' to bloom. What she did for your mother before she died was priceless." Mrs. Wise placed the pot on the porch beside her.

Mr. Thatcher backed down the steps. "What should I do with this check?"

"That's for you to figure out," Mrs. Wise said, rising from the step.

"You don't think this Mrs. Lily would want it?" Mr. Thatcher asked, holding it up to Mrs. Wise.

Mrs. Wise smiled. "Doubt that she would." She walked down the steps toward her garden. When she reached the edge, she turned toward Mr. Thatcher. "There's a garden in your heart too," she said.

Mr. Thatcher looked over at me then looked down at the check in his hand. "Worthless," he said and placed the check in his pocket. He pulled the tie down from over his shoulder, placed it back around his collar and tightened it. He turned toward the road and began to walk away.

Mrs Wise sat down on the grass and began to hum. "That check was worth a lot of money," I said.

Mrs. Wise stopped humming. She looked up at me. "Money ain't never worth the pain it causes. That man, Mr. Thatcher, wasn't nothin' but the face of selfishness and greed. American capitalism. It come in different sizes, shapes and colors. It come in many disguises. And that brooch is priceless. There ain't no amount of money Mr. Thatcher could offer that equal to how much it meant to Mrs. Lily," she said, then began to hum again.

Chapter 30

On Wednesday morning there was a funeral, the rising of the sun and rain. Women, men and children stood outside the doors of the school building on St. John Road where they would normally wait on Sunday mornings for the church bell to ring. Mother and I were among the crowd waiting for the doors to open. Mrs. Wise stood in front of us with a bouquet of daylilies. There was a bright yellow ribbon wrapped around their fresh-cut stems. She was singing "I Believe," and those who were close by and could hear her sang along.

The bell rang, and the church doors opened. Mrs. Wise continued to sing as she walked in front of us. The rest of the crowd focused on making their way through the doors. Mother moved slowly, tightly clutching her bible. I wrapped my arm around hers and walked beside her. When we reached the inside of the sanctuary, an usher approached us.

"Good morning," she said. "Where would you like to sit?"

"Good morning," Mother answered.

I looked around for Mrs. Wise. She was making her way down the middle row toward the front of the sanctuary. "With her," I said, pointing at Mrs. Wise. The usher handed us a small paper booklet then lead us toward Mrs. Wise. When we reached her, she was already sitting in the third row directly in front of the pulpit. Mother stood back to let me into the row of seats. I sat beside Mrs. Wise, and Mother sat on the other side of me. Mrs. Wise had her eyes closed and hands clasped together. She was praying. When I looked over at Mother, she had tears in her eyes. I looked back toward the pulpit, silently wondering if it was appropriate to cry, and waited for the funeral to begin.

Pastor Starks, the head of Mrs. Cooper's church, approached the pulpit. "Good morning and God bless," he said.

Those of us in the congregation repeated, "Good morning and God bless."

"It is a blessing for us to be here this morning," he said. "We are here to celebrate the home going of our late Sister Cooper."

Voices in the crowd answered, "Amen."

"Today is not a day to be sad," he said. Pastor Starks opened his bible. "It is a day to rejoice."

The voices in the crowd answered, "Amen."

I held back my tears.

"Yes, we will miss the physical presence of our dear Sister Cooper, but her spirit will remain with us always," Pastor Starks said. "Amen. Let's turn to First Corinthians." He hurriedly flipped through the pages within his bible. "I will read for you chapter fifteen, verses forty-two through fifty-eight: This is how it will be when the dead are raised to life. When the body is buried, it is mortal; when raised, it will be immortal. When buried, it is ugly and weak; when raised, it will be beautiful and strong. When buried, it is a physical body; when raised, it will be a spiritual body...The first Adam, made of earth, came from the earth; the second Adam came from heaven. Those who belong to the earth are like the one who was made of earth; those who are of heaven are like the one who came from heaven...."

The people in the congregation, and those in the choir, nodded in approval of what was being read. The woman sitting in front of me wearing a large black hat continued to wave her white handkerchief and repeated "amen" after each pause. Mrs. Wise sat silent with her eyes closed and hands clasped. Mother held her head down and continued to wipe her tears. I stared at the closed pearly white casket at the side of the pulpit and wondered if Mrs. Cooper was resting peacefully within it. Pastor Starks cleared his throat and took a sip from a glass of water. Then he continued: "What I mean, friends, is that what is made of flesh and blood cannot share in God's Kingdom, and what is mortal cannot possess immortality. Listen to this secret truth: we shall not all die, but when the last trumpet sounds, we shall all be changed in an instant, as quickly as the blinking of an eye. For when the trumpet sounds, the dead will be raised, never to die again, and we shall all be changed. For what is mortal must be changed into what is immortal; what will die must be changed into what cannot die. So when this takes place…then the scripture will come true: Death is destroyed; victory is complete!"

The congregation clapped and shouted "amen." Pastor Starks wiped his brow, took another sip from his glass and continued: "Death gets its power to hurt from sin, and sin gets its power from the Law. But thanks be to God who gives us the victory through our Lord Jesus Christ!"

Pastor Starks closed his bible. "Will the people of this church shout 'amen.'" Everyone rose and shouted, "Amen." Mrs. Wise stood. She bowed her head and closed her eyes. Pastor Starks began to speak again. "I'd planned to give the eulogy after the reading but a dear friend of Sister Cooper's and of the church, of course, will be giving the eulogy this morning. Let's first listen to our gifted choir." He walked to his seat and sat down. The choir began to sing, and everyone in the congregation began to clap. I stood and wiped my tears, listening to the words of "Just Give Me Jesus." Mother placed her arm around me. "It's okay," she said. Then she began to sing along.

Once the choir was done, everyone in the church took their seats again. Pastor Starks returned to the pulpit and opened the booklet that had been passed out by the ushers. "Sister Wise, please raise your hand so the church can see you, and please make your way to the front here." He pointed in the direction of the casket. Mrs. Wise started toward the front. Mother and I stood and moved out of the row to let her through. As she was passing she gently squeezed both of our hands. Mrs. Wise stood just below the pearly white casket. Pastor Starks walked to the edge of the stage and handed Mrs. Wise a microphone. He then walked back to the pulpit, took another sip of water then took his seat. "Sister Wise is gonna share a few words with us about the lovely Sister Cooper," he said, talking into the microphone from his seat.

Mrs. Wise placed the daylilies she held on the stage below the casket. She faced the congregation, put the microphone up to her mouth and began to hum the words to the song she had lead earlier. The choir began to sing along.

Mrs. Wise continued to hum while the choir sang, then she lowered her head. The choir lowered their voices. When Mrs. Wise completed her prayer, she then placed the microphone on a metal folding chair near her. "I never liked those things," she said. People laughed. The choir became silent, and Pastor Starks smiled and nodded. Mrs. Wise walked away from the stage, closer to the congregation.

She began the eulogy: "I believe for every drop of rain that falls, a flower grows." Mrs. Wise paused for a moment. "Sister Cooper was a flower, you know? She had the beauty, dignity and strength that a flower do, and I say that a flower have strength 'cause it go through struggles too. It have to make it through the storms just like we do. And when you look out and see the flower has made it through the storm, it remind you of the strength it has. Give you hope. Well every time I looked out my window and saw Sister Cooper at my garden, I couldn't tell the difference between her and the daylilies she planted there. Those were her favorite flowers. They was one and the same. For her, they was the hope in the world, and for me and most other people in our community she was the hope. Whenever folks around us seemed to be goin' astray or if she was dealin' with something personal, she would come on over to the garden, sit at the edge near her daylilies and pray. It was then that hope was renewed. One time when she finished prayin', I remember her sayin', 'Seems like the rain made them grow some.'

"I smiled and said that's a sign they livin' not dyin'. She nodded 'cause she knew what I was really sayin'. I meant, sometimes we ain't gon' like the rain. Most times we rather have nothin' but the sunlight, but then here come the rain, and sometime it come real hard, and sometime it stay long. But when it come we got to let it feed us so we can keep growin' and livin'. That's what a flower do. It let the rain feed it. That's the way it keep growin'. When it's growin' we know it's still livin'. I'm not talkin' 'bout what we seein' on the outside either. I'm talkin' 'bout life on the inside. See, 'cause when we look at what's on the outside, it just lead us to confusion.

"We get confused like when we see that part of the flower has been broken 'cause the rain came down hard. That make us think the flower ain't no good anymore. But when there's life on the inside, then it starts to make its way on the outside, and then we see a new piece start to grow again. You see? That drop of rain—sometime it only take one, especially when it come down hard—caused a part of that flower to become broken is the same drop that give it a reason to grow again. Grow a new part. And that part is made stronger. It let the rain feed it. When we let the rain feed us, we keep growin'. We keep livin'. That's the way of God. Yes, it is.

"God show us the mystery and beauty in life right here on this earth. In this life. We don't have to wait to see it 'cause it's right here on this here earth, in this here life. The earth that our weary feet walk on, that our weary bodies rest on, there is life with all its mystery and beauty bein' born. You see, Sister Cooper didn't wait for the restoration of heaven's Garden of Eden that we've been told will come in the afterlife. She found heaven's garden here on earth.

"Our Mother give it to us. And God has given us in this life our kingdom. It is found in the garden of our hearts." Mrs. Wise pressed her hand against her heart. "The kingdom is in here. It is in our hearts. Sister Cooper found the kingdom in her own heart. Yes, she did. And when she found it, she shared the gifts of the kingdom—of her heart—with us." Mrs. Wise held her hand firmly to her heart. "So when we look at this casket, don't let it make you all confused. People here talkin' 'bout death and all. Sister Cooper is alive. She still a part of us. She in our hearts livin' and growin' with each of us. She feedin' us."

Mrs. Wise turned toward the stage and picked up the bouquet of daylilies, then she made her way over to the steps and ascended onto the stage. When she reached the casket, she untied the yellow ribbon and spread the twelve daylilies across the top. "She planted the seed. And I believe for every drop of rain that fall, a flower grows." Mrs. Wise clasped her hands, closed her eyes and began to pray.

The church was silent. Pastor Starks fidgeted in his seat as he watched Mrs. Wise in prayer. He waited for a moment then rose and began making his way to the pulpit. Once there he cleared his throat and said, "Well. Church let us say amen."

Chapter 31

Green is a color in the rainbow. The sunlight always makes it brighter after it rains. I always loved green, especially the grass, trees and apples.

Mother said she lived on a farm when she was a child, and there were fruit trees in their front and back yards. There was one with shiny green apples growing from it. Every time Mother thought about the fresh shiny green apples back home, they made her mouth water. When she thought about her childhood days, she said they reminded her of a time of innocence. I never thought much about living on a farm, but when I thought about the fresh shiny green apples, they made me wish I had one for myself. Sometimes I could taste the sweet-sour taste of fresh farm apples. It made me want them more.

The feeling was the same when I met the boy with green eyes, a few days after Mrs. Cooper's funeral, while taking a walk in the park behind my building. After my twelveth birthday, Mother began allowing me to visit the park that I used to sneak to with Tanya.

Melancholy and lonesomeness had overwhelmed my heart since Mrs. Cooper's passing. I cried a lot, especially after both Mother and Mrs. Wise told me it was okay to. I understood that change meant new beginnings, but not all change found a trusted place in my heart—at first. Until it did, my heart struggled with its own vulnerabilities. When the conflict was most intense, I took walks. Sometimes they took me— where didn't always matter.

The first day I saw the boy with green eyes it seemed the strife in my heart took a moment of repose. Within that time my dreaming had carried me through to another place. He didn't notice me on the first day. I watched him from the park bench behind my building where I sat writing in my journal. He was tossing a ball around on the court with others. It seemed his green eyes glittered whenever he smiled, which he did often. He seemed happy. The shine in his eyes made me want to reach out for it—happiness—and sprinkle some of it on my heart. I wrote about him in my journal. About my dreams. He had become my fresh shiny green apple.

The second time I visited the park, he was in the company of his shadow only. He played with his handball on the crack-ridden court. I thought once and then a second time about making myself noticeable, but doubt's hand was heavy on my shoulder, so it kept me on the bench. There was still the green glitter of rainbows in his eyes, but the brightness reflected in his would not paint itself into mine. Sadness had already poured its dull, lifeless colors into mine leaving room for nothing else, so I sat and watched him, hoping doubt would eventually lift its hand from me.

A week went by before I saw him again. During the time I was away from the park I filled most of my journal writing about him, about my dreams. I still did not know his name, so he became the words that made pictures in my mind. The third time he spoke to me.

"Come here alot?" he asked. He sat on the bench beside me. With my mind preoccupied by words I had written and pictures I had created, I hadn't seen him walk over.

"Not that often," I answered, closing my journal.

"What you write in there?" he asked, looking down at the cover.

"Different things," I said, shrugging.

"Like what?" he asked, silently reading the words on the cover.

"My thoughts, mostly."

"What you think about?" he asked, smiling.

"Different things," I said, smiling back.

"That's your favorite answer?" he asked, tossing a small black rubber ball back and forth between his hands.

"No."

"What's your name?" he asked.

"Rose," I answered. "What's yours?"

"Dice." He looked down into his hands.

234

"Dice? Who gave you that name?"

"My friends. They say I'm always gambling with life."

"In what way?" I placed my journal on the bench between us.

"I like to take chances. I'm not scared to take risks, you know?"

"What kind of risks do you take?" I shifted to face him.

"You ask a lot of questions." He leaned back on the bench. "But I like that. I don't know. Relationships I guess. Doin' things that most people scared to do."

"Like what?" I picked up my journal and placed it on my lap.

"I don't know. Maybe one day you'll find out." He grinned.

"My favorite color is green," I said, changing the subject and looking down at the cover of my journal.

"Oh yeah?" he said. "You like my eyes then?" He was looking into mine.

"Yes. They're pretty."

"Pretty? That's a word for girls," he said.

"So what word should I use?"

"Cool. I like that better."

"Cool? Okay."

"You look young. How old are you?" He squeezed the black ball.

"I'll be fifteen in September."

"In two months. September what?"

"On the twenty-first. How old are you?"

"How old do I look?"

"I don't know." I shrugged. "Sixteen."

"Close."

"Seventeen?"

"Closer."

"Eighteen?"

"Yeah."

"Oh." I sat upright again.

"That's too old for you?" he asked. "You look a little concerned about my age."

"I don't know."

"You know," he said. "I'm too old for you?"

"Well, I thought you were younger. I didn't realize you were that much older than me." I fidgeted with my journal. "You're not old, but I'm only fourteen."

"Don't matter. Only thing that matter is what's in here and here." He pointed at his head and heart.

"I guess," I said. "You don't have a girlfriend?"

"Haven't found the right one yet. Been lookin' for a while but she hard to find. Maybe I just found her." He bit down on his lip and slightly tilted his head upward.

I felt a warm sensation on my face. I wondered if he could see the difference in color in my cheeks. I averted my eyes and observed the jagged cracks in the cement below me. A dandelion had been crushed, it appeared, under someone's foot. "I don't know why, but I like dandelions. They're not really flowers, but I think they are."

"You tryin' to act like you didn't hear what I just said, but I hear you. Yeah, they say a dandelion is a weed. Look like a flower, but ain't nothin' but a weed."

"When they change from yellow to white, I like to pick them and blow on them while making a wish." I could feel the warm sensation in my cheeks leaving.

"There's one right over there." Dice jumped up and jogged over to where a single dandelion grew from another crack. He picked it, jogged back to the bench and sat. "I'm gonna make a wish." He closed his eyes and said, "I wish for you." He blew on the dandelion.

"You were supposed to make a silent wish," I said, laughing.

"I wanted you to know what I wished for." He threw the stem in back of him.

"I wasn't supposed to know."

"And why not? Everybody got rules. The world got them. You got yours. I got mine. My rules say I can wish out loud if I want. If I want everybody in the park to hear my wish then they can. But I just wanted you to hear it." He leaned back on the bench again.

I smiled and averted my eyes. "Okay." I picked up my journal and stood. "I should probably get going. I've been here for a while."

"When you coming back? I'm usually here playin' ball during the day, except on Fridays. Go in to work a little earlier." Dice stood.

"I don't come here every day," I said. "Just when I feel like takin' a walk."

"When you plan on takin' a walk again?" Dice reached for my hand. "I usually like to go for walks when the sun just rising and the sky is blue and clear."

"I might take one tomorrow. It depends on how I feel." I gently pulled my hand away.

"Well feel like takin' a walk up here to see me, okay?" Dice reached for my hand again. "I can't hold your hand?"

"I guess you can," I answered. "I'll see you tomorrow."

"Sounds good." Dice kissed the back of my hand then let it go. "I'll see you tomorrow." He winked.

I smiled and nodded. "Okay."

When I reached the bottom of the hill, the warm feeling in my face dissipated. I walked slowly and looked back up the hill several times. I saw that Dice was watching me each time I looked back. I took the long way home that day, keeping company with the sunlight and blue clear skies. The day made me wonder how it would be to walk in the light of morning with the green glitter of a rainbow beside me. The nights would keep me dreaming of the walk into the sunlight of morning. A morning with a rainbow.

The park was empty when I arrived. The next day woke from its dream with big, bright sunlit eyes. Summer poured itself out over everything—the grass, trees, butterflies, birds and bees. Fresh-cut grass permeated the air, a smell not often found in the parts where I lived. Trees stood tall and commanded a respect that power usually does, butterflies paraded their freedom, and birds sang in soprano while bees danced with glee around the bloom of dandelions. It seemed summer's voice was made audible through those things born of Nature, whose children had invited me in to their mother's womb to be born into life again. So when the leaves of the maple tree waved me over, I walked past the bench and found a grassy spot in the shade. I picked a dandelion. It had magic and would tell me if Father still loved me. I picked one petal then another until the head of the dandelion was bare and golden petals were sprinkled on the grass in front of me. Before I released each petal, I repeated over and over, "He loves me. He loves me not." Soon I had cleared the head of three dandelions. I thought about a fourth but the voice of a tenor interrupted me.

"Thinking about another man, huh?" Dice spread himself out on the grass near me.

"No....Well, I guess." I was flustered by Dice's sudden appearance. "I was thinking about my father."

"Oh yeah?" Dice wore a childish smile. "I was hoping you were thinking about me."

"We don't know each other that well yet. I just met you yesterday." I began to play with the golden petals in the grass.

"It's such a thing as love at first sight, you know?" Dice continued to give me a childish smile. "Plus, you said you like my eyes." He fluttered his eyelashes.

I smiled and averted my eyes. "I do like your eyes. They are—"

"Cool." Dice interrupted me. "Remember not pretty but cool."

"I remembered. I wasn't going to say pretty."

"You weren't gonna say cool either. I can tell."

"Did you go for a walk this morning?" I asked, still playing with the golden petals.

"Naw, didn't have a chance to. Had some other things I had to take care of this morning. Wish I had though. My morning walks always make me feel better during the day. Take my mind off things." Dice rolled over on his back and looked up into the leaves of the maple tree.

"What kinda things?"

"Just things in general. You know, like work and stuff like that." He closed his eyes.

"Well, I don't work so I don't know," I said, studying his features. A bee circled his thick brown hair. "There's a bee around your head."

"That's okay. Won't bother me as long as I don't bother it." He kept his eyes closed.

"I like bees, but I just don't like when they get too close to me. I get a little nervous. I think they can sense it 'cause that's when they start chasing me." I placed my journal on the side of me farthest from Dice and folded my legs Indian style.

"You make bees sound like a dog," he said, opening his eyes. "As far as I know, they don't bother you until you start hittin' at 'em. That's the only time they bother me, but when they come at me, that's the end of 'em. Don't play around with no bees. Got stung once and don't want to experience that again." Dice rolled onto his side and faced me. "Ain't a good feelin'."

"I've never been stung by a bee. I got bit by a dog once. Right here." I placed my finger on the side of my behind.

"How the dog bite you there?" Dice asked, placing a dandelion stem between his lips.

"I was running, and the dog chased me. I was so scared that I jumped up on my friend's back, and the dog jumped up and bit me right here on my behind. I was six when that happened." I laughed at the memory.

Dice laughed too. "That's funny," he said. "You gonna let me see what's in that journal today?"

I pushed my journal under my leg. "No. My thoughts are private. For me only."

"You talk about your father in there?"

"Yeah."

"Your father alive?" he asked, moving the stem between his lips.

"Yeah. I think so," I said, looking down at a bee that had landed on the dandelion petals.

"You think so? You don't know?" Dice looked over at the bee too. "You ain't scared?"

"Not yet," I said, avoiding his first two questions.

"So, you don't know if your father is alive?" he asked again.

"I think he is, but I haven't talked to him in a long time. He used to call me on my birthday." Dice stared into my eyes. "He stopped calling, so I don't know where he is or what he's doing."

"My father around, but we don't talk much. He ain't never been a real father to me. Never was able to depend on him. Left my mother when I was young. She still speak to him though. Sometime she act like he never left us. Pisses me off." Dice rolled on his back and looked up into the sky.

"I wish my father was still around. He was a smart man. He used to talk to me about everything. It was like he knew everything there was to know about the world. He knew the good and the bad. He used to tell me all the time how important it was for Americans to know the truth about our history, especially blacks. He said if we knew more, things would've been different for us, but most of what we know about

American history is told by the people who win and make the laws—the few rich and powerful white people."

"Wow, that's deep. That's the kinda stuff you got written in that journal?" Dice rolled on his side to face me.

"A little bit. I have other stuff too. I like to write poetry and words to my favorite songs. And I like to write about the things that make me dream."

"And you ain't gonna share none of it?"

"Nope."

"What if I wrestle you and take your journal?" Dice grabbed my arm.

"I won't let you get it." I grabbed my journal with my other hand and pushed it farther underneath me. "I don't want anybody to see what I've written."

"Man, you real shy, huh?" Dice let go of my hand. "We gonna have to work on that. Gotta take risks, especially in this world."

"I do take risks, but some things are for my eyes only. The things that I write in my journal are for me only," I said, still holding on to the edge of my journal.

"Man, you a tough one, but I like that. You got a personality." Dice began to pick at the small print on my jeans. "So when did your father leave?"

"He didn't leave us," I said. "We left him. My mother said he had changed too much, and the change wasn't good."

"You mad at your mother for leaving him?" Dice asked, looking up at me.

"Kinda." I looked away. "Sometimes I get mad at her. I blame her for the way things are. She's always saying it was for our own good, but things didn't really get better after we left. Seemed like things got worse."

"How?" he asked, studying me.

"In a lot of ways," I said, looking away from him again. "Sometimes it's hard for me to put everything into words. I just feel it inside, and those emotions don't always have words that I can fit them into."

"I feel that way sometimes. That's when I turn on my radio and listen to music. Seems like there's always a song for every emotion, for every pain." Dice sat up and put his back up against mine. "Man, if it wasn't for music, I don't know what I'd do."

"Sometimes you have to listen for the music that's inside. That's what Mrs. Wise told me."

"Who told you that?"

"Mrs. Wise. A good friend of mine."

"Sound like she deep too."

"She is."

"You hear that?" Dice looked over his shoulder.

"Sounds like someone's coming," I said, moving farther away from him.

"Look." Dice pointed toward the bottom of the hill.

I sat up straight and looked. A man was climbing up the grass on his hands and feet. "I think that's Proverbs," I said.

"Proverbs? Who that?" Dice asked, still looking at the man.

"He's from around here. I haven't seen him in a while though."

Proverbs made it to the top of the grassy hill. He stood with his back slightly bent and wiped the grass and dirt from his torn pants, then straightened up and looked in our direction. He shook his head. "Look like the devil's playground." He laughed and then began to walk in the other direction.

"He looks bad. I mean real bad," Dice said, staring at Proverbs with a disturbed expression.

"He looks a lot worse than he did when I last saw him. I think it's been at least two years." I lowered my eyes and shook my head. Proverbs's face appeared sunken in, his eyes distraught and lifeless. His body had shrunk and seemed to have dissipated into almost nothing. His clothes hung loosely on his body, and he walked as though he could barely keep himself from falling over.

"That's how my aunt looked when she had AIDS." Dice shook his head. "She had sores all over her body just like that. She was a junky."

"I know he drinks a lot, but I don't know if he started doing drugs. I guess it doesn't make a difference 'cause whatever he's doing, it's killing him." Tears began to well in my eyes.

"A lot of people who live around here got AIDS, you know?" Dice said. "A man living in my building dying from it. He a junky too."

"There was a girl named Shawna in my third-grade class. She died of AIDS sometime last year. It was in the community paper. When I showed the paper to Mrs. Wise, she said we are like roots. When we become severed from our Mother, death begins its claim." I wiped my eyes.

"Our mother?" Dice asked, confused.

"Our Earth Mother," I said. "I wrote something in my journal that I read in this book about Africans. I can read it for you."

"Cool," Dice said. "Cool. I'm listening."

I pulled out my journal from beneath my leg and flipped through the pages. When I found what I was looking for I read out loud: "Most of us [the world] have lost our connection with her. Our Earth Mother. Our ancestors worshipped, cherished and protected her. They kept her healthy and so her children were healthy. But she has been poisoned and is continually being spoiled more and more through the ages. Now her children are suffering, and they are dying with her."

"So do that mean that we all dying?" Dice asked. "We all have become disconnected and poisoned?"

"Seems like most of us are," I said, closing my journal. "What we see in our community is just a microscopic version of what's in the world. Mrs. Wise told me that too."

"Damn. That's some shit." Dice stood and began to pace. "Why it seem like black people doin' the most sufferin' though? That's what gets to me."

"Because somebody keeps writing our story for us. When we start writing our own stories, maybe things will change," I said. I remember Father saying this to me during one of our conversations about American history and slavery.

"What you mean by that?" Dice asked, stopping in front of me.

"There's books about us. A lot of them telling lies. They tell us what we are and what we aren't. They mostly telling us what we aren't. You know, like we aren't human and stuff like that. But we know the truth—at least some of us do. So we need to write our own stories telling that truth. If we don't write it then we need to live it."

"Man. All that you just said is some bull." Dice began to pace in front of me again. "I'm already livin' the truth, so why would I want to write about my truth when I ain't got nothin' positive to say about it?"

"Because it's like holding a mirror up to your face. You're either gonna like what you see or you're not. But the living truth is right in front of you, giving you the power to change it. You can write your story and make it end any way you want." I stood from the grass and picked up my journal. "It's starting to get late."

"Writing about the truth, especially my own, is easier said than done. But I gotcha though. I gotcha." Dice walked up to me and grabbed my hand. "When am I gonna see you again?"

"Maybe tomorrow, but I don't know yet."

"What can I do to make you know?"

"Bring the sun with you," I said, smiling.

"Can't promise that the sun won't have a little rain with it." Dice winked. There again appeared the green glitter of a rainbow. "But I'll bring the sun. I'll definitely bring the sun." He kissed the back of my hand and let it go.

I smiled and said "Good-bye." As I began to walk away, my memory painted in my mind a tree decorated with fresh shiny green apples.

Chapter 32

The wind carried back around for another season shortened days of sunlight, selfish with their brightness and warmth, prolonged starless and somber nights and nine months of school. I was happy with School's last departure, considering during its visit in my life it agitated more unwanted thoughts in my mind—mostly on the contradictions of love—than what was usual. On most occasions I tried to keep my head clear of thoughts that angered and saddened me, such as Tanya and Mr. Dickens's relationship and Mother and Mr. Girard's. During the last school year, it seemed there were more empty dreams invading my mind because of who and what were contained in them. I'm not sure which relationship—Tanya and Mr. Dickens's or Mother and Mr. Girard's—made me most question love. Perhaps it didn't matter. But the season carried within the wind a time for school. I supposed history had proven, in certain cases, that a building with books and teachers was essential for the growth of brain cells, so school made sure to keep with the wind and find its way back around.

Before school started, I had several more dreams about fresh shiny green apples. My desire for their sweet-sour taste had grown since my first encounter with the boy who had green eyes and called himself Dice. During our times together, I had learned of his relationship with the sun. On the days we would meet at the park, he always made sure to lift up the window of the world to let the sun shine through. A bit of the sun's golden dust had sprinkled itself into my heart. And so laughter made me forget about the other things life brought with it. The season in my heart

245

had begun to change. When the new season was in full bloom, another window opened for me to escape through.

When August's days were getting shorter—the new season was drawing nearer, and it seemed the sun set earlier—Dice decided we should begin meeting at his place. Most of my visits to see him were late afternoon, when he had gotten home from work. Most times he would work a full eight-hour day, but sometimes he would work in the mornings and take the afternoons off or would skip work altogether. I tried not to encourage his decision to miss work, but I never refused to see him when he did. Although our relationship was still new—we had been seeing each other for little over a month—my heart was growing fonder of Dice, and I always longed to see him when we weren't together. I was sure he felt the same way about me because of the smile on his face every time he opened his door to let me in to his world. Plus, whenever we were together in his one-bedroom efficiency, he did everything he could to accommodate me. He said he always wanted to make sure I was comfortable.

Dice rolled up his shirt sleeves and moved his bed closer to the window. "This the window where the sun shines through the most," he said. "That other window over near the door don't attract the sun like this one do."

"I like it over there," I said, leaning on the windowsill near the door. "Makes it easier for God to watch you."

"God ain't gonna watch me," he said, straightening out the sheets. "Never watched me before, so why He gonna start now?"

"How do you know?"

"'Cause chameleons can't be watched." He fell back onto the bed. "Can't see 'em in the tree no matter where they at."

"You're not a chameleon," I said, walking over to the bed. "I see you wherever you're at."

Dice pulled the sheet over his face. "Can't see me now."

"Yes, I can," I said, laughing and trying to wrestle the sheet off.

"Let go." Dice laughed and pulled me down on top of him. "What are you gonna do now?"

"Nothing," I said, still laughing.

"I didn't think so," he said, kissing me on the neck. "Are you ready for me yet?" he whispered into my ear.

"Ready?" I asked, lifting my head to look into his eyes.

"Yeah. You ready for me?" He rolled on top of me.

"Um, I don't think I'm ready yet," I said, still looking into his eyes.

"When you think you gonna be ready?" he asked, rubbing his hand between my legs.

"Um, I don't know," I said, biting gently on my bottom lip.

"School startin' in a couple of days, right?"

"Yes."

"You ain't gonna be tryin' to find a new boyfriend while you there, right?" He shifted onto his side, lowered his head and began to kiss one of my breasts.

"No," I said, closing my eyes.

"I'll get jealous if you do," he said, unbuttoning my shirt.

"I won't have time," I said with my eyes still closed.

"Those books gonna keep you that busy? If that's the case then you won't have time for me either, right?"

"No. I won't have time for more than you and my books."

"You mind me kissing you here?" Dice was still kissing one of my breasts.

"No."

"What if I kiss you down there?" he asked, moving his head slowly toward my navel.

"I'm not ready for that yet," I said, opening my eyes again.

He looked up at me. "It's just a kiss."

"I know, but I'm not ready." I shifted away from him.

"So tell me what you're ready for."

"What you're already doing."

"I have to get ready for work in a few minutes, so I'll let you off this time," he said, lifting his head and looking over at the clock. It was the first time he had made the decision to work the evening shift. He rose from the bed. "I'll walk you to the door."

"I'll walk out with you."

"I have to take a shower and stuff like that. Stop by tomorrow if you can. Around the same time." He grabbed my hand and pulled me up from the bed.

"Okay," I said, buttoning my shirt and walking toward the door.

Dice ran over to the door. "Let me get that for you." He winked. "Lookin' forward to seein' you tomorrow."

"I'm looking forward to seeing you too," I said. I walked out the door into the hallway. It was dark and gloomy. The only reflection of light came through the open door of Dice's apartment.

"I'll keep the door open until you reach the bottom," Dice said.

"Thanks," I said, descending the steps.

"Don't trip over nothin' on the way down. There's always some kinda trash on those stairs."

"I won't. There's enough light to see the stairs," I said, slowly stepping down onto each.

"Might be a body at the bottom, so step lightly." Dice laughed.

"I hope not," I said, looking toward the bottom. When I reached the last step, I turned back and said, "Good-bye."

"See ya," he said, then the light disappeared.

Mrs. Wise was at the garden with Mrs. Lily when I reached home. I walked over and joined them. Mrs. Wise was cutting fresh tulips for Mrs. Lily's new place. She had gotten an apartment closer to the home for girls where Violet was. Violet remained at the home to attend and finish school there. She was in the eleventh grade. Mrs. Lily's apartment was in a community that was funded by the same people who owned the home for girls. Mrs. Lily said the two-bedroom apartment was in a place called Mount Berry, only thirty minutes away from Violet. She was happy to be moving out of the condemned building where she had lived for twenty-two years, especially considering she was the last to move out. Most of the apartments in the four-story building had been boarded up for years. The state had been waiting for the other tenants, including Mrs. Lily, to move out before they boarded up the rest. There was a notice on the front entrance of the building that read, *Tenement not suitable for occupancy.*

"Look like you glowin'," Mrs. Lily said, studying my face and straightening the ruby-red angel brooch pinned to her dress.

"Me?" I asked, smiling and admiring the brooch. Mrs. Cooper had it on the day I attended church with her. Sunday was the only day she would wear it.

"Ain't talkin' to Sister Wise. And ain't nobody else here but you and me, so I guess that mean I gotta be talkin' to you. Ain't that what it mean?" Mrs. Lily was smiling.

"I guess so," I said, smiling back, still blushing.

"So who put the glow on your face?" Mrs. Lily asked.

"Nobody," I said, averting my eyes and smiling.

"That nobody got a name?" she asked. She turned toward Mrs. Wise. "They at that age now when they interest change from dolls to boys. I remember those days. Don'tcha, Sister Wise?"

"I remember." Mrs. Wise nodded and smiled. "I remember when Solomon captured my heart. I was a young girl then. He captured it and never let it go. Ain't let it go until the day he left this earth. If I ever got a thought in my mind to leave 'im he was makin' sure that my heart wasn't leavin' with me. I tell you that man was somethin'. Indeed he was."

"Had too many loves in my life to remember any of 'em good. Seem like one just come right after the other. Don't know if it was 'cause I lost interest too quickly or 'cause they did. But one finally got me for a while. That was Violet's father. Stayed in my life long enough to watch Violet open her eyes for the first time, but then he was gone soon after. Still don't know why, but I didn't fret over it too much. I had my baby girl, and she had me. We had each other, so wasn't no room for the past or lonesomeness to creep up on us."

"His name is Dice," I said when it grew silent again.

"Dice is his name, huh?" Mrs. Lily said. "Any special reason for the name?"

"He said his friends gave 'im the name 'cause he like to gamble with life," I said. "I don't know. Something like that."

"You hear that, Sister Wise?" Mrs. Lily turned back to face Mrs. Wise who was tying a white ribbon around the stems of the tulips. "Whatcha thinkin' about that?"

"Sounds like a flirt to me," Mrs. Wise said. "Like to flirt with death."

"With death?" I asked. "He doesn't flirt with death."

"You know what I mean, Sister Lily," Mrs. Wise said. "Take a lot of unnecessary chances. Them the ones you gotta be careful of."

"Uh-huh," Mrs. Lily said, nodding. "Them the ones you gotta be careful of."

"It's just a name," I said.

"A name with meanin'," Mrs. Wise said.

"But it don't really describe him." I sat down at the base of the oak tree. "He's nice to me. He's always making me laugh, and he hasn't taken any unnecessary chances that I can see."

"Time, baby," Mrs. Wise said. "Time."

"Always tell it plain," Mrs. Lily said, shaking her finger at me. "Time always tell it plain."

I leaned my head back against the trunk of the oak tree. "How long am I suppose to wait until I know?" I let out a sigh.

"What exactly is you waitin' for?" Mrs. Lily asked.

"I want to know if he really loves me," I said.

"There's always signs, baby," Mrs. Wise said.

"What kinda signs?" I asked.

"When's the last time you tended to Love?" Mrs. Wise asked, referring to my flower. She knelt at the edge of the garden and removed a leaf that had fallen from the branch of the small rosebush.

"I haven't been paying much attention to Love lately," I said.

"When you was tending to Love, what kinda things did you learn?" Mrs. Wise asked. She placed the green leaf in a small tin pail.

"A lot of things, I guess." I leaned my head forward and looked up at Mrs. Lily. She nodded.

"After you planted the seed, did it take time to grow?" Mrs. Wise asked.

"Yes."

"When Love started to grow, did it seem healthy to you?" Mrs. Wise picked up another leaf and placed it in the tin pail.

"Yes."

"Did Love need things to keep it healthy and growin'?" Mrs. Wise asked.

"Yes."

"Name some things for me." Mrs. Wise sat on the step and looked at me with tenderness in her eyes. Mrs. Lily walked over and sat on the step beside her.

"The sun, the rain, and sometimes I had to water Love and talk to it and sing to it," I said.

"And when you did these things, did it still take some time for Love to grow?" Mrs. Wise was still looking into my eyes.

"Yes."

"Did other things happen in the process of Love's growin'? You know, like some days the sun didn't come out from behind the clouds. Some days we didn't get enough rain or we didn't get any rain at all. And some days you wasn't around to give Love the tending it needed."

"Yes."

"But with the things you did, things that helped her grow and be healthy, what finally happened?" Mrs. Wise asked. Mrs. Lily looked over at Love, smiled and nodded.

I looked over at Love. "She blossomed," I said.

"She blossomed." Mrs. Wise nodded. "She blossomed. In the end what we saw was a sign of a healthy flower that grew into something fine. Something beautiful. But before we could see what was gonna be in the end, there was things that happened in the beginning and in the middle. The things that happened in the beginning and in the middle, mostly the things you did, was the signs that let us know what we might expect at the end."

"He's been good to me," I said. "He makes me laugh all the time."

"How long have ya been together?" Mrs. Lily asked.

"It will be two months soon," I said.

"It's still the beginning, baby," Mrs. Lily said.

"Yes, indeed." Mrs. Wise nodded.

"How long does true love take? Isn't it different for everyone?" I asked.

"It'll be in your heart," Mrs. Wise said. "You'll start to feel a blossomin' in your heart. Right now the flower still a seed."

I sighed and leaned my head back against the oak tree. "But I feel something in my heart already."

"Time, baby," Mrs. Wise said. "Time."

❦❧

School opened its doors again. On the first day, some walked through with minds so plagued with their yesterdays that nothing new could enter, while others walked through with omnivorous minds waiting to be fed. Which group one was a part of depended on certain things that changed from day to day, but mostly it was contigent on a simple thing: habit. Some people made it a habit to be angry so there was always an excuse for the status they held in the world. Some made it a habit to smile upon the world 'cause they knew the only world that really mattered was the one lived from the inside out. But the learning came slow to some and to others not at all.

Mr. Lockheart, my homeroom teacher, was one of the ones who smiled upon the world. He was always smiling.

"Good morning. Good morning. Good morning." Mr. Lockheart sat at his desk with a smile, watching the door and greeting everyone who walked into his class.

"Good morning," I said when I passed his desk, walking toward my seat.

"Good morning to you." Those who were already in class laughed at the girl who had just spoken. "Mmm, he look good," she said, turning toward the class. Mr. Lockheart laughed heartily. He was a tall, slim dark brown man with a shiny bald head. He wore a dark suit and tie.

"You sure your name ain't Mr. Heart?" a girl sitting in the back of the class asked.

"Nope. Mr. Lockheart is the name."

"'Cause our hearts is connecting right now," she said. "It's singing to me. *Pitter, pat.*" She patted her heart.

Mr. Lockheart as well as the class laughed. "Good morning," he said to a boy who was entering.

"Good morning," the boy responded.

"Hat off please," Mr. Lockheart said to the boy.

"That's cool," the boy said. He reached up for his hat and pulled it off.

"Looks like we almost have twenty-four," Mr. Lockheart said, standing with the attendance sheet in his hand. "I believe we're waiting for three more. We'll just wait a little while longer."

"Are you our homeroom teacher?" a girl asked.

"Yes, I am," Mr. Lockheart answered.

"You look too young to be a teacher," another girl said.

Mr. Lockheart grinned, showing all of his front teeth. "No. Not at all," he said.

"Are you gonna be here all year?" a boy asked.

"Plan to be," Mr. Lockheart answered.

"How old are you?" I asked.

"Thirty-three," he said.

"You look a lot younger," I said.

"Thank you," he responded, then walked back to his desk and sat down. "Well, it looks like we're going to have some latecomers or some absentees." Just as Mr. Lockheart got the last word out, another boy walked through the door. "Good morning."

Without looking at Mr. Lockheart, the boy answered groggily, "Good morning."

"Okay. I guess I should start calling your names now. I think it's a good idea to learn each of your first names and for each of you to learn one another's name. So I am going to call attendance by using your first name rather than your last. How does that sound?"

Lots of students chimed in.

"Okay," Mr. Lockheart finally said. "Asia?"

"Here."

"Bailey?"

"Here."

"Bernie?"

"Present."

When Mr. Lockheart completed the list of names, he placed the attendance sheet down on his desk then walked over to the blackboard. "Can someone read this out loud for me?"

I raised my hand. "I will."

"Thanks."

"Improvise. Life is a song sometimes without a lyric," I read out loud.

"Can someone tell me what that means?" Mr. Lockheart turned to face the class.

A boy named Ethan raised his hand. "I know."

"Explain." Mr. Lockheart sat on the corner of his desk and faced Ethan.

"We got the music, but ain't no words for it, so we gotta make up our own," Ethan said.

"Very good." Mr. Lockheart stood back up. "Anyone else?"

A girl named Sage raised her hand. "I think I know," she said.

"Let's hear it." Mr. Lockheart approached Sage's desk and listened.

"Well, what it mean to me is, I'm listening to a song, and it don't have no words, but it's a good song so it make me wanna dance, so I just make up my own dance," she said.

"Another very good one." Mr. Lockheart walked back to his desk. "Anyone else?"

No one raised his or her hand. I thought about raising mine, but I had suddenly become nervous about sharing my own thoughts. I remained quiet and wrote on a blank page of my notebook: *Life becomes our own song and dance made up as we go along.*

"Rose, how about you? Do you have a thought or two you would like to share?" Mr. Lockheart approached my desk.

I quickly closed my notebook and laid down my pen. "No," I responded.

Mr. Lockheart walked back toward the blackboard. "Well, we've had a couple of very good thoughts that were shared. Actually, they were excellent thoughts. What I would like each of you to do is think a little more about what I have written here and write down in your notebook what your thoughts are as they relate to these words: 'Improvise. Life is a song sometimes without a lyric.' Can each of you do that for me?"

"I'll think about it," a boy named Maxwell said.

Mr. Lockheart turned to face him. "That's exactly what I want you to do. Think about it." He gave a friendly smile as he responded. Maxwell lowered his eyes and picked up his pen. He began to write in his notebook. "Well, class, we have about three more minutes before the bell and then you'll be off to first period. So my last words for the day are, everything that you do in life counts. It all adds up, so do your best and make life worth it. And lastly, each morning I will share a new thought with you. Some will be my own, some will belong to others and some will be yours. I'm always listening to you. I'm not here to teach books and lessons, but I am here to teach you."

The bell rang.

Every morning, Mr. Lockheart had a single word or a phrase written on the blackboard. When the students became more comfortable with one another and with him, he began to randomly call on us to read the word or words out loud or to give a meaning as to what we thought they meant. Sometimes he would use a student's explanation as the reflection for the next day. He said that our thoughts mattered and motivated him.

Starting my day out with Mr. Lockheart kept me motivated throughout the school day. At the top of each page in my notebook I had a new meditation written down and circled. I would always refer to one or more before the start of each of my classes. One of my favorites was shared by another student in homeroom. He said, "The only way the world gonna know that I matter is if I show it that I do." Sometimes I would sit and fill an entire page with my own thoughts while in another class. Sometimes I would write repeatedly on the same page, *The only way the world gonna know that I matter is if I show it that I do,* then I would rip the page out of my notebook, fold it up and write Dice on the front of the small square of paper. He was always saying he didn't matter. During the times I visited him, I would leave the small square of paper under his pillow. Sometimes I would see the paper balled up and thrown into the small garbage can that was in the corner of his room. But that didn't matter because I knew he had read it.

Dice and I were reaching our four-month mark. During the third month, we hadn't spent much time together, mostly because he was working and I had started school, but it seemed we were becoming closer. When we were together, he would usually have a small gift for me or would find ways to make me laugh, especially when I was feeling low when I thought about Father or Mother and Mr. Girard. But sometimes Dice was distant and didn't want to talk much. Sometimes we spent our short times together in silence. I would lie back on his pillow, close my eyes and dream myself into another reality. Dreams were reality too. They were real.

I hadn't seen May, who had transferred to the white school across town, or Patrice, who had transferred with May and moved away to live with her Afrocentric aunt, all summer. May started to spend every summer away at camp, and Patrice stopped coming around since she moved in full-time with her aunt. According to Patrice, the world had shown her something different, something she liked better, that was better for her. When May first told me this, I felt like I had lost another friend. Tanya still didn't speak to me and avoided me every chance she could. Every so often when I ran into May, we would sit and talk, mostly about the books we had read and boys. She was seeing a white Italian boy named Vincent at the school she attended. She said he drove a car and always took her places, but I had never seen him or his car in our neighborhood. I didn't mention it to her. May had a way of denying reality. I did mention Dice to her.

When I first said his name, she wrinkled her nose and said, "What kinda name is that? What's his real name?" After she said it, my face turned warm because he had never told me his real name. He said he didn't like it because his father had given it to him. I didn't press him because the times that I did about other things, it made him angry. I told May the same thing I told Mrs. Lily and Mrs. Wise, "He likes to gamble with life."

May said, "He sounds like fun."

One day I felt the urge to talk to May about sex. I thought she might be surprised when I mentioned to her that I was interested in talking about it, but she wasn't. She had already experienced her first time with Vincent, and when she told me, she smiled hard. The day we talked about sex, I asked a lot of questions.

"When did you know it was right?" I asked while we were sitting on her front steps in the cold. It was November '78.

"When I first met Vincent, I knew he would be my first," she said. "He was different."

"Different in what way?"

"The first time we met, we talked for two hours, mostly about all the books we both had read. I really enjoyed our conversation and didn't want it to end. The whole time we talked, he was gazing into my eyes. I knew he already loved me. Seeing the glow of deep affection in his eyes made me adore him too. My heart melted." May blushed as she talked.

"How long did it take before it happened?"

"What do you mean? How long were we seeing each other?" May folded her arms around her.

"Yeah."

"We kissed after the second time we saw each other. That's what we did for about three weeks, then one day it just happened. When it did, we were in his car. He said that was where he wanted his first time to be. It was a little uncomfortable initially but it still felt right to me." May smiled. She was still blushing.

"Did it hurt?"

"Something terrible." May wrinkled her nose and made a face. "At first I thought I was going to die, but then I just drifted outside of myself and let it happen naturally. It felt better the second time though."

"When I'm with Dice and he puts his hand down there, I start feeling things," I said, looking away from May. "When he touches me in certain places, I want more."

"I remember that feeling. I still have it, but it was a lot stronger before the first time. When Vincent touches me down there, it still makes me want more, but not like the first time." May looked away.

"I want it to always be that way," I said. "I wanna always have the same feeling."

"Maybe you will."

"Why don't you have the same sensations that you had before the first time?"

"I don't really know."

"Are you in love?"

"I don't really know," May said. "Sometimes I think I am. But sometimes I look at Vincent, and I don't see him the same way."

"Why?" I asked. "Is he different?"

"No. He's the same. I guess it's because I want him to change."

"Change in what way?"

"I want him to look at me differently," she said. "The only thing he sees is a smart, pretty black girl who loves to read the same books. He doesn't see just a smart pretty girl who loves to read the same books."

"But you are a smart, pretty black girl."

"Why can't I just be a smart, pretty girl?" she asked, facing the other direction.

"What's wrong with being a smart, pretty black girl?"

"If I was just a smart, pretty girl then he would love me differently. He could see me as his wife and the mother of his children, but he said he can't see it. Not because he doesn't want to, but because his parents won't let him see it. Who are they to decide?" May continued to look away.

"Maybe he'll change," I said. "Maybe time will let him see things differently."

"Maybe not," she said somberly. "He says he has too much to lose."

I didn't have an answer, so I tried to change the mood. "Well, I don't have to worry about that. Dice doesn't have anything to lose but an old bed, some old sheets and an old refrigerator and stove. Oh yeah, and an old trash can," I said.

May laughed. "I guess that makes you lucky."

I laughed too. Then I thought, *I'm not sure if it makes me lucky or not.* I hadn't thought about it enough. May and I didn't talk again for a long while after that day.

Chapter 33

A few days after I had spoken to May about sex, I wanted to talk to Mother, not about the same thing I talked to May about, but about relationships, specifically. I had never felt comfortable talking to Mother about anything that had to do with boys. I still found it hard to discuss my period with her, but I felt like I still hadn't gotten all the answers I was looking for. I wasn't sure what answers I needed, but there was an emptiness I began to fill within my relationship with Dice.

Mother was sitting at the kitchen table reading the Bible. I walked up behind her and put my hands around her eyes. "Guess who?" I said.

"You got me?" she responded.

"Guess who?" I asked again.

"A young girl who used to live here," she said, "but she's hardly around. Not sure if she still livin' here or not."

I removed my hands from around Mother's eyes. "I still live here," I said, walking around her to sit on the opposite side of the table.

"Somethin' or somebody's been keepin' you away," Mother said.

"What are you reading?"

"Don't try to avoid an answer to what I just said," she said. "I'm curious to know what or who it is. Let me know somethin'. I been tryin' not to bother you about it when you are here 'cause I know how you teenage girls like your privacy. I just bring your plate to your room 'cause that's where you bring it yourself and let you do your own thing in your own way. I've been your age before, so I know how it is. The only thing I pray is that you make good choices, and that you the one makin' the choices and nobody else but me of course. You know sometimes a mother gotta

259

step in and help out a little. That's part of her duty. Wouldn't be a mother if she didn't. So what is it—or who is it—keepin' your company?"

"I have a friend I hang out with every now and then," I said.

"A friend, huh? What kinda friend you talkin' about?" Mother pushed the bible aside. She clasped her hands in front of her and rested them on the table.

"Just a friend."

"Sounds like a friend who's a boy," Mother said.

"He is a friend who is a boy," I said, smiling.

"So tell me about him."

"Like what?"

"Anything. You know, like what you like about him."

"He's funny. He makes me laugh a lot."

"What else?"

"He can be thoughtful sometimes."

"Not all the time?"

"Most of the time."

"Why not all the time?"

"I don't know."

"Tell me some more."

"He's cute and has green eyes."

"Well it's good to be attracted to him, but don't be deceived by those green eyes. Remember the world got its own perception about beauty—green eyes, blue eyes, brown eyes, and deep, dark midnight eyes. The color of eyes ain't got nothin' to do with what's real in the heart. Don't be deceived by the world's perception."

"I don't let the world deceive me."

"Yeah, it's easy to think that. Real easy." Mother moved the bible back in front of her. She flipped through the pages until she found what she was looking for. "What I'm waiting for you to say is he honors me, he respects me, he hopes the best for me, he likes me, he loves me, he appreciates me, he thinks I'm beautiful. Is any of this true in your relationship with him? What's his name?"

I let out a big breath of air. "You're not gonna like his name."

"Do you like it?"

"Not really."

"What's his name?"

"Dice."

"Dice, huh?" Mother said, nodding. "What name was he given at birth?"

I shrugged. "He doesn't like it because his father gave it to him. He doesn't have a good relationship with his father."

"So why Dice?"

I let out another big breath of air. "His friends gave it to him."

"And the reason is?"

"Because they said he likes to gamble with life."

"Does he?"

"I don't think so."

"You spend enough time around him to know?"

"We spend time together after school. Not every day, but at least two or three days out of the week."

"How long is that time?"

"Each time?"

"Yeah, I guess that's what I'm asking."

"A couple of hours."

"Do you know what he's doin' the rest of the hours in the day?"

"Mostly working."

"How do you know?"

"Because that's what he tells me."

"Right, that's what he tells you," Mother said. She turned another page in the bible. Then she began to read. "Love is patient, love is kind. It does not envy, it does not boast, it is not proud. It is not rude, it is not self-seeking, it is not easily angered. Love does not delight in evil but rejoices with the truth. It always protects, always trusts, always hopes, always preserves." Mother lifted her head and looked at me. "That's from First Corinthians, chapter thirteen verses four through seven."

"You don't have that kinda love with Mr. Girard," I said, growing angry.

"What I don't have, you must seek."

"When are you gonna seek something different? When are you gonna tell him not to bring his lazy, no-good ass back into this apartment again?" I quickly rose from the table and stared down at Mother. My lips began to quiver, and my hands began to shake.

"I have an answer for you, but I see you're not ready for it." Mother looked up at me with hurt and resentment in her eyes. Then she lowered her head and began to turn the pages in her bible again. I stood there and stared at her, waiting for something more, but she gave me nothing more.

"It's just a name," I said then walked away.

Mother remained silent.

ॐଃ

Mr. Lockheart had written a new thought for the day on the blackboard. When I sat down at my desk, I wrote it in my notebook: *Money can buy you books but can't buy you brains.* When I looked around the class, it appeared everyone else was writing the thought too. Mr. Lockheart was sitting at his desk smiling as usual and wishing everyone a good morning as they walked through the door, and he was checking off the names of those who were present. After the second week of school, Mr. Lockheart always had perfect attendance in his homeroom. On Friday morning of the second week he said when kids were motivated to learn, it made him proud to be a teacher, and although he was young and very handsome, everyone took him seriously, not only as a teacher but as a man of his word. Hidden behind Mr. Lockheart's smile, there was an enlightened mind that understood the worth of a fearless child. On the day before, Mr. Lockheart wrote on the board, *When fear is conquered, our own limits cease to exist.*

A boy named Charles had raised his hand and said, "I don't understand that one, teacher."

Mr Lockheart answered, "Nothing makes you afraid to live, love or learn to your fullest ability."

"I ain't afraid now," Charles said.

"That's a blessing, son," Mr. Lockheart answered with a smile.

When the bell rang, I waited in my seat for the class to empty. When it was only Mr. Lockheart and me, I rose from my seat with my books in my hand and approached his desk.

"Hello, Rose," he said, looking up at me with a smile.

"Hello," I said. I looked behind Mr. Lockheart at the blackboard and pretended to read again the thought he had written down.

"You have a question for me?" Mr. Lockheart asked.

I looked back into his face and studied his eyes. "Yes," I said.

262

"What is it? Ask away," he said.

I hesitated for a moment, then I asked, "How do you know when a person really loves you? And how long does it take for a person to love you?"

"Wow. Those are pretty deep questions." Mr. Lockheart rolled his eyes then began to twiddle his thumbs. "I have to think about this a little." He thought for a moment longer. "If you don't mind me asking, is it someone specifically that you're talking about?"

I began to feel a warm sensation growing in my face. "Yes," I said.

"Would you mind sharing?"

"My boyfriend."

"That makes it a little easier for me," Mr. Lockheart said. "How do you know when a person really loves you? Well, I would say it's mostly by the way he treats you and talks to you. If he's always kind to you and always uses kind words when speaking to you, then I would say he really loves you. Of course, we are all human, so sometimes we slip up a little, and out of frustration or stress or whatever we might be going through, something nasty might come from our mouths or make us react in certain ways, but that's when you have to be smart and be able to distinguish between the two. When you're in a relationship, it's important to learn whether someone is being ugly because that's just the type of person he or she is. Am I answering your first question?"

"Yes," I said.

"How long does it take for a person to love you?" Mr. Lockheart asked. "Well, let me think about this one." He continued to twiddle his thumbs. "It's different for everyone," he began. "It's hard to give a time frame. If I look back at my own relationship with my wife, I would say it took both of us some time before we knew we really loved each other, I mean from the perspective that we knew we didn't want to live without each other. I would say it took about a year, but for some it takes a shorter time, and for others a little bit longer. Different strokes for different folks, you know what I mean?"

"Yes," I said. "It'll be five months soon."

"I guess that's long enough for you to know whether or not he loves you," Mr. Lockheart said. "Do you love him?"

"Yes."

"How do you know?"

"Because I'm always kind to him, and I care about him, and I try to make him a better person."

"Has he become a better person since you've been together?" Mr. Lockheart asked.

"I think so."

"Have you become a better person since you've been together?"

I shrugged. "I think so."

"The best advice I can give you this morning is this: Always be good to yourself. When you're good to yourself, you won't want or accept less from anyone else. Be good to yourself and love yourself and know that you deserve it." Mr. Lockheart rose from his seat. "You have approximately five seconds before your first class. Try to make it there before the bell rings.

"Thank you," I said then hurried for the door.

Chapter 34

Dice was asleep when I arrived. I knew he was home although he hadn't answered the door. I continued to knock and waited for ten minutes. When he did answer, the door was unlocked, but I had to open it for myself. "Did you hear me knocking?" were the first words to come from my mouth after stepping over the threshold.

"I didn't hear anything," Dice said groggily.

"The music isn't on," I said, closing the door and locking it.

"What's that suppose to mean?" he said, falling back onto his bed. He pulled the sheet over his head.

"I don't know why you couldn't hear me," I said. "The door is right here, in the same room. Plus, you knew I was coming over today. I told you that I was when we talked over the phone. I haven't seen you in a week."

"I'm too tired to listen to you nag," Dice said. "Anything else on your mind besides complaints?"

I sat on the bed beside Dice. He still had the sheet over his head. I removed it and said, "I have a new thought for you." I pulled out the folded sheet of paper then placed my purse on the chair beside the bed. "Actually, I have two." I opened up the sheet and placed it on top of Dice's stomach.

Dice picked up the paper then sat up. "Money can buy you books but can't buy you brains." He rolled his eyes. "Duh," he said. "When fear is conquered, our own limits cease to exist." He rolled his eyes again.

"Do you understand them?" I asked, encouraged by the thoughts.

"Yeah, I guess. They can mean something different for everybody. It depends on who reading 'em."

"When I read the first one I thought, money can buy all the material things in the world but it can't buy things like love and happiness. We make love and happiness for ourselves. Money doesn't buy 'em."

"That sounds right," Dice said, folding up the sheet of paper. He slid back on his bed and rested against the windowsill.

"When I read the second one, I had a few thoughts but the one that made a lot of sense to me is the one Mr. Lockheart shared in class," I said, reaching for the piece of paper.

"That's the teacher you got a crush on, right?" Dice looked over at me.

"I don't have a crush on him. I just think he's handsome, that's all," I said, opening the piece of paper.

"Same thing," Dice said.

"No, it isn't. There's a difference. Anyway, I wrote down what Mr. Lockheart said on the back. He said when you conquer your own fears—the ones inside—nothing makes you afraid to live, love or learn to your fullest ability. Nothing." I folded the paper. "Where do you want me to put this one?"

"Put it in the top drawer with the rest I saved," Dice said. "He leaned his head back against the window and looked up at the ceiling.

While placing the small square of paper in the top drawer, I noticed the others that I had given him were tucked under a folded shirt. "It isn't that many in here. Where are the rest?" I asked.

"The ones I kept in there," he said. "Just put it anywhere."

"I was gonna put it with the rest."

"I said put it anywhere," Dice said, sounding annoyed.

I closed the drawer, walked back to the bed and sat. "Something wrong?"

"A lot of things is wrong," he said. "Too many to name."

"Name one."

"When you gonna be ready for me?" he asked. "What's makin' you afraid to live, love and learn to your fullest ability?"

"Nothin'."

"So what you waiting for?" Dice looked at me. "You asked me if I loved you, and I told you I did. I make you laugh, and I bring you nice gifts. What else you lookin' for?"

"Nothin'," I said. "I just need to know in my heart."

"Your heart should already know. Don't you love me?" Dice stared at me.

I turned away and looked out the window. "Yes," I said.

"Why you lookin' away?"

I turned back to face Dice. "Yes, I love you," I said.

"So help me to understand why the wait."

"I don't know."

"How much more time will you need before you know?"

"I don't know."

"What do you know?" he asked. "You startin' to sound like my k—" Dice quickly cut himself short. He looked away and leaned his head back against the window.

"Like your what?" I stood from the bed, walked to the chair, placed my purse on the floor and sat.

"It ain't important."

"If it's not important, then say it."

"That's why I'm not gonna say it, 'cause it ain't important."

"You do that all the time. You get ready to say something then you stop. It makes me think you're hiding something." I picked up my purse.

"What are you doin'?" Dice asked, sliding across the bed toward me.

"Maybe I should leave."

"Don't act like that," he said, taking my purse out of my hand. He placed it back on the floor. "Come over here with me." He pulled me toward him. "Come on." Dice pulled me back onto the bed. I rested my head on his pillow and looked out the window up into the sky. The sun was fading into the horizon. There was a burst of orange behind the clouds. "The sky looks pretty," I said.

"You do too," Dice said, kissing my neck.

I closed my eyes. Dice gently massaged my breasts. He began to kiss them softly then moved toward my navel. His hand followed and stopped between my thighs. He rubbed me until I began to softly moan. I reached for his head and ran my fingers through his hair.

"Do you like that?" he asked as he began to kiss between my legs. I gently cried. Dice unbuttoned my pants and began to slide them down. My legs began to shake nervously. "It won't hurt," he said. When he had gotten my pants off, he stood and looked down at me. He then removed his pants. I had never seen an erect penis. Seeing it made me close my eyes again. I began to think about my conversation with May and her first time with Vincent.

I began to grow more nervous. When my legs began to shake again, Dice repeated, "It won't hurt." He gently rubbed the inside of my thighs and began to kiss me there. The touch of his lips made me want more. I began to moan again. Dice slid his body onto mine. I held on to him and squeezed him against me. I could feel his penis between my legs.

"This your first time?" he asked.

"Yes."

"Nobody ever been in you before?"

"No."

"Nobody ever kiss you down there before?"

"No," I answered again with my eyes still closed.

"Open your eyes and look at me," he said. I opened my eyes and looked into Dice's.

I began to feel the pressure of his penis between my legs. I closed my eyes again.

"Open your eyes and look at me," Dice repeated. I opened them again, and this time the tears began to build within them. The pressure grew, and I began to moan louder. "It hurts," I said.

"Move with me," he said. He opened my legs wider.

I began to move, following the same rhythm as Dice's lower body. The pressure continued to grow, and my moans grew louder. "It hurts," I said again. The louder I moaned, the more the pressure grew. Then I felt the moisture. Dice had released himself. He moaned then rested his head on mine. The lower part of my body had grown numb. The tears continued to fall. Dice remained still on top of me, and I remained silent, hoping the pain would never return. Dice lifted his head and noticed my tears. "It hurt that bad?" he asked.

"Yes," I said, wiping the tears from my eyes.

"My first time wasn't no fairytale either," he said, lifting himself from on top of me. "So now we always gonna have something in common." He grabbed a towel from behind the chair and wiped himself. "I have to get ready for work." He threw the towel down onto the bed, walked over to the sink and began to wash his face. When he was done, he looked into the small oval mirror that hung above it. "My first love broke my heart. That was my mother. Then my kid's mother tore it apart. Now all women gotta pay for what they did to me. I don't trust any of you." The truth had finally made itself clear within the looking glass.

I slowly lifted myself from his bed. My tears would not stop, and I had no words, no sound. I picked up the towel he had thrown down onto the bed and wiped his fluid and my blood from between my thighs. I felt a burning sensation. Each time I touched myself, the pain grew. When I looked down at the towel again and saw my blood, my tears came faster; I silently wept. Dice remained in front of the sink gripping both sides. He looked down at the running water and shook his head. If there was a tear in his eye, he wouldn't show it by looking at me or saying a word. We both remained without words. I reached for my pants and put them back on. I picked up my purse and coat and walked toward the door. I unlocked it and placed my hand on the knob. I turned back and looked at Dice. He had not moved or lifted his head. I turned the knob, opened the door and stepped over the threshold into a black and lonely hole.

It was cold and dark outside. The streets were filled with cars quickly passing one another. In the air were sirens, screams and a bitterness that seemed to suffocate my lungs. And those who had been slighted by life occupied the corners and alleyways. Their world was a lonely one without the hope of a sunlit future. They had, at times in their lives, reached for a dream, but those dreams remained elusive. And at this moment so had mine. My sadness had grown deeper. My pain traveled the distance between the physical and emotional. That distance was not far. While witnessing the world that was hurriedly enfolding me, I had almost forgotten about my own physical pain, the burning sensation between my legs, but when I began to think about what seemed like an endless journey home, the feelings I felt had begun to plague me all over again.

"Hey, pretty girl. You walkin' like it hurt," a strange voice shouted. "Need something for the pain?" There was laughter.

"She ain't got a voice," a woman shouted. "That's like most of us. Ain't nobody ever listenin' anyhow." There was laughter.

"Yaw ain't got nothin' betta to do but to bother somebody," a man shouted. "I guess it make the world less lonely. Let us know somebody in it wit' us." There was laughter.

"Hey, man, give me another hit of that," another voice shouted. "I'm startin' to feel lonely, and she ain't feelin' real good right now." There was laughter.

There was laughter and tears.

When I walked into our apartment, it was quiet. There was no music. Mother was sitting at the kitchen table silent and reading. I could see her shadow on the wall. I hurried into my room and quickly undressed. I opened my bottom drawer and hid my stained panties underneath my sweaters. I placed on my robe and discreetly made my way into the bathroom. I locked the door and ran the water for my bath. I sat on the edge of the tub, holding myself and letting my tears fall freely. I silenced my cry although I wanted to give it a voice. My scream was at the bottom of my throat, choking me until I let out a breath of air. When the tub was filled halfway, I removed my robe and stepped into the warm water. I rested my head against the back of the tub. The water moved in subtle waves between my legs. I gently touched myself and thought, inside of me, this sacred place, a strange seed was planted. A seed whose fruit was bitter. I closed my eyes and dreamed, but not of fresh shiny green apples.

Mother came to my room that night. She knocked on the door. I didn't answer and pretended to be asleep. She opened the door with my plate in her hand. "Dinner is ready," she said. I remained motionless and voiceless. "You should eat something. It won't take you long."

I turned over in my bed and looked up at Mother. "I'm not hungry."

"You should eat something. It ain't healthy to go to bed on an empty stomach."

She placed the plate on the table at the foot of my bed. "I brought you some ginger ale too."

"I'm not hungry," I repeated. I then turned back over and closed my eyes.

"Well, I'll just leave it here for you just in case you change your mind." The door opened. "We need to talk," Mother said still standing there.

"What is there to talk about?" I asked with my mouth pressed into my pillow.

"Things," Mother said. "Things that might be important to you."

"I don't wanna talk right now."

"That's alright. Maybe you'll just listen then." Mother closed the door again then sat at the foot of my bed. "You mind if I turn the light on?"

"No," I said. I pulled the cover over my head.

Mother turned on the lamp. "Got some news today," Mother said. "Pretty sad news."

"About what?"

"Mr. Dickens. He was taken away earlier this evening. He's gonna be away for a while."

"Taken where? What did he do?"

"Well." Mother sighed. "I don't know exactly where and in simple terms, he was having a relationship with a minor."

"I'm not surprised."

"You're not?" Mother asked, seeming to be taken aback by my response.

"No. Not really."

"Did he do somethin' to you?" Mother asked, concerned.

"No."

"All this time I was thinkin' Mr. Dickens was a nice man. At least he seemed to be. He was always very friendly and was in church practically every Sunday. I wasn't there myself, but I always seen him either coming or going there. And he used to sit out on the front steps in the summer and play gospel. Good ole gospel songs too. Almost every summer you could rely on him being out there with that radio on until it was time for him to go to work. Sometimes I used to watch him. He used to make me laugh. When he thought nobody was lookin', especially after Mrs. Wise left the garden, he would light up a cigarette then he would inhale until he couldn't inhale no more, nearly choking himself, then blow out one smoke ring after another. He always looked like he was having so much fun. I tell you I would've never thought he could do what he was doin'."

"I could."

"Did he do somethin' to you?" Mother asked again, more concerned than the first time.

"No."

"You sure?"

"Yes."

"You startin' to make me worried."

"Who was the minor?" I asked with my head still covered.

"Well this is the part that's gonna shock you the most," Mother said. "I hope it doesn't hurt you too much. I know you already goin' through some things right now, but you gonna find out anyway so I might as well tell you. You listenin'?"

"I'm listening?"

"Little ole Tanya." Mother gave a long sigh. "Can you believe that?"

"No," I said, pulling the cover tighter around my head.

"I can't believe it either. Little ole Tanya. You're fifteen now, so that makes her only sixteen. She still a baby," Mother said. She slapped her leg. "What would make her want to be with an old man? She's such an attractive girl. I mean really attractive. I know there was plenty of boys givin' her the eye. In God's name, why would she lay down with Mr. Dickens?" Mother was silent for a moment. "In God's name why?"

"I don't know."

"Lord, what is this world comin' to? I mean it has happened a hundred times over, but I never thought it would happen this close to my home. I tell you, Ms. Ross nearly lost her mind when she found out who Tanya was pregnant by. It wasn't easy for her to find out either. Tanya told her some big ole lie about getting pregnant by some boy at school. Ms. Ross asked his name and where he lived. I don't think Tanya knew her mother was planning to pay him a visit. Ms. Ross went over to the boy's house today and confronted him and his parents. The boy denied everything. He said he had never slept with Tanya without using a condom. Plus, the last time they were together was about a year ago. Tanya is four months pregnant. Poor child. Pregnant by that old man.

"Ms. Ross got back home, and she was mad. I heard her down there screaming at the top of her lungs. I didn't know what was going on, but I heard Tanya crying, and my heart melted. I heard everything they said to each other. It hurt me just listenin' to 'em back and forth at each other. But the truth finally came out. Tanya told Ms. Ross who she really was pregnant by. Next thing I know the police was here and escorting Mr. Dickens to their car. The look on his face. I don't know, but I wouldn't have wanted to be in his shoes. What do you think about that? How does it make you feel?"

"Sad."

Mother let out another long sigh. "Ms. Ross needed to know why. Why did he do it? Any mother would've wanted to know. Any mother would've wanted to know why. She walked over to the car and talked to Mr. Dickens for a long while." Mother sighed again. "When the car finally pulled off and Ms. Ross was standing outside by herself, I went down to talk to her. I wanted to make sure she was okay. She told me what he said. She said that poor man was raped when he was a young boy by an older woman who lived in his neighborhood. A woman close to his family. He used to run errands for her. Lord, how a woman could do such a thing to a child is beyond my understanding. A young boy? That woman ruined his life. Lord, he told Ms. Ross he has never been able to let a woman into his bed since that happened to him. She said he broke down and cried. Cried like a baby."

I kept silent. The tears ran down my face, and I couldn't stop them. I pressed my face into my pillow and pulled the cover tighter around my head. I cried, but I didn't know for who or what I was crying.

"Ms. Ross sent Tanya over to her sister's. I guess that's where she'll remain until her child is born. Tanya cried like a baby too. Boy, did it make my heart melt. Lord, are you okay?" Mother gently patted my back. "I'm sorry if I'm depressing you." I remained voiceless and continued to cry. Mother sat for a while at the foot of my bed. When my sobbing began to cease, she rose. All I could think about at that moment was the expression in Mr. Dickens's eyes whenever I saw him. It was always a despondent one that made me think only of these words: Simon says cry, because he's crying too.

Chapter 35

I stayed in bed for two days crying, only leaving it when necessary. Mother became worried. Each morning she brought my breakfast into the room and placed it on the table at the foot of my bed. "You have to eat something," she would say. Each night she replaced the full plate of breakfast with a plate containing my dinner, and each night she would let out a long sigh. I still had not touched my plate. Because I had missed a day from school, Mother had phoned Mr. Lockheart to tell him I was feeling under the weather but that I would be in school on Monday. They spoke for a long while. I could only hear her muffled voice, but he gave her a message for me: Love life even in your struggles, when it is hardest to love it, because life is all.

Mother cried when she repeated the words Mr. Lockheart had given her. She pressed her head into the small of my back, resting it there, and we cried together. Finally after some time had passed, Mother lifted her head and said, "It was suppose to be different for you. Your father and I promised each other it would be different for you." She began to gently pat my back. "I don't exactly know when things started to go wrong, but on the day when you came into life, we decided things would be different for you. We thought we were doin' all the things that responsible parents are suppose to do for their child. We made sure you had everything you needed, mostly all the necessary things that are required to live a full and happy life. We both worked hard and always had a decent place to bring you home to. You always had a good meal and nice clothes. We made sure you was receivin' good love and good knowledge. The kinda knowledge that makes you strong and positive. Your father used to always say school ain't enough. You ain't never gonna get the kinda knowledge you need to make you strong in mind and positive in heart by just goin' to school. He was right about that.

"So he read to you and taught you things that you would never learn in school. Some things was a little radical, but they were things that was good for you to know. Things about war and stuff like that. You was young, but that's the time when you plant the seed and begin to cultivate it. Ain't that what Mrs. Wise is always sayin'? It was our duty as parents and conscientious people to make sure that life was fair to you, and so we did what we could to prepare you for it. We used to think that we was prepared for it. That's when life was good to us. For a while, life was good to us."

Mother sighed. "But then stuff started to happen. Things in the world that we couldn't control. Since the beginning of time, as we know it, there was always something in the world that man couldn't control, but when you was prepared for whatever it was, it didn't matter as much. But it seems like, as the world continues to evolve, things just keep gettin' worse rather than better, and we becomin' less and less prepared. You would think that life would be better with all that we've thought up and invented to make life easier. But life ain't gettin' easier. The world growin' to be more and more selfish, which make the world harder to live in and harder for us to be prepared for.

"Your father cared about all people, and he put his whole heart into the things he believed in, made him vulnerable to them. I used to tell 'im that he was bein' foolish and that he had to protect his heart because the world ain't a place where you can just throw your heart out to it. But he didn't listen to me. He just kept throwin' his heart out there, and each time it seemed like the world was throwin' it back, all broken up into small pieces. It was you and me that had to put him and his heart back together again.

"I know you remember some of those times. It wasn't always easy. As time moved forward, it was becomin' harder and harder to put the pieces back together because the world didn't always throw his heart back with all the parts still there. Throwin' his heart out into that cold place, he began to lose himself and wasn't able to find himself again. It seemed like the world cut the pieces out of his heart and buried them somewhere where he would never be able to find 'em, no matter how hard he searched for 'em.

"I tried hard to keep you from seein' him all bruised up and with only fragments of himself left. I tried real hard, but you loved your father too much to stay away from him. You had to be there to see 'im, no matter what condition he was in. It made him love you even more for it. I loved you for it, too, and wished I was as strong as you were, but when the world cut him down, when he wasn't whole no more, I started to lose parts of myself too. I started to become weaker. Every day I was becomin' weaker. Slowly I started to feel myself dyin' too."

Mother began to sob again. "Why the world the way it is is beyond my complete understanding. Your father thought he had a grasp on it. Perhaps he did, but the truth, in the way he knew it, helped him and hurt him. Some parts of it he could deal with and other parts he struggled with and couldn't seem to keep his grasp on it. It's all there. In his journal. Every bit of what he learned, what he knew and was still tryin' to understand. It's all there, and I know you want to read it. All of it. But I'm afraid that it will do to you what it did to him. I'm afraid.

"I'm sorry that I've been keepin' it from you, and I know you mad at me for it and mad at me for other things, too, but I'm afraid. I don't want you to become what he became. My hope is that only the good parts of him will live in and grow in you. That's my hope even though you learned and experienced some of the bad already."

"Why hasn't he called or tried to come and see us?" My tears continued to soak into my pillow.

"'Cause he has nothin' else to give," Mother said.

"Just being here is enough."

"It wouldn't be enough for him."

"But it's not right."

"It seems that way, I know," Mother said, still patting my back. "It seems that way."

Then she sat silent. I waited for her to continue. There were still things that she had not said yet. Things I needed to know.

"You left Father," I said, "but you won't leave Mr. Girard." I finally removed the cover from over my head, sat up in bed and leaned against the headboard.

Mother let out a long breath. She lowered her head then raised it again. She began rubbing her hands together. "I've been thinking long and hard about this one. Mostly 'cause I knew I would have to give you an answer one day. The answer is not a simple one, so I can only give you the best I know. A lot of why Clarence is still here—in my life, in our lives—is 'cause of your father."

Before Mother could continue, I interjected, "What does my father have to do with you and Mr. Girard?"

"I'm not blamin' your father. It's myself that I blame, but your father played a part in my reasonin'." Mother looked over at me. "All those years that your father and I was together, the years that things wasn't so good between us, I was doin' everything I could to save him, but the world had a tight grasp on him and wouldn't let him go. Seemed like that grasp was much stronger than mine. I even used you at times, thinkin' it would give him another reason to fight off that vicious, tight grasp, but it was too strong.

"When I started to think I had completely lost him, I gave up. I just gave up. Didn't want to but I did. I told myself I was doin' it for us, but mostly for you. But the guilt afterward was the deepest, most hurtful feelin' I could ever remember. It ate away at everything inside of me, and I couldn't stop it. I didn't know how. You saw the change in me when we moved here. You remember how different I was then and the years after. I know you remember 'cause you kept remindin' me of how different things was. I know you was remindin' me 'cause you wanted me to change things again, make things better again. But rememberin' just made what I was feelin' inside worse."

Tears welled in Mother's eyes again. "And I couldn't do nothin' about it. I didn't have the strength to. Then when I met Clarence, I thought everything had changed. I could laugh again, and mostly I could love again. Not in the same way that I love you. It was a different feelin'. Just different. But it's hard for me to explain right now. When Clarence came into my life, I felt my heart beat again. I had almost forgotten I had one. I thought that it dropped completely out of me." Mother shook her head. "But he made me feel the beat of my heart again. The music that was inside of me."

Mother gave a weak smile. "But then after a while, things started to change between us. It got so bad that we couldn't look at each other without sayin' a mean word. The kinda words that hurt and seem to live in your heart forever. There's some that still livin' in my heart and just won't seem to go nowhere. I think the only thing that make me forget is when I'm concernin' myself with you and when the music is playin'. A song is playin', and it carries me away with it. Those are the only times I forget."

Mother was quiet for a moment. "Even though there was happiness in the beginning, things was never fully right between Clarence and me. I was still harborin' guilty feelings in my heart that had nothin' to do with him and everything to do with your father. Clarence still had pain in his heart 'cause he lost the very thing in his life that gave him meanin'. He said life had stolen his child from him. He hated life for that and could never find it in himself to forgive. These are the things that was livin' and growin' inside of us. Things that was spoilin' us. Killin' us.

"One day he told me the only way he could forgive and live life again is if I gave him a baby. I nearly lost my mind that day. The way that I was livin', I knew I could never bring another child into this world. I just couldn't do it. After that day, he completely stopped livin', and I started to remember your father again. In the same way, he stopped livin'. I didn't want to go through the same thing twice, so I tried harder to save Clarence. Harder than I had with your father. All of this time I've been tryin' to save him. Hoping that I could save him. I been tellin' myself that if I could save him then I could finally rid myself of the guilt that's been livin' in my heart for so long. The guilt that's been there since your father. But it seems like Clarence is content with death."

Tears ran down Mother's face. I looked away from her and stared at the empty space on the wall. I tried to find the strength inside of me to go to her, but my own pain and anger held me in place. I sat there staring at the empty space on the wall and cried.

There was a knock on the door. Mother wiped her eyes and slowly lifted herself from my bed. I could feel my anger growing. I knew it could only be him. I knew Mr. Girard had come only to remind us of his suffering.

"Who is it?" Mother answered.

"You know who it is," Mr. Girard answered irritably.

"Who you lookin' for?"

"Maxine? Open the door." Mr. Girard knocked harder.

"She don't live here," Mother exclaimed. "And ain't nobody else home, so you got the wrong address."

"Maxine, why you playin' games?" Mr. Girard pounded louder on the door. "Open the door."

"The Maxine you used to know moved. She don't live here no more. Please leave, and don't come back." Mother turned the music on and played it loud. The knocking persisted for a short time then it stopped. Mother walked back into my room. "He ain't welcomed here no more. Death ain't welcomed here no more." Mother looked over at me and stared into my eyes. "We gonna be alright." A tear rolled down her face. "We gonna be alright." She closed the door.

It was Sunday. I rose from my bed and walked over to my window. The day was still young, and the sun poured itself out over the cold, bare earth. There seemed to be no sound coming from the outside. All was clear and quiet. I put my pants and boots on and removed my coat from its hanger and put it on too. There was no one at the garden, and I needed at that moment to be there. When I reached it, I sat on the edge of the cold grass for a moment with my eyes closed. I wondered if God was there with me. I opened my eyes again then began to push my bare hands down into the earth. I pushed them down as deep as they would go, reaching back into my mother's womb, hoping to become connected to her again. I began to cry. My tears fell freely into the earth. I cried for both my mother and me.

Printed in the United States
59726LVS00004B/1-102